WHICH WITCH

Is wild?

KERRIGAN BYRNE • TIFFINIE HELMER
CYNTHIA ST. AUBIN • CINDY STARK

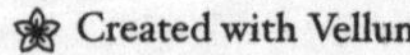 Created with Vellum

*To everyone who feels like it's the end of the world.
Because it isn't, not until this shit starts happening.
You're going to be fine.*

AERIN

KERRIGAN BYRNE

❦ I ❦

Aerin de Moray was about to commit a cardinal sin. This decision stemmed from a biological imperative and, though she knew she would live to regret it, she was unable to avoid it any longer.

Her sisters just didn't understand. How could they? Her appreciation for the darkness remained a sensitive subject with them. One she didn't dare broach just now. She wished she could explain it to them, that she could make them see. That they would open their minds and just give her a chance to prove that her way wouldn't result in the acid taste of disappointment they all feared.

Sure, the darker you went, the more uncertain the outcome, but if things turned out the way she hoped they would, the way they *should*, then the result could be a miracle. And wasn't that worth the risk of it all?

Sometimes the first try of anything new left a bitter taste in your mouth, but that didn't mean you gave up like some weak-willed pansy ass. *No*. You learn to accept your new reality and, instead of fighting and fearing it, you acclimate. You evolve. You acquire an appreciation for the darkness, and learn how to use it to accomplish goals. To further your agenda. So you live to fight another day.

Aerin's deep, preparatory breath chilled her lungs as she stared straight ahead at the long portal through which her salvation would be found. Once she opened that door, there would be no turning back.

Fuck it. She was doing this.

Because if she didn't, she'd be useless and powerless.

Because no matter who, or what, she encountered down that shadowed corridor, she would get what she needed and be the better witch for it.

Because, though some might see this as a betrayal, she couldn't find another way.

Because everyone at the *Mason de Moray* mansion made weak-as-shit coffee. And she needed something dark, strong, and black Goddess-damnit.

She'd stood in front of her fridge this morning glaring at its contents with disgust overflowing the brim of her tolerance and oozing down as rage on the other side like so much hot lava.

Then she'd looked into her full mug of coffee and the fact that she could still see through the liquid to the bottom of her mug nearly caused a bitchsplosion that would have rivaled the one that had left Ambrosia's Brews and Charms, their Cafe and Tea Shoppe, a smoking crater in the middle of town.

No more. She'd told herself. No more sugar substitutes. No more nut milks. (heh nut milk). No more coffee brewed to the same consistency as tea. Her identical sister, Tierra, was pregnant, and everyone else was indulgent. But *this* was the Apocalypse, and if there was ever a time to *carpe* the shit out of a *diem*, it was *now*. How was she supposed to save the world (or become one of its new benevolent overlords, she hadn't decided yet) on little more than coffee-flavored water?

Aerin stood in front of the glass door to Better Living Through Coffee, one of Port Townsend's premier coffee shops, and let a shiver roll down her spine caused by equal measures of guilt, need, cold, and humiliation.

Guilt, because even though Ambrosia's was little more than scorched earth after the Devil went all Inquisition 2.0 in there, Aerin still felt like she was cheating on Tierra's cafe.

Need. Because coffee. 'Nuff said.

Cold, because she'd overestimated the warmth of one of Tierra's flowy shirts—er knit poncho thingies.

And humiliation, because she was wearing one of Moira's micro-mini jean skirts and muthafucking flip-flops.

In public.

On purpose.

Aerin reached for the door, preparing to lunge in. It was that or yark on herself, which might improve the outfit.

"Allow me, m'lady," beamed a masculine voice as bright as the missing sunshine and smooth as his own velvet waistcoat.

Aerin tensed. It was im-fucking-probable that there were two men who spoke with such antiquated diction in a town of less than ten thousand. And yet, she'd known without a doubt that the gallant gentleman reaching to hold her door open for her was *not* Julian Roarke, known to the bible-reading types as Pestilence.

Because *that* elegant douche lord knew better than to show his perfect, ethereal face in her fucking presence. Lest she smite it mightily.

With a shovel.

❧ 2 ❧

The perfectly symmetrical curls of the gentleman's silver handlebar mustache lowered as his pearlescent smile lost some of its confidence, but none of its authenticity.

Aerin couldn't decide if she was pissed or pleased that it wasn't Julian Roarke.

"Forgive me if I overstepped one of your boundaries, dear lady, as I consider myself the most progressive of male feminists. But permit me to remind you that, whilst many of the folks who roam our streets are technically dead, chivalry is not." He made a wide gesture for her to proceed him into the shop.

Ugh. Zombies. Another thing on her list of things to brood about over coffee.

He'd obviously mistaken her dark look conjured by thoughts of Pestilence as disapproval of his kind gesture.

"No, I appreciate it," she muttered, the thwack-thwack of her foot attire, for lack of a better word, ostensibly even more repugnant in his bespectacled presence as she shuffled through the door. What she wouldn't give for her Manolo Blahnik pearl satin pumps in cobalt blue right about now... "I was just a little distracted," she offered by way of apology.

"It is of little consequence," he assured her. "I tend to have that effect."

Her eyebrows lifted at his audacity. Five apocalyptic seals had been opened. The world was experiencing conquest through the violent overthrow of governments (totally the fault of Nick Kingswood). War was devouring a fourth of the global population and repaving the streets in blood (Thanks a lot, Drustan Geddais). Virulent strains endangered the third world with devastating pandemics threatening to cross continental barriers and obliterate life as they knew it. (Eat a bag of dicks, Julian Roarke) And on top of it all, the blood of the fucking dead was rising up and crying for vengeance, creating pandemonium in the streets. And those whose souls were damned stayed behind to devour innocent flesh and pilfer souls for she-Satan (i.e. Zombies) How this walking anachronism thought her distraction had a THING to do with *him* was pure vain bullsh—wait a sec, was that a rapier hanging from his belt?

Aerin stopped in the narrow hallway to take him in, indeed distracted.

His silver hair and well-kept beard hinted that it once might have been gold, which must have been stunning next to eyes the color of rich, European chocolate. He was ageless in that enviable way of Patrick Stewart and Liam Neeson. Like a fine scotch whisky. An age defying fifty-five, or a well-worn thirty-five. It was impossible to tell.

He dressed like he'd waltzed out of the pages of an Oscar Wilde novel, but for the sword, which was more Shakespearean than Victorian.

"Permit me to introduce myself." He executed a perfect bow from the waist. "I am Sir Norman Barriston, a humble IT professional by day, but by night president of the Port Townsend Tourist Association, establisher of the local Arts Council, Historical Society, and the

Victorian, Steam punk, and Sailboat festivals, respectively, and also the proprietor of the popular local Bed and Breakfast, Ye Olde Constabulary."

Aerin tried not to be impressed, but this guy wore more hats than just the stovepipe one he returned to his curls and expertly tilted at an angle that even she had to admit could be described as "jaunty." Though she couldn't remember using that word before.

"Uh, nice to meet you," she said, unsure if she was losing her mind, or he had. She attempted the kind of smile you give to blabbery toddlers and people who want to sell you stuff at the mall. The one that says "no offense, but please leave me alone. It was nothing personal, she just hadn't had her coffee. Turning, she followed olfactory senses toward the café.

"And you are?" he prompted, falling into step with her. They walked shoulder to shoulder down the narrow hall, and Aerin was half afraid that he'd offer her his arm as an escort.

She bit the insides of her cheek, for the first time in her life ashamed to own her name. It was the reason she'd worn this accursed getup in the first place. Up top, she was hippie bangles and one too many necklaces, her hair swept into a loose and feminine bun.

And her nethers were draped in pure *haute de* hillbilly.

She could maybe pass for her identical sisters, Moira or Tierra at a glance, and had she the foresight to pilfer a leather jacket from the hall closet; she could have added Claire to the mix.

"I'm...thirsty," she answered, deciding that her "trust no one" motto had gotten her this far, she should probably keep it up.

"I see." His cheeks, painted a doll-pink by the outside chill, lifted in another patient, indulgent smile. "A gentleman must leave a lady her mysteries. That I have learned in my extensive experience with women."

She nodded, trying not to feel awkward. "So Norm—"

"A great deal of people call me *Sir Barriston*. I'm not saying you must, just that a lot of people do," he said in a voice that suggested she must.

"Sir Barriston," she amended, deciding not to point out that she doubted he'd ever been knighted by the Queen, but hey stranger things had happened. *Were happening.* "What's with the sword?"

"I'm so glad you asked." He rested his hand inside the intricate cage, and Aerin had a sudden fear that he might draw it right there in the narrow hall. "I also teach combat fencing Tuesdays and Saturdays at the local community center, and a little bit of aerial yoga."

Of course he did.

"My lady wife loves a man who can riposte, if you know what I mean." He somehow was able to look naughty and innocent simultaneously. "Besides, you can't be too careful these days. The world has recently upgraded from dangerous to hazardous." He punctuated his insinuation with a jolly wink and a tip of his cap.

"You're not wrong about that, Sir Barrison," Aerin agreed as they turned the corner into the café. "Not wrong in the least."

Aerin was able to slide to the cafe counter under the radar as they entered due to the hearty welcome Sir Barriston received from the local crowd. He took a moment to pose in the doorframe, and modestly accept the well-deserved adulation.

Aerin shook her head as she ordered the most obscenely large Shot in the Dark Latte with extra foam. She worried for people like Norman Barriston, a man on the fringes of society who sought their solace in this haven for the extraordinary, the bizarre, and the extraordinarily bizarre. When people were taking to the streets with AK-47's and such, what good could his one foil sword do? He was charming as fuck, but not very effective...and if she, Moira, Tierra, and Claire didn't figure their shit out soon; lovely people like him would be the first to die.

❧ 3 ❧

A s Aerin waited for her drink order, she took a moment to peruse her surroundings. When had the lumberjack look come back? Had she missed something? It was like Nirvana'd had sex with Paul Bunyan and squeezed out an alarming number of beards and man-buns.

A great deal of the women in this particular coffee shop wore Birkenstocks and expensive fleece, or presumably their boyfriend's oversized flannel shirt.

Aerin shuddered as she retrieved her order and weaved her way through the crowd. She never thought that she'd yearn for the urban gypsy feel of Ambrosia's with all its fringe and tassels and eclectic clutter. But this place smelled of sandalwood and weed, and if it messed with her palette as she enjoyed her first decent cup of coffee in days, she was going to be I-fucking-rate.

Lifting on her toes to slide into a tall barstool facing the window, Aerin allowed the din and bustle of the busy coffee shop to fade into her periphery. The multitude of dizzying problems she faced hustled and clamored for her undivided attention like day traders at the stock exchange. All she needed to do was pluck one from the rapidly spinning rolodex and get to work.

After she hunched around a mug roughly the size of a soup bowl with the darting eyes of a suspicious addict, she pondered the white caps of the Puget Sound out the window as they were tossed about by a growing wind.

She was a fucking problem solver wasn't she? The goddamned President and CEO of a multinational corporation. She'd been taking names and kicking ass all over the place since before she'd accidentally helped to bring about the apocalypse. All she needed to do was approach this from a familiar angle.

This whole Apocalypse thing was like an impending merger, really. Or maybe more like a hostile corporate takeover. The players nothing more than an amalgamation of the good, the bad, and the ugly.

The good: Aerin and her sisters. Well... good*ish*. Like, she kinda *did* read from the back of the Grimoire and use forbidden dark necromancer powers and stuff, but it was to save her sisters from being eaten by a horde of zombies so it totally counted in the good column. Right?

At least Claire thought it did... But Moira and Tierra? Not so much.

Pausing to contemplate, she took a sip of her latte, already feeling the vasodilating effects of the copious caffeine wash through her veins.

Fuck it, this was *her* list, and in *her* list she went in the good column. Her actions, however reproachable, were well-intentioned, and she would apologize to no one about them. Her sisters were alive in no small thanks to her, and she'd do whatever it took to keep them that way. She had to admit, that using dark necromancer powers *had* been a risky move. And that the zombies she'd briefly controlled were the corpses of the dammed, because the remains of those souls who were not under the thrall of the devil could not be reanimated *buuuuuuut*...

It was probably fine.

Deciding that self-introspection might, at the moment, illuminate more shadows than she was prepared to face, she moved on to...

The bad: Top of that list was the Princess of Darkness, her-fucking-self, Lucifer. Six hellish feet of pure blonde bombshell *bitch*. Powerful, sexual, and utterly ruthless, she would do anything to get the four of them to break the seals and bring about the end of the world. All she-Satan wanted was to wait for humanity to implode and swoop in like some cosmic vulture to pick over the bones. According to every myth, religion, and story, she'd coveted this pile of spacerock from the beginning, and she'd stop at nothing to get it.

Hell, she'd already done plenty to put herself at the top of the de Moray shit list. You know, aside from being the reason for all suffering and evil and stuff. Like, taking over the local coven and turning them into her own personal army of *succubitches* who now called themselves the Sisters of the Serpent. Then there was trying to poison her pregnant sister, Tierra, with brimstone kryptonite. Or, trying to burn Tierra at the stake. A foiled attempt on her life that left Ambrosia's the aforementioned crater of nothingness in the middle of town.

Who knew brimstone was so flammable?

Boy, now that she thought about it, Lucy really did want Tierra dead, didn't she? Maybe because her earthy sister was carrying death's super seed and may or may not spawn the biggest badass that ever lived. Aerin considered that if her niece or nephew was powerful enough to make Satan nervous, she'd better start thinking of great birthday presents now to get on his or her good side. What *did* one buy the possible antichrist? Maybe that was a list for another time... she needed to get them all through the fucking apocalypse first.

So now that the zombies she'd once had in her thrall

had been entirely dismembered when she'd sicced them on the Horsemen, the only person who had any control over the undead was Lucy. As far as they understood it, dear old Beelzebitch owned the undead's souls, and it would be a cold day in hell before she coughed them up. Their only chance of regaining a soul for their empty meat sack was to ingest it through vital organs and brains.

Ugh. Talk about reinforcing a stereotype.

Aerin straightened, struck by the beginning of an idea. She'd been wondering all this time, why would Lucifer work at cross-purposes with her own self? She needed the four witches alive to open all the seals, and they had two left, so why, then, would she try to burn Teirra at the stake? Or talk Conquest into making Moira his very own witch kabob?

It made no sense, unless...Lucy knew of a way to break the seals without the de Moray witch's magic.

Julian had warned Aerin, back before he'd betrayed her, that the zombies would be after the de Moray sisters, specifically, because if one was lucky enough to absorb her soul, they'd also acquire her powers.

Probably, that meant that if Lucy was in control of that *zombie,* she'd also wield the handy elemental magic power attachment.

Sobering thought, that.

Aerin had to admit she would have done the same were she in Lucifer's dominatrix boots... and it was scary how similar Aerin and Lucy approached things.

Blinking that thought away, she moved on.

To the ugly: There was plenty ugly about this predicament. Uglier than the contents of Moira's shoe closet.

This situation with the horsemen, for example, was one methane-infused cluster fucksplosion. Not only had War been boning Claire in the astral realm, (and no, that wasn't a euphemism for anal), Conquest and Death had been *quite literally* boning Moira and Tierra. Respectively, of course, like not together in some sort of twisted twin fetish or whatever.

Not to mention this entire time Aerin had been doing her damndest to get Pestilence to throw *her* a bone, but they kept getting interrupted. *And then* he'd gone and decided that she had to die. And that was just a dick move, even if he thought he was saving the world and shit. Nothing killed a lady-boner faster than attempted murder.

She could still see the regret swimming in his soulful eyes as he'd turned away, allowing his brothers, the other three horsemen of the apocalypse, to advance on her, their aim being her death. He'd gone all Pontius Pilot on her ass, washing his hands of her and melting into the mist. His conflicted pain almost hurt and infuriated her more than a decisive action on his part. Would that he were a tyrannical douche weasel, like Nick Kingswood, or a blood thirsty meat-head like Dru. She could have hated him less, somehow, if carnage and murder had been weaved through his blood into a tapestry of years innumerable.

But the sheen of moist hopelessness in his gaze haunted Aerin until she about wanted to gouge out her mind's eye.

He said he'd fallen in love with her. He'd looked at her like he somehow hoped she'd redeem herself.

And when she hadn't, he'd left her to die.

Luckily, as it turned out, witches *can* fly on broom sticks. And that had saved her ass, if not her heart.

At the moment, she didn't know if the organ in question hadn't just shriveled and died right there. Because she was pretty certain that was the last time she'd ever felt it beating. Now, it seemed, an empty void pulsed with a bleak chill to a familiar rhythm. And though she could still laugh, function, and fight when she needed to, she was *so* cold all the time.

Aerin embraced a ray of cheerfulness stabbing through the gloom brought on by no small amount of coffee and the fact that Moira had destroyed the Horsemen's compound with a ginormous wave.

That ought to keep them distracted from trying to kill her long enough to finish her latte at least. She hoped.

"We have the same buns." A smooth, masculine voice sliced into her consciousness like a wire through hot wax.

"Excuse the shit out of me?" Aerin glanced up into possibly the clearest hazel eyes she'd ever seen. They regarded her from an intensely masculine face tanned the color of her calfskin leather Jimmy Choo ankle boots.

Damn. He was *fine*.

Loose jeans slung low from lean hips, though his tight t-shirt stretched over muscles honed by physical labor. She wished the open flannel button-up revealed a little more of the swells of his chest.

Aerin couldn't see his ass, as he was facing her, and she was pretty certain he couldn't see hers, as she was sitting on it, so she just narrowed her eyes at him, trying to arrive at the point he'd made about buns.

His handsome mouth just lifted in a lazy grin, and a sexy dimple peeked through neat stubble as he pointed to the lush dark hair he'd secured into a messy knot at his crown. Some-fucking-how, it added to his masculinity instead of detracting from it.

Now that she'd registered it, she realized that they did, indeed, sport similar hairdos.

"That's great." She hadn't meant to sound entirely as bitchy as that had come out, but she was under a lot of pressure what with the world ending and all, and frankly, he wasn't really her type.

She turned her back to him, sipping on her coffee and fixed her eyes on the gathering clouds.

"The coffee's pretty decent here, isn't it?" he asked as he settled onto the stool next to her with the slack-limbed ease of the confident alpha male.

So he obviously didn't get hints, either. Sometimes the pretty ones didn't have to be smart.

Aerin closed her eyes and got right with the Lord before turning to bite his head off. One show of her inner bitch and he'd be out the door faster than you could say "Timberland Boots."

"Look, Brodie or Jake, or whatever you name is--"

"It's Brock." There was that fucking dimple again. Damn she was a sucker for those.

"Of course it's Brock," she snarked, blaming the flip-flops for letting this blue collar mud puddle think he even had a chance. Had she been wearing couture, he would have known she was not his type and moved right along. "I'm sure you're great and all, but I have--"

"You have hair that reminds me of a blood moon I saw once when I spent the summer working coffee bean farms in Colombia," he said with a bit of dramatic nostalgia. "We all just sat and stared up at the sky knowing we'd never see something that beautiful again, but here you are."

Wha? Aerin stared at him dumbly, using her empathetic abilities to read him. He wasn't a liar, and yet, he wasn't being honest.

Intrigued, she leaned closer.

"Your eyes are just as silver," he continued. "Your skin as velvety smooth as the espresso we sipped in our hammocks." He cast his eyes down as though he'd suddenly become shy. "I haven't been able think straight since you walked in. In times like these, I love that you remind me of that summer."

"Speaking of smooth, Brrrrock, you surprise me." She drew out his name, unconsciously throwing sex into her sarcasm. Damn but it had been too long since she'd gotten laid.

"What's your name?" he asked, flashing her another slow half smile that made her abruptly glad she was sitting down as her knees were not exactly stable at the moment.

"I'm...Tierra?" She went with it, as she promised she wouldn't give away her identity to anyone.

"Is that a question?" he chuckled.

"Tell you the truth, I don't feel like myself these days," she admitted into her mug.

"These days are dark," he remarked, meeting her solemnity with some of his own. Looking into his eyes without the crinkle of a good-natured smile, Aerin thought he might be older than she'd initially assumed. He looked harder. Wiser. With a sad sort of anticipation vibrating in his aura. "You looked like you were thinking heavy thoughts, just now," he continued. "I wanted to make you smile."

She flashed him a smile without any teeth. "Is that all you wanted, Brock?"

He looked at her for a long time with a storm darkening his eyes from hazel to grey. "No," he answered. And again, he was telling the truth.

But not quite.

"What else do you want from me?" she asked.

He leaned in closer and took her hand from where it rested on her lap. His palms were calloused, rough like a man used to swinging an axe or a sledgehammer. Their rasp against her perfectly moisturized skin sent a thrill through her that hardened her nipples to the point that even the silky inside of her bra felt abrasive.

"I wouldn't generally say this so soon," he admitted with a sexy, coy smirk. "And if I wasn't afraid that the world was about to end, I'd take longer to get to know you. But what I really want is to get you out of here, and bang you up against the brick wall until you scream."

All moisture deserted Aerin's mouth and headed for

her panties. She considered the frank, clear face of the solid hunk in front of her as her body woke up and paid attention for what seemed like the first time since... well since He-who-shall-remain-nameless, and fuckless, had last touched her.

Why not? She asked herself. Claire was taking out her anger with Dru on her zombie ex-boyfriend, Tommy. Why the hell not grudge-fuck a hippie? Surely, it was the lesser crime. Brock was the antithesis of Jul— that pecker head she wasn't thinking about. Inelegant, inarticulate, rough edges and bulky brawn. Maybe a decent wall-banging by a hot, hard, somewhat dangerous stranger would do her some good.

"All right, Brock," she purred before she slammed the rest of her coffee that had barely cooled enough to not blister her throat. Setting the mug aside she slid off her seat. "Let's get out of here."

The alley between the coffee shop and the bookstore next to it was so narrow Brock had to turn sideways to fit through. Aerin followed, her hand tucked into his as the chilly wind tunneled through the space, whistling with an intensity that seem to be fueled by their wild, reckless intentions.

The black and charcoal pebbled beach made a chalky sound against their frantic movement as it shifted unsteadily beneath her flimsy foot attire. The rocky beach stretched to the north behind the long wall of Victorian buildings that comprised downtown Water Street. The water, a mere two yards away, tossed against a long and empty pier by gusts that seemed to mirror the surge and wane of her excitement.

Windows adorned a great deal of the coffee shop's rear exterior, but the bookstore was solid brick, and so that became the spot where Aerin found herself trapped between a Brock and a hard place.

His rough hands conveyed none of the careful worship or veneration of... that one guy she wasn't thinking about while seconds away from shagging someone else. She wrapped her arms around the man who'd trapped her against the wall and went in for hot, slippery kiss.

Seizing her wrists and thrusting his leg between hers, he imprisoned her hands over her head, which added a jolt of delicious anxiety to her arousal.

Rough ardor became pain, and then shocking violence. He kept both her wrists prisoner in one hand as something light and leather slipped over her head, and a cold stone settled at the hollow of her throat.

The wind abruptly calmed.

What the holy fuck?

Brock's voice changed from silk to steel as he glared down at her, eyes glowing with victorious hatred. "Gotcha, bitch."

❈ 4 ❈

The sudden change left Aerin frozen with astonishment for the precious second it took to process the fact that when he'd told her the truth about wanting to bang her up against the wall, he'd not meant that in the sexy way, but the murdery way.

"Can't a bitch get laid around here without the man trying to kill her?" she lamented, struggling against his hold.

His heavy brows flinched in a way that told her she'd surprised him with the vehemence of, in her opinion, a very valid gripe.

"No, Brock, you most certainly do not 'got' me, you grunge-wannabe mud-swilling shit stain," she said from between teeth clenched with a dark, dark rage. "I'm *Aerin* de Moray, modern druid priestess and elemental air witch. I'm one with the wind, motherfucker, and I'm *out* of here."

She made to teleport away from the danger as specters of several men darkened the already gloomy beach with sinister shadows. A scream escaped her throat as whatever he'd slipped over her head sent a shock of hot pain from her chest right into her veins. It was as though her very soul, the source of her power, was singed by whatever amulet branded the delicate skin in between her clavicles.

Stowing her magic instantly, Aerin sagged against the bricks and would have crumpled had Brock not been holding her upright.

A chuckle rippled through the men who had spilled from a few narrow alleys and began to close in. How a laugh could be smug and ominous at the same time beat the shit out of her, but Aerin didn't have time to be pissed. She fought her spasming lungs for gasping breaths, trying to form a plan. She counted maybe eight men through her vision blurred with pain. Nausea roiled in her gut, mixing with a dark and acid hatred that seemed to pulse from whatever talisman at her neck held her hostage.

"Who?" she wheezed, rather pathetically she was mortified to note. "Why?" She gave a few feeble efforts against the hand that still held her wrists, but yielded no result.

A man separated himself from the approaching enemies and drew up behind Brock. Next to her muscular captor, he seemed small, thin, and unthreatening. But his aura pulsed with strength, and Aerin was struck by the force of his charisma a full second before she was struck by the back of his hand.

"Regard not them that have familiar spirits, neither seek after witches, to be defiled by them." The cadence of his voice hailed from an American South a great deal more genteel and civilized than Moira's backwater Parish. Dressed in a sober linen suit only a few shades darker than his silver/gold hair, he clutched a book that seemed only a few centuries newer than their own Grimoire.

Brock shifted to the side with obvious deference to the older, smaller man, his hold on her intensifying painfully as though protecting *him* from *her*.

The man brandished the book at her with both

hands, and the gold inlay cross on the cover told her exactly from which book he quoted. "The fearful, and unbelieving, and the abominable, and murderers, and whoremongers, and sorcerers, and idolaters, and all liars, shall have their part in the lake which burneth with fire and brimstone: which is the second death."

Brimstone. The word permeated the throbbing in her cheek. Was that what they'd slipped around her neck? It wouldn't be the first time she'd tangled with it. But before, it had made her stronger.

Before... when she used dark magic.

The darkness she felt glowing from the amulet...*that* was familiar.

"Second death?" she parroted him hoarsely, biding her time until she could figure out what to do. "I think you're confused there, General Lee, I haven't even died a first time, but I could point you in the direction of a few people who have, and are just begging for a second death. Have you not noticed the hordes of undead?"

He leaned close so Aerin could clearly read the pious disgust oozing from eyes as hard and dark as marbles. "Thou shalt not suffer a witch to live." He enunciated every word with abject clarity.

Panic threatened to gallop away with her wits like a herd of stampeding horses. Aerin fought black spots in her periphery as she struggled against hyperventilation.

She couldn't control her breath.

She couldn't control the air.

Without her magic, she was damn near helpless.

"You have done well, Brother Brock." Placing a hand on her would-be lover's shoulder, the obvious leader of this band of misfit toys doled out some positive affirmations from the brainwashing handbook (Vol. 1) before turning back to her with a look so acerbic, she fought a backwash of coffee-flavored bile.

"Do you know who I am?" he queried with a self-importance that would have made Kanye West super proud.

She blinked. "Colonel Sanders?" She wasn't being particularly snarky, as the dead *were* rising, and he might be a bit sore that Moira made better fried chicken. He *did* look like the guy on the bucket.

"Shut your whore mouth, witch." Brock ground his elbow against her throat, cutting off her oxygen supply.

"I am the Reverend Bill Blanding. My ancestors have been hunting and killing your kind since before the Romans, the Greeks, even the Macedonians."

That he spoke these words with an unhurried air was made even more disturbing due to the fact that Aerin's lizard brain was doing its utmost to survive by flailing her limbs and bending her spine in unnatural angles. Searching for air. For power. For any hope of escape or survival.

One of Moira's flip-flops flew off with a powerful kick and smacked one of the men in the face, and she was too panicked to even enjoy it.

Bill Blanding. Hadn't Moira mentioned she'd seen something about him in the papers? Would Aerin die regretting the fact that she read nothing but the financial section?

"You can breathe your last breath safe in the knowledge that your sisters will be following you to the grave in short order." He visibly savored this fact like a glass of sweet tea on a hot Louisiana afternoon. "I will make sure that they—"

"I say, you fellows!" A top hat peeked around the alley, followed by mild, mustachioed features and a familiar impeccable suit. "I hate to barrage you with harsh language, but I must insist that you cease this most ungentlemanly conduct forthwith, and with all subsequent alacrity, before I am forced to call you to answer for your crimes against this lady."

Aerin screamed in a breath as Brock's forearm relaxed one millisecond away from completely crushing her windpipe. "Get lost," he ordered. "This isn't your affair."

"That's the thing." Sir Barriston's eyes danced with good-humored regret as he took a few sure steps forward, simultaneously drawing his foil from its scabbard. "My honor will not permit me to allow you to continue on your current course of action."

The Reverend stepped toward him and said in a voice like corn silk, "She is in league with the devil, and per our Lord's good word, must be destroyed. We have no quarrel with you, and ask that you move on."

"Not...working...with...Devil," Aerin managed to pant. "She's...a thunder....cunt."

Blanding shot her a look of pure hatred. "I assure you, sir, that this woman and her kin are responsible for these biblical scourges now threatening our very existence."

"Nevertheless, she is a lady—though I'll admit she doesn't speak like one—and my gentleman's code will not permit me to allow such behavior. And so you leave me no choice." Sir Barriston bent his knees and assumed a very Musketeer-like stance, one hand behind his back and the other, the one with the sword, pointing directly at the Reverend.

"*En garde*."

❧ 5 ❧

Aerin was forced to admit that she'd been wrong. It didn't happen very often. Like hardly ever. But she'd sorely misjudged Sir Barriston regarding his effectiveness, because he, apparently, was a bad ass.

The hand behind his back hadn't just been placed there for the sake of an appropriate fighting stance. Aerin had thought she was going to watch him die when three of the ten men reached for handguns, but the eloquent innkeeper merely produced a few throwing daggers and had disarmed two of the three with masterful aim before they'd even had a chance to thumb the safety.

"I am able to count ambidexterity among my many blessings." He strategically moved to place Brock and the Reverend between himself and the third gunman. "Now unhand the lady before I'm forced to demonstrate to you just how pointy this sword really is."

"Yeah." Aerin supported his threat, as she was still too breathless to fabricate one of her own, and really didn't want Brock to choke the shit out of her again.

She couldn't really blame the group of fanatics for the time it took them to react. They had to be dealing with a whole lot of inner *WTF?* Sir Barriston was a lot to process and that was *before* he started talking. It took twice the time for these ignoramuses to flip through their mental dictionaries what with all the three-syllable words and such. The bright ones were a lot more difficult to brainwash, so the Reverend Blanding wasn't leading a team of geniuses here.

Blanding's eyes narrowed as he turned to Barriston with the demeanor of a man on a holy mission. "If you're in league with this she-devil—"

"Again," Aerin interrupted, her voice gaining some strength back. "The devil and I are on opposite sides. At least I'm *pretty* sure."

"You can join her in hell," the Reverend finished, as though she'd not spoken. He gestured to the remaining eight men to attack.

Barriston advanced, his sword whipping through the air with a resounding swish. He would have sliced through the Reverend's middle had a bruiser with a bowie knife and his asp-wielding friend not gotten there first.

The asp provided a decent counter-weapon to the fencing sword as they traded a few attacks back and forth. Ultimately Sir Barriston's skill won out, and with a few deft strikes, the water lapped their blood from the pebbled beach.

A gunshot startled everyone, and chunks of brick sprayed the swordsman but, thankfully, the bullet missed.

"Ah ha! I see you brought a gun to a sword fight, what a shame. Let us see if the rest of you chaps are as fleet-footed as you are fanatical." Sir Barriston wisely leaped behind the brick building.

Aerin was about to use Brock's momentary distraction against him with a sound kick to the balls when a trio of familiar motherfuckers stepped from the alley.

"I thought I sensed a disturbance in the force," said Dru, as he wrenched the gun from the shooter's arm and pistol-whipped him. It appeared that the action took as much energy as swatting a fly, but the rather hefty gunman tumbled ass-over-end until he came to a stop several feet away, holding his shattered jaw and moaning.

Most of the men had made chase after Barriston, and therefore missed the arrival of the absolute last person on earth that Aerin wanted to see.

❧ 6 ❧

J ulian Roarke looked more like a gothic GQ model than one fourth of the reluctantly genocidal Horsemen of the Apocalypse. Every one of her molecules stood up to pay attention to his devil-may-care stride, even the ones that were pissed as fuck.

"What the hell is this, a witch-killing convention?" she bitched, glaring daggers.

All hope that she would escape this alive drained out of her as three of the Four Horsemen slowly approached the corner of the building where the Reverend and Brock still had her trapped against the brick wall.

If they thought she was Tierra, she might have a chance, as everyone was pretty sure they'd need her alive to get Death out of hell where she'd accidentally sent him.

Drustan Geddais, aka *War*, checked the clip and slid it home before taking aim and painting the brick with the brains of the two witch hunters that hadn't chased sir Barriston.

"I've said it before, and I'll say it again," Dru's midnight eyes inspected the .45 with frank appreciation. "I'm damn glad we made that pact with the Druid

King, Malcolm de Moray, a thousand years ago to stop the Apocalypse. Because if we hadn't, I'd never have had the pleasure of playing with these." He spun the gun a few times spaghetti-western style before pointing it at the trio.

Aerin froze, her eyes trained on War's twitchy trigger finger.

She didn't want Julian to be here. Didn't want to be fascinated by the silver striations in his otherwise ebony hair. Didn't want to face the regret mirrored in his beautiful blue eyes.

And she would. Because she couldn't help it.

If he was near, she was drawn to him. For Julian Roarke, the virulent bastard known as Pestilence, was a plague her heart just couldn't seem to fight off. She was immune to his lethal touch, but not to his killer charm. And she knew that in the end, his face would be the last thing she would seek before the darkness took her.

But Damn it all, she would hold out as long as she could, purposely looking everywhere but at him.

"Step away from the bitch," Nicholas Kingswood stepped ahead of his comrades, his hand smoothing a rather lovely Brioni Two-Button Colleseo suit down his impressive torso.

"I think you meant, witch," Aerin corrected.

"No," he said with a droll smirk. "I didn't."

Incensed, Aerin took a moment's break from her terror to appreciate how the dark oak color of his suit illuminated bronze highlights in his waves of hair only shades lighter than the richest German milk chocolate. He took control of the situation as only Conquest could, with the smile of a shark, the presence of a Caesar, and *omg*, were those Bruno Magli suede loafers?

Oh shit and holy fuck, she thought, tears of pure, gut-wrenching panic stinging her eyes. *I'm going to die in a jean skirt and flip-flops! er, flip-flop...* Singular. Like the tear rolling down her cheek.

A sob escaped her as the Reverend brandished the book in front of him like a shield. "I am charged with a sacred duty by the power of this holy bible to stop this witch from conducting her evil."

"We are *in* that fucking book," War said severely.

"Oh?" Brock challenged, "which one?"

"Revelations," Conquest answered. "And our sacred duty trumps the shit out of yours, so hand her over and I don't rip your spine out through your throat." Nick shrugged as though he thought it a perfectly reasonable condition.

"Do what you must." Blanding thrust his chin up. "Vengeance is *mine*, sayeth the lord."

"Well that witch is mine, sayeth my fist," Nick countered before squinting the couple yards up at Aerin. "Er, she's one of ours."

Aerin had kept her lashes swept down as their eye color was the only thing that visually distinguished one de Moray sister from another, and she didn't want Julian to know it was her.

"Which witch is she?" Dru queried. "I don't think its Claire, but beyond that..."

"How can you claim to be in this most ancient holy text? For surely you are no angels," the Reverend asked, his accent thickening with what she suspected was fear.

"Actually, there is some debate on that," Julian cut in pensively, his proper British diction sliding like the most expensive silk over chords so previously plunked with the artless strains of an Evangelical. "Whilst we're not the winged seraphim in that version of ancient mythology, we were fashioned by the creator in her image and given a heavenly task in which--"

Aerin couldn't take this anymore. Brock's hold was tightening on her throat again, and Julian's voice was causing her heart to squeeze with the same breathless pressure. "They're in *every* ancient text, you ignorant douche canoe," she interrupted. "You're arguing with three fourths of the fuckwits of the Apocalypse. So why don't you just do your job and kill me, because I'll be goddamned if they get the fucking pleasure, *capiche?*"

Dru, Nick, and Julian glanced at each other. "It's Aerin," they said, mystery solved.

"Nice flip-flop," Conquest snarked.

"Don't start, asshole, I've heard you look pretty in an apron."

Nick's brilliant eyes narrowed, but he muttered, *"Touché."*

"Leave her with us, and we'll see justice done." Julian's long wool coat hid what she knew to be an impeccable, if somewhat outdated, suit and an even more perfect physique as he took an unthreatening step toward the minister.

"How can we be satisfied that you are who you claim?" Brock called over the shoulder of his leader.

Julian's ice-blue eyes settled on Brock with a falcon-like alertness. "How, indeed?" No one moved as he more glided than walked over the stones toward them. With a chilling calm, he removed his glove and placed it on the nape of Brock's neck, which was exposed by his up-swept hair.

Aerin couldn't smother just a bit of a victorious surge of smugness beneath the fear that she might be the next one to die.

Bye Bye, Brock, she thought as her captor released her and staggered backward, his hands falling to his sides as though he found them too heavy to hold aloft anymore.

But Julian didn't let go. Not when Brock started to sniffle. Nor when he began to cough, and then strangle, blood running from the corners of his lips. He didn't let go when the witch-hunter's smooth skin erupted in boils, or when his hair began to fall out. Nor when every pore and orifice began to bleed and his lungs filled with his own fluids.

Julian didn't let go until Brock's organs liquefied, his joints disintegrated, and he collapsed into a disgusting puddle of gore onto the stones.

"Satisfied?" Pestilence queried, replacing his glove.

The Reverend dropped his book and fled.

✻   7   ✻

As quickly as she could, Aerin tore the talisman off of her neck and made to teleport out of there. Though it wasn't as painful as it had been before, the thing still pulsed with tangible power from where she held it away from her by its leather thong, and prevented her from using her magic.

She was going to have to drop it in order to escape, but if she did, she'd be leaving one very powerful unknown weapon in the hands of three men more ultimately dangerous than a few bible-thumper inquisitor wannabe's.

"We're not going to hurt you, Aerin." Dru held up a staying hand.

"Fuck off," she snarled stepping away from them and inching along the brick wall. "You think I trust a *word* you say?"

"How about a *thank you* for saving your life?" Nick suggested, changing the subject.

"How about you make up your fucking mind?" Aerin shot back, grateful for another outlet for her ire. "First you want to kill me, and then you rescue me. What gives?"

"At this point, your death might prove more dangerous to our cause than your life," Dru explained. "We've come to offer you a truce, of sorts."

Aerin's eyes narrowed, but she lowered the talisman. "Okay," she breathed out slowly, trying not to let her fear and anger get in the way of logic. "I'm listening."

"We think that Lucy might have figured out how to harness your powers, maybe even your souls, if you die." Nick Kingswood dropped that bomb before he paused to inspect the damage, glancing around them. He visibly noted dead bodies on the ground, and the two live men who'd had their gun hands skewered by Barriston's well-thrown knives struggling to stand and escape. "They can't overhear this." Nick didn't have to say more than that as War put bullets right between their eyes without even looking.

Aerin flinched as the gunshots echoed off the brick and resounded across the water with a sharp and ominous augury. She'd seen the bodies of the dead, and the undead, but to watch the princes of the biblical scourge snuff out human lives without so much as a blink was more than a little unsettling.

They were killers. Each and every one of them, in their own way, lived for human suffering.

And yet were plagued, for lack of a better word, with a conscience. With humanity... of a sort.

"We should discuss this elsewhere," Julian suggested with a furtive glance at Aerin. "We won't be alone for long. Either the police, the undead, or the devil will be drawn to this place."

"You're nuts if you think I'm going *anywhere* with you." Aerin summoned her chilliest glare, the one that shriveled the balls of many men who dared question her authority as President and CEO of Westwind Tech. "The police are keeping the zombies busy and are working double time trying to deal with this whole apocalypse thing, so spill the beans, and make it quick, and tell me about what fresh hell we have to deal with."

"Don't blame us." Nick shrugged. "You have Tierra to thank for this."

Aerin hid a wince. She thought she knew where this was headed and didn't want to follow them down the road to hell paved with Tierra's good intentions.

As per usual, Julian explained. "There's a vulnerable instant between the moment a person dies, releases their soul, and death or one of his reapers come to collect it. Because Tierra, in a fit of temper sent Death to Hell, Lucifer now can count our brother's potent soul as one of her own."

Yup, that's exactly where she thought this was going. Well...*Fuck*.

"But he's not dead, right? So how is that possible?" She grasped for any hope she could.

"He's unable to die, but are you familiar with the adage that possession is nine-tenths of the law?" Julian queried.

Aerin nodded, dread thickening in her already sore throat.

"Eternal laws are not often very different from mortal ones, many of the things that rule your world and the Other World are the tangible constructs of belief. Currency is only such because you've assigned it a specific value. National boundaries only exist because someone drew a line on a map. Government is only powerful because people allow themselves to be governed."

For the first time since they'd met, Aerin sensed anger beneath Julian Roarke's generally implacable facade. *Just what did he have to be mad about?* She wondered as he continued.

"You humans are ruled by fear, and you use faith to counteract that fear. But your faith is not contained to a benevolent or vengeful creator; it is split between a deity above...and one below. Faith is an instinct of the soul, and it is that belief that lends a deity power."

"I thought we were going to keep this short," Aerin bitched. Half because she wanted him to get to the point, and half because she was afraid of what he would say next.

"Hell is a place from which there has historically been no escape, no redemption, and no forgiveness. Hell is *her* domain, and whilst Lucy holds Bane in her clutches, it gives her a certain... power over the dead. Now, if she wants, she can play reaper, and she doesn't have to answer to Death, himself, because he's imprisoned and, essentially, powerless."

Well. Fuck.

Again.

Aerin swallowed around a dry tongue. She couldn't say that she blamed Tierra for her fit of temper. There were those pesky pregnancy hormones to deal with... and who wouldn't have been pissed upon learning that she'd been secretly married, er, soul-bound without her permission? Aerin couldn't say she wouldn't have done the same were she in her sister's place, especially because there was no way Tierra could have known her actions would carry such weighty consequences.

But because of it, they were royally fucked. Like sideways.

"So you're telling me that demon bitch now has the ability to steal *our* souls and *our* powers if we die, and she doesn't even have to use the zombies to do it?" Aerin used a technique she'd used in the corporate industry just to keep things straight. Repeat what you don't understand. What you don't want to hear. Put it in your own words.

"We think so," Dru answered.

"You *think* so?"

"We're pretty fucking sure," Nick confirmed. "Lucy was there when I shot—when Moira went into the water, and when your sister was saved, the devil blew a gasket."

"She's not exactly keeping her plans a secret," Dru remarked wryly. "I don't think she feels that she has to."

"She's powerful, Aerin," Julian's voice had become more urgent than she'd ever heard it. "More so than ever as fear is beginning to build and she feeds upon that. She's closer to attaining her goal of world domination than she's previously been..." He didn't say that it was Aerin and her sisters' fault.

He didn't have to.

❋   8   ❋

"So, let me get this straight," Aerin held up her hand. "The only reason you've decided to stop trying to murder the four of us is because you don't want Miss Mephi-*syphilis* to nab our elemental powers before we gain entrance into the afterlife?"

"That's the only reason we've decided to stop trying to murder *you*," Conquest clarified, fingering the diamond cufflinks beneath his suit coat. "We'd actually regret the loss of your sisters."

Ouch, kinda. Aerin shrugged it off, used to people not really liking her.

Not caring if she lived or died.

From the moment she'd been thrown off a high rise building by a well-meaning witch, to the orphanage, group homes, foster care, and so on, she couldn't reach back into her memory and touch a single person who'd truly cared. She was just another unwanted soul.

The expendable de Moray witch...

"If we can figure out how to get Death out of Hell, our problems should be solved and we can go back to trying to kill each other," Nick said.

"I'll take it." She sounded more indifferent than she actually felt and was proud. "The enemies of my enemy

39

are my friends... for now," she amended. "But know that we make no apologies for trapping Bane in hell as he totally deserved it for being a devious douche nozzle. And don't think for one second that I've forgotten that you skewered Moira," she pointed to Nicholas.

"She asked me to." He held up his hands to portray his mock innocence. "Both times."

Aerin flipped him off which only deepened his smirk.

"And you," she turned to Dru. "You're the whole reason Claire is with that zombie freak. You're messing with her head, and her heart, and that's just... well it's fucking uncalled for is what it is."

"That's not your business," Dru growled.

"Christ." Aerin pinched the bridge of her nose. "You even *sound* like her. I don't know what's going on there, but you two need to seriously figure some shit out before the world explodes."

"You speak as though we've already lost," Julian murmured.

"And I sure as shit ain't talking to *you*," she spat in his direction. "You're the worst of the lot! You are a Machiavellian liar, Julian Roarke, and I wish it was *you* rotting in hell."

"I never lied to you." Julian's eyes shimmered with sincerity from a face the study in masculine symmetry.

"You said you loved me!" She hated the plaintive note of hurt beneath her righteous anger.

"I *never* lied," he repeated, paying no heed to the two very uncomfortable-looking men to his right.

Their eyes locked, and Aerin not only saw but felt the truth emanating from him.

Which pissed her off.

Then why didn't you fight for me? she wanted to scream at him. Of course, she knew why. Because Julian held his honor, his goddess-given duty above his own desires, his feelings, his very life.

And hers.

Well, you know what? That just wasn't gonna work for her. If she was going to love someone, she wanted that love to defy the laws of nature, nay, the very Gods. Every single bitch ass one of those narcissistic tool bags who put them all in this situation in the first place.

"Yeah… we're going to go see what's happening to that guy with the sword," Dru nudged Nick toward the alley down which Barriston had taunted the other men away from her. "I haven't seen a fencing stance that great in nearly three hundred years."

"I could stand here a little longer." Nick shoved back, not wanting to miss the drama.

"We're leaving them *alone*," Dru insisted. "Speaking of people who have shit to work out."

Aerin barely noted their exit as she stared, unflinching, into Julian's eyes.

All right, she guessed they were going to do this, right here, right now.

She wished he didn't look so wild, his black and silver hair loose to his shoulders in disarray, his eyes flashing hot, silent promises. To see him like this was surreal. The consummate and collected scholar, the brooding and pensive gentleman, these were the iterations of Julian Roarke she'd been introduced to thus far.

But this man, this *immortal* advancing on her was different.

In every rendering of him she'd Googled, he was a dark, sinister, skeletal being. An inescapable affliction. Something you couldn't outrun, outwit, or hide from. No king nor Emperor could defeat him. No warrior could oppose or withstand him. For he was the unseen terror. Those touched by Pestilence *begged* for Death, the brother that followed him, to grant them oblivion.

Release.

Aerin realized as he closed in on her that, though

he'd made multiple attempts on her life, she'd never truly been in danger from him.

Not until now.

$$\text{❀ 9 ❀}$$

Julian saw Aerin open her mouth, preparing to defend herself—or to cast aspersions at him, he couldn't yet tell which—and something drawn tight and cold inside him snapped.

Not this time, he thought as he yanked her into his arms and stopped her words with his mouth. He didn't have much of a frame of reference, having never kissed another, but there was nothing in the world with a sweeter texture than Aerin's lips. When vitriol and curses weren't spilling from them with dizzying alacrity, she had the most alluring mouth and accompanying voice he'd encountered in a handful of millennia.

She made a sound, whether protest or submission, he couldn't be certain, and didn't much care.

She didn't *get* to be angry. Not this time. She didn't get to charm and exasperate him with the dichotomy of her foul words and beautiful lips. Not this time. She didn't get to dictate the course of their passion.

Not. *This*. Time.

Not when he'd seen that witch-hunter's hands on her body. Not after he'd watched her kiss another, paw at him, rub herself against him in a hollow rendition of the ardor they'd once shared.

Aerin de Moray would learn once and forever that,

though he was not her first lover, he would certainly be her last. Because any man who'd dare touch her would rot from the inside out.

He'd make sure of it.

Even as the thought imprinted itself into Julian's mind, he knew it was archaic, barbaric even, but he didn't care. These lips, this mouth, and the woman attached, they *belonged* to him. And the world could go to hell if he'd ever be without her again.

Because to kiss her was to taste heaven. To touch her was to feel divinity. He couldn't imagine what making love to her was like, but in a handful of moments he wouldn't have to.

She tasted like rich coffee and salted caramel when his tongue slid past her lips. He lapped at her, showing her in slick, strong thrusts of his tongue just who was in control this time.

She, of course, was no passive, sibilant recipient of his passions. She met his challenge with a dueling tongue, battling his control with wild abandon. Surging against him, as though to press him back, she brought every curve and inch of her against him, but he refused to budge. Instead, he grabbed each of her wrists, much as the man he'd melted had, and imprisoned them against the brick of the building, effectively rendering her his captive.

Their lust had teeth, sharp and hungry, ready to tear what they needed from each other with a desire that bordered on desperation. He wanted to punish her for allowing another man to touch her. He was equal parts need and anger. He wanted to spank her. To pull her hair. To hold her down and ride her into a lathered submission.

To have her up against this wall.

And so he would.

He'd thought it would be different than this... that their joining would be an exploration of all things denied him for untold millennia. That he would revel in the contact of flesh, in the binding of molecules, in the exploration of their powers and how they could combine them to culminate in a sweet, delicious gluttonous feast of a man eternally starved.

But he was past that now. Past all reason. All hope of control and relish was lost the moment he'd seen that man touch her. He might have spent the endless span from pre-history to this moment learning to be a cultured and erudite man, but in his core he was as much a beast as any of his brothers.

And his territory had been breached.

The rip of her flimsy shirt and bra was just white noise to the roar of his blood in his ears. Then his hands were full of her breasts, the warm weights softer than anything he could have imagined. The tips puckered against the cold, and the friction his palm created against them. In the past he would have written odes to the perfection of these glorious, feminine orbs. But there was no time for that. There was no time to make love.

This was naught but fucking.

Tearing his mouth from hers, he sank his teeth into the delicate curve where her shoulder met her neck as he freed himself from his trousers.

"Julian," she gasped out his name on a low moan as a shudder undulated down her entire body. "We can't—"

"We will," he countered, sliding his hands behind her and lifting her so her legs split wide enough for him to fit between them. "Don't you *dare* tell me to stop."

He pressed his cock against the apex of her thighs. With her skirt riding almost up to her waist, only her panties separated his sex from hers. He could feel her slick heat, the answering moisture of her body soaking through the thin scrap of silk and lace and beckoning to the aching length of his need.

He bared his teeth at the exquisite torture of it, ready to claim her. To brand her as his own.

Something in her quicksilver eyes changed, deepened, and the unexpected shock of it gave him only a momentary pause.

Vulnerability. An open exposure he'd never expected. Not from her. Fear. Hurt. Maybe something else. He was too hard and starved to tell.

"Aerin I—"

"Don't stop," she whispered, and wrapped her legs around his waist. Coat and all.

Apparently now was not the time.

He couldn't agree more.

Then her panties, that saturated and insignificant barrier, were thrust to the side, and he drove into her with such force, a raw sound ripped from them both.

In that moment, tens of thousands of years of languages escaped him, leaving him with only one word to describe the experience.

This.

This was what he'd eternally sought. *This* woman. *This* sensation. *This* wet, aching, wild pleasure. There was nothing beyond this or above it.

Above her.

Today he'd found a new Goddess to worship.

This.

They didn't kiss again. Didn't speak. His every muscle was locked, including his jaw, so he stared into the liquid lightning that flashed in her eyes.

Her tight feminine flesh pulled at him as he withdrew and speared her again, and again, driving her higher against the rough brick. He was not cruel, but neither was he kind. A dark beast within him reveled in the carnal, savage things he'd never even conceived of.

The wet, sharp sounds their body made as he mercilessly drove deeper. The high, tight note of pain in her gasps. The blood of his enemy, the man who'd dared to touch her, only feet away. The taut flesh of her ass gripped in his hands. The sting of her nails scoring his shoulders through his shirt.

Spurring him on, making wordless demands whilst pulling him deeper, faster, harder. Her beautiful face contorted into something primal before a savage cry preceded a spasm of the muscles that engulfed him so sweetly.

Only a few primitive words returned to him in great, pulsing waves that started in his spine and gathered in strength and potency with every thrust.

Fuck. Yes. This.

Mine.

With that, he was ripped away from himself. White hot pleasure shot through his body, his bones, and lanced his very soul. He emptied it into her in incredible, jetting pulses. His love. His loss. His pain and darkness. His pleasure and need. His incomprehensible power, and his ultimate helplessness. Whatever made him more than a man, but less than a God.

And she took it gladly. Greedily. Until every last throb and shudder had coursed through them both and feathered across their flesh, escaping into the gathering wind.

He remained inside her for a breathless moment, his eyes locked with hers as they panted and pulsed with the last vestiges of the aftermath.

It all rushed back to him in a swarming charge clogging his throat with the things left unsaid between them. The words. The reasons. The guilt. The love. He wanted to plant his emotions inside of her just as powerfully as he had his body. For how could he convey... how could he make her understand? How was there not a language from here to the cosmos that could adequately express the depth of his feeling for her?

"I love you," he whispered.

He read something different in her expression every

time she blinked. Pleasure. Doubt. Uncertainty. Indecision.

Then resolution.

She reached a trembling hand to her side, and before the realization permeated his bliss-muddled thoughts, something slipped from her fingers.

She was gone before the amulet clattered to the stones.

A erin appeared in the *Maison de Moray's* kitchen, assembling her molecules with the last bit of strength she had left and took a moment to orient herself on trembling legs.

"What the shit?" Tierra gasped in astonishment, causing Clare and Moira to look up from where they were sorting herbs on the island to dry.

More Horseman repellant, Aerin guessed. Too bad she hadn't armed herself with that earlier...

Something sharp stabbed her in the chest, right behind where she clutched the ripped blouse over her breasts. It felt like grief and weakness and fear, pressing down on her shoulders with such a weight, her knees hit the cold floor of the kitchen with no small amount of force.

She was still slick between her legs, still pulsing with aftershocks of explosive pleasure around emptiness. Her underwear was in disarray, her bra torn, and—oh balls—was that mascara staining the tears falling from her chin? Shit. Shit. *Shit*. She was such a mess.

In every sense of the word.

She didn't want to do this in front of anyone. Didn't want to do it at all. But, it seemed, her heart had decided to break down and take her body with it.

The gentle hands of her sisters stung against where the brick wall had abraded her back. They surrounded her where she curled into a ball like a protective wall of magic and concern.

They all spoke at once.

"Who did this? I'll kill them." Claire hissed.

"Was it Lucy? The Horsemen? Zombies? The Sisters of the Serpent?" Tierra demanded.

"Are you bleeding? Where are you hurt?" Moira soothed.

Aerin opened her mouth to inform them that she was okay, that they didn't need to worry about her; she'd be off the floor any second.

Only a dry sob escaped on a wave of pain.

Tierra was right, *what the shit*? Why had she run? How could she have just *left* Julian there with his dick *literally* hanging out?

What was she afraid of?

That he would come to his senses after so thoroughly robbing her of her own.

She'd never been attributed a great deal of emotional maturity, but she was self-aware enough to recognize panic when it stabbed her in the heart. She'd done what she always did when she was not in control and could see no way to take it back.

She'd run.

No, not run. It was more like a strategic retreat. She just needed to regroup before facing him again.

It had been in his possession that she'd lost herself. He'd made it clear in no uncertain terms, somehow without even saying a word, that he was claiming his territory. That he was throwing down the gauntlet.

And, Goddess help her, but she wanted him to... but...

"Aerin," Tierra took her face in gentle hands and lifted it to meet searching verdant eyes. "Did someone attack you? Were you... have you been..."

"Can't rape the willing," Aerin muttered bitterly as another hot tear branded its way down her check.

Her sisters just looked at her.

"Yeah, okay, bad joke," she admitted. "Help me up?"

The thing about sisters like this was...when you couldn't stand, when you didn't think you could get off the ground, they lifted you.

Every time.

Moira wrapped an extra soft throw around her shoulders and it felt like a hug. Tierra and Claire took each of her elbows and they were her legs until she was settled at the table.

Tea appeared, and alcohol. Then snacks, sugared and salty, so she could hand-craft whatever she needed for self-medication.

The next tear that fell was because of them. A grateful one.

Once they were settled around the four-person table at their respective places in the correct directions, north, south, east, and west, they patiently waited for Aerin to explain.

She didn't know where to begin, so she ate chocolate instead, and washed it down with whisky.

The wind had chased the storm clouds away, and the late morning sun cast its eye through the stained glass above the bay window, warming her in a kaleidoscope of color.

It was too early to be drinking.

But after the morning she'd had... down the fucking hatch.

"Julian?" Claire correctly guessed.

Aerin couldn't say anything around the golf ball sized lump in her throat, so she just nodded and drank some more, letting the warmth of the alcohol release the knot in tiny, burning increments.

"He...I...We..." She poured another shot and knocked it back.

"Did he hurt you?" Moira asked carefully, wrath lurking behind the gentle concern in her eyes.

Aerin stared into the empty glass for a long moment before shaking her head. "Not yet."

"Then what *happened*?" Tierra prompted, her impatience showing. "Who ripped my shirt?"

"He said he loved me," Aerin murmured, still looking no one in the eyes. "And then he ripped your shirt."

"Oh, sheeeeit," Moira moaned.

"I know." Aerin's forehead met the table.

"Goddess knows, my panties have dropped for the 'L' word," Claire confessed. "More than once. And to be honest I'm kind of impressed by Julian. Didn't think he had *that* kind of fire in him."

"Neither did I," Aerin said. But he had it. And then some.

"Was it at least good?" Moira asked. "You know, up until the runnin' away part?"

Aerin straightened, her sister's lack of judgment giving her a little courage to lend voice to the fears paralyzing her. "It was soooo... good." Understatement of the century. It hadn't been good.

It had been the best.

"*He* is so good." It was what she'd meant to say. "And I'm... well I'm..." She tried to pluck good descriptors out of the air. Ruthless. Ambitious. Selfish. Bitchy. Unstable. Fucked up. "I'm other words than good," she finished lamely.

She'd never been good *enough*. For anyone.

"You're too hard on yourself." Tierra reached across the table and took her hands. "You're a good woman, Aerin."

"A good sister," Moira agreed.

"A good witch," Claire chimed in.

Aerin shook her head, unable to accept their platitudes. "I've sabotaged every chance I've ever had at a healthy relationship."

"Welcome to the club." Claire smiled wryly, tossing her straight, heavy hair over her shoulder.

They all nodded in agreement.

"I've done ruthless, calculating things to get ahead in business," Aerin continued.

"You had no one to rely on but your own self," Moira's eyes met hers, their aqua depths swimming with understanding. "That don't foster feelings of team-work and shit like that. You had to fight harder to break the glass ceiling."

They weren't getting it; she had to try harder to make them see. There were no excuses for her actions, no forgiveness for her dark tendencies and indecent ways.

"I let my own power and magic seduce me. I read from the back of the book." Shame flooded her.

"As dangerous as that was," Tierra said. "You were trying to help."

"Partly," she confessed. "At first. But then I thought... I thought maybe we *should* take over the world. That maybe an apocalypse was due. That the devil was right, and not only should we fulfill the prophecy but overthrow her and take her place."

Silence met her admission, and Aerin couldn't lift her gaze above the striations of oak in the antique table.

"I was going to try to talk you all into it," she forged ahead, certain that each word was a nail in her coffin and her sisters would be the ones hammering them home. "I thought, if we're all forsaken by the Goddess anyway, why the hell not, you know? Why not embrace destiny instead of fighting it? It doesn't seem to be working, anyway. That's what I didn't tell you. That's why the Horsemen decided to kill *me*. They know. They can see my damage and my darkness, and they know that I'm...That I'm not worthy."

The tears fell again and Aerin swiped at them with impatient fingers, awaiting her sisters' reprimands.

Claire spoke first. "I have to say, I've had similar thoughts. We're in a really bad position here, and maybe we're not supposed to be fighting the prophecy, but giving into it."

"No!" Tierra slapped a palm on the table. "You *guys*, fate is not decided for us, you don't just give in to it. We make our own path, even if the woods are dark. Come on! We decide whether to end the world or to save it. And we decide *together*." She thought for a second. "As long as it's saving it, because that's the decision I've decided we're making."

She was serious, but they all gave in to a little laugh. Classic Tierra. Eldest sister and Mother Bear. Especially now.

"Here's what I think, for what it's worth," Moira cut in. "We are the elements. We are the seasons. We are the directions. Tierra and I, we're earth and water. Feminine signs representing growth, healin', life, light, and such. Claire and Aerin, y'all are the opposite of that, but maybe not in a bad way. This universe, it's about balance. Fire and Air are masculine signs. Passionate and chaotic. Destructive and cleansing. The way I see it, how could our light exist without the ballast of your darkness? How could we make the right decisions without contemplating the wrong ones? And who says, just because Tierra and I often make the most compassionate choices, that it's always the right one."

Mutely, they all stared at her in wide-eyed surprise.

Moira just shrugged. "Maybe the correct answer lies in the middle."

Aerin wanted to hug her, but if she moved her arms it would be a half-naked hug, and that would be weird.

In her flippant, wise way, she'd validated not only Aerin, but them all.

And the rift that had been open between the sisters, both light and dark, became a little smaller.

"Yes, we should totally explore that." Claire smiled at Moira. "But let's get back to the part where Aerin finally took Julian's V-card, he tells her he loves her *again*, and she teleports away... Because I thought *my* love life was fucking complicated."

Aerin made a noise half laugh, half anguish. "I've... never said it before, the 'L' word, and before you guys, I'd never had it said to me, either. I don't know what to do."

"Do you love him?" Claire asked frankly, her artfully kohl-lined eyes glowing amber with curiosity.

Aerin closed her eyes, assaulted by fresh pain. "I don't know. I don't know how."

"We'll help you figure it out," Moira offered kindly. "We're all kinda in the same boat."

Speaking of fate. What were the odds that the four witches and the Four Horsemen of the Apocalypse would have connections like they did? Something to consider.

"We're just glad you weren't attacked," Tierra added. "You know, in the way that *doesn't* end in orgasms."

Aerin cringed. Here she'd been crying about her relationship issues when they had bigger problems. Like deadly ones. "Well... I sort of *was*, but I think they're dead now." She worried about Sir Barriston. Hoped that he'd fought off her captors, or that at least the Horsemen had gotten to him in time.

"What?" her sisters screeched in union.

"Yeah..." She took a deep breath, wondering where to begin. Lucifer with Death's powers? Witch Hunters? Reverend Blanding?

"The good news is that the Horsemen have called a temporary truce against us in exchange for our help in defeating Lucifer," she said, doing her best to soften the blow.

"And the bad news?" Claire asked, her eyes flaring.

Aerin turned to Tierra. "We have to get Death out of Hell."

Tierra's eyes widened. "But... I don't know how to do that. It sort of just... happened."

"Well, if we don't want the world to go, quite literally to hell, we're going to have to figure it out."

❦ 11 ❦

"**Y**ou got laid." In Nicholas Kingswood's sardonic baritone, the words conveyed more accusation than congratulations.

Julian ignored him, tossing the amulet down on the library desk behind which his conquesting brother held court like a tyrannical Caesar.

They were, after all, in a castle. Since their woodland bachelor retreat had rather been leveled by Moira's temper tsunami, they'd been forced to seek refuge elsewhere. Manresa Castle had provided just the right amount of familiar creature comforts as, through the ages, castles had been their particular residence of choice.

There was just something timeless about a stone fortress, especially now when everything was made of glass and steel and plaster.

Nick barely glanced down at the artifact before him, instead studying Julian with intent and perceptive eyes. "Finally danced the old Barnaby, eh? Ground the corn? Hauled the ashes? Took the bald-headed hermit to the alley? Broke your teacup? Danced the mattress jig? Licked the clicket—" Nick broke his tirade of archaic euphemisms when he finally took a good look at what Julian had thrown down in front of him. "Sweet baby antichrist, I haven't seen one of those since... let's see... since the de Medici's, I believe. Or was it the Borgia's? Didn't Da Vinci steal one from them to save a witch he liked once?"

"There was no clicket licking." Julian had snagged on one particular vexing and alternately alluring idea. "And how can you tell if I... had congress or not?"

Dru entered, dressed in his usual uniform of jeans and a black t-shirt, unceremoniously munching on a sandwich the size of his head. "You should always lick the clicket," he admonished, his adopted persona of sexual sage ruined by the mustard clinging to the corner of his mouth. "Lick it before you stick it," he said around a generous bite. "I'm pretty certain that was one of the original Ten Commandments."

"Yes, I think it was bumped off the tablets when the whole *thou shalt not lick thy neighbor's wife's clicket* became such a big fucking deal," Nick recalled.

"Don't be ridiculous," Julian muttered, wondering if one could strain an eye by rolling it too often. Though he pondered...what would Aerin have tasted like, that soft and supple flesh in which he'd buried himself again and again until...

"Though, it's been argued that those particular rules don't apply to us," Nick pointed out, ignoring him. "What with the 'Thou shalt not kill' thing being totally obsolete, as it's sort of our reason for existence."

"We're not being ridiculous," Dru said, flashing a wicked smile. "There are some rules worth following and others that aren't. But, I think the one about oral sex was extra important... Why do you think the bush was burning in the first place? Know what I mean?"

Nick shrugged. "I thought the whole burning bush thing was some ancient sexually transmitted infection caused by you-know-who." He feigned a covert action behind a hand while pointing at Julian's blushing face.

Pestilence lamented that even after thousands of

years, his brothers could be so infuriatingly juvenile as he watched Dru and Nick bump knuckles. "*You* are both going to burn in hell for blasphemy," he groused.

"At least we'll be together," Dru remarked, and the room's atmosphere immediately turned sober at the reminder that the fourth Horseman in their ranks was currently doing just that.

Burning in hell... or whatever Death did down there. They'd done all they could to get him out, now they had to rely on some pretty unreliable witches.

"The amulet," Julian reminded them, trying not to consider just how Nick had figured out just what he and Aerin had done. "Do you think it's significant?"

"Oh, it's significant as fuck." Nick picked it up and conducted a thorough examination. "There are only four of these in the known world," he marveled, allowing the Baltic amber to shimmer in the rays of the afternoon sun, illuminating the effervescent orbs encased within. "Created by an evil Macedonian Necromancer some handful of millennia ago, I believe. Darkest of the dark magic."

"Air, encased in amber from the original tree of life." Julian reclaimed the amulet from Nick's clutches. "The only thing that could render Aerin de Moray powerless. Curious, that a few upstart Americans could get their hands on a relic such as this." Something they should most definitely investigate.

"It is fortunate that we now have it," War inserted.

"Would that we had the other three amulets." Nick's eyes took on the dreamy expression of a tween girl contemplating the capture of Justin Beiber. "They would be at our complete mercy."

Julian's forehead wrinkled. "They only work against the witches."

"I know," Nick countered. "I was referring to the witches."

"You're terrible." Shaking his head, Julian pocketed

the amulet, not comfortable with it in anyone's hands but his own.

"Only on the days I'm not feeling ambitious."

"So..." Dru cut in, swiping at a place on an ancient tome where he'd dripped some pastrami and cheese grease. "You and Aerin just finish hate-fucking or what?"

An exasperated noise echoed through the library before Julian realized that his own throat had produced the sound. "That wasn't what—How the devil do you two know what transpired? You didn't—you weren't —*watching*, were you?"

Dru shrugged. "We were enjoying the shit out of watching Barriston fence with those witch hunters."

"Then how?"

Nick stood. "Relax, Jules, we just *know*. You live with a guy for a few thousand years, and you get to know him pretty well."

Dru made a gesture of agreement. "We haven't seen someone so pent up since Alexander the Great had that bout with erectile dysfunction."

"Those were the days," Nick chuckled. "But we totally get it. It's either have her against the wall or explode. Welcome to being a dude."

Troubled, Julian caressed the amber amulet in his pocket with his thumb, hard and smooth as any gemstone, and a hundred times more valuable. "It's not how I imagined things would progress between us," he confessed.

"Join the fucking club." Dru turned the page, not looking up from his book. "None of us were ready. We always knew this time would come. The end of days. We knew that we'd have to fulfill the prophecy. But I sort of thought we'd be helping some old hags put down a populace of fucktards who'd already destroyed their planet. That we'd be helping the Goddess sweep the board clean and create something new. Something better."

Nick made a bitter sound. "Instead we're caught in-between Satan and her forces of darkness, and some unpredictable beauties with a fucked-up destiny."

They each reflected for a silent moment, perusing the torn-apart library full of what was left of the ancient texts they'd salvaged from the ruins of their cabin, and what else they'd imported from Julian's Chateaux. They'd been immersed in frenetic and fruitless study for days, trying to figure out how to get their captured brother back.

A pall of hopelessness threaded its way through the room weaving a heavy blanket of doubt and darkness. Through their bond, each man could sense the maelstrom of bleak questions and bleaker decisions that needed to be made.

Were they fools to challenge fate? Were they wasting precious time and energy fighting a battle that could not be won? Should they have allowed the Apocalypse to commence some thousand years ago? Should they allow it now?

"It *can't* be now." Julian slammed his fist against the wall with an uncharacteristic show of temper. Shards of stone peppered the ground as the entire castle seemed to shake with the force of his frustration. "Humanity has yet to make the final decision. They think that we are the destroyers of worlds, but that just isn't so. We're little better than the clean-up crew. Cosmic janitors, if you will. For a time, it certainly seemed that humans would bring about their own demise, but look at all the pinpoints of hope in their dark tapestry. They're starting to revive the feminine divine, to return the ideal of equality for all man and womankind to this earth. The majority of them want to combine ideals, to find common ground, to facilitate peace and prosperity. They are rising up against those in power who would continue to damage the earth upon which they live. They are beginning to revolt against oppression. Against destruction. Against evil...but they need more time. Time I feel we must fight to give them."

"How do we fight destiny?" Dru stood, his lunch half-forgotten.

"We go to the witches," Julian said. "We convince them that we're on their side."

"As long as their view aligns with ours," Nick pointed out. "As far as I know, they're split down the middle."

"I believe we can find common ground," Julian insisted. "We can all concur that we can't stomach the idea of Lucifer winning the day."

"Fucking A," Dru agreed, before his dark eyes turned pensive. "The question is, how do we approach them? They're still pretty convinced we're out for blood. Specifically, their blood."

They stared at each other, their minds working furiously.

"We could just...go over there," Dru suggested, his face screwed into a grimace.

Nick let out a caustic snort. "Don't be an idiot, they'd zap us with that fucking horsemen repellant the second we showed our faces."

"Well I didn't say we'd go in unarmed."

"Yeah, like that inspires confidence." Nick stood and made his way around the desk. "Hey ladies, we come in peace, don't mind all these weapons, we just don't trust you."

"You have a better idea?" Dru held out his hands in a gesture of encompassing defiance. Or of crucifixion, one couldn't be completely certain.

Julian pulled out his cellular phone. "Perhaps we could...phone them or maybe send them one of those electronic correspondences people are so fond of? Contact them through social media or the like."

Neither of his brethren would meet his gaze.

"Tried that," Dru muttered.

"Me too." Nick regarded his phone on the desk as though it were the enemy. "I sent like... a million texts."

Pensive silence descended again.

"There's only one thing left to consider," Dru finally said.

"What's that?" Nick asked.

"WWDD..." Moving to the window, Dru stared out the casement at the specter of a riderless pale horse. "What Would Death Do?"

"We can't leave his perspective out," Nick agreed. "He'd break down the fucking doors and force them to listen."

Julian winced. "Indeed, and look where those tactics landed him."

Dru hissed in a breath through his teeth. "Good point... I say we give the house a wide berth. Meet on neutral ground."

"Agreed." Nick crossed his arms over his chest. "Let's not give them a chance to..."

Julian blinked as his vision blurred. The castle seemed to wrinkle beneath him, and a strange vibration started in his bones and rippled outward, as though the very space between his molecules was being ripped apart.

He reached out to steady himself, and gripped nothing. Opened his mouth to protest, and found he didn't have one.

Just as panic began to spear him, the sensation vanished, and he found himself in a very different place, indeed.

A bedroom. Done in white and black arabesque with wispy curtains and a bed that might as well have been a cloud.

"Excellent," Aerin purred, moving to stand from

where she'd been cross-legged in a circle of candles. "It worked."

Dumbfounded, Julian only stared for a few breathless moments, trying to orient himself.

"Dru was right," she said as she walked toward him, clad in a creamy, translucent robe. "You and I have some shit to work out."

❊ 12 ❊

Julian had never been driven to his knees. Not by any personage either God or man.

And plenty had tried.

However, the wave of reverential lust at the sight of Aerin's breasts thrusting proudly against the gauze of her gown—if such a garment deserved the distinction—threatened to buckle his legs from beneath him.

"You...summoned me here." The blatancy of his bewildered statement was cringeworthy, but he focused most of his attentions on not retreating from her seductive advance.

"I did," she admitted coyly, her eyes glowing quicksilver in the lantern light. "Like I said, we need to talk."

"Aerin," he warned hoarsely, putting his hand up against her advancement. "We both know that...that... garment isn't at all crafted for the conduction of conversation."

"This old thing?" she purred. Somehow, his outstretched hand was captured by hers, and then placed on her body, curving around one perfect breast. "Well, if you don't want to talk, there are other ways to occupy your mouth."

They did, indeed, have so many things to discuss, Julian conceded. But it would have to wait. It would have to wait until after he indulged one encompassing curiosity that had consumed him in the moments since Drustan had brought it up...

Before another word was spoken, Julian would find out just exactly what Aerin tasted like.

Everywhere.

With a speed belonging only to the revenants of the Other World, he dragged her against him and claimed her mouth.

Her lips were soft and familiar, though Julian wondered if he'd ever accustom himself to the electric charge of her touch. The husky sound she made rippled over his skin like silk and velvet, a sensual abrasion of sound and desire.

He knew she was angry with him. That his deeds had caused her pain, yet still their kiss was soft and achingly sweet. Julian drew his lips over hers again and again, the tenderness he felt for her blooming to the surface, melding with her ire and softening it.

Something about this kiss held more power than any magic spell or prophecy ever could. Aerin made him feel like a man. *Only* a man. A creature of blood and bones and hunger and lust. Nothing more. Not a soldier of destiny. Or a destroyer of souls innumerable.

A man making love to his woman. To the woman he loved.

With a moan made of equal parts pleasure and torture, Julian ran his hands down the dramatic slope of her back as it dipped into a narrow waist and flared into an ass that filled his kneading palms. Gods, there was nothing in heaven or on earth so perfect as Aerin de Moray's ass. As the feel of her lush curves pressed against his stark angles.

He'd yearned for so long. For a lifetime

For an eternity.

The scent of her, of storms and spices, frayed the edges of his sanity.

Picking her up, he split her legs around him as he walked them toward the white cloud of her bed, devouring her lips the entire way. Gently, he lowered her onto the bed, pressing her to lie back, though her legs dangled over the side.

Standing over her, he let his eyes drink their fill of the utterly erotic sight of her stretched beneath him like a pagan delicacy as he rid himself of his shirt. Her skin glowed creamy and iridescent in the candlelight, like the gossamer wings of a dragonfly.

Slowly, with blatant lust shining from her moonstone eyes, she parted her robe, and then parted her thighs.

It was then, and only then, that he hit his knees.

Thousands of languages deserted him at the sight of her. Thousands of prayers and spells, of curses and compliments. There was nothing to say no words applicable enough, no prayer appropriate enough. Not for an altar like this. Pink and pretty, shamelessly inviting him to worship.

Julian never wanted anything like he craved the pale body glowing beneath him. He couldn't remember a time he'd been so hard. So out of his mind with need. So fucking insatiable with lust.

And yet. A reverent patience drove him to chart the insides of her thighs. To rest her legs on his shoulders. To kiss the divots of her knees, then the thin skin protecting tiny blue veins of her inner thigh, until she made some foul demand on a breath so desperate, the words were unintelligible.

Though the sentiment was decidedly apparent.

"I've waited for more years than you can comprehend for this, Aerin de Moray," he rumbled, letting his hot breath waft over the damp petals of her bare sex. "I'll not be rushed."

This woman, *his woman,* was not one to beg. But the look she sent him down her luscious body was full of command and promises of retribution. Beneath it, though, if one looked deeply enough, a plea underscored it all.

And Julian knew he could never deny her. Not even if she asked him to damn the entire world.

His gaze never leaving her lips, parted in silent demand, he let his hot breath once again caress her intimate flesh before lowering his mouth to taste it.

Her ragged sound echoed his sentiment as she tossed her head back in equal parts relief and frustration. She tasted *wild*, like salt and carnal sin as his tongue slipped and snaked around the folds of her body.

She would beg, he decided, settling his shoulders between her thighs, pressing them ever wider. He would worship her. But she would beg.

Testing the entry to her body with his tongue, he found the slick desire he sought in abundance. He split her open with a sinuous lick, latching on to the exposed nub of sensation he'd uncovered, enjoying the tortured rasp of her increasingly desperate breath.

He abraded the soft pearl with quick, playful motions, and then long circular ones. His curious finger found her opening and sank inside her. She was so wet, so incredibly slick, that he glided in with no resistance, welcomed by the velvet warmth of her body.

She gasped and moaned, writhed and bucked beneath his ministrations, and a masculine thrill of victory speared him with feral desire. Tight sounds tore from her in hitches and sobs as his tongue circled and flicked, teased and tormented her to the edge of release, only to deny her.

The third time he pulled back, she literally growled at him. Reaching down she clutched at his hair, only to be thwarted yet again.

"What's the magic word, Aerin?"

"Fuck," she gasped.

"No, my love, that is what we're about to do...I'm

sure you know a slew of magic phrases, but there is one, in particular, that is the most powerful. It will get you what you want."

"Don't make me say it," she said from between clenched teeth.

He curled his knuckle inside her, flicking at her clit with his tongue. Then he pulled back, delighted to note that her hips curled off the bed, seeking him.

"Please," she begged.

Ever the benevolent immortal, he gave her what she asked for with his hand and his mouth. Her legs gripped at his shoulders, her hips surging, pressing her sex against his mouth as he feasted like a Roman in the throes of Saturnalia. She moaned his name.

And then she screamed it, loud enough to drown out the surge of wild, tempestuous wind battering against the old bones of the mansion.

Once her spasms of pleasure melted into little quivers, Julian withdrew his fingers from inside her and undid his belt. He distracted her with tiny licks and soft nips on her sex, reluctant to end his feast.

She collapsed to the bed in a puddle of pale limbs and shimmering hair, her hand resting on her head, the very essence of a Waterhouse painting. "Fuck me," she breathed, as though awestruck.

"If you insist." With a self-satisfied smile, Julian prowled up her naked body, settling his bulk atop her. He kissed her again, pouring an eternity of deprivation into her open mouth. He knew his lips were no longer gentle. That they were rough and demanding, perhaps even agitated. He knew he forced her to taste the essence of her pleasure on his tongue.

But it had been long enough. Now was the time to claim what was his. What would forever belong to him.

Heart thundering with the strength of his desire, he drew her knee up his waist to grant him easier entrance before surging forward. He didn't stop until his entire length was buried in the succulent warmth of her body.

How, he marveled, had anyone ever convinced themselves that this act was a sin? Nothing else existed so close to divinity as this place, this soft place close to the womb of a magical woman.

"Take me," he breathed, sinking into her again, staring down into those lovely, lovely silver eyes, and uncovering all the secrets that she shared with no one. "Take all of me."

"I will," she gasped, lifting her hips to meet his. "I do."

He couldn't stop to consider the full extent of the meaning in his words to her. *Take me. Take my heart, my soul, my needs, my emptiness.*

Take all of me.

It was too much for any one woman to hold.

But she did. She held him so sweetly in the cradle of her thighs he thought he might expire from the bliss of it.

Julian had the strange notion one does when they're certain that this had happened before. That in some other lifetime—in another place—they'd met like this. They'd felt like this.

They'd loved just like this.

He forced his mind away from thoughts of fate and destiny and focused on the tight sheath of her flesh already pulling tremors of pleasure from the base of his spine. He slid his hand beneath her ass and set an erotic rhythm with his hips, one she met with thrusts of her own.

I love you, he thought.

Her fingers threaded into his unbound hair, her features shimmering with lust, pleasure, vulnerability and fear.

"I love you, too."

At her words, a bolt of lightning touched down in

the garden, sparking the world with light as brilliant and blinding as the sun. Answering sensations exploded within him with a force he could not comprehend and a power he had no name for. Greater than the Gods. More potent than prophecy.

Aerin wrapped her arms around his back and locked her legs about his hips, clinging to him like one would an anchor in the storm. She screamed her pleasure to the sky, her body clenched around his in an endless shudder of ecstatic release. The contractions of her sex sent even more violent pleasure into his own until his orgasm became a spiraling cataclysm of sensation. Crippling. Destructive. And full of the redemption they both sought.

Thunder rumbled in answer to the lightning, and the electric build of the storm that accumulated over the sea held the whisper of danger on the wind. Though as Julian watched the woman he loved come apart in his arms, he could think of nothing as dangerous as she.

Once the storm of their passion passed, they lay entwined for a silent eternity, contemplating the meaning of things. Of the lightning. Of their admissions to each other.

Of their love.

"Say it again," he rumbled, nuzzling at the downy skin of her temple and placing a kiss on her sharp cheekbone.

"Fuck me," she sighed.

He smiled against her hairline. Nothing with this woman would be easy. Then again, he wouldn't even know what to do with easy. It wasn't a concept he had much experience with.

"No," he said patiently. "The other thing."

She gave an undignified snort. "You get one 'please' a day, buster, don't get greedy."

"Don't deny me, Aerin," he said seriously, rolling on top of her. "Tell me you love me. Give me your heart."

"I can't." A veil of tears shimmered in her eyes and she fought them down, valiantly. "If I give you my heart, then I give you control. I give you power. The power to break me. I can't...I shouldn't have..."

A tender laugh escaped him, and he adored the wrath gathering in her eyes. "Don't you know that I already gave you the control? Don't you understand that you've had it from the beginning? From the moment I saw you in that airport. From the moment I touched your hand."

"You tried to kill me, twice," she reminded him archly.

"Because I knew how dangerous you were. How much power you could wield. Not only over me, but over the entire cosmos. I knew, in that moment, that if you set your cap at world domination, not even Lucifer could stand in your way. I want you to be the companion of my life, but the thought of you as an overlord is utterly terrifying."

"Well...in that case..." She kissed him, mollified. "I love you, Julian Roarke."

"And I love you." He caressed the silk of her hair, marveling at the color. "I want you to know that I never wished you harm. I thought that your demise would save the world from certain destruction, and that my personal hell, my curse, would be to forever walk this earth without you. But now I—*we*—think that maybe there's another way."

"We being..."

"Nick, Dru, and I. Though we'll have to wait for them to arrive to discuss it with your sisters."

"They'd better take a while," Aerin said before thrusting her hips up and using the momentum to reverse their positions, rolling him to his back. "Because I'm not finished corrupting you. *Cum* to the dark side, Julian Roarke, and I'll show you how fun sinning can be."

❧ 13 ❧

Lucifer seethed.

As *the* agent of evil and insuperable ruler of her own otherworldly realm, she'd never before had to deal with the kind of disrespect and *bullshit* she'd been subjected to by these self-important mortals. She had to merely but whisper her whims, and her minions obeyed. If a tiny sliver of displeasure showed upon her face, they cowered. Her name, nay, the very *idea* of her was to be feared. Hated. Reviled. Not bandied about like a riddle meant to be solved.

There was no solution for the hell she was about to unleash upon this world.

Beginning with Port Townsend.

Julian was hers. *She* was meant to be the one to corrupt him, to initiate him to the sins of the flesh. To beat him into submission until he worshiped *her* on his knees.

Just who the mother fuck did Aerin de Moray think she was? Better yet. Who did she think she was dealing with?

Merging with the shadows in a brimstone wisp of smoke, Lucifer had found the crack in the wards and filtered into the de Moray manse with no more tangible shape than a breath. She'd slunk through the rooms of the house, following the pulse of wicked desire to the Air Witch's chamber in time to watch them fuck in the shower, eliciting another bout of wild lightning to whip across the cloudy sky.

Lucy's out-of-control emotions made it more difficult for her to hide herself, to remain anonymous, but she had the dark will of the ages on her side, and somehow managed to contain the magical pulses of her fury.

She'd gone about this all wrong, Lucy decided as Aerin stepped from the shower and towel-dried her admittedly impressive voluptuous body before slipping on a filmy white satin robe.

How could she have been so blind? The perfect opportunity had been there all along. She'd tried the conservative approach before, and should have known that it would fail. There was no tempting a druid to the dark side. Not completely. Not if you left them their free will.

If you wanted something, *someone,* you had to take by force.

And Aerin de Moray and she shared an element.

Better yet, they shared a proclivity for dark magic. And it was that dance with the darkness that left Aerin vulnerable to what Lucifer was about to do next.

RELAXED AND PLEASURED BEYOND IMAGINING, JULIAN padded out of the bathroom with a towel about his waist, still not comfortable giving up his habitual modesty. Regardless of every illicit thing they'd only just done.

Aerin had traded her filmy white robe for a silken black one and was coiling her hair in a serpentine knot above her head.

"Hello lover," her eyes burned up at him like liquid

smoke, and her lips curled into a smile that was at once familiar and unsettling.

She looked different than she had all night. Their newfound intimacy, the vulnerability she'd revealed, had somehow...dissipated.

Perplexed and disappointed, Julian reached for her. It was as though she'd donned not only a change of clothing but a change of skin.

"Is everything all right, darling?" he inquired, pulling her into the circle of his arms.

"Everything is just as it ought to be, *my lover*," she said against his chest.

A pang of warning speared him. Maybe it was the way she'd emphasized the last two words. The possession in which he'd thought to enjoy, somehow chafed.

Enough for him to pull away.

The act of dressing gave him an excuse to avoid her touch, which saddened him. Just what was he missing?

A tug at his otherworldly senses informed him of Nicholas and Dru's approach. They'd finally decided to bite the bullet, as it were, and brave the dangers of the de Moray territory to come after him.

He was glad they'd waited. That they'd not... interrupted.

But now...

He cast a covert glance at Aerin, at the only woman he'd ever fallen for, and was surprised at his *lack* of desire.

Perhaps it was nothing. They'd spent many hours in each other's arms, reached climax more than was possible for most humans.

Maybe he was just depleted. Maybe he needed a moment to build the lust back. Though, he'd not thought that possible. Not with how insatiable he'd been all night.

The doorbell rang, and Aerin's head whipped around at an almost unnatural angle.

"My brother's are here," he informed her, trying to put her at ease.

"Not all of them," she murmured with the ghost of a smirk.

"Not all of them," he echoed. "But that's the purpose of our visit. Like I said, we want to talk about finding a way to rescue Bane from Hell. To release him from Lucifer's clutches.

"Well." She lifted her eyebrows over eyes sparkling with an anticipation he didn't at all expect. "Let's go meet them." Gliding to her door she opened it and sashayed through, moving with a sensual swing to her hips that hadn't been there before.

Rather overdone, in Julian's opinion.

"Come, lover," she beckoned. "I'm just *dying* to hear what they have to say."

GLIDING DOWN THE GRAND AND WINDING STAIRCASE of the de Moray manse, Lucy let her hand trail along the banister with a possessive sort of glee. Lord what power coursed through her, what pure elemental bliss.

She'd previously underestimated these witches. She understood that now. Not since the dark ages had she felt this kind of unmitigated strength.

What a pity, really, that the devil's magic was—like all deities—linked to faith. To belief and worship. But no longer. Now entirely new opportunities presented themselves like the prostrate forms of the hopeless damned.

Beneath her fucking Jimmy Choo sling back heels.

One of these prospects was beneath them all, quite literally, as a writhing tortured Horseman. Her plaything. Her possession.

The other, was regrettably still inside her. Or, rather, Lucy was inside the air witch. In the most intimate possible way. This was a penetration of the soul.

An intrusion of the mind. A rape of Aerin de Moray's very self.

A secret smile lifted the corners of her mouth as Aerin's creative and emphatic curses screamed from the dark cage where Lucifer had imprisoned her awareness. Of course, Lucy planned to get rid of Aerin eventually. But she'd have to gain more power first. More souls, more fear, and more electric sex with Julian Roarke. How delicious it would be to make Aerin watch as Lucy crushed everything and everyone she cared about.

"You don't deserve that shit-eatin' grin, Aerin de Moray." At the bottom of the stairs, Moira wagged her finger like an Italian mama, her other hand resting on a hip thrust out as far as it could to in order to convey the proper amount of censure. "We all know who caused it and, while I can't rightly judge y'all for taking the train to pound town, we don't appreciate a Horseman in the house without our knowing it first."

"And I don't appreciate you both knocking three crystals from the chandelier!" Tierra lamented. "That's *Irish* crystal imported more than a hundred years ago. Do you know how much they'll cost to replace?"

"I can afford it." Lucy found that adopting Aerin's sultry sense of sarcasm wasn't much of a reach from her usual diction.

"You bet your ass you can," the earth witch muttered.

Was this what sisters tiffed about? Was this how it felt to live with family, among equals? It was rather novel to break with the regular stuff, like the scraping, the moaning, the gnashing of teeth and so forth. A family... experiencing such a thing hadn't occurred to Lucifer until now.

"We might not have time to replace anything." Claire blazed into the foyer, her hips swaying as much as her leather duds would allow. Woman after her own heart, the devil mused. "What with impending fucking

Apocalypse and the remaining Horsemen trying to in-filtrate the house."

"Infiltrate?" Tierra fretted. "Are there more Horsemen inside the house other than Jul--?"

The doorbell rang just as Claire reached for the handle and yanked. Though the heavy door barricaded her view, Lucy knew exactly who stood on the opposite side.

Julian was a silent presence behind Lucy's back, and she loved that she stood between him and his brothers.

In more ways than one.

God this was the most fun she'd had in centuries! She had to clutch the banister to keep from clapping her hands with child-like delight.

Claire stood her ground and said nothing, directing a simmering, unamused glare toward the porch.

"Hey," rumbled Dru's deep voice.

"Hey," Claire echoed.

Even the Lady of Lies had to wince.

Awkward as fuck.

"Is uh... is Julian here?"

"How'd you get past the wards?" Claire ignored the question.

"What wards?" Nick queried. "They're down."

"What the shit?" Tierra whirled on Aerin. "Did you do this?"

Lucy was going to deny it, but then she realized that she was utter shit at the innocent expressions. Always had been. "How else was my fuck buddy going to get in?"

She could tell from the chilly shift in the at-mosphere behind her, that Julian wasn't thrilled with his new moniker. Well, tough. You mess with the Devil, you still get horns.

That truth never changed.

"You going to invite us in, or what?" Nick demanded.

"You can stay right where you are," Claire said. "We'll send Julian out with the rest of the trash."

"I beg your pardon?" Julian's effrontery hit her in another chilly wave.

Claire went to shut the door in their faces and was thwarted by what Lucy imagined was Dru's boot.

"We're here to offer a truce." He bit out the words as though they cost him a great deal.

"Oh, you mean you'll stop trying to kill us for a second now that you're only three strong?" Claire snarked. "Thanks a million, but we'll take our chances."

Moira slid gentle fingers over Claire's jacket shoulder as she padded around her to peek out the door. "Maybe we should hear them out."

Claire yanked away. "As the only one who's not fucking one of these yahoos at the moment, I maintain that the smart thing to do is toss Julian to his brothers, slam the door, and put the wards back in place."

"I dare you to endeavor to throw me anywhere," Julian challenged.

"Lucifer has Bane in her realm, which means she has use of his power." Nick gave them the reader's digest version.

The sisters only paused for a moment before throwing open the door and admitting Dru and Nick into the foyer.

Julian stepped around her to join his brethren, without reaching for her.

Strange. She'd thought he'd be more considerate to the witch he'd just spent hours making love to. Lucy descended as well, though she stayed a few stairs above them all.

"We came to talk to you," Dru addressed Tierra, looking more worried than she'd seen him. Maybe ever. "To ask, to beg you if necessary, to bring Bane back. If you do, our ceasefire will continue, and we'll work with you stop the Apocalypse."

"The hell you will," Lucy hissed. Though her lips snapped shut when they all turned to stare at her. "What I meant was... why should we believe a word you say?" Using Aerin's imperious tone, she knew by their mirroring frowns that she'd pulled it off.

"Because despite any differences we have, none of us want Lucy to achieve her goals." Nick was obviously trying to be charming, but Lucy knew the gall that seethed just below the surface. She could tell by the way he avoided the water witches' knowing aqua gaze.

So Conquest had finally found someone he feared. My, my, it really *was* the end of days.

"What do we have to do to get him back?" Dru gritted out.

The earth witches' eyes filled with tears. "I don't know. I'm not really even sure how I--" her hand went to her stomach. "*We*, put him there."

Fascinating, Lucy thought. So Tierra couldn't have done it on her own. She had help... from Killian Bane's child. A familiar stab of fear pierced her and she smothered it with cold, pure rage. What if Death and Druid of creation made a baby? What kind of power would it wield?

Lucy barely paid attention to their paltry brainstorm as her eyes fixed on Tierra's softly protruding stomach.

She had Aerin now... but perhaps she'd gone after the wrong sister.

TIERRA

TIFFINIE HELMER

❧ 1 ❧

Tierra would pay for dumping him in Hell.

The thought of all the many deviant acts he planned for her was the only thing keeping Killian Bane from going bat-shit crazy. After he punished her, he'd take her over and over again until there was no fucking question in her mind to whom she belonged.

Just as soon as he got out of Hell.

Which had to be any day now.

Surely within the hour.

His brothers were working on a plan and would be implementing it soon, of that he had no doubt. But they were sure taking their sweet ass time.

From the moment he'd landed in this pit, he had become Lucifer's favorite pet, and she'd made it her mission to demonstrate on him, Death himself, all the demonic practices that had bred fear in the populace since the time of Adam and Eve.

The bitch was downright creative, he'd give her that.

Currently he was naked and shish kabobed to the wall of a rank crypt after having undergone a variety of tortures only a sadist of the highest order could dream up. Copper spikes pinned him to the brimstone walls, leeching his powers and keeping him in a state that was somewhat close to human. It wouldn't kill him. He was a fucking immortal, but if left too long, it might end him in a catatonic state. Copper was one of the few elements that had the ability to affect him. And the three-foot-long stakes pinning him to the wall burned like a son of a bitch.

Rods pierced the sides of his neck, a few through his triceps and the skin under his ribs, and if that weren't enough, two in his thighs and calves as well. He wasn't going anywhere without divine intervention. She'd left his hands and feet alone as she found that too offensive even for her, stating personal reasons.

The Bible spoke of Hell as an all-consuming fire where the inhabitants burned endlessly for eternity with no chance of relief, but that wasn't true. Hell was tailor-made for each individual. Arachnophobes were deposited into a room filled with spiders. Germaphobes swam in cesspools of bacteria, while those afraid of heights continued to fall from immense cliffs. Whatever would evoke the highest emotional response was implemented. He didn't want to consider what happened to child molesters. He'd heard rumors, and he really couldn't fault the practice Lucy had chosen as punishment for that particular heinous crime.

Death's private Hell was either being trapped in a tomb or buried alive in a grave, which Tierra had now accomplished *twice*. He was a tad more claustrophobic than he'd like to admit, and Lucy had outdone herself. The air was stifling and infused with sulfur. Water dripped on his face until he thought he'd go mad. Not rhythmically, which could resemble white noise. No, the dripping changed, morphed with his emotions. Fast, disjointed, sluggish, violent at times until the dirt floor he stood on with bare feet turned to soul-sucking mud. Cold, damp, and desolate.

Tierra had a lot to answer for: rejecting him when she'd discovered he'd bound her to him for her protection—a romantic gesture she should have appreciated—and then opening the Hell Mouth and dropping him here, a power far beyond her capabilities. He could only assume she'd had help.

Help in the way of their unborn child.

It was the only explanation for how Tierra had thwarted Lucy when she'd tried to burn her at the stake.

Hadn't that been a sight to behold?

A smile curved his lips at the memory, and he promptly bit it back. He was mad at her. *Furious*. He'd suffered much because of her, and she would feel his wrath once he was free. He'd start with her on her hands and knees, her mouth around his—

"Killian?"

His heart stopped at the sound of her voice. She couldn't be. *Not here*.

Timidly, Tierra entered his cell, dressed in a flowing gypsy skirt, bangles wrapped around her wrists and ankles, singing with bells with each graceful movement. A gauzy peasant blouse in the purest white graced her upper body. The fine cotton billowed and hid her pregnancy. *His* child, the one they'd created the day he first had her delectable body five months ago. Her long reddish-black hair cascaded around her in wavy rivulets and he ached to touch her with the hunger of a concentration camp victim.

"Tierra?" She couldn't be real. He didn't want her to see him like this, strung up like some voodoo doll. She had to be an illusion, one Lucy planned to taunt or torture in front of him. He swallowed, not knowing if he'd mentally survive it.

"I've come to rescue you," she said, her voice breathy.

How? *How* had she gotten here? But then, how had she sent him here to begin with? "Are my brothers with you? Your sisters?"

Maybe there was a chance . . . hope sprouted in his chest.

"No, it's just me."

Shit.

"Leave!" he barked. "I don't want you here." Lucy had been trying to strike a deal. She'd promised to release him if he gave over his first-born. He would perish in Hell before she got her fake nails on his child, but if she found Tierra . . .

She rushed toward him, her hands feeling like fire brands on his frigid chest. He craved the warmth, but the touch was too much. Painful.

"Don't." He winced. "She'll be here any moment. Get out. *Now.*" He put every ounce of strength he had left in the words, yet they sounded whiny and pitiable.

"I can't leave you like this. I'm so sorry for sending you here in the first place. Please tell me you don't blame me."

Oh, he blamed her.

Hadn't he just been relishing the ways to punish her? But seeing her now, standing in front of him, and knowing what Lucy would do to her if discovered—fear devoured the sliver of hope.

"Please, Tierra, think of your sisters, the baby. If you have any feelings for me, you'll leave now. I couldn't bear it if something happened to you."

"Do you love me, Killian?" she asked, her voice shy, her eyes downcast.

Did he? He had lived for so long, had many dalliances, and remembered a few women he'd taken to bed fondly, but love? Did he even know what love was?

"Are you willing to die for me?" Her hands trailed over his stomach, the touch raw and unwelcome. "I know about the deal. Why won't you take it? Be with me. I've missed you."

"To give up our child would be like giving over my own soul. I can't do that."

"You're forgetting something, Killian. I don't want this baby. I've considered aborting it."

"*No*." A painful fist clutched his heart. "You don't mean that. I've seen you. Your hand protectively covers your belly, the mother bear in you fighting to the forefront whenever it's been threatened. You love our baby."

"No, I don't. It's changing me, making me do things, crave things that are unnatural. Scary, dark evil things. This child was never meant to be born. It's an anomaly, a freak of nature. Please, take the deal. If not for yourself, do it for me."

"Look at me, Tierra. Look me in the eye and tell me that." Suspicion started to clear his senses. The woman he knew would never consider aborting the life growing inside her, regardless of the creature that fathered it. She was an earth witch and therefore abhorred the idea of killing anything.

"I can't. I'm so ashamed of how I feel. And I'm scared, Killian, scared of what you and I will unleash on the world. How can we be that selfish?"

"Kiss me. Let me taste you, feel you against me." He held his breath as she slowly lifted her head toward his.

Their lips met, and bile rose in his throat. He yanked away from her. A crafty smile spread over her lips, and her silvery eyes met his.

Not Tierra, but Aerin. *That bitch*.

Had Aerin completely gone dark then? Was that why she was here? Certainly not to save him, not after he'd come so close to killing her.

She tilted her head back and laughed. "Took you long enough." She trailed a finger farther down his chest, and it felt as if an electrical current followed in its wake. "And here I'd lowered myself to dress in this hideous outfit. Though, granted, they are comfortable if not more suitable for the homeless. Did you know your precious Tierra wears the hand-me-downs of her relatives? Trunks and trunks of dusty clothes are packed away in the attic and she *shops* out of them. I think that's more than a bit crazy." She slid her smoky gaze down his naked body and studied his manhood, her fingers brushing close. "I have to know—you're the fourth Horseman of the Apocalypse, an immortal who could have any woman he wanted. Many women for that matter. So what kind of hold does Tierra have over you?"

He gritted his teeth as bile rose higher in his throat. Had Aerin made a deal with Lucifer? She hadn't seemed the type who needed or wanted anything from anyone else. So what could the Devil offer Aerin de Moray that would have her signing on the dotted line? It had to be power. Everyone knew Aerin was hungry for more, but would she have willingly sacrificed her sisters to taste it?

He didn't answer her question. Instead, he asked one of his own. "What have you done, Aerin?"

"Oh, I've done plenty. Answer my question, and I'll tell you all about it. Do you love Tierra?"

"Why do you care?"

She laughed and turned away, gliding to stand in the middle of the room. The bells on Tierra's bracelets sang with her nimble movements, causing his heart to ache.

"Well, for one, it would explain a lot. Why you'd forsake Lucy, a sexy, powerful immortal—who I'll admit to having a little crush on myself—for a lowly earth witch, and why you aren't willing to do the one thing that would spring you from this prison. Can't imagine you're enjoying your . . . stay."

"Do your sisters know you're here?"

"There's a lot my *sisters* don't know about me." She smirked. "As I'm sure there's plenty your brothers don't know about you. Come on, you can tell me. Do you love my sister or not?"

"It's none of your business. That's between Tierra and me."

"Ah, still upset with her for putting you here. But, you see, I'm not leaving until I get an answer."

"I don't give a shit what you do."

"Oh, you might." She held her hands out to her sides, and sparks flew from her fingertips, flashing into lightning. The lightning instantly sought out the copper rods skewering him to the wall. His body bowed and convulsed from the electricity arcing through him. A scream escaped him regardless of how he tried to contain it. The pain was too much and needed an outlet.

"Wow, wasn't that intense." Aerin ambled over to him, her eyes wide with fascination. "Tell me, how did that make you feel?"

"Fuck you."

She laughed, the sound unlike anything he'd heard Aerin utter. "You should be so lucky."

"Julian won't be happy to know what you're doing."

"Fuck him. Oh, wait, been there, done that. Disappointing, I can say. Virgins are so much work. All those questions, the teaching, it was downright frustrating. Really not worth all the hype. But then you took Tierra's virginity, so I bet you understand where I'm coming from—er, not coming that is."

His mind reeled. Julian and Aerin *slept* together. If Lucy found out . . .

Aerin was playing a dangerous game. Lucy would be beyond furious if she knew Aerin had taken Julian from her. The term, "Hell to pay," would take on a whole new meaning. He wondered if she'd considered that before she made her deal.

"What did you give up, Aerin, in your deal with the Devil?"

"That's just it. I didn't give up anything. Well, I have to train under Lucy, get back at the Horsemen, and make sure the Apocalypse is successfully accomplished, but those were things I already wanted. So it's a win-win for me, and a loss for you since you're my first

Horseman to geld. No wait. I'm pretty sure I gelded Julian. The man is useless now that I've ridden him into oblivion."

Aerin walked over to the wall and turned a large valve to a water main.

"You've been down here a while," she continued. "A lot has changed back home. And unless you want to answer my question, I guess we should step this up a notch. I do believe I have a knack for torture, and I love hearing you scream." She held her hands out to her sides again. She levitated up from the floor, her icy eyes glowing demonic in the shadowed room.

Water bled from the walls, pooling at his feet, and lightning flew from Aerin's fingertips again.

☙ 2 ❧

"Where's Aerin?" Tierra asked, entering the kitchen to find her sisters eating breakfast and studying ways to get Killian out of Hell. Claire was on the computer, and Moira was deep in the pages of the Grimoire.

"She's sure been gone a lot lately," Claire muttered. Her hair hung in a sheen down her black silk top that she'd paired with even blacker jeans.

"And bitchier than normal, have y'all noticed?" Moira bit into a pop tart. "Gotta be her time of the month, but doesn't that only last like five or six days?"

"Maybe for her it's longer," Claire added. "Lately she seems to be in a constant state of PMS."

"I miss having a period."

They both looked at Tierra like she was crazy.

"Hey, pregnancy makes PMS seem like a cake walk. The bloating, the cravings, the freaky dreams. Everything is so much more intense. And my breasts hurt." She adjusted them in the constricting bra.

"Lose the boulder holder. Does wonders for me." Moira shimmied her shoulders, her breasts moving freely under the blue Bubba Gump Shrimp t-shirt. She'd given up on the threadbare tanks as the weather had turned much cooler with fall settling over the Northwest. She even wore a full pair of jeans, instead of the cutoffs. Granted, they were torn at the knees and frayed at the hem, but she at least had more skin covered for a change.

Tierra put the kettle on to heat and pulled out organic fresh eggs. Glancing around for Cheeto, she grabbed the bacon.

Good. The pig was MIA, too.

While she'd always eaten a vegetarian diet, this pregnancy required more. Since the horrific day she'd devoured a bag of Moira's pork rinds, she'd given into the cravings as it kept the morning sickness at bay. Rather than fight it, she decided a balanced diet of organic and processed foods was called for. Hence the bacon.

"It's the back pain for me," Moira continued. "I'd do about anything not to feel those aches every month. Well, except get knocked up. Sorry. Okay, yeah, I can see why you would miss your period."

"Let's get back to where Aerin is," Claire said. "We need her help. It's like she has a second job or something. Have you seen her work on her computer lately?"

"No, I haven't." Tierra held up the knife she was using to slice an apple, gesturing with it for emphasis. "That *is* weird, now that you mention it. Her laptop is like an extra limb to her."

"Maybe she and Julian are sneaking away for a bit of the old lust 'n' thrust." Moira set aside Grim and thickly buttered a biscuit. "They about tore this house apart the night she snuck him in. I'd sure like to know how she managed that."

"You and me both, sister." Claire grunted an agreement. "Actually, Julian didn't seem too pleased with her at the impromptu meeting we all had. He seemed more confused. Definitely not lover like."

"The man hasn't had sex in like . . . *ever*," Moira said

around a mouthful, using her tongue to swipe at a glob of butter off her lip. "He might need some tutorials."

"Sure sounded like they'd enjoyed themselves," Claire muttered. "I don't think the chandelier will ever hang the same."

Tierra agreed. The thing had swayed and bounced, dangling in the room under Aerin's bed. She needed to make a note to have it reinforced. The crystal chandelier was a family heirloom, brought over from Ireland a hundred or so years ago by their great-great grandmother.

The bacon started to sizzle, and her mouth watered. She cracked an egg, even though it wasn't the egg she wanted. It was the pork she craved. And didn't that bite? But she needed a big breakfast if she was going to face what she'd faced every day since she had sent Killian to Hell. She'd been plagued with guilt and something else she didn't want to put a name to.

"Find anything yet?" she asked her sisters.

"Nothing in the Bible," Claire said. "I've gone through both the NIV and King James' versions until I was cross-eyed. Then I tackled the Koran, the Egyptian Book of the Dead, and the Witches Bible. Nothing. I'm perusing the Hortus Deliciarum now."

"The what?" Tierra asked.

"It's a medieval manuscript that came up in my Google search. I'm grasping at anything really."

"Anything in Grim?"

Moira shook her head. "He's not speaking to me, so I'm trudging through page by page. Sorry, darlin'."

"Hopefully the Horsemen are having better luck. After I eat something, I'm going to search through the attic. I remember boxes of old books. Some are journals. Maybe there's another witch's grimoire up there, and it will have some insight."

"Have you considered that no one has been able to

escape Hell?" Claire pointed out. "If they had, wouldn't there be rumors?"

Moira kicked Claire under the table. "Just because nobody has don't mean nobody will."

Moira and Claire shared a look.

"It's all my fault." Tierra slumped against the counter. "How was I to know opening the earth and saying those words would actually send him straight to Hell?"

"Now, sugar, don't go beating yourself up." Moira rose from the table, walked over, and draped a comforting arm around Tierra. "We all do things when we're off kilter. And I for one, think he deserved what he got treatin' you to the Horsemen version of a shotgun wedding."

"Inexcusable," Claire agreed. "If a man married me without my permission, he'd be lucky to retain his balls. Hey, wait." Claire rose and started to pace.

"What?" Tierra and Moira said together.

"Give me a sec. I'm thinking."

While Claire paced, Tierra loaded up a plate with eggs, bacon, apples, blueberries, and a thick slice of artisan bread spread heavily with butter and freshly made orange-ginger marmalade. It was enough food to feed a lumberjack. Moira carried Tierra's peppermint tea to the table for her, and they both tucked themselves in and waited.

She'd foraged through half her meal when Claire finally turned toward them. "I think we're looking at this the wrong way. We don't need to get Death out of Hell." She pointed to Tierra. "You do."

"Excuse me? You want me to go to Hell?" Tierra laid a protective hand over her expanding belly.

"*Claire*," Moira chastised.

"No, that's not what I mean. Think about it. You said they were bound. There has to be a way to reach him through their bond."

"Ahh, I'm reading you, sister," Moira said, nodding her head.

"Well, someone needs to clue me in." Tierra picked up a piece of crisp bacon and devoured it with savage pleasure. Hmm, maybe she should dip some bacon in chocolate? Her stomach rumbled. Most definitely.

"You said you were having freaky dreams," Claire said, retaking her seat and typing into the search engine on her laptop. "What kind?"

Tierra squirmed in her seat.

"Oh, it's that way, is it?" Moira smirked. "Having you some cum slumbers starring your baby daddy?"

"No, nothing like that. And don't call him my baby daddy. It's weird." She couldn't imagine Killian Bane as anyone's daddy, let alone her baby's. No matter how much she tried, she couldn't see the fourth Horseman of the Apocalypse changing diapers. If the little tyke was bullied at school and Killian was called in, he'd most likely take the offending kid's soul rather than reason through the situation.

"Yet cum slumber doesn't weird you out?" Claire commented.

"What should we call him then?" Moira asked. "Drive-by sperm donor, ye old knocker upper, wham bammer thank-you ma'ammer? No, I got it. Spawn slinger. Yeah, that's gonna stick. Hehehe, see what I did there?"

Claire laughed. "How about baby batter blaster, Johnny Applecock, Colonel Cockknocker, or killer egg splitter?"

They dissolved into a fit of giggles.

"Very mature." Tierra sipped her tea, wishing she hadn't said anything. "Can we get back to your idea, before you make me throw up my breakfast?"

Claire sobered first as Moira wiped tears from her eyes. "You're not still getting sick, are you? I thought you had that under control once we cleansed the house of Lucy's brimstone."

"Yeah, doing better. Don't worry. Tell me your idea."

"Right. First, what kind of dreams are you having?" She held up her finger to silence Moira. "Let's stay on track. You and I can revisit this conversation later. Aerin's gotta hear these names, too."

Great. Tierra picked up another piece of bacon. Jinx, her black cat familiar, wandered in with Doctor Lector, Aerin's bat, riding on his back.

"Would you look at that?" Moira exclaimed. "It's a catbat, or batcat. I feel a superhero joke in there somewhere."

"Wonder why those two are hanging out together?" Claire asked.

"Lector is missing Aerin. He and Jinx are playing point guard," Tierra informed them.

"How do you know that?" Moira asked.

"They told me."

"Told you?"

"Uh, yeah, remember when I put on the crown that I found in the Standing Stones? Well, I can talk to the animals now. Cheeto and Kai are sniffing out zombie leftovers in the garden. That can't be healthy. They have the grounds today while Jinx and Lector are patrolling the manor."

"Add research on the familiars to our growing list." Claire wrote down on her note pad. She loved making lists.

"What else have they told you?" Moira asked. "Did Cheeto tell you how he breaths fire and where the hell he came from?"

"I'll have to ask him. But I can tell you that he thinks of Nick as 'the hairless mansack.' In Cheeto's mind, the only man worthy of you has a curly tail, breathes fire, and trots around on all fours."

"Aww, ain't that sweet."

"Anything from Kai?" Claire leaned forward.

"He's skittish around me and doesn't like to share information. Maybe if you were in the room, I'd get something out of him."

"Well, shit on a stick, this just opened up a whole new world."

"Can we not mention shit at the table?" Tierra pushed her plate back. She'd consumed most of the food and felt beyond full. She inched her chair away from the table and leaned back. With the baby, there didn't seem to be a lot of room for her other organs, and she'd just stuffed her stomach, adding to the uncomfortable feeling.

"Crap, I just got a flash of the tongue-curbing you'll expect us to do once the little tadpole gets here," Moira said.

"Fuck." Claire swung her hair over one shoulder and started to play with the ends. "You're right."

"*Claire!*" Aunt Justine pounded down the stairs and ran into the kitchen. With her bright red newly-dyed hair in disarray and the color in her face flaring with anger, she looked exactly like a boiled lobster. "You *have* to do something about Tommy. I found *skin* in the shower drain. It's time you put that . . . *man* to rest for good."

Silence followed her statement. Tommy, Claire's first love who had recently been resurrected from the dead, was the elephant in the room no one wanted to bring up.

"I'll talk to him and have him use a different shower."

"Not mine." Moira shuddered. "Sorry, I can't believe I'm about to say this, but I agree with Aunt Justine."

Claire looked at Tierra. "And what do you have to say?"

"Pregnant with Death's spawn, here. I have nothing to offer."

"What? You're always up for a lecture," Claire sneered, her mood smoldering.

"Is that how you see me?"

Moira shrugged. "You're pretty good at it. And to be truthful, you're usually on point."

"Claire, this is something you have to decide for yourself," Tierra said. "You love Tommy, so you have to choose if you can have a life with him the way he is or love him enough to let him go."

"I killed him once. I can't do that again. You're asking the impossible."

"I'm not asking you do to anything." She placed her hand over Claire's. "I understand how much you care for him. Maybe search your heart and figure out how much is guilt and how much is real love."

"I don't give a fig either way," Justine said. "I just don't want pieces of flesh clogging my drain. Now, who is going to go up there and take care of it? I need to shower. I have a meeting with the insurance agent about the claim on Ambrosia's. Remember *your* business, Tierra? The one that blew up?"

Like she could forget, since she'd been set afire at the stake by the Devil herself right before the explosion. "Aunt Justine, use my shower. It's a zombie free zone. And thank you for meeting with the insurance adjuster. I really appreciate it."

"Well," Justine harrumphed, placated. "Fine, I guess that will have to do for now." She pointed to Claire. "But you need to be responsible and clean up your mess." She stomped out of the room.

"Old bat," Moira murmured under her breath, but her normal fervor wasn't in the insult. Either she agreed with Aunt Justine or they'd come to some sort of understanding while they'd both been held prisoner by Conquest.

Claire tightened her hold on the pen she held. "Let's get back to work. Tierra, dreams. Tell us about them."

Where did she start? "They're really graphic, disturbing. Killian is there."

"See, I told you they were about him," Moira exclaimed.

"But they aren't sex dreams. He's being tortured in Hell. He's pinned to a stone wall with copper rods and . . . and I'm there doing the . . . torturing." It sickened her, the things her subconscious had dreamed, and his screams tormented her throughout the day.

"*What?*" Both Claire and Moira said together.

"You're the last person who would torture someone," Moira added.

"It's me, but not me. She gets off on hurting him. I can't make sense of it. I've consulted dream dictionaries and interpretations. None of them fit."

"Walk us through the dream," Claire said, busily writing down her every word.

"Killian's been offered a deal. If he gives up his first born, he's free to go, but he refuses. No matter what I —she—does to him, he won't take the deal."

"How is he being tortured?"

"How isn't he? It's horrific. And I'm the one who is doing all those unspeakable things to him. Lightning shoots from my fingertips, and water pours down on him. He's electrocuted over and over again. His screams . . ."

"Okay, stop." Moira swallowed, clearly affected by the picture Tierra painted. "We get a clear enough idea. Don't we, Claire?" She angled her head in Tierra's direction, and Claire studied Tierra.

Tierra knew her color had leached out of her face as she felt light-headed and dizzy.

"Maybe we should take a break," Claire suggested.

"It's so real." Tierra looked at Claire and then to Moira. "You don't think it's a dream, do you? You believe that what's happening to him is in real time. Oh, good Goddess," her words ended on a whisper.

"This is good—" Claire started.

"Good! How can it be good knowing how much he's suffering for the sake of our child?"

"Tierra, focus. If you're seeing these images, that means you and Bane are connected through your bond."

"And since you're connected, you might just be the key to getting him a one-way ticket outta Hell," Moira finished.

TIERRA'S HEART HURT AS SHE ENTERED THE ATTIC. Could Moira and Claire be right and those horrific dreams—the ones that woke her in full body sweats—be *real*? Could her senseless action have resulted in the punishment she envisioned? She hadn't meant for anything like that to happen. She'd just wanted Killian as far away from her as she could get him.

Well, she sure as hell had accomplished that.

She'd been furious with Killian for taking her choices away, for tricking her into doing what he wanted without consulting her.

Could that be why she'd dreamt of herself as his torturer?

It made her sick. While her breakfast was staying put, everything else inside her was in turmoil. She had to do something. But what? Where was the answer?

Tierra regarded the attic space with its rough plank floors and walls. Trunks lined one area, and shelves stacked with boxes reached to the angled ceiling on the other. Windows flanked both ends of the room, letting in the gloomy, cloud-covered skies promising rain. What she wouldn't give to see the sun shining instead of the oppressive veil outside threatening to completely close her in.

Moira and Claire were searching through everything they could on magical bonds, and she needed to do her part. While hunting in the attic for clues was probably a waste of time, she didn't have any other ideas, and she needed to physically be doing something. Not researching and speculating. Neither of which were her strong suits.

She needed something solid. Family was her strength. Whether living or dead, she always found solace in family.

She'd seen journals packed away in one of the trunks. But that had been ages ago when she was a teenager. At the time, she'd been looking for answers on why she'd felt part of her was missing. She'd had no idea that three parts of her had been stolen at birth until she performed the spell that called her sisters home.

The spell she'd found here in their grandmother's personal grimoire.

If her ancestry had all been witches clear back to Malcolm de Moray, there had to be more family grimoires or journals that could offer up something helpful.

She wished Aerin would return.

On the other hand, going through the many trunks and boxes would be useful, even though Aerin hated it up here. Mainly because they were making her wear old clothes that Tierra treasured, and Aerin considered junk. In Tierra's opinion, Aerin had never looked better. She'd lost that don't-touch-me veneer with the softer, more relaxed style. Now that they'd made a temporary truce with the Horsemen, and the Horsemen weren't trying to kill Aerin, she'd be able to return to her overpriced designer wardrobe.

Tierra bypassed the area that held the clothes. She'd gone through them enough times to know she wouldn't find the books there. Instead, she focused on the north corner.

Securing her hair on top of her head with a pencil, she got to work.

Hours passed and still no luck. She sat back on her haunches and wiped sweat from her brow. There had to be an easier way. She was a witch, damn it, and this called for a little help. Adapting a mini version of the spell that she'd used to call her sisters home, she began to chant.

> *"Keeper of what is lost, hear me now,*
> *reveal to me what I seek,*
> *What is now hidden, return to me,*
> *by earth, air, fire, and sea ..."*

SHE REPEATED THE SPELL FOUR TIMES AND THEN waited. It didn't take long. She jumped to her feet when the steel shelf unit in front of her slid aside as easily as if it were on castors. A ray of sunlight poured into the room, highlighting the wall behind.

Okay, that was weird. But then weird was becoming the new norm.

Unfortunately, her spell revealed nothing but a blank wall. Her shoulders slumped in defeat, but she quickly straightened when the wood began to pulse. Cautiously, she ventured forward. Edges of the wall beamed with light, forming a door and then a crystal knob.

Her hand shaking, she reached for the doorknob. It twisted freely, and the door swung open on silent hinges to expose a room dusty with neglect.

A wooden altar stood in the middle of the area. Across from it was a stained-glass window that depicted the Standing Stones on Siren's Cry. How had she never noticed this window from the outside of the house before?

How long had this room been hidden and why?

"*Tierra*!" Moira hollered, running up the stairs. "Grim just lit up like a freakin' light bulb." She rushed into the attic with Claire on her heels, the Grimoire in her hands glowing as if fire burned within its pages.

Moira's mouth fell open, when she spotted Tierra inside the secret room. "Holy shit."

"What is this?" Claire asked. "How?"

"I wasn't having any luck with trunks so I did a simple seeking spell. I think my spell broke someone else's."

"You had no idea this was here?" Claire asked.

Tierra shook her head. "I don't think anyone did, at least not for a very long time." She wiped her finger in the dust on a shelf and held it up to show.

Moira strolled toward the altar and set the heavy Grimoire on top. The pages hummed with a moan that sounded like pleasure. Moira jumped back. "Well, slap my ass and call me a weasel. Would you look at that? It's like he belongs here."

"You think the Grimoire is a he?" Claire entered and wandered the space with its floor to ceiling bookcases.

"Damn skippy. He's a smarty pants, ain't he? And right now holding out on us."

"I know a lot of women like that, too. Our own sister who is suspiciously absent is one." Claire picked up a mason jar filled with something suspended inside the liquid. "What do you think is in this?"

"Please don't let it be eye of newt." Moira shuddered.

Tierra walked over to see what Claire held. She took the jar from her and blew dust from the top and unscrewed the lid. She sniffed the contents. "Witch hazel with stalks of aloe, I'm guessing."

"Thank the Goddess," Moira said. "Any idea who this room belongs, too?"

A book suddenly flung itself off the shelf landing on the floor in the middle of them.

They all jumped. Tierra's hand went protectively to her belly, while Moira covered her heart. Claire remained composed.

"I'm thinking that's a clue." Claire reached down and picked up the book. Tierra and Moira huddled around her as she opened it.

The book was leather bound with a complicated Celtic knot and the four elements, represented like a compass, embossed on the front. Claire opened it, and the scent of lilacs filled the room. Scrawled on the inside flap in flowing cursive was a note.

If you are reading this, welcome blood of mine. I don't know if you are my children or grandchildren, maybe even later generations. If the sealed door revealed itself to you, you are welcome in my sanctuary.

"Sanctuary?" Moira said. "Come on, read more."

"I'm getting to it, if you'd stop interrupting," Claire said.

First, don't let anyone know of this place, as they will want to use the items and information I've gathered for their own gain. Replace the wards with your own spell and keep it hidden.

Moira looked around. "Where's Aunt Justine?"

"You saw her leave an hour ago," Claire said. "Now hush."

Moira grumbled something Tierra didn't catch, and if Claire did, she chose to ignore it.

This room and its contents have been my life's work, preparation for the coming Apocalypse. I pray that has been thwarted before now. If it hasn't, and my daughters are reading this, I'm sorry to leave you such a weighty birthright. That was not my intent. My utmost desire is for my four elemental daughters to live healthy, happy, and prosperous lives.

"Is this . . . our *mother's* journal?" Tierra asked. "It's her sanctuary?"

"Let me get to it," Claire said.

I knew you would be tested, and for that I apologize. I hope that I am with you to help guide you along your way. If I'm not—as I fear will be the case—the following is an account of how you came to be, and from whom. Your grand legacy.

Forever my love,

Mirelle de Moray

Silence followed, and they all held their breath.

Moira was the first to speak. "No, I don't want to read it. Put it away."

"We have to, Moira," Claire said.

"I've had enough of dead relatives and tragic tales."

"Moira, you can't be serious?" Tierra asked.

"You bet your pregnant patootie, I am. It's bad enough knowin' our mother died birthin' us." Moira backed up and pointed to the book Claire held. "Now I gotta be told that our daddy's dead, too."

"You don't know that," Claire said.

"Yes, she does," Tierra said. "We all do."

"It's like we're living in one of them Disney movies," Moira continued when Tierra and Claire looked at her funny. "You know, when the kid is orphaned at birth and then has to go on some sort of epic quest and finds their true love, and all that sappy happy crap. Well, last time I checked, none of those singin' orphans was 'sposed to cause the end of the world. There ain't no happy endin' for us."

"We don't know that," Tierra said.

"Are you forgetting the prophesy? Four elemental witches from one woman, or line, however you want to interpret it. It's a crap shoot that I never signed up for."

"Moira," Tierra began, moving toward her.

She backed up farther. "Don't you pull that motherin' thing on me. I hate this. All of it. Why can't we just be normal?"

"All right, that's enough," Claire said. "I'm not going to coddle you like this one." She pointed to

Tierra. "Buck up, Moira. It's the hand we were dealt whether we like it or not. Avoiding what our mother has to tell us won't change that. Knowledge is power and we need all the fucking power we can get right now. So shelve those insecurities. We don't have time for that bullshit."

"Claire," Tierra chastised, "she's hurting."

"We're all hurting, and the hurt won't stop until we start acting like warriors instead of little girls. I thought they grew women stronger down in the south. There's got to be more to you than cooking up a mean fried chicken."

Moira straightened her shoulders. "There's a hell of a lot more to me that that, and right now all of it is about sick and tired of piecin' together my past from attic trunks and magic books."

"Shouldn't we wait for Aerin?" Tierra asked, hoping that would give Moira a little time to come to terms with the situation. Not to mention, she wouldn't mind a little time herself.

"Probably, but we aren't going to. She should be here and she isn't. When I called her earlier, she said she was busy and hung up on me. I'm not waiting on her a minute more. I need to know what shit we were born into and why." Claire looked at Moira. "Are you going to stash the tears and grow a pair or what?"

"Bitch," Moira said without heat.

"Damn, right. And you'll thank me for it someday," Claire said.

"Well, that's not today."

"Are you in or out?"

"In," Moira mumbled, shifting her flip-flops in the dust on the floor.

"Say it like you mean it, or there's the door."

"Fine. Yes, I'm in." Moira's color was back and with it her resolve. "Goddess damnit, but you're a tough witch."

"Fucking A." Claire moved to the stained-glass window. A padded seat was built-in and covered in a swirling floral pattern of turquoise and red. "I suggest we get comfortable."

"Could we dust first?" Tierra asked, wanting a little time to fortify herself for what would be unveiled within the pages of their mother's journal.

"A little dust never hurt anybody." Claire sat and dust poofed around her. The following sneeze belied her words.

"Bless you," Tierra and Moira said together.

"Come on," Claire said. "There's enough room for the two of you on this seat."

With no other way to stall, they walked over and sat.

Claire turned the page and started to read. And what she read had them rethinking everything they believed or could possibly have dreamt.

$\mathscr{H}$ 3 $\mathscr{H}$

Jinx raced into the room, letting out a screeching yowl. Doctor Lector wasn't far behind with his high-pitched, ear-piercing cry. He flew around the room, dive-bombing the three of them who sat on the window seat, dealing with the information they'd just read in their mother's journal.

"What the fuck is wrong with them?" Claire asked, ducking to avoid Doctor Lector's latest swoop.

"Someone's trying to break through the wards." Tierra scooped up an agitated Jinx who clawed higher and perched like a gargoyle on her shoulder.

"Can't we get some friggin' peace?" Moira slid her feet into her flip-flops. "I've a mind to scalp whoever's out there."

"Moira, stay here and guard the room." Claire went into fighting mode. "And keep that crazy bat in here." She swatted at and missed Doctor Lector as he came for her again.

"Just because I'm a sappy wreck doesn't mean I'm staying in the house. The sister with the bun in the oven should be the one to stay."

"Hey!" Tierra objected. "If anyone is staying behind it should be Claire. Both Moira and I have our wands. *You* stay."

Moira gave Claire a satisfied smirk. "And find a spell to hide the room while you're at it, sis."

"Fine." Claire smoldered.

"Kai will fetch you if you're needed," Tierra added, trying to simmer Claire down.

Jinx continued her grating meow while keeping her balance on Tierra's shoulder, as she and Moira flew down the many flights of stairs. Cheeto and Kai were outside on the front porch, waiting impatiently. Kai's tail was a bottle brush in blazing colors, and Cheeto snorted smoke from his nostrils, his little hoofs prancing in place. His compact, pink body trembled as though any minute he'd belch a fire ball.

None of the familiars knew the intruder. So it wasn't the Horsemen. Since she and her sisters had made their temporary truce with the guys, the wards had been lowered for the Horsemen.

So this threat was something new.

Moira was right. Couldn't they get a moment of peace?

An incredibly tall man with a mean whipcord leanness stood at the gate, feet spread far apart, ready for any threat. He wore a long duster jacket, heavy boots laced to his knees over buckskin leather pants, and an old top hat wrapped in tapestry with clockwork gears pinned to the brim along with a blue-black raven's feather. He could have stepped out of cosplay meet-up or maybe ComicCon. He looked like the perfect geek with his steampunk getup. He had a salt and pepper handlebar mustache over a grim set mouth, and his eyes were covered with blue, rounded shades even though the sun was hidden behind boiling purple clouds.

"You the witches?" he barked in a deep, raspy voice as if he regularly inhaled brimstone instead of air.

"Who wants to know?" Moira volleyed back.

"Name's Reaper."

Tierra and Moira shared a look. Was he an actual

reaper or had he just adopted the name? No mother would christen their child with such a name, of that Tierra was certain.

"What can we help you with?" Tierra asked.

"You can start with lowering these blasted wards, and tell me what you did with Bane."

Tierra and Moira shared another look.

"What's your business with him?" Tierra asked.

Rather than answering, he followed with another question, his wintry gaze arrowing in on Tierra. "You the witch that sent him to Hell?" He lowered his John Lennon shades and regarded Tierra over the rims with distain.

"What's it to you?" Moira jutted out her hip. Cheeto plopped at her feet, and a sulphuric fart tainted the air. Reaper took a step back with a look of horror as the smell reached him. Cheeto's farts were a better deterrent than the wards.

"We need Bane back."

"Who are *we*?" Tierra asked. Were there more . . . *men* out there like this reaper guy in Killian's employ—for lack of a better word?

"His operatives. Do you have any clue what's happening to the souls that we can't reap now that Bane is stuck in Hell? Let me paint you a picture. They can't cross over. Have any idea what happens to souls who have no place to go?"

Tierra swallowed a lump in her throat.

"*Ghosts.*" He spit out the word and curled his lip in disgust. "I've been elected to see what you're going to do about it."

"Lucifer is holding his death-dealing ass," Moira said. "Why don't you talk to her?"

"I've tried. She isn't answering my calls."

"Wait a damn minute." Moira shook her head as if to clear it. "You can like *pick up* the phone and call the Devil?"

"Not quite, but in a sense. This is wasting time and souls are piling up. I want this fixed. Pronto."

"We're working on it," Tierra murmured.

"Work faster. If you don't produce Bane by All Hollows' Eve, I'm delivering the lost souls here, and *you* can deal with them." With that he turned, his coat flaring out behind him in a wave of lethal shadows. In a blink, he was gone.

"Those poor lost souls." Tierra released the breath she'd been holding in a whoosh as guilt settled heavy on her shoulders. Jinx growled and leaped down, slinking away with a twitch of her tail. Cheeto picked himself up and followed, joining up with Kai who'd stayed as guard at the front door.

"Yeah, well, we'd better figure out something fast," Moira muttered. "I don't relish being haunted by vengeful spirits. Who would've thunk zombies would be preferable to ghosts?" She shuddered. "At least we could fight them."

"I'm so tired." Tierra rubbed at the ache in her lower back, wishing she could curl up and take a nap.

"Sleep is good. Maybe you can reach Death, and we can settle this before it gets further out of hand."

Tierra stared at Moira. "And how do I *reach* him?"

"I don't have the answers, but you can't deny you have a connection. If you can see him, he should be able to see you."

"He does see me. He sees me *torturing* him."

"It's *your* dream. Take control of it."

"Don't you think I've tried to stop myself? The things I've done . . . if I can somehow reach him, he's going to want me dead."

"Not until you push out that tadpole." Moira pointed at Tierra's ever-growing belly. "Come on, let's get a drink—er, tea for you. It's been a hell of a day."

And it wasn't over yet.

Tierra's Prius zipped up the drive and jerked to a

park in front of the old carriage house. Aerin climbed out of the borrowed car dressed in a black Prada pantsuit with killer stiletto heels. She'd slicked back her hair into a dominatrix bun anchored with sharp silver pins the length of daggers, and painted her mouth a shocking blood red. She reached into the backseat and pulled out four large bags printed with the Sak's 5th Avenue logo.

"Well, aren't we living in high cotton," Moira commented, taking in all the bags.

"Aerin de Moray, we've been trying to reach you all day," Tierra said, "and you were *shopping*?"

"Don't nag. A girl needs some retail therapy every now and then."

"Not during the Apocalypse!" The waste of time and money boggled Tierra's mind. Regardless how much money Aerin had, there were better things she could be doing with it than shopping.

"Hey, if I'm going to die, it isn't going to be in anything you two wear. Ever heard the saying, 'I wouldn't be caught *dead* wearing that?'" She gestured with her booty at Moira's torn jeans and thread-bare t-shirt. "Or *that*." She shuddered at Tierra's loose-fitting dress styled three decades earlier.

"The seventies are back in style."

"No, Tierra, they aren't."

"We thought you were with Julian," Moira said, following behind Aerin as she sashayed up the steps into the house.

"He's become a bore. All he wants to do is *talk*. So I took myself off to Seattle." She traipsed into the kitchen and set the bags on the table, and then reached for the bottle of bourbon. "Look at me. I have a body made for sin, and the man's had a dry spell that rivals Death Valley. He should be drinking me down like a glass of cool water." She poured herself two fingers, shot it back and closed her eyes as the fiery liquid burned down her throat. "Anyone else?" She held up the bottle and waved it in the air.

"Hit me," Moira said, sidling up to the table.

"I'll call Claire down. We need to talk." Tierra turned to leave but found Claire entering the room.

"Saw the car drive up." Claire glared at Aerin. "Do you have any idea what we've been dealing with today? You should have been here. At the very least, you should have answered your damn phone."

"I answered it."

"And hung up on me."

"Gucci was having a sale, and Aerin's credit cards needed a workout."

"So we're now referring to ourselves in the third person?" Claire took the bottle from Aerin and grabbed glasses for her and Moira.

A somewhat surprised expression appeared on Aerin's face that was quickly masked as sarcasm. "Sue me. I've had a few frustrating days."

"And the rest of us haven't?" Tierra asked. "We're in this together, Aerin. We can't just call it quits for the day and take off. What if you'd been hurt or something? There are Bible thumpers and witch hunters gunning for us."

"Goddamn, but you're a worry wart." Aerin grabbed the bottle back from Claire and flopped into a chair, re-filling her glass. "I couldn't face another day searching dusty old books for something that would save Death from the all-powerful Lucy. As far as I'm concerned, you did us a favor, and the Great Dragon can have him."

"*Aerin*," Moira chastised and then turned to Tierra. "She didn't mean it."

"Yes, she did." Tierra set the kettle down on the burner with a clang.

"Yeah, I did." Aerin nodded.

"What's gotten into you?" Claire asked. "Since you

slept with Julian, it's like you are possessed or something. You've been bitchier than normal."

"And that's saying somethin'," Moira muttered.

Aerin blanched and looked at the three faces staring at her and cursed. She crossed her legs and took a moment to gather her next words. "Okay," she gritted out through clenched teeth. "I'm off my game a little, I guess. This is all *new* to me . . . what with Julian all up in his lofty tower." As apologies went, it lacked regret, but did explain her actions.

"Look, sugar, we know you care for him, but you can't treat us like day-old dog doo," Moira said. "We're your sisters."

"I like handling things my own way."

"But you don't have to." Moira leaned in with concern. "Let's talk about it. Unloading will do you good."

"No." Aerin tossed back another swallow. "I want to get drunk. Any objections to that?"

"Actually, that's the smartest thing you've said since you returned." Claire pulled out a chair and sank into it, sliding her glass over for Aerin to fill.

"Gettin' befuggered probably ain't the best use of our time at the moment," Moira said.

"The telling will be easier for all of us if we're less emotional," Claire added, motioning for Aerin to add more to her glass. "And definitely easier for her to hear if we indulge."

"Sure, easier for you guys," Tierra muttered.

"Tierra, honey." Moira pointed to the pantry. "On the bottom shelf behind the five-pound bucket of sugar is a bag of pork rinds. Help yourself."

It galled her that the thought of pork rinds had her mouth watering and took away the feeling of being left out of the drinking, penalized because of her pregnancy. She found the bag and ripped into it, stuffing a few fried pig skins into her mouth before taking the last seat at the table with her cup of rose petal tea.

Aerin gave her a look of horror but smartly didn't comment. "So fill me in. What great tragic thing did I miss?"

The three of them started talking at once.

"Whoa, one witch at a time!"

"You two begin," Clarrie said. "Tell us who the guy was trying to get past the wards."

Moira pointed at Tierra. "Since this falls in your koi pond, you tell 'em."

"Apparently, with Killian in Hell, souls can't move on to the next realm. They're stuck here on this plane as ghosts. If we don't rescue Killian before All Hollows' Eve, Reaper and his cohorts plan to dump the lost souls here for us to deal with."

"Wait, so if Death's not here, souls can't cross over?" Claire asked. "How is that possible?"

"He's the power that opens the gates to Heaven and Hell," Aerin said. "Without him here, his power is absent, too." She paused when they all looked at her. "I think I heard Julian mention it."

"How many souls are we talking?" Claire asked.

"There has to be thousands of people who die every day," Tierra said apprehensively. "More so now with the worldwide spread panic of the End of Days and wars and rumor of wars reported daily. And he's been gone . . . a long time."

"Shit." Claire grabbed the bottle and topped off her glass, passing it to Moira who did the same. "I'll add ghosts to the growing list of concerns."

"Why All Hollows' Eve, do you s'pose?" Moira asked.

"It's the time of the in-between," Aerin said. "Known also as Halloween and Samhain. It's the day that crosses from the light half of the year into the dark half, when the veil is thinnest between the Other World and ours. Hell, Heaven, Purgatory, and *Tir na Nog* are closer, more accessible, straddling the line between life and death."

"How do you know all of this?" Claire asked.

"Must have read it in one of those books you keep foisting on me." Aerin shrugged.

"So why do we dress up in costumes for Halloween?" Moira asked.

"Wearing of spooky costumes is to scare off other ghosts, and treats are left to trick the dead into leaving believers alone. At least, I think that's the idea. Doubt it fools the average demon," Aerin added with a smirk. "I read that some Irish man named Stingy Jack played a trick on the Devil and was cursed to wander the Earth searching for salvation he'd never find, lighting his way with a candle stuck inside a hollowed-out turnip. Hence Jack o' lanterns. But knowing the woman like we do, I bet she shrank his dick to the size of a radish."

"With everything we've now come to believe, there might be some truth to this." Tierra stood and grabbed a calendar. Retaking her seat, she pointed to the date in question. "All Hollows' Eve is a week away."

"You thinkin' what I'm thinkin'?" Moira asked.

"That's the night we can rescue Killian." Tierra nodded.

"It's not only that," Claire added. "When you were out talking to this reaper guy, I read further in our mother's journal."

"You found Mirelle's journal?" Aerin asked, going perfectly still in her chair.

"Oh, we found much more than that, but before we show you, you guys all need to hear this." Claire took a deep breath and began. "Our mother's element was earth, like Tierra's. Probably explains how she's been able to see and converse with her in the Standing Stones, but our father was a Druid and not from this time."

"What do you mean, not from *this time*?" Aerin eyes sharpened.

"Our mother brought him through the Standing Stones. Through time. Malcolm de Moray isn't our great-great grandfather a thousand years removed. He is our *grandfather* and our father is his son, Stian the Wanderer, and our grandmother Vian was a demon whom Malcolm freed from Hell."

❧ 4 ❧

"Wow, I don't even know what to do with this?" Tierra said, falling back in her chair. Their father was a Druid from another time and their grandmother a demon? The good news? There was a record of someone being released from Hell, finally. "How did our grandfather rescue her?"

"It didn't say. I'm sorry, Tierra," Claire said. "But there has to be more information in our mother's sanctuary that will hopefully help."

"Sanctuary?" Aerin sat up straighter. "What are you talking about?"

"Come on, we'll show you what we uncovered today while you were off *shopping*." Moira stood and led the way upstairs to the attic. "Tierra had the inspired idea to try a spell to find something hidden and uncovered a secret room. We've all agreed not to tell Aunt Justine."

"No problem here," Aerin agreed. "I can barely handle being around the simpering old crone."

They entered the dark and dusty attic.

"Where is it?" Aerin asked, twirling around, searching.

"Give me a minute." Claire positioned herself in front of the metal shelving units. "I performed a cloaking spell similar to the one that we used when we flew on the brooms. We might want something stronger though." Claire recited her spell, and the steel bookcase silently moved aside, revealing the door within the wooden wall.

"Nicely done," Tierra said, turning the knob and opening the door. She waved her hand to show Aerin, who looked at her suspiciously.

"I don't see anything."

"You can't see the room?" Moira asked. "It's there plain as the over-priced shoes on your feet. You see it, right, Claire?"

"Yes." Claire regarded Aerin with puzzlement.

Aerin's shook her head again. "Seriously, there's nothing there but a wooden wall."

"Let's see what happens when I enter the room," Tierra said, doing just that.

"Whoa, Tierra just disappeared," Aerin said.

Moira shared a look with Claire.

Claire held her hand out to Aerin. "Take my hand. Moira take her other one. Maybe since you weren't here for the unveiling spell, you can't see it unless you're holding onto one of us."

Aerin took Moira's and Claire's hands. When Claire entered the room, Aerin screamed and dropped the connection, cradling her arm next to her chest. "What the shit are you trying to do to me? That burned like frostbite." She held up her red-marked hand that looked like it had been scalded.

"Ice?" Tierra retreated from the sanctuary back into the attic. Aerin blinked at her, obviously able to see her now.

"Maybe with me and Moira each holding onto her, my fire turned to ice?" Claire suggested, looking down at her own unmarked hand.

"I s'pose," Moira agreed slowly. "What doesn't make sense is why Aerin can't see or enter the room to begin with."

All three stared at Aerin with suspicion.

"Quit looking at me like that."

"What did you do, Aerin?" Tierra ventured closer, her eyes narrowed. "What aren't you telling us?"

"Excuse me?" She retreated a step.

"Have you been performing spells from the back of the book again?" Tierra asked, doubt growing like a weed inside her. "You promised. No more black magic."

"Back off, Tierra." Aerin stood her ground.

"Cool your jets or I'm dumping cold water on the both of you." Moira planted her hands on her hips. "Let's not go jumpin' to conclusions. There could be a helluva lot of reasons why Aerin can't see the room."

"What the fuck do you mean by that?" Aerin asked, her tone blistering like an arctic wind.

"Tierra brought up a good question," Claire pointed out. "Besides the Necromancy spell, what else have you been up to? Have you really been spending time with Julian during your disappearing acts?"

"I told you I went shopping today, and I have the receipts to prove it. Good hell, what do you suspect me of?"

"Enough bickerin'." Moira stepped next to Aerin. "Attacking each other ain't helpin'. Been there done that. Remember how that turned out? We've just gotten on better footin', and I ain't in any hurry to ruin it. We've enough to fight without fightin' each other."

"She's right." Tierra released a breath and hated herself for what she'd been thinking and for accusing Aerin. "I'm stressed out and not sleeping well. I shouldn't have taken it out on you. I'm sorry, Aerin. Forgive me?"

Aerin narrowed her eyes and seemed pumped to let loose with a string of insults. "Guess I could have communicated my whereabouts better. You're forgiven, but that doesn't mean we have to hug it out. Right?"

Tierra smiled as relief washed over her. She and

Aerin had been at odds more often than not, and it hurt her heart to have a cantankerous relationship with anyone, let alone her sister. "No hugs needed, I promise."

"This still doesn't answer why Aerin can't see or enter our mom's sanctuary," Claire said.

"Could it be the residual effects of performing black magic?" Tierra asked.

"Seems the most likely explanation," Claire agreed.

"So how do we scrub the evil outta her?" Moira asked.

"Excuse me? I'm not . . . evil." Aerin shuffled on her heels, not making eye contact.

"Fix you then, cleanse your aura," Moira clarified. "Evict the darkness squatting inside your soul. Whatever you want to call it. Point is, the information our momma left in that room might be our best chance at getting Tierra's baby daddy out of Hell, and it don't do us a lick of good to have you trapped outside."

"Wait," Claire said. "I was able to take Mom's journal out of the room. Until we can figure a way for Aerin to enter the room, we'll just grab the items we need and bring them to her."

"First we need to do what Moira suggested," Tierra said. Maybe purging Aerin would help with her constant bitchiness. They'd all benefit from that.

"I don't need cleansing," Aerin scoffed. "What are you going to do, baptize me?"

"Or something," Claire muttered. "Let's at least get Grim and see what he has to say."

"Good idea." Tierra rushed back into the sanctuary and picked Grim off the altar and tried to return to the attic. Grim refused to budge past the threshold. "Hey, guys. Something's up with Grim. He doesn't look like he wants to leave the sanctuary."

"That's crazy," Aerin said. "The book's been hanging around the house, even took a trip out of it when War stole it."

"Well, he's found a home he likes," Tierra said, struggling with Grim. "I seriously can't make him leave. Maybe give me a hand?"

Claire reached for Grim, and he flew out of Tierra's hands, landing back on the altar in a poof of dust and stubbornness.

"Well, that complicates things," Claire muttered.

"What in the hairy hell is going on?" Moira asked, looking from the sanctuary to Aerin. "It's like he doesn't want to be around *you*."

"The book's been around me plenty of times," Aerin said. "So that doesn't make any sense."

"Except since the sanctuary has been found," Tierra said, "could Grim have more to reveal now that he's in the room?"

"Might be," Claire murmured, tapping her lip in thought. "It would explain why he isn't willing to leave. It would follow that the room itself has a certain amount of power, too. What with all the artifacts and such."

"What do we do now?" Moira asked.

"I've had about enough for one day," Tierra said. "I'm exhausted." The weight of her guilt and her pregnancy were taking its toll.

"Yeah, you look tired as a one-finned fish durin' spawning season," Moira said. "How about Claire and I consult Grim, you go to bed, and Aerin . . . well, you can clean up the kitchen, I guess."

"You're putting *me* on kitchen duty?"

"It isn't like you're good for much else right now," Claire pointed out. She gave Tierra a worried look. "You do look wasted, Tierra. Try and get some sleep while Moira and I search for a solution."

"I hate to leave this all to you." But a nap sounded heavenly. Tierra stumbled through the doorway of the attic, feeling like her limbs were heavy tree stumps.

"Get some rest," Clare said. "We need you on top of

your game, too, since we're down a witch. Aerin, help her to bed before she collapses."

Aerin grumbled something under her breath, but took Tierra's elbow.

Everything went black then flashed to red. Nausea hit her so fast that she dropped to her knees and dry heaved.

"What the shit!" Aerin jumped back to avoid anything Tierra might project on her shoes. She grabbed Tierra again, and the insinuating wave of darkness caused Tierra to convulse.

Tierra heard screams as she collapsed in a heap on the floor. She felt immobilized yet conscious of her surroundings.

"*Tierra!*" Moira screamed, reaching for her only to be propelled back ten feet. She pushed herself into a sitting position and cradled her hands next to her chest. "Flaming toad-twats, that hurt."

"What's wrong with her?" Claire rushed over and got a similar jolt when she reached for Tierra.

Aerin stood off to the side, regarding her sister with skepticism.

"What did you do, Aerin?" Claire asked, kneeling next to Tierra, being careful not to touch her.

"Nothing. I just . . . took her arm."

"Tierra, honey, can you hear me?" Moira asked, venturing closer, but staying far enough away to avoid another shock.

Trapped within herself, Tierra tried to talk. She could hear them, see them, but responding seemed beyond her. She was cocooned tightly within a shell. Frozen, yet not cold.

"Grim!" Moira exclaimed. "Before Aerin touched her, she'd been holding him."

"Grim wouldn't hurt her," Claire said.

"And neither would Aerin. It's gotta be somethin' else."

"It has to be the *spawn*," Aerin sneered. "She should have gotten rid of that thing months ago."

"Hush your mouth about that," Moira said. "We all agreed."

Claire ran for Grim. Moira hovered like a worried hen over a hurt chick, while Aerin kept vigil far away in the corner, her expression cryptic.

"All Grim is giving me is 'How to perform an exorcism,'" Claire hollered from the sanctuary.

"He can't mean the *baby*, can he?" Moira asked, horrified.

"*Finally*, someone is making sense," Aerin commented.

"One more word about that and you're fixin' to get the world's first Manolo Blahnik enema," Moira said. "As much as I hate suggesting this, maybe we oughta call the Horsemen."

"Are you insane?" Aerin asked. "Men are useless when it comes to pregnant women."

"You got a better idea?" Moira challenged.

"I like Grim's," Aerin grumbled.

"What Grim is showing me isn't an option. She's too far along," Claire said from within the sanctuary. "We need a doctor, preferably a magical one. Does anyone remember the name of Tierra's doctor? She's in her second trimester. All sorts of issues could be popping up."

"Actually, I don't think she's seen a doctor yet, on account of having canceled multiple times due to the Apocalypse."

"There's a midwife among the members of the coven." Aerin pulled out her phone and started dialing.

"Did Julian bang the brain right outta your head? The coven tried to *kill* Tierra." Moira stood and reached for her phone. "I'm calling Nick. He may be a narcissistic domination-hungry asshole, but I sure as hell trust him more than those back-stabbing witches. Claire, before anyone gets here, hide that room again."

Tierra couldn't hold onto the thread of consciousness a moment longer and gave into the welcoming darkness.

❧ 5 ❧

Sharp murmuring voices came at Tierra from across a dark void. Too many voices, a jumbled mix of men and women arguing.

"You called us here to help a *pregnant* woman?"

"What the hell do you expect us to do? Unless you want us to kill her?"

Focusing, she tried to make sense of the conversation, narrowing in on the one calm, clear tone.

"I believe she's developed a force-field of sorts." The deep timbre sounded like it came from Julian. "As near as I can tell, it seems to be a combination of the flight-versus-fight response. The fight, shocking anyone who tries to touch her, and the flight, sheathing herself in a protective force field. Describe the situation before she collapsed?"

"That's just it," Claire said. "Nothing was really going on. Aerin tried to help Tierra to her room to lie down since she was exhausted."

"All four of you up here in the attic, doing nothing?" Nicholas Kingswood's disbelieving tone carried easily to Tierra and had her heartrate quickening in response. Conquest had killed her once. Now that she was down for the count, would he again shoot her with his deadly arrow?

"I think she's waking up," Moira said. "The force field, or whatever you want to call it, just shimmered. Tierra, can you hear me?"

Tierra blinked her eyes open and found herself surrounded by her sisters, three Horsemen, and another woman with cropped dark hair, and a pear-shaped body whom she'd never seen before.

Something heated inside her and radiated outward, flinging everyone across the room.

"Holy shit!" War hit the wall with a resounding thud.

"What the fuck!" Nick followed, picking himself up off the floor and smoothing his steel-gray suit jacket and adjusting his silver tie.

Julian was slower to gain his feet, but the first to cautiously venture closer, studying Tierra, his thoughtful eyes moving to her womb. "Definitely a force field, but I don't believe it's emanating from her."

"The *spawn* is doing this?" Aerin asked.

Julian spared her a disapproving glance. "Stay back, Aerin. If you were the last to touch her, she or the babe, might consider you a threat."

"*Me?* Why? I'm her sister." Nervously she secured a stray hair back into its tight bun.

"That's what we need to figure out. For now, it would be wise for everyone to keep their distance." Julian inched closer. "Tierra, can you hear me? Blink or nod if you can."

Slowly, Tierra blinked. She couldn't move, no matter how much she tried. The feeling was comforting, like being swaddled tightly in a blanket, yet she couldn't stay this way. Her breathing increased and spots swam in her vision.

"Do you hurt anywhere?" Julian asked, his tone soothing and supportive. "Blink once for yes, twice for no."

She took stock of herself, feeling fine other than not

having the ability to twitch even a pinky, which was disconcerting to say the least. She blinked twice.

"Good," Julian said. "You're doing fine. No one here is going to hurt you." He turned to the occupants of the attic, taking in each one in turn. "In fact, let's clear the room. Limit whatever or whomever she or the babe deems a threat."

"Shouldn't that include you?" Aerin said.

"Uh, I actually agree with Pestilence here," Claire said. "Aerin, you should be first to leave as this seems to have started with you."

"That's bullshit," Aerin fumed. "There are *three* Horsemen here, and you want *me* to leave first?"

"I don't care who leaves first," Julian said, his jaw clenching. "Just get out. For now, Moira and the midwife can stay, since they are healers. As there is a band of witch hunters and religious fanatics picketing outside the wards, why don't the rest of you figure out how to disperse them? In a non-violent manner, if you please. We don't need to increase their fervor. The babe might be reacting to them instead of what is happening inside this room."

Grumbling followed Julian's statement, but they traipsed from the room, leaving the wide-eyed midwife who had taken up residence by the trunks, and an anxious Moira.

"Anything in particular y'all would like me to do?" Moira asked, hovering opposite Julian on Tierra's other side.

"Inch as close to her as you can without triggering the force field. I'd like to know how far it extends."

Moira held her hands up in a non-threating manner as if Tierra had a gun held to her head. She shuffled closer in her flip-flops, until she was about three feet away. "I can feel a . . . charge in the air. A kinda hummin'." She looked down at Tierra. "It's just me, little tadpole, your Auntie Moira. I ain't gonna hurt you, dumplin'."

Julian gave Moira an approving nod.

"Tierra," Julian addressed her. "I want you to concentrate on your breathing. Measured slow inhales and exhales. That's it. Perfect. No one here has any aspirations to harm you or your child. Isn't that right?" The frightened midwife gave a jerky nod, and Moira gave her a worried but reassuring smile. Julian continued, "I, for one, am eager to meet my brother's offspring. While he is . . . away, you and the babe have no better champion than I. You are safe with me. Blink twice if you believe me."

Tierra released a cleansing breath, surprised that she did believe him, and blinked twice. Her hand twitched and a shower of white and pink angel fire blossoms cascaded around her, dissolving the force field and allowing her to move. She sat up and Moira instantly enfolded her in a bone-crushing hug.

"Goddess almighty, but you scared the bejeezus out of me."

Tierra wrapped her arms around Moira, breathing in deep her comforting scent of summer sea breezes and magnolias. "I'm okay. Just would like to know what the hell happened."

Julian was the one to answer. "The infant is more in tuned to outside forces than you realize. Now, I'd really like to know what was transpiring when all this began."

Tierra shared a look with Moira. "Really it was nothing. I was going to lie down. Could it be that I'm just exhausted?"

"I highly doubt that. Exhaustion seems an odd reason to have the fetus react in such a strong manner."

"What about the Bible thumpers and witch hunters outside? Could they be causing this?" Moira suggested, though Tierra knew she didn't believe that any more than Tierra did.

"Unlikely as the wards are doing a fine job keeping the riffraff out, and by your accounts, she went into this state before they arrived. They could be adding to the stress though." Julian adjusted the leather gloves covering his deadly hands. "It would be a good idea for the midwife to examine you." He turned and spoke to the midwife in question. "Do you know who I am?"

"Y-yes," she answered, visibly quaking.

"Then you are aware that one touch from me will be your last."

She gave a jerky nod, swallowing audibly.

"Take great care with Tierra. Your very life depends on it. Understood?"

"Y-yes."

"Your allegiances lie with her now, and not the Sisters of the Serpent. What you have witnessed and will witness goes no further. If I hear that you failed in following my directives, it won't be only you I will infect, but all who originate from your gene pool."

"Y-yes, sir. I promise."

Julian stared at the midwife for a second longer, seeming to be satisfied. "I'll take my leave of you then. Tierra, I'm glad that you are feeling better. After the midwife has examined you, and if you feel up to it, I'd like a moment of your time."

Tierra gave him a jerky nod. How did Aerin allow this deadly man to touch her? Just being under his steely stare was enough to make her feel queasy.

Julian exited the room, and Tierra released a relieved breath.

"Damn, but he's a scary son of a bitch," Moira muttered. "Gives me a case of the all-overs. Let's get you up and off this dusty floor. You there, snatch-miner, give me a hand."

The midwife rushed over, and between the two of them they got Tierra to her trembling feet. "Whoa, I'm dizzy."

"Have you eaten enough today?" the midwife asked.

"Sorry, but what's your name?" Tierra asked.

"It's Lila. Lila Sullivan."

"Sullivan?" Tierra did a quick mental search of the citizens of Port Townsend. "Are you related to Sunny?"

"Yes, she's my niece. Her father Basil is my brother."

"Well, then you'd better take to heart what Pestilence told you," Moira said. "Sunny's like a family member to Tierra and the rest of us."

"I know, and thank you for helping Sunny and her family during these dark times. And just so you're aware, I wasn't present, nor did I have any part in what the coven did to you at Ambrosia's."

"Good to know," Moira said, guiding them down the stairs and into Tierra's room.

They helped her onto the bed, and Jinx jumped up and nuzzled Tierra. "It's all right," Tierra assured her familiar, who curled up next to her.

"That remains to be seen." Moira turned to Lila. "Do your thing, but remember, I'm watching your every move."

Trembling, Lila opened a black bag that Tierra hadn't noticed before and took out a stethoscope. "How far along are you?"

"She knows the exact date of conception," Moira muttered.

"Just shy of five months."

"Have you felt the baby kick?" Lila asked.

"No, should I have?"

"Tierra's li'l tadpole's been kicking ass," Moira muttered.

Moira was right, so why hadn't Tierra felt it moving inside her? Worry swamped her. She'd tried to pick up books on pregnancy and couldn't make herself read them, as if doing so made her situation real. On some level, she knew without a doubt she would do anything to save her child, but on the other hand, it was incomprehensible—with zombies, the looming Apocalypse, and her sending the baby's father to Hell. The amount of things she could deal with was limited. And this pregnancy was *huge*.

"At this stage, you might not even know what the sensation feels like," Lila said. "Many first mothers disregard their babies movements as gas."

Lila raised Tierra's dress to under her breasts, revealing her swollen belly. Moira covered her lower body with a quilt, giving her a much-needed sense of privacy.

Lila placed the end of the stethoscope on her distended stomach, moving it left to right, and then she stopped. She checked her watch and gave Tierra a reassuring smile. "I'm picking up a very healthy heartbeat. Would you like to hear?"

Tierra nodded, words suddenly failing her. Lila handed the stethoscope ends to Tierra, and she worked them into her ears. Her throat closed with emotion as she heard the quick fluttering of her child's heartbeat. It was rapid and strong and very, very real.

"Can I listen?" Moira asked softly.

Tierra nodded and wiped away tears that had appeared from nowhere.

The stethoscope was transferred to Moira. Her eyes widened, and a huge grin lit her face. "We'll don't that just beat all."

"I'm going to feel around your abdomen." Lila's hands were warm and confident as they moved over Tierra's belly. "You're too thin. What have you been eating?"

Moira laughed. "Pork rinds and bacon are about the only foods she's been able to keep down."

"How bad is the morning sickness?" Lila frowned. "You should be over the worst of it by now."

"She's had a rough go of it." Moira supplied when Tierra couldn't bring herself to speak. "What with members of *your* coven poisoning her with brimstone."

"Brimstone?" Horrified, Lila snapped on a pair of latex gloves, fished out a disinfected wipe and began searching for a vein to stick with a needle. "I need to take some blood and have it tested."

Tierra tore her arm out of Lila's grasp. "No. No blood." She held Lila's startled look longer than what was comfortable.

Lila slowly lowered the needle. "I would never use a witch's blood in that way. This is just to help you and the fetus. It will give me a better idea of what we're dealing with."

"And just what kind of lab would you send it to?" Moira asked.

The last thing they needed was for her and her unborn child to become a science experiment or for someone else to get hold of de Moray blood. Like the coven or worse, Lucifer.

"No lab," Lila reassured. "I have my own clinic, and everything I do will be kept confidential. I won't even tell my staff. You can trust me."

They didn't need to bring up Julian's threat. It was there to see in Lila's pallor.

Still, there was no way Tierra would freely give up her blood. From her earliest age, she had been trained to never allow anyone to use her blood. She had routinely burned hair and nail clippings and had never given blood. She wasn't about to start now—not with the stakes this high and so many enemies at their gates.

Tierra shook her head. "Taking my blood isn't an option."

Lila slowly nodded. "All right, we'll try other things first." She exchanged the needle for a blood pressure cuff and wrapped it around Tierra's arm. After a few minutes, seeming fine with the reading, she ripped it off, writing the information down on a notepad.

"From what I can tell, at this point, you seem in okay health other being too thin. I need you to eat more than pork. Instead, more fruits and vegetables, and lean meats. Stay away from tuna and foods high in mercury. Drink lots of water, and eat small meals throughout the day. That should help with any remaining morning sickness." Lila produced a notepad and wrote down instructions. "I want to see you in my office tomorrow. We'll perform an ultrasound and see if we can gain information that way. Here is the address." Lila tore off a piece of paper from the notepad and handed it to Tierra. "Is there anything else I need to know about this baby?"

Moira and Tierra shared a look. How much should they tell her? She'd already witnessed what the baby could do up in the attic. Moira shrugged, leaving it up to Tierra how much to share.

"Uhm, the father is the fourth Horseman of the Apocalypse, and before today, the baby has performed some other tricks."

Lila's coloring went whiter, and she jerked her hands back from Tierra. "The father is . . . *Death*?" Death came out in a shocked whisper. "How—how is that even possible?"

"Believe me, you aren't the only one askin' that question," Moira said. "But then Tierra's obviously a fertile-Myrtle earth witch."

Lila swallowed and took a minute to compose herself. It didn't take her long to get her emotions under control. She was more like her niece Sunny, and bounced just as well, which reassured Tierra. "So, what other supernatural things has the baby performed?"

"Well, at Ambrosia's when the coven attempted to burn me at the stake . . . it was the baby who saved me."

"How?"

Tierra placed a protective hand over her belly. "It, uhm . . . increased my powers, rather significantly." She couldn't share that it also opened the mouth of Hell and sent its father there for a time out.

"That's not completely unheard of," Lila said. "I've come across other witches who have mentioned this same phenomenon. Obviously not to the extent that you have, but that's most likely due to the magic the fetus has inherited from the father. Chances are you'll experience more instances like what happened today whenever your baby feels threatened." She paused and took a deep breath. "I guess we'll find out together. This will be one for the books. Not, that I'll tell this to anyone," she quickly added.

Tierra shared another worried look with Moira.

Why would the baby feel threatened by Aerin?

"Until I see you tomorrow, I want you to rest. I'm sure you've been overwhelmed and haven't taken time for moments of quiet. Understandable with what you're dealing with, but you have more than yourself to think about now." Lila stood and gathered her items, packing them away in her bag.

"Lila, is there any way to tell if the baby is . . . *wicked?*" The word was hard to say, when everything inside Tierra told her it couldn't possibly be so.

"Actually, many mothers worry about that, too. Normal women and magical. In a sense, you have a parasite taking over, and it feels alien. I don't want you to worry. Stress is something we need to eliminate as much as possible." She covered Tierra with the blanket, petted Jinx who'd curled next to Tierra's shoulder, watching over the exam like a personal guard. Jinx purred, giving Tierra more assurance that Lila didn't mean them any harm.

"Moira, can I speak to you outside?" Lila asked, picking up her bag.

"Sure. I'll be right back, Tierra."

Tierra watched them leave, figuring Lila would give Moira further instructions to keep her calm and resting comfortably. But how did she do that when Killian was still stuck in Hell, their child projected powers of its own, witch hunters and religious fanatics stood outside their gates, and now ghosts and reapers threatened them all?

6

A short, heavy knock sounded on her door, pulling Tierra out of the wicked spiral of "what ifs."

"Come in," she hollered.

Julian entered her bedroom, looking out of place among the velvet and satin bedclothes and the riot of colorful silk scarfs discarded this way and that. "Is now a good time for a chat?" he asked.

When would entertaining Pestilence in her bedroom ever be good timing? Tierra gave a shaky nod, curious as to why he wanted a word with her.

Jinx arched and hissed, the hair on her back standing at attention.

Julian came to a stop in the middle of the room, raised a challenging brow at Jinx, and then cocked his head to the side. "That is one very ancient feline."

"How do you know?"

"Call it a perk, if you will, of being an immortal. It's easy to recognize another."

Her familiar was immortal?

Tierra gathered Jinx—who made a low guttural growl—in her arms and tried to reassure her that Julian didn't mean them any harm. At least she hoped he didn't. Could his wanting to talk to her be a ruse to infect her with something that would kill both her and the child she carried?

As if picking up on her scattered emotions, Julian slowly locked his leather-clad hands behind his back and planted his feet wide apart. An "at ease" stance if he was in the military, but then Tierra figured he sort of was. The Horsemen were the first line of defense before any army had been formed on Earth.

"For as long as there have been witches in your ancestry, that cat has been linked to the women in your family. But as interesting as the history of your familiar is, that isn't what I wanted to discuss with you." The lines on his face deepened, and he took a fortifying breath. "I'm troubled about Aerin. What happened today with the fetus solidifies some of my concerns. I believe she is being seduced by the dark arts."

Tierra met his cool, clear eyes. "She hasn't been spending time with you, has she?"

"Today is the first I've seen her since our . . . interlude in her bedchamber a fortnight ago."

That night the de Moray chandelier's crystals had broken due to the gymnastics being performed above in Aerin's bed.

"I would like you to inform me about what really happened in the attic earlier." Julian didn't break eye contact, nor did he move. He stood like a statue, as if attempting to come off nonthreatening, but his mere presence had everything inside her at high alert. Though her child didn't seem overly concerned. Maybe she could take comfort in that?

"How did you know the baby created the force field?"

His mouth twitched as though amused by her question. "Since being informed of your condition, I've read everything I could find that might give us some insight into what the child could be."

"What did you read about babies and force fields?"

Could there be documented proof of other magical be-ings such as the one she carried?

"It's of no matter."

"No, really, I'd like to know." What if this book could help her deal with the changes and magical powers her child had already demonstrated.

"I found a chronicle . . . Actually, it was set not far from here in the Hoh Rainforests on the Olympic Peninsula near Forks."

"*Twilight?*" she blurted. Julian Roarke, Pestilence, the third Horseman of the Apocalypse had read *Twilight?*

"Not actually *Twilight*," he reluctantly admitted. "But the fourth book in the series, *Breaking Dawn.* The book brought up a concept that I found interesting as it talked of a vampiric-human child with magical proper-ties that protected itself while inside the womb."

"Did you read the whole series? How did you even come across the book?" It was fascinating to know that Julian had read the teenage saga that had captured so many women of all ages with its sweeping romance and teenage angst. Tierra hadn't made time to read it, but Sunny had devoured each and every book and con-stantly talked about Edward and Bella. Although, Tierra couldn't remember Sunny mentioning anything about a magical baby. She wondered briefly, if Julian would be team Edward or Jacob? Most definitely Edward.

"I attempted The Google, and the book appeared." Julian adjusted his stance as though uncomfortable with the subject. "I pursue many topics and have a wide va-riety of interests. The information I researched seemed consistent enough to spark the idea that something similar was happening with you. I started investigating the possibility when you had escaped Lucifer's clutches at Ambrosia's."

"You realize *Twilight* is fiction, right?"

"Many things that have been written off as fiction

have some basis in fact. Case in point, most believe that witches are fictional."

"Touché. Did you found anything else?"

"Other than the legendary barrier of the Gates of Alexander, but that doesn't really apply here. The same with Merlin when he erected a force field and encased himself inside a cave for many years. I did find a similar reference to a magical fetus able to protect itself in a television program titled *Charmed* that aired in the 1990s. It seems to be a phenomenon with twentieth century fiction writers. Now that I have revealed the . . . source of my information, what really transpired earlier in the attic?"

"It's like we already said. I was tired, and Aerin tried to help me to my room."

He regarded her with skepticism as if instinctively knowing she hadn't revealed the whole truth. "How did you feel at the time?"

How much should she tell him? Definitely not the truth that Aerin's touch had filled her with feelings of darkness and despair . . . and a wickedness that surpassed anything Tierra could imagine.

"I don't feel comfortable with this conversation." Jinx picked up on her conflicted emotions over betraying her sister, and let out a long screech that would make a lion retreat.

Julian narrowed his steely eyes. Instead of being intimidated, Jinx hissed at him. "My intent is to help Aerin. She . . . she is important to me."

"It wasn't long ago that you tried to kill her. Why should I trust you now? Just because we agreed to work together to try and get Killian out of Hell doesn't mean that you have her, or *our*, best interests at heart."

"You are perfectly correct. We don't. But there are worse things than death, worse than the end of the world. I believe Aerin's very soul is in jeopardy, and I would do anything within my power to keep her soul pure."

"You're asking me to betray her."

"That I am not. Help me bring her back from whatever precipice she's flirting with."

Tierra took a deep breath and released it. Could he truly care for Aerin? It was true that he hadn't been able to touch another soul without destroying that person, except for Aerin. Taking a leap of faith, Tierra revealed, "When Aerin touched me, I felt . . . devoid of life, a darkness so deep that it swallowed the light. What could she possibly be doing to give off those vibes?"

Julian took the news like an expected blow. "I don't know, but I plan to do everything in my power to find out."

THAT BASTARD.

Lucy sat astride Aerin's broom, hovering outside Tierra's bedroom listening to her and Julian discuss Aerin's latest behavior. Interesting that it had taken this long to raise any suspicions since she had possessed the darkest one of the four sisters for a while now.

Aerin beat inside her head, a combination of threatening, vulgar swearing—impressing even Lucy—and pathetic pleading that was getting incredibly old.

Lucy slapped her back. It surprised her that Aerin had enough strength to fight her after all this time. Other victims Lucy chose to wear like a suit, retreated to dark corners and whimpered.

Not Aerin.

Somehow Lucy needed to destroy her—starting with her mind.

These de Moray bitches were too powerful for their own good.

Just that one probe in the attic with Tierra had shown her that.

She had planned to switch Aerin for Tierra. A little push to put Tierra under her spell and then full possession once she moved Tierra to her bedroom.

Fucking fetus.

The brat had to be destroyed, and fast.

She was the fucking Antichrist. Not this *baby*.

Yet, these witches had found Mirelle's sanctuary, and even though Lucy possessed Aerin, she hadn't been able to find her way in. Once the sisters were asleep, she would give it another try. So far they'd found out that their father was Malcolm's son. Did they know that Malcolm's line descended from the Goddess?

Obviously not, or they would've told her. She still had time. But time was running out and the threads she held were becoming taut.

Julian hadn't lain with her. He couldn't stomach her, the Queen of Hell, even though he'd fucked Aerin the corporate whore. Maybe she needed to be *sweeter?*

Ugh.

Of all the sisters, Aerin appealed to her the most. They were so similar. But Julian must sense more than Aerin's attitude. He was the most perceptive of the Horsemen. After all, Aerin's own sisters hadn't a clue she was possessed by Satan.

Though Tierra had reservations, it seemed.

Attempting to burn that fertile witch at the stake had been a miscalculation on her part. She saw that now. Not taking into account the brat she carried and whatever powers it had from Bane, deemed that a failure. That was on her. She knew better than to react with emotion rather than cold calculation.

And once again, she reacted rather than thinking it through. Nudging Tierra in the attic had been a moment of opportunity. If they'd been alone, she would've gotten past whatever magic the fetus projected. The temptation of possessing the witch with Death's spawn had been too great of a lure, and she hadn't calculated the consequences.

The idea of overtaking a *pregnant* woman always made her want to vomit. She'd done it before but not with a fetus tied to Death. As far as she knew—and she knew plenty—only one time before had a situation similar to this been recorded.

When the Goddess had knocked herself up with that Druid.

Some of the greats had been birthed from Lucifer. Starting with Cain, Nero, Vlad Tepish, Hitler, Genghis Khan, Osama bin Laden, and her favorite all time pet project, Countess Elizabeth Bathory. She stuck around after the birth of that baby, raising her through her formative years. Grooming her.

She missed her, but then she did treat herself to the occasional conjugal visits in Hell. Such a diabolical soul, Elizabeth. Lucy made a mental note—one that had Aerin cringing for hidden corners—for another date with the greatest serial killer of all time.

Lucy had high hopes for Death's spawn. One way or another, she would find a way to either kill it, or control it. For now, she'd—

Doctor Lector flew at her from out of nowhere, surprising her into a shriek. Wasn't that embarrassing? Damn flying rodent.

Normally she liked bats. Not this one.

He came at her again, almost wobbling her off the broom. She snatched him out of the air, pinching his wings between her manicured fingernails.

"Think you can get the best of me, do you?" Maybe she would fry him up in lard and feed him to the pregnant witch? Doctor Lector gave a high-pitched screech that had Lucy wincing. "That's it, you flying rat. Let's see how Aerin likes this." She crushed the bat in her fist and tossed the remains away like so much trash.

Aerin screamed inside her head and beat against the barriers Lucy had imprisoned her in.

Lucy smiled in satisfaction. That was fun. Now who else could she crush?

Killian Bane.

Her smile widened. She had just the thing to make him to beg.

7

K illian slumped against the copper rods holding him in place, having endured another of Aerin's sadistic sessions. The more he refused her demands, the more she amped up the electrical works. During their last episode, she had wrapped him in a web of lightning until he felt like a fly sucked dry by a spider.

He had suffered torture many times throughout his existence, and even though he was an immortal, he didn't know how he could endure much more. She couldn't kill him, but if she kept this up, she might break him.

After he'd refused her demands, blessedly she had left him in a huff of colorful swear words. He hoped she was frustrated enough to give up soon.

What if Aerin was the opening act, warming him up for Lucifer? It would totally be something the Devil would do.

He needed to take this brief respite to recover and remember why he needed to stay strong.

Tierra and the babe.

They were what kept him steadfast and resistant, even though his body begged him to take the deal and end his misery.

He heard a commotion from outside the room and

raised his head, eyes struggling to focus. Four lackeys brought in a bed of copper nails.

What did Aerin plan to do with that?

Part of him didn't give a shit, the other part started to sweat.

Aerin supervised the low-level demons, barking out orders that they followed without hesitation or comment. It sure hadn't taken her long to work her way up to management.

"Chain him first then strap him face down on the bed," she instructed. "You might've withstood what I've done to you so far." A crafty smile spread over Aerin's lips as she addressed him. "But not what I have planned for round two."

Round two? The torture he had already endured should classify as more than that.

Even in his weakened condition, he struggled to be free as the demons yanked out the stakes and manhandled him chest-down onto the bed of nails. Every part of his body pricked with the leaching copper points, sending pain to areas that he believed had lost their ability feel.

He'd been wrong.

"Restrain him good and tight."

Two demons, their eyes soulless, held him down as others secured chains around his neck, hips, and thighs, locking them to metal plates bolted to the stone floor. Aerin ran her hand through his hair and leaned down to whisper in his ear. "I want you to feel every nail pierce your skin."

Actually, it was a relief from the copper rods staked through his muscles, and he had the added benefit of lying down. Not that he would inform her of that. How many days had he stood on his feet without relief?

Time had ceased to exist in this literal hell hole.

Aerin ran a sharp fingernail over the full tattoo inked over his back, a gift from the Goddess as ancient as time, depicting a fallen angel with a massive feathered wingspan. The black-hooded skeleton figure held a scythe with the River Styx flowing at his feet while fire and brimstone burned behind him.

"Tell me, Bane, how do I go about getting your wings to extend?" Aerin purred as she traced the lines of the inked feathers.

Why would she possibly want to know that? But he was afraid he already knew the answer.

"I've always wanted a coat made of feathers, and your wings would make a marvelous accessory."

"Release me, and I'll gladly sever them for you myself." Taking his wings would be in a sense a form of castration, but if they got him released, he would gladly pay the price.

"Now what would be the fun in that?" Her laugh cut like razorblades, and he heard a knife slide free of its sheath. "I'm afraid this might hurt a little."

TIERRA WOKE ON A STRANGLED SCREAM, HER BODY bathed in cold sweat.

No, no, no!

She threw back the covers and raced for the bedroom door, hollering for her sisters. Claire and Moira met her in the hallway.

"What the fuck, Tierra?" Claire asked, clutching her robe, her hair a mess.

"Is it the baby?" Moira followed, wearing a tank top and thin straps of lace for underwear, pairing the outfit with unicorn tube socks.

"Get the book! We have to help Killian. She's cutting him, trying to amputate his wings." Tierra ran up the stairs to the attic, not waiting to see if they followed.

"For *Goddess's* sake, slow down before you take a tumble," Moira said, running on her heels.

"Where's Aerin?" Tierra ignored Moira's warning and busted through the attic door. Claire recited the spell, revealing their mother's sanctuary.

"Where else?" Claire cursed. "She sent a text saying she was spending the night with Julian."

That would be another lie and something to deal with later. Right now, Killian needed whatever she could do for him. "We can't wait for her." Tierra entered the room, her white nightgown flowing around her legs. She laid her hands over Grim. "Protection spell." The pages surged in a whirl and stopped on the spell she had ordered. She would have to modify it a bit to fit her needs.

"Just how are you going to protect him?" Moira asked, flanking Tierra on the south side. Claire took the east corner. "You can't reach him. We've already tried."

"I was there. *I saw.* I might not know how to get him out, but if I can see, maybe I can cast." She looked at them to help her. "Please. We have to find a way."

"I have an idea." Claire turned and grabbed an olive-colored book off the shelf. "I read in here about trances, waking dreams. If we can put you in that state, maybe we can do something. No guarantees." She pointed to Moira. "Light four white candles, and set them in the directions of east, west, north, and south."

"You got it, sis." Moira hurried and followed Claire's instructions.

Claire found the page she was looking for, her lips moving as she silently read. "Okay, we need lavender oil, ground valerian, and passion flower root. Yes, there on that shelf."

Moira grabbed the items. "What do I do with them?"

"Mix a teaspoon of valerian and passion flower in a cup of blessed water." She turned to Tierra. "Lie down on the window seat, put the pillow behind your head, and get as comfortable as you can."

"I can't find the blessed water," Moira said, scanning the items stocked in the room. "Wait, yes I can." She closed her eyes and reached out with her witchy senses. "There you are." She grabbed the jar of sanctified water and poured it into a chalice, mixing in the herbs. "Holy Hannah, this smells like the tail end of a horse."

Moira brought the goblet over to Tierra who reached out for it. "Hold on, do we have any idea what this will do to the baby?"

Claire paused. "Not a clue. Tierra?"

Panic had her thoughts in a tizzy. She knew the answer to this question but couldn't find it in her chaotic mind. Both passion flower and valerian root were common for aiding sleep. She was sure the passion flower was fine but not so much on the valerian root. She closed her eyes and said a small prayer to the Goddess. "We have to risk it."

"Knowing the parents, you could probably feed that tadpole a dynamite and nitroglycerine cocktail, and it'd be right as rain," Moira muttered, relieving Tierra.

"Right, forgot we weren't dealing with a purely human fetus here." Claire knelt next to the window seat. "Now drink, but only if you're sure."

"I'm sure."

"Got the spell in your head?" Claire asked.

"Yes." Tierra drank and shuddered as the vile mixture slid down her throat. "Good Goddess, that's awful."

"Smells like shit, gonna taste like shit," Moira said.

"All right, here goes nothing." Claire picked up the lavender oil and anointed Tierra's forehead, temples, and chest, over her heart. "Aerin's going to get a piece of my mind as soon as she shows her slutty self. She should be here."

"Don't worry about her," Tierra said. "There isn't time. We'll deal with her later. What's next?"

"Moira, I need you to act as her anchor."

Moira picked up Tierra's feet, sat down on the bench, and cradled them in her lap, rubbing her soles. "This work?"

"Hell if I know. I guess we're about to find out." She turned to Tierra. "You're sure about this?"

"We're wasting time with questions. Let's do this."

Claire swore. "Okay, I need you to breathe in four times and let each breath out slowly. Close your eyes and envision Bane as you saw him in your dream."

Tierra shuddered but followed Claire's instructions. She relaxed her muscles one by one as she fell under the thrall of Claire's soothing voice.

"I'm going to count to fifty. Think only of Bane. Search him out. That's it, slow your breathing."

Claire's voice hummed in the background as the room and space disappeared, and suddenly she was in the tomb with Killian. She gasped, seeing the image of herself wielding the knife slicing into his back. She covered her mouth as bile rose in her throat.

"Tierra, calm down. Breathe." Claire's voice sounded as if it came across the sea from another continent. But it was enough to center her. "Nod if you can see him."

She nodded, a whimper escaping her. Her eyes widened as she took in the horrific scene and breathed in the rank smell of the room.

"Concentrate on the spell, Tierra."

She swallowed and began.

"Goddess of day and night, protect this man in my sight.
In this place and in this hour, I call upon my power,
erase the damage that has been wrought,
and protect him from the evil that is sought.

I command that my will be done by the bond that binds us
three.
So mote it be . . ."

A CELADON POINT OF LIGHT GREW BEFORE HER UNTIL it surrounded Killian in a translucent bubble. His torturer screamed and flew back, as though repelled, hitting the stone wall and falling into a heap of unconsciousness.

Tierra watched in fascination as the cuts on Killian's back knitted together until they were but a memory. His skin glowed under the verdant sphere, and he gasped in a fortifying breath. He lifted his head and looked in her direction.

Could he see her?

"Tierra?"

Her heart swelled in her chest, and she reached for him.

❧ 8 ☙

"*T*ierra!" Claire yelled. "Wake up!"

"Come on, sugar, come back to us." Moira gripped her feet, her nails sinking into Tierra's flesh.

"Ouch," Tierra murmured, trying to free herself from Moira's clutches. She felt like she was mired in mud, her movements sluggish, her limbs heavy. "Let go."

"Thank the Goddess," Claire breathed. "Open your eyes, yes that's it. Focus on us, Tierra."

"She doesn't look good," Moira said. "Tierra, if you don't snap out of it, Claire's going to light you on fire and then I'm gonna dump you in ice water."

"I'm good," Tierra croaked out in a voice raspy with exhaustion.

"No, you're not. You're as pale as the underside of a gator and as cold as beer in a cooler." Moira rubbed her hands up and down Tierra's legs. "Get a blanket," she told Claire.

Claire disappeared but quickly returned, smothering Tierra with a quilt, tucking it around her until she couldn't breathe.

"I'm okay." *I think*.

"Did it work?"

"He saw me, called me by name. I think the spell

worked better than I'd planned. It repelled me—his at-tacker—and then this beautiful, moss-green sphere en-veloped him. His wounds began to heal. We've got to save him before I—*she*—does more to him."

"We will, Tierra." Claire shared a look with Moira that was anything but reassuring.

"We *have* to." Tierra sat up, clutching the blanket around her shoulders. "This is all my fault. I have to fix it."

"Now, sugar, don't go gettin' upset again. Remember what the midwife told ya."

"Don't tell me not to get upset. Upset is all I know right now!"

"Uh, Tierra." Claire looked toward the outside wall. "Might want to dial it back. Whatever it is that you're doing."

"Fiery frog's foreskin!" Moira jerked to her feet. "How're you *doin'* that?"

Tierra had no idea. The wood that made up the out-side wall had come alive, similar to what had happened when she had been almost burned at the stake. The planks rounded their edges and pulsed with life. Sud-denly she knew what she needed to form. A magical push of energy and the slats of the wood rippled, mor-phing into roots, twisting and tying themselves until they created the shape of a door.

"Where the hell do you think that goes?" Claire asked, her amber eyes wide.

"Only one way to find out." Tierra stood and reached for the leaf-shaped knob.

"Wait!" Moira grabbed her arm. "No person in their right mind opens a door that is *four stories* off the ground."

"Doubt it opens to the backyard," Tierra said. "Maybe it opens to where Killian is?"

"Oh, no, you don't." This time Moira yanked her

back. "You're not gonna open a door to Hell that *leads* into our house."

"Did you make the door, or did the baby?" Claire asked.

Tierra narrowed her eyes. "What difference does it make?"

"It makes a difference. You know that," Claire said.

"I fashioned the door." Though she wasn't one hundred percent sure she accomplished it alone.

"Why?" Moira asked.

"I'm not altogether sure, but it has something to do with rescuing Killian . . . and answering more questions. I think. It's all a bit fuzzy."

"Ha, see, another reason not to open a magical door," Moira said. "Y'all recall what happened in *The Witch, the Lion, and the Wardrobe.*"

"Now you're grasping. Besides we aren't in a wardrobe. And I think it's *The Lion, the Witch, and the Wardrobe.*" Tierra wrapped her fingers around the leaf-knob again, her wand suddenly appearing in her other hand. "I'm opening the door. It might be a good idea to be ready for whatever is on the other side."

Moira's wand materialized, too.

"*Great*. Remember that I don't have a wand," Claire said. "Hell, couldn't we at least take a moment to get dressed? We're in our pajamas. Plus, I wouldn't mind packing some heat."

"Sis, you're always packin' heat." Moira smiled. "Alrighty then, open the damn thing."

Tierra twisted the knob.

❧ 9 ❧

The door slid silently open under Tierra's hand. Excitement and a twinge of fear mixed together to create a heady cocktail. Her senses sharpened, and she viewed the misty landscape beyond the threshold.

The door in the attic had opened *inside* the Standing Stones.

Claire gasped, the sound full of reverence and wonder.

"I'll be a buggered gnat," Moira whispered.

Goddess, she loved being a witch. Times like this reinforced that the world did revolve around magic, and she was incredibly blessed to be a part of it.

Storm clouds danced over the full moon, causing a blue, silvery light to flirt over the stones not unlike a lover's caress. The stones glowed as if constructed out of deep sea pearls, while leaves drifted lazily, more than ready for the long slumber promised around the corner. Fragrant whiffs of smoke from someone's campfire tinted the crisp, moist air laced with undergrowth mulching the rich soil beneath their feet.

Tierra dragged a deep breath into her lungs and held it, savoring the feel of the cooling air and the chill of the ground beneath her bare feet.

"Who the hell is that?" Claire asked as a tall man

morphed from the mists, running and yelling at them, his long duster jacket blowing out behind his long legs.

"Reaper," Tierra said. "What's he doing here?"

"*No!*" Reaper yelled, swinging his arms sharply to the side in a gesture to stop. "Shut the door!"

Suddenly the mist floating around the stones divided into individual apparitions. Hundreds of them streamed toward them like a hungry flock of birds. Eerie wails and high-pitched screeches seethed through the midnight air, causing goose bumps to rise on Tierra's flesh and fear to flow in her veins. A deep fluttering rat-a-tatted in her stomach. Could the baby be warning her?

Now would be a good time for that force field.

She and Moira raised their wands as the spirits flew their direction, while Claire formed a fireball. All were useless as the angry souls swarmed.

"Holy spankin' spirits!" Moira shrieked.

"*Shut the goddamn door!*" Reaper gained ground, but he was still too far away, swatting at the troupe of ghosts swirling around him.

An icy punch hit Tierra as a ghost shot right through her. The surreal sensation knocked her to the ground and stole her breath. Claire screamed, encased in a glacial mass of specters, while Moira waved her wand, adding rain to the mix that pierced like needles and did absolutely nothing to fend off the poltergeists.

As suddenly as it began, it was over.

Heart beating fast in her chest, Tierra thought it would surely escape its confines as she struggled to her feet, holding the underside of her belly.

"You goddamn idiots!" Reaper advanced, no longer hampered by the spirits. A chilling silence settled over the stones. "Do you have any fucking clue what you've done?"

Tierra was beginning to get an idea.

"What *we've* done?" Claire fired back. "What did *you* do?"

"These are our *stones*, our *sacred* place," Moira informed him. "How *dare* you turn it into a pokey for poltergeists?"

"There is nothing on this earthly plane that can contain lost souls except for standing stones. And you, in your stupidity and ineptness, have released them into the world."

"How many?" Tierra asked, her voice weak with the growing implications snaking through her mind like ivy choking an oak tree.

"*Thousands*," Reaper gritted out through clenched teeth. "I've been gathering and holding them here until you released Death and the gates were reopened so they could properly be placed in Heaven or Hell. Instead, you just freed the fucking lot on an unsuspecting populace who have no idea how to deal with them."

"Come on, they're spirits. What trouble can they really cause?" Claire asked. "It's not like they can touch anything, or communicate with anyone." This last was said with Claire's special brand of bravado.

"Some will be harmless, wandering lost and wailing in misery for an eternity, and that is the smallest percentage of the batch. The others will learn, adapt, haunt, torture, and seek their vengeance."

Oh, good Goddess. Tierra swallowed the lump of dread that formed in her throat.

Reaper wasn't finished nailing his point home. "You have no idea the chaos you've just unleashed, but you're about to find out. And it's all on you. Deal with it. I'm outta here." With a swing of his long duster coat, and a slap of his steampunk top hat against his buckskin pants, he gave them his back and disappeared into the night.

❄ 10 ❄

"**W**hat have *you* done?" Aunt Justine demanded, her face scrunched in wrinkles of outrage, hair standing straight up in bright red spikes making her look a lot like a troll doll.

"I'm getting really tired of people asking us that," Claire muttered, falling into a chair at the table, exhaustion radiating off her.

"You didn't wake to being felt-up by a backwater *ghost* who called himself Skunk. A *man* who has a tail *and* a penis." Justine shuddered with revulsion, grabbed the edges of her robe and twisted the fabric into a knot at her throat.

"Not Skunk Hurley?" Moira asked.

"A man like that can take you coming and going," Claire said. "Sorry, punchy over here. Say, wasn't that the name of the guy you lost your virginity to?"

"Don't remind me." Moira slid into the chair next to Claire's. "I should give Uncle Sal a call and catch up on the parish gossip. I've heard nothin' about Skunk bootin' the bucket."

"Apparently he drowned in some swamp after a night of trying to pickle himself in moonshine," Justine informed her. "Stunk like rocket fuel and sludge."

"Yeah, sounds like him. He still here?"

"*Yes!* Him and what seems like a convention of the unrest. Can't go anywhere in this house without being spied on or run through." She shuddered again. "Feels like your insides have been dipped in a glacial lake. So, again, what the hell did you girls do?"

"Better have a seat, Aunt Justine," Tierra said. "It's been a long night. I'll make some tea." She busied herself in the kitchen, so tired she couldn't think straight.

"Might want to brew some coffee. We're going to need something stronger than tea." Claire gestured to the morning view out the window. "Aerin just pulled in the drive."

"Before she gets here, Julian said that they haven't slept together since that first time weeks ago." Tierra lit the flame under the kettle and then rested against the counter. "She's been lying to us about where she disappears to."

"Now wait a snake-suckin' minute," Moira objected. "Just because they haven't continued doin' any naked noodlin', don't mean they aren't spendin' time together."

"Julian also said that yesterday was the first time he'd seen her since the night they slept together. He's worried that Aerin's into something . . . dark." Tierra took a deep breath and let it out in a rush. "I'm worried she is, too." She couldn't shake the overwhelming wickedness she felt when Aerin had touched her in the attic.

Aerin stumbled in, her hair a mess, half of it plastered to her skull with what looked to be matted blood. There was also a nasty bruise forming on the side of her face. "What are you guys doing up so early?"

"Splendid," Aunt Justine said, her lips twisting into a sneer. "I'll get the first aid kit, and then you girls are coming clean." She harrumphed out of the room.

"What in the blue blazes have you been up to?" Moira asked.

"I not only have the end of the world to deal with, but a multinational corporation to run," Aerin said. "And the internet here is shit."

"Good Goddess, what happened to you?" Tierra rushed over and almost reached for her sister before a look of hatred flickered briefly in Aerin's eyes. It was gone so fast that Tierra figured she must have imagined it. With the long night of seeing Killian, and then releasing a gaggle of ghosts, she couldn't trust her faculties completely.

Aerin dropped her bag on the floor and kicked off her heels. "I got shanghaied by . . . uhm . . . witch hunters or Bible thumpers. I really can't tell the difference between them anymore. One surprised me and threw me against a stone wall." Her silvery eyes never left Tierra's.

A cold shiver skated down her spine, and Tierra took a step back, and then another. An outlandish idea spun around in her head.

Could Aerin be the one torturing Killian?

The teakettle whistled, and she rushed to turn off the heat.

She had to be insane to even consider it. The woman with Killian had been wearing Tierra's clothes, and yes, Aerin was the spitting image of her except for her eyes. Then again, so were Claire and Moira.

Come on, how would Aerin even get into Hell?

Unless she'd delved deeper into the dark side than Tierra had suspected? Knowing the Devil and her love for disguises, Lucifer most likely concocted an illusion to further torture Killian. That made more sense. Guilt washed over Tierra at even thinking such ridiculous things about Aerin.

If Aerin had dabbled more in the practice of dark magic, Tierra loved her, and she would find a way to bring her back from the edge.

Moira rushed to Aerin and inspected the side of her

head. "Damn, girl, that was some hit. Must have rung your bell harder than a sinner on Sunday. Let's wash the blood away, and I'll get y' all healed up." She headed to the sink to wet a cloth.

"What's the other guy look like?" Claire asked. "And why were you out there alone?"

"I've been alone most of my life. I can handle myself."

"Sure you can." Claire gestured to Aerin's disheveled appearance. "Just look at you."

"Bite me." Aerin pulled out a chair and went to sit, but a ghostly old man appeared in her place. Aerin stumbled back. *"What the fuck?"*

"Yeah, you missed a bunch of shit while you were off doing whatever." Claire glared at the ghost, who slunk off the chair and floated from the room. "*Shoo*! That's right you, goblin ass-grabbers, stay out of here!" Claire hollered up at the ceiling. A windy wail, sounding a lot like laughter, followed her words.

Moira, with cloth in hand, stood behind Aerin and carefully began to clean the cut, using her healing touch to knit Aerin's skin back together and erased the colorful bruise marking her face.

Justine returned and slapped the first aid kit down on the table. "Well, guess you don't need *this* anymore." She folded her arms across her chest, and Tierra was surprised when she didn't tap her foot. "Now that *she's* been dealt with, I'm through waiting. Start explaining yourselves."

Claire carefully reported on the night's events, leaving out the protection spell they performed for Killian and the door Tierra had formed that led to the Standing Stones. By the time she finished—blaming the release of the ghosts on Reaper—Tierra had set a tray of tea and cookies on the table, as well as a French press full of coffee.

"Well, that's . . . an interesting development," Aerin

said. "I think my coffee's going to need a bit of Irish this morning."

"For once, I'm in agreement with you." Justine grabbed the whiskey, pouring a very healthy dose in her cup and taking a chair.

"Is that really a good idea?" Tierra protested.

"Hey, you didn't get assaulted in your sleep by a tail-wagging, stubby-penis redneck. So, don't judge me."

"Not judgin', just hurry and pass the bottle, old woman," Moira said.

Tierra frowned as the whiskey bottled was emptied. "Don't we have enough *spirits* to deal with? We shouldn't be drinking more."

"The answer is probably not, but I'm going to anyway," Claire said.

"How are you going to clean up this mess?" Justine asked. "I can't live here with that zombie Tommy and a bunch of ghosts."

"I'll help ya pack." Moira smiled sweetly. "After all, what are nieces for?"

A chorus of yips, squeals, and screeching meows echoed from the front of the house.

"I can't take anymore drama!" Aunt Justine yelled, tipping her Irish coffee back and drinking the remains.

They all looked at each other, and then hurried to slide their chairs back from the table and ran toward the ruckus.

Moira shot through the door, leading the way around the house to one of the flower beds bordering the foundation. There amongst the mums, they found Doctor Lector crumpled on the dirt, both of his wings bent at impossible angles. Shallow breaths lifted his little chest, and his black, beady eyes swam with pain as he looked up at them.

The other three familiars surrounded him in a protective circle, Cheeto nudging him with his stubby nose, giving a worried little snort. Doctor Lector released a pitiful sound that clutched at Tierra's heart.

"Doctor Lector," Aerin whispered. "What the hell happened?"

Tierra tried to understand the familiars but couldn't make sense of what they were saying to each other. It was like they were attempting to perform a spell.

Kai and Jinx linked tails with Cheeto and started up their chorus of yelps, mews, and squeaks again.

"Holy toad scrotums, would you look at that?" Moira exclaimed as Cheeto carefully spit on each of the breaks in Doctor Lector's wings. The spit shimmered an iridescent aqua in the sunrise, and the bat's little bones began to pulse and weave together.

"Now that's not something you see every day—or like ever," Claire said.

"How the fuck are they doing that?" Aerin asked, her tone shocked and somewhat more annoyed than normal.

"It makes sense that as our familiars, who are immortals in their own right—I'll explain about that later—have their own magic which coincides with our elements," Tierra answered, remembering her conversation with Julian the night before.

"We've seen Cheeto's saliva 'heal' Aunt Justine's surly attitude before," Claire said. "We might want to bottle some of that stuff and have it on hand."

Kai let out a high-pitched howl as Doctor Lector suddenly shot into the air, his wings flapping as good as new. But he didn't return to them. Instead, he flew high up into the dark shadowed eaves overhanging the attic.

"How'd he get himself hurt in the first place?" Moira asked. "It's like he was . . . crushed or somethin'. Who would've done such an awful thing?"

"I'm trying to find out." Tierra knelt next to the three remaining familiars who all spoke at once. "Come on, guys, let Jinx tell me. I'm not so good yet with fox or swine speak."

Jinx meowed long and mean.

"What's she saying?" Aerin said.

"Shh. I'm trying to make it out." Tierra listened, her brow furrowing in concentration, as Jinx gave her an earful. "An ancient evil outside the house. Something about a wolf in sheep's clothing. I think. It's disjointed since Doctor Lector was in so much pain. Jinx isn't clear on the details either."

"The only dark evil around here is the four of you," a raspy voice echoed around them, followed by the ghostly image of a bearded man sporting a man bun. "*And you all must die.*"

Claire immediately whipped her water pistol from the pocket of her robe, loaded with Horsemen repellant that she'd armed herself with when they'd returned from the Standing Stones. She shot off a stream of blueberry scented liquid that passed right through the newcomer.

The ghost threw back his head and gave an eerie laugh. "Can't kill me, *witch*. I'm already dead."

"Who the freak are you?" Moira asked.

Three Horsemen appeared, sitting astride their legendary horses, their razor-sharp hooves digging deep, cutting crescent moons into the thick grass of the front lawn.

"Brock somebody or other," Julian said, urging his horse forward. "He's the witch hunter I killed protecting Aerin's . . . virtue."

"Virtue?" War said in a dry, droll voice. "Is that what we're calling it now?"

Brock took one look at the Horsemen and scattered into a misty cloud, disappearing into the upper story of the manor. Tierra doubted they'd seen the last of him.

"Can't leave you alone for a minute without the four of you making a shitty situation shittier," Conquest said. "Morning, Moira." He tilted his head in greeting, his eyes lighting with lust at the sight of her in the tank top, lacy underwear, and unicorn tube socks. "Nice outfit."

Moira flushed, but her tone was sarcastic when she addressed him, "What are *you* doing here?"

"Heard there was something strange going down in the neighborhood," Nick said, with a smirk.

"Probably you shouldn't try to be funny" Moira said. "Doesn't suit you."

"Who else you going to call? I'm the closest thing to a Ghostbuster you've got." Nick aimed a grin at Moira. "Spirits have a healthy respect for immortals."

"That wasn't respect when I was taking care of personal business this morning," Dru said. "It was voyeurism, plain and simple. No one spies on me in the john and gets away with it. We need Bane back. Now."

Dru's last word echoed over the landscape, his midnight eyes slicing over toward Tierra. With his no-nonsense military cut and rough-stubbled jaw clenched to reveal the vein throbbing on the side of his chiseled face, he didn't look like he was up for explanations or excuses. War wanted results.

Tierra backed up a step, and the earth trembled under his horse's hooves, causing the horse to snort and stomp its hooves, chopping the grass underfoot.

"You want to join your brother in Hell?" Claire warned. "Just keep it up."

"Don't threaten me," Dru said, teeth clenched, eyes cold.

"Don't destroy my lawn." Tierra schooled her expression into the best poker face she could manage, but she cringed over Claire's threat. Sending another Horseman to Hell was the last thing she wanted to attempt. Besides, she doubted she could do it again, certainly not on command.

Jinx hissed, her hair standing on end, further agitating the horses. Cheeto shot off a fireball at Nick that had his horse rearing, almost unseating him. Kai's thick, bottle-brush tail quivered, and he created a chittering sound that grew louder and louder. Claire scooped up the fox before he could release his sonic boom.

"Enough!" Dru barked. "We're wasting time with these . . . *squabbles*. There are battles to be won." Under his breath he muttered to his fellow Horsemen, "I knew this fucking *truce* was a bad idea."

"I suggest we compose ourselves, confine the familiars, and have a civilized discussion." Julian dismounted his black horse and sent him away into the forest. He stood there regarding his brothers with impatience, until they, too, dismounted their horses and sent them off.

From what Tierra could read from the horses, they

were similar to the witches' familiars, with powers of their own, yet tied to each Horseman.

Interesting.

"Where's Killian's horse?" she asked out of curiosity.

Julian regarded her with . . . approval? "You've figured it out, haven't you?"

"What has she figured out?" Aerin asked. "What are you talking about? Stop doing that sharing of the look thing and tell us what you're thinking."

Julian settled his piercing gaze on Aerin. "Tierra, would you take a promenade with me?"

"Uh . . ." Tierra looked from Aerin to Julian and then to Moira and Claire, who both shrugged their shoulders. Aerin fumed, and the air quivered with electrical currents.

"She's not going anywhere with you," Aerin sneered. "From now on, no witch consorts with any Horseman. If we're to work together, that's exactly what we do. *Together*. No more secrets."

"She's right," Claire said. "There should be no secrets between us." Though the statement was directed toward Aerin more than anyone else.

"Are you suggesting that we reveal our mysteries?" War asked. His eyes turned slumberous as he strode toward Claire. "Be careful what you wish for, my fire witch."

"I'm not *your* fire witch." Claire narrowed her eyes, and Tierra was afraid that she would attempt to burn him like a slab of bacon in front of her. And that would most likely ruin her new-found favorite food.

Tommy appeared from around the corner of the house. Dru straightened, and Tierra thought she heard his spine crack. Tommy cocked his easy surfer's smile and sauntered over to Claire, draping a possessive arm around her shoulders. "What's going on here?"

"Unhand her, you undead piece of filth," Dru ordered.

Oh, this wasn't good. Just what they didn't need, a pissing match between Tommy and Dru over Claire's confused affections.

"Sure, you can have her," Tommy said, his smile turning crafty, his bright blue eyes flashing to black. "What's left of her." A butcher knife appeared from behind his back, and Dru bellowed a warning. Claire jerked to the side, saving herself from a lethal stab to the heart, but Tommy's downward swing still found purchase high in Claire's shoulder. She went down with a shriek of pain and surprise.

In less than a blink, Dru swung his sword at Tommy, the blade sinking deep into his chest. His body shimmered as Dru yanked the sword from his heart, yet a maniacal laugh was all that escaped Tommy as Brock, the witch hunter, slid free of his body.

"Now that was more satisfying than I believed it would be," Brock sneered. "Can't wait to stick it to the rest of you *witches*."

"*Claire!*" Tierra and Moira screamed, rushing forward but stopped short as Dru roared, swinging his broadsword in a wide arch at Brock, intent on taking off his head. It went right through his neck, the plasma displacing and morphing back together with no damage done.

"Seems that being dead does have its advantages." Brock looked at Aerin, Moira, and then settled on Tierra. "Yes, I do believe I'm going to enjoy this." He disappeared on another sadistic snicker.

Dru was the first one to recover and reach Claire. Gathering her up in his arms, his fingers gently investigated the bleeding wound.

"I'm okay. Just hurts like a *sonofabitch*." Claire struggled in Dru's embrace. "Put me down. Oh, my Goddess, Tommy!" Claire freed herself and rushed toward

Tommy where he lay on the grass. "I can't believe *you* stabbed him." She sent an accusing stare at Dru.

"*He* stabbed you. *I* was protecting you."

"I can protect myself."

"Yeah, that's *clearly* apparent."

"I hate to pour acid on this little tête-à-tête," Nick drawled, "but what would you like to do about the *press* that just caught that little scene on video?" Nick gestured to the swarm of journalists snapping pictures and filming from outside the gates.

When the hell had they shown up?

"Should we all take them out, or send a small posse?" It was obvious that Nick relished the idea of conquering a batch of enterprising journalists.

Great, just what they needed, more documented proof.

"Nick, you and Aerin gather up the evidence they have collected," Julian instructed. "Moira, see to Claire. Tierra, you and I need to take that stroll."

The last thing Tierra wanted to do was take a walk with Pestilence, but she didn't see where she had much choice.

She nodded to Moira. Claire's condition was the most important. That and the press.

"Just don't kill them," Tierra said. "Take the evidence, but leave them breathing."

"Are you serious?" Nick scoffed. "Of course we're going to kill them. Silence them forever."

"You do that and we will have journalist ghosts snooping around us all the time," Tierra said. *Damn, bloodthirsty Horseman.*

"Oh, for the days when a little bloodshed was a simple proposition," Nick muttered, stomping off with Aerin, who looked like she would rather be cleaning toilets than be paired with Conquest.

Moira flanked Claire, and she and Dru helped Claire inside the manor with Tommy fretting apologetically over his part in causing her injury. It looked as though

Dru's blade, and Brock's spirit possession, hadn't caused Tommy any harm, which was a further concern.

If the witch hunter could possess him, what would keep the other spirits from doing the same? Any ghost with a score to settle now had a weapon they could use, and it resided right under their own roof.

Julian cocked his head toward the lower lawns that housed the new drying shed where Sunny—with Justine's help—had taken over running the online business, what with Ambrosia's now nothing but ash.

The day promised a rare break from the encroaching winter. The cloudless lapis sky reached into the stratosphere, and the wind held its breath as though in anticipation. Puget Sound reflected an aqua sheet of antique glass below the towering cliffs turning shades of cinnamon and nutmeg beneath the stately evergreens. The scene belied the tension that had taken root inside her, and Tierra wished she could take the day to lie on the grass, soak in the heat of the sun, and commune with nature. It had been too long since she'd linked with Mother Earth, and she missed it more than she could express.

"I unearthed something of consequence," Julian began, walking alongside her, his hands linked behind his back. His black hair, shot with blades of silver, glinted like hematite in the sunlight.

Tierra waited him out as he gathered his thoughts.

"The Standing Stones have the power to act as a portal through time and space. While I didn't find anything about traveling to the Underworld, legends do speak of entering the Faerie Realm through the stones."

She wasn't about to tell him that she and her sisters had already thought of that. Their father had traveled here from a thousand years ago, so it was the only logical deduction. But the Faerie Realm was new.

"So Faeries are a thing?"

"Unfortunately. Malicious buggers. When endeavoring such a feat, you must ground yourself to this plane, or you will be at risk of being taken, or worse."

What would be worse than that?

"There are . . . things, creatures, which could return with you." He stopped and turned to face her. "I assume that you and your sisters planned to use All Hallows Eve to attempt Bane's rescue?"

Slowly, she nodded, not sure how much she should share of their plans. Truce or not, she didn't want to open them up for the Horsemen to enact a coup the second Bane returned.

Julian tightened his jaw for a moment. "I advise against it. The veil is too thin during the in-between."

"We can't wait. All Hallows Eve is tomorrow night. We must perform the spell."

Julian shook his head, his black eyes fathomless with knowledge and secrets. "You must do it tonight. And you must do it alone."

"*Alone?*" No, she needed her sisters and went to say as much when he spoke again.

"Aerin can't be present. Trust me, and listen. You've reached Killian in your dreams, haven't you?"

"Y-yes." Should she tell him about last night? Maybe it was the long night of no sleep and releasing ghosts upon the world, but Tierra found herself revealing last night's events, keeping quiet about the sanctuary and the hidden door that led directly to the Standing Stones from the attic.

"You say that you saw yourself torturing Killian?" Julian questioned, his brow furrowing. At her nod, he paced a distance away and looked over the Sound. She gave him a moment before joining him.

He spoke without looking at her, "It's imperative that you do the spell yourself. I know this is daunting, but you've reached Killian on your own before. I have faith that you are the key to releasing him. You had the power to send him there, and only you can retrieve him.

To have your sisters present could, and most likely will, create problems. Either the attempt will be disrupted or you will lose one, if not all of them, to the Grave."

Reaching into the pocket of his long coat, he pulled out a black velvet pouch. "What I'm about to give you cannot be shared with anyone else. No one can know of its existence." Carefully, he held the pouch by the strings so she could take it without coming into contact with him.

She took the pouch and released the ties, coaxing the heavy item from the fabric. A black tourmaline fell into her palm. Blacker than any other tourmaline she'd ever seen, it was roughly three inches long and an inch wide, and its age seemed immeasurable. Oblong and jagged, it covered her palm, power radiating through her at the contact, grounding her to the Earth in a way she'd never felt before.

A startled breath escaped her, and it took a minute to recover. "What? Where?"

"The stories attached to this stone are ancient and bloody. That is why you cannot let anyone know you possess it. I've had it in my collection since I acquired it from the Knights Templar the day they were massacred. Legend has it, that the stone was mined from deep within the Carpathian Mountains. A place some in the know refer to as 'The Cradle of Life.'

"I'm sure you are aware that black tourmaline is revered for its ability to repel negative ions, repress electromagnetic fields. It will aid in shielding your body and the babe from the effects of radiation you will most likely encounter, in order to reach the Underworld."

The stone had more than the normal properties of regular tourmaline. So much more. Tierra recognized the unlimited battery life glowing from within, charged from the sun. Her earth charka fairly vibrated in excitement.

"Do not get too attached," Julian continued. "I will

need this returned posthaste. Those who have sought the benefits of the stone, ended up being seduced by its power. It is not meant for mortals."

"But I'm a witch."

"Yet still mortal. The tourmaline alone will see you safely to Hell and back, but you will need to perform your other rituals. You'll know which ones. The harvest moon will be at its peak at midnight. You must be ready. Tell no one of what we've spoken of here today. To release this stone into your hands could have dire consequences for us all. Heed my words, Tierra de Moray. Tell no one."

She gave Julian a shaky nod, enraptured by the iridescence of the stone pulsing in her palm.

"Tierra, I must hear the words." Julian's commanding tone grabbed her attention, and she glanced up at him, surprised he was still there. "Promise me."

"I promise to tell no one."

"Good." Julian gave her a short nod. "Now, cover the stone, and cast a cloaking spell over it. Perform the ritual before the harvest moon begins its descent. Do not wait another day. It's imperative more than ever that we have Bane back tonight."

Tierra entered the house, and instead of checking on Claire, she ran upstairs to her bedroom and hid the black tourmaline in the bathroom amongst the tampons she wouldn't need for months yet. One perk of pregnancy. She thought about hiding the stone in the sanctuary, but worried she might be found out. No one would question her running upstairs to use the bathroom, as lately she always needed to pee.

She hated that she wasn't being honest with her sisters, hated keeping something from them, but Julian's intensity had convinced her. Ignorance, would keep them safe.

Returning downstairs, she found Claire and Moira in the kitchen. There was no sign of Tommy or Dru. Good. She didn't relish dealing with those two. Moira stood next to Claire, wrapping a sling around Claire's arm to take the weight off her shoulder.

"How are you feeling?" Tierra asked.

"Better now that those two halfwits are gone." Claire picked at the label on the beer bottle in front of her. "Men are more trouble than a monsoon."

"Actually, I enjoy a good monsoon," Moira said. "Besides, it was kinda romantic how they fought over you." She tightened the knot on the sling. "There, baby that shoulder, no heavy lifting, and I'll apply more healing salve in a few hours. Hope you don't mind that I added a bit of Cheeto's spit to the mix?"

"Not at all. That pig can spit on me anytime, what with how his spittle healed Doctor Lector. Thanks, Moira. Already feels normal." Claire lifted her arm halfway and then winced. "Well, maybe not completely." She picked up her beer and took a long draw.

"Aerin isn't back yet?" Tierra asked, opening the fridge. Goddess, but she was tired and hungry. She didn't know which to satisfy first and figured if she didn't silence her stomach, there would be no chance at sleeping.

"Not yet," Moira muttered. "Hope her and Nick don't kill each other."

Tierra pulled out the leftover pepperoni pizza, grabbing an apple for good measure. Her eating habits were atrocious lately.

"I'll take a slice of that, too," Moira said, taking a chair and leaning her head on her hand.

"Make that three," Claire said. "No, don't bother heating it up. For once, I'll eat it cold."

Tierra set the pie on the table and handed out napkins, not bothering with plates. She took a few bites to quiet the gnawing in her stomach before broaching the next subject. "I think we need to talk about Tommy."

Claire's eyes heated. "Not now."

"Claire, you realize that if Brock can possess him, other ghosts can, too."

"Somethin' to consider, sis," Moira said around a mouthful. "We won't know who's wearin' him each time he walks into a room."

Claire rubbed the back of her neck, winced again, and traded the pizza for her beer. "I'll think of something, but I don't want to talk about men right now."

"Okay, now can Tierra tell us what Julian wanted to

yap about?" Moira asked, going for another piece of pizza.

Claire drained her beer and sat back in her chair with a sigh. "Lay it on us."

What should she tell them? She couldn't outright *lie*, but then she couldn't tell them the truth either. If they had any inkling of what she planned to do, they would either stop her or force their way into her plans. "Pretty much the same old. Gotta get Killian out of Hell. He's real upset over the release of the ghosts."

"Aren't we all? Goddess, I need a fucking vacation." Claire laid her head down on the table.

"Oh shit, we're going to be late!" Moira jumped to her feet. "Your ultrasound appointment is in fifteen minutes. Hurry, we need to get dressed."

"Can't we reschedule?" That was the last thing Tierra wanted to do. She needed a nap.

"No, we need to check out the tadpole, make sure he isn't sportin' horns or somethin'. Come on." Moira pulled Tierra out of her chair and pushed her toward the stairs. "Besides I wanna peek at my little niece or nephew."

"Claire?" Tierra asked, glancing back. "Want to come?"

Claire shuddered. "If it's okay with you, I think I'll have another beer and try to get some sleep. The ghosts seemed to have quieted down, probably busy figuring out how to rattle chains or something."

"Shouldn't we wait for Aerin?"

"The last thing that chick wants is anything to do with babies." Moira gave her another push. "Get a move on."

"I SEE YOU'VE TAKEN MY ADVICE TO HEART," LILA said sarcastically, regarding Tierra with a critical eye. "When was the last time you slept?"

"Uh . . . "

"Could that have anything to do with the ghosts being reported about town?"

"Uh . . ." Tierra answered intelligently again.

"Thought so." Lila sighed and grabbed a bottle from the tray and squirted a glob on Tierra's exposed stomach. "Let's take a look, shall we?"

Moira planted herself next to Tierra. "So, we're really gonna to see what's happenin' *inside*?"

"Ultrasounds give us a pretty good idea. At least it will let us know if we need to do more tests."

"More tests?" Tierra stiffened.

"Nothing to worry about," Lila reassured her, laying a comforting hand on her shoulder. "You're supposed to be reducing stress, remember."

"How do I do that when you say stuff like *more tests*?"

"Breathe, and take a look." A grin split over Lila's mouth. "There's your baby." She pointed to the screen as she maneuvered the wand-like thing over Tierra's belly. "Never ceases to amaze me. This is the best part of my job, that and delivering a new soul into the world."

Tears popped into Tierra's eyes, and a rush of . . . *love* overwhelmed her. There on the screen in black and white was the image of her baby. It was hard at times to make out, but she could see legs and arms. Suddenly she felt movement inside her.

"Holy Mother of Earth!" she exclaimed. "I-I think it just moved."

Lila smiled. "Sure is a swimmer. Lots of movement. That's a good thing." She pressed some keys on the computer, and the image froze. "Just taking some measurements here." A few more clicks and she moved the wand again.

"So . . . like can you check its hooves—er, little footsies?" Moira asked.

"Here." Lila moved the wand. "Ten toes on each foot."

"Ten!" Tierra tried to sit up, but Lila pushed her back.

"My bad. Ten toes total. Five on *each* perfectly formed foot."

"Phew, 'bout gave us a heart attack there, doc," Moira said. "What about a tail? What? Like you weren't a wonderin', too."

Tierra remembered Skunk Hurley and Aunt Justine's early morning rant. "Does it have a tail? Seems to the theme of the day. Just go with it."

"This is going to go down as one of my most interesting appointments ever," Lila said. She maneuvered the wand. "No tail. Wait . . ."

"*Wait?*" Tierra and Moira said together.

"For a minute there, I thought I could determine the sex of the baby, but it crossed its legs."

"Think I'd do the same if anyone were pointin' some sonic wave gun at my lady bits," Moira said, enraptured with what she saw on the screen. "Hey, would you look at that. I think it just waved a flipper at us!"

"No, must be a reflex . . ." Lila gasped as the baby pressed its hand against the wall of the womb and held it there. "That's . . . interesting." She moved the device and the baby followed its movements across Tierra's abdomen. "Apparently your child is *very* aware of what we're doing. Astonishing."

"How is it doing that?" Tierra asked.

Lila shrugged. "Your guess is as good as mine. I've never seen anything like it," she whispered.

The baby held up its other hand, and the ultrasound machine sparked as though zapped with a power surge.

Lila jumped back on an exclamation.

"What just happened?" Tierra asked.

"I-I think it just killed my *machine*." Lila attempted to reboot the apparatus.

"How could it do that?" Moira asked. "It's just a baby. Hear that, Tierra, just a baby."

One that had the ability to detect its surroundings from *inside* the womb, communicate, and kill appliances. Sure, *just* a baby.

"No horns, tails, or cloven hooves," Moira attempted to soothe. "Ten toes, too, remember?"

A rapid succession of kicks that she couldn't disregard as gas, rippled the skin of her stomach.

"Holy shit," Moira said, jerking back. "Don't that hurt?"

"Not at all." Tierra smiled and stroked the mounded curve of her belly. Whatever grew inside her was her child, and she suddenly wanted it more than she wanted anything.

❧ 13 ❧

T ierra looked over the gathered items.

While ghosts continued to haunt the manor, sending Aunt Justine shrieking to sleep elsewhere, Tierra prepped for the night ahead with Jinx eyeing her every move. Turned out, one hiss from the cat and the wandering souls scattered like leaves on the wind. Her sisters assumed she was tuckered out, and she was, but sleep would have to wait a little bit longer. She hoped she didn't screw anything up.

On the bed lay her crystal bracelets of jasper for aid in pregnancy and astral travel, bloodstone for courage and emotional clarity, strength and energy—damn but she needed that more than she liked to admit—green aventurine to help realign her spirit with her body, and she was good to go.

Wait, was she missing something?

Jinx meowed from the bed, sitting on her haunches, and regarded Tierra's preparations ready to hand down judgment.

"I know. You've made your objections clear. Here." Tierra laid a sheet of paper on the night table. She'd written a letter to her sisters, conveying her love and regret to them, in case she didn't return. "If—no ifs, this will work—but just on the slim chance things don't go as planned, please give this to my sisters *if* I'm not home by sunrise."

Jinx meowed again, the sound low and long in her throat.

"You're not changing my mind. So knock it off."

Jinx wasn't about to let it rest and started up a caterwauling that Tierra feared would have her sisters rushing to check on her. She stopped what she was doing and faced the cat, giving Jinx her full attention. "Wait. Say that again." Jinx swatted her paw in exasperation and began yowling again.

"Why, that's . . . brilliant."

Jinx let out an approving purr strong enough to vibrate the bed.

Tierra located her henna and stripped off her clothes. She proceeded to apply a tree of life on her distended stomach, giggling at the tiny fluttering from the baby as it followed the strokes of the applicator.

Why hadn't she thought of this? Too tired to think, obviously.

Trees were symbols of physical and spiritual growth. They represented fertility, provided sustenance, and brought together the temporal worlds. Places of birth and death, of worship and sacred shrines that had been documented since the time of Adam and Eve. Not to mention, trees anchored themselves to the earth with their deep-seeded roots—part living and feeding underground, the other cleansing the air and reaching toward the heavens.

While the henna-painted symbol dried, Tierra slipped the crystal bracelets over both wrists and around her ankles. She picked up the black velvet pouch with the black tourmaline Julian had given her and tied it to a long piece of twine hemp and slipped it over her head. It rested between her breasts, and she immediately felt that deep spiritual connection with the Earth again, stronger than any link she experienced before. Next, she weaved the plants she'd gathered when Moira had checked in on Claire, whispering to Tierra that she planned to have a come-to-Jesus-talk with her about Tommy.

Supposedly, Aerin had headed to the store to stock the pantry. Apparently, she had a craving for dark chocolate and they were out. Claire added more beer and whiskey to the list, and Moira announced that she had a hankerin' for boiled canned peanuts. Tierra doubted Aerin would be able to locate that particular item. But it gave her the time required to visit the solarium and harvest the plants she needed.

Now, she braided mugwort leaves into her hair for aid in traveling through gateways to other dimensions, peppermint for repelling evil spirits, rosemary for health and wellbeing, and mandrake for help in locating one that you loved.

She hesitated on the mandrake. Love was a powerful word, and she wasn't sure exactly what she felt for Killian. Fear, longing, respect, and definitely sexual attraction . . . but love?

Deciding it couldn't hurt, she weaved that in, too, but limited the amount as the plant also tended to heighten physical desires, and she didn't need sex getting in the way of her rescue mission.

Following that, she added the flowers of belladonna for the dark element she'd need and balanced it with angelica. She washed off the henna and admired how the plant had dyed the tree of life symbol in the skin of her abdomen. She might need to make the symbol permanent. Getting a tattoo had never tempted her before, but she wasn't looking forward to when the henna would disappear from her skin.

Last, she reached for the golden crown in the shape of stag antlers and placed it on her head. Everything inside her heightened, sharpening her eyesight and in-creasing her hearing. The cut flowers in her hair bloomed brighter as though they'd been resurrected. She regarded her reflection in the full-length mirror. She looked like a fairytale nymph and figured Mother Earth would be proud of her efforts.

She donned a thin, white cotton shift for the journey to the Standing Stones. The other essential items she needed were located in the sanctuary. Now she had to figure how to get into the attic without anyone noticing her.

Jinx leaped off the bed, not about to leave her alone, and they quietly snuck out of the bedroom and up the flights of stairs.

Only one ghost crossed their path and immediately dispersed when Jinx hissed. Tierra felt around the door to the attic, not willing to turn on a light, and carefully recited the spell that would uncloak Mirelle's sanctuary.

"This is as far as you can go," she whispered to Jinx, leaning down and stroking the cat. Jinx lifted her nose and left a kiss on her cheek. "Take care of them if this goes upside down. Please know how thankful I am for your devotion to my family." Jinx rubbed up against her shins, letting out a pitiful meow, a menacing mandate to keep her ass safe or else.

Once inside, Tierra reversed the charm, once again hiding the room. She lit a candle, gathered the other items she needed, placed them in a basket, along with salt for the circle, a small ceremonial knife, and the smelly blend of herbs Claire and Moira had helped her concoct the last time she'd seen Killian.

Taking a deep breath, Tierra conjured her wand, turned the leaf-shaped knob, and opened the door to the Standing Stones.

The swollen harvest moon had risen to its zenith, shining red and gold over the Standing Stones, bathing them in shades of copper and bronze. The air was still, almost reverent, the chill of the night bearable as the day had been so unseasonably warm.

Tierra strode to the middle of the stones, poured salt on the dormant grass, and cast the circle. She lit candles and placed them north, east, south, and west, offering up a small prayer to the Goddess.

Centering herself, she slowly released the tie at her throat, and the shift pooled at her feet. She stood naked, a symbol of fertility and strength, in the moonlight. She reached for the knife and sliced her palm, the blood seeping into the soil, a small sacrifice to what she was about to ask of the Earth. She drank the potion and began reciting the spell.

> *"Powers of mountain and glen,*
> *deliver me to Killian.*
> *Allow safe passage and return.*
> *In this sacred place and in this hour,*
> *I command that my will be done,*
> *by the bond that binds us three.*
> *So mote it be . . ."*

THE GROUND TREMBLED BENEATH HER FEET, WIND gusted and wailed, and the majestic stones before her shimmered.

In a blink she was gone.

❦

KILLIAN STRUGGLED AGAINST THE CHAINS THAT bound him to the bed of copper nails. He had to get free. Whatever had happened the night before proved that Tierra had been trying to rescue him.

It went against everything in his nature to have a

woman save his ass, but then another woman was bound and determined that he wouldn't survive and be the same man after her special brand of treatment.

She wanted him to be a pet, housebroken, and submissive.

Never fucking going to happen.

Tierra had gifted him with renewed strength, somehow healed him of his injuries, and prevented him from further harm.

Now if he could just break these chains.

A pinpoint of jade flickered in the dim light and grew, gleaming into the loveliest shade of green he'd ever beheld.

Tierra appeared like a vision in the dank, hell hole in front of him.

She was . . . *enchanting.* An earth goddess. Nay an earth *warrior* goddess. Naked and wild, with leaves and flowers entwined in her titian-colored hair that flowed down just shy of brushing her shapely hips. The Druid King's golden crown regally sat upon her head, while colorful crystals twinkled at her wrists and ankles. Jeweled and silver rings adorned her fingers, yet it was the intricate tree of life—with Celtic symbols interwoven into the roots and leafy branches—gracing the supple mound of her belly that drew his attention. Beneath that tree, his child flourished.

How had she known to anchor herself to the Earth in such a manner?

She took his breath away. His heart galloped in his chest, and his body swelled with need. A *need* so encompassing that his whole body shuddered.

"Killian!" She rushed toward him. One hand clutched her wand and the other reached for him, but she stopped as though she didn't know where to touch him first.

"Tierra?" *It's really her, not a mirage.*

She studied the chains and then directed those

lovely long fingers wrapped about her wand toward the copper links. A few whispered words, and the metal links bent to her will until they broke.

He dragged a full breath into his lungs, something he hadn't been able to do with the restraints holding him down against the sharp nails.

"Can you stand?" she asked, her voice full of concern. "I don't know how to raise you off the nails without hurting you further."

He placed his hands on the nails, and they pierced his palms as he pushed against them. But it was enough leverage to help him roll off the needle-sharp points. Tierra caught him in her arms when he hit the floor.

"Hold onto me. I have you."

He could bloody well do anything now that he'd been released of the leeching copper. He tried to rise and stumbled, falling back to his knees. Well, maybe he would need a moment. But time was something they didn't have. He had to get her out of here before she was discovered.

If Lucifer got her hands on Tierra . . .

He couldn't bear to think of that scenario.

"Hold onto me." She knelt beside him and locked her arms around him. "We're getting out of here." She closed her eyes and started to chant.

> *"I call upon air, earth, fire, and sea,*
> *return us safely back to the earthly sphere,*
> *By the power that binds us three,*
> *So mote it be . . ."*

SHE CHANTED IT FOUR TIMES BEFORE STOPPING, HER arms tightening where they squeezed him. "Something's wrong. It's not working." Panic made her words choppy. "Why isn't it working?"

"You're channeling your sisters' powers through the elements, right?"

"Yes."

"Eliminate air."

She swallowed but didn't comment as if words were beyond her. She nodded, her eyes glistening, her voice trembling as though tears swam close to the surface, and began the spell again.

> *"I call upon earth, fire, and sea,*
> *return us safely back to the earthly sphere,*
> *By the power that binds us three,*
> *So mote it be . . ."*

A DISPLACEMENT OF SOUND AND SPACE AND KILLIAN suddenly found himself kneeling within the protection of the Standing Stones, Tierra still wrapped naked around him.

A growl started deep in his belly and traveled up his throat until he bellowed into the sky. Power seethed inside him, his presence in the earthly realm returned what had been drained of him, healed what had been done to him.

Tierra scrambled away, as a shaft of light from the harvest moon engulfed him. Pleasure, similar to a swimmer gulping a deep breath after being underwater too long, spread throughout his body. His wings slowly extended, stretching from their confines, the feathers shivering with eagerness to fly. He raised his arms to the sky in a prayer of thanksgiving.

Completely returned to his full power, Killian lowered his arms, his wings still extended, and stared at Tierra, passion and need running hot in his blood.

She had a lot to answer for.

She must have read the intent in his eyes, for she stumbled back a step, and then turned and ran for a white piece of fabric discarded on the grass. He reached her just as she grabbed the cloth.

"You will not need this." He tore the shift from her grasp.

"Killian—"

"We can talk after." His mouth swooped down and took hers. She stiffened in his arms, her naked body fully aligned against his bare skin. His wings caged her, leaving his hands free to investigate the changes that had happened during his incarceration.

She'd blossomed since the last time he had her in his arms. Her breasts were fuller, her hips a tad wider. She'd also lost weight. Weight she couldn't afford to lose.

A startled gasp escaped her when he palmed her breasts rougher than he'd intended.

"Killian, we can't." She tore her mouth free.

"The hell we can't." He took her mouth again, but then the thought came to him. He'd been absent a while, what if there had been complications with the babe? "Will having sex hurt the child?"

"Uh . . ."

He saw the desire to lie in her eyes and curled his lips into a predatory smile when she couldn't bring herself to utter it. "You owe me."

"*Owe you?*" Her green eyes flashed a warning.

"You sent me to Hell in the first place, so yes, you owe me, and I'm going to make you pay. Starting now."

"Killian—"

He dropped to his knees in front of her, tipping her back into the cradle of his wings, and worshipped at her center with his tongue.

She'd been all he'd thought of in Hell. All the things he wanted to do to her—with her. The many ways he would take her, let her take him. Exhaust himself within the heat of her body until Heaven and Hell, and the bloody human race, didn't matter. Only she and the magical child they'd created mattered. They were a new Adam and Eve for this soon to be post-apocalyptic world, creating a better human race, one that revered the Earth, replenished her riches, and fucking recycled.

"*Oh, good Goddess*," Tierra cried, her fingers digging into his shoulders. He reveled in the pleasure of her nails piercing his skin in small crescent moons. His fingers and tongue delved deep and sure, knowing how she liked to be touched, just how much pressure to give, to keep, how to suck and flick until she shattered.

He growled, relishing how she came apart in his grasp. Hungry to take more, to give more, he stood and backed her up against one of the stones. "Hold onto me. I have you." It was his turn to repeat the words that she spoke when she'd freed him from his chains in Hell.

Trembling in his embrace, she smartly obeyed, wrapping her arms around his shoulders. He grabbed her thighs and hiked her up, and took her body with one deep thrust.

Tierra gasped, and her head fell back on her glistening porcelain shoulders. He'd planned to take her hard and deep, imprinting his body onto hers in his need to conquer. But that one smooth, wet slide into her silken heat stilled him in place, completely captured by the pleasure of being inside her and the wanton picture of her in his arms.

Her lips were red and swollen like crushed rose petals from his rough kisses, her skin flushed under the glow of the persimmon moon. He stared, enraptured. Wearing the golden crown, with white flowers of belladonna and angelica as well as the many shades of green foliage entwined in the tresses of her thick reddish-black hair, she turned his need to master into one of wonder and reverence.

A stirring began in the center of his chest. He recognized the yearning much lower as he'd been dealing with its effects since the moment he'd first seen her at *Siren's*. But not this feeling. This was intense and vicious, yet also somehow gentle and caring.

He was Death, the fourth Horseman of the Apocalypse, and he did not fucking *care*.

Yet, he knew it for a lie. This woman had bewitched more than his body, she'd stolen his heart.

Tierra raised her head and looked at him when he held her against him without moving, gazing at him questioningly. Slowly he lowered his mouth and softly took her lips. She sighed into his mouth, her arms tightening around his neck as she tried to get closer to him. He began to move in a slow dance, a lazy ocean kissing the shore, a gentle flap of wings from a raven riding a summer's breeze. He made love to her, giving more of himself than he took.

She gasped his name, her thighs clenching around him, and he knew she was close. Still he didn't increase his pace, drawing out the pleasure, cataloging each expression, painting awe and pleasure over her lovely face.

This face was worn by another, the one who tortured him. He couldn't believe he'd ever mistaken Tierra for Aerin. In his eyes, they didn't look a thing alike.

Tierra was her own unique woman, created especially for him.

His climax began to build at the base of his spine, and he tried to hold it back, not wanting to have this connection, this magic, end so soon. But he was lost within her as she came, shuddering around him, her inner muscles milking his cock until he finally broke and thrust heavily inside her again and again. He bellowed her name as his world exploded and then realigned into something new and wondrous.

Breathing heavy, he dropped his head to rest alongside hers, cradling her against his hammering heart. The realization of how much she meant to him —and what he could lose—almost dropped him to his knees.

He didn't know how long they stood clenched together, but he knew it wasn't long enough to satisfy him.

"I need to get back," Tierra whispered.

His arms constricted around her in reflex. He couldn't let her go. Wouldn't.

"Besides, your brothers will be anxious to see you. There's also a bunch of lost souls that need rounding up. The town and the manor are plagued with their haunting."

"I can't let you return to the manor," Killian murmured, his lips in her hair.

"What did you say?"

"You heard me."

She shivered in his arms, becoming aware of how serious he was. "Why?"

He didn't know if she was asking why he didn't want her returning to the manor or if there was another reason. He wasn't ready to voice how deeply he felt for her. It would take some time for him to get used to the fucking idea himself.

"In Hell, Aerin was the one who devised ingenious ways to torture me. It's why calling upon the element of air in your spell didn't work."

"You're wrong. How would Aerin have gotten to Hell when it took everything I had to reach you? No, I don't believe it. It had to have been Lucifer wearing some disguise."

Yeah, wearing Aerin and dressed in Tierra's clothes.

"I've already thought of that, and you aren't going to

like my conclusions. I'm sorry to inform you, Tierra, but Aerin's been possessed by Lucifer."

Tierra froze in his arms, her eyes wide and swimming with emotions, but she took the news better than he'd thought she would. "How?" Her voice cracked on the word.

"It's one of Lucifer's favorite tricks. She's mastered the ability to possess someone with just a touch." Now it was his turn to stiffen when Tierra's eyes turned hard as emeralds. "Did Lucifer try to possess you?"

"Y-yes, I think so, but the baby created a force field and kept her out. *Oh goddess*, I need to get home. I need to save Aerin and warn Moira and Claire." She struggled fiercely in his arms.

"That isn't happening, not until Aerin has been dealt with."

"And you think you can what . . . *keep* me?' She pushed uselessly against his shoulders, twisting her body to free herself from his ironclad embrace.

"You're mine, Tierra," he growled, holding her so tightly against his chest that he could feel her rapid beating heart against his. "I will do *anything* to keep you and our child safe. Returning to the manor is not an option, not with the Devil in residence."

"I just traveled to Hell and back and saved your sorry ass. I can deal with Lucifer and Aerin. I can *save* her. If you don't let me go, I'll send you right back to where I found you." The ground trembled under his feet as fury and fear bloomed in her eyes.

"No, you won't. Now that I am free, I have the power to open the gates to other realms. Places no one will ever find us, places you won't so easily travel back from." He gave her a wicked, possessive smile, liking this new plan more and more.

His arms clamped her tight against him, and he shot off the earth, before Tierra could split the earth's crust open and swallow him again. He captured her mouth to silence the spell she chanted in an attempt to free herself from him.

His onyx-black wings soared wild and sure, shooting them through the atmosphere, through the golden topaz rays of the morning sun to a place and time where they would never be found.

MOIRA

CYNTHIA ST. AUBIN

❧ 1 ❧

She was going to pay for this.

At least, Moira de Moray was pretty sure she'd be frowned down by just about every witch, wizard, warlock and their spell-belching toads for stooping to the levels she was fixin' to stoop to.

And Lord love a duck, she was stooping.

Naked as a jaybird, wand in hand, and leaning over a bathtub of water just south of scalding, Moira searched her scattered brain for the right words.

Or...words, anyhow.

Please dear Goddess, I'm choked with troubles,
make this bathtub filled with bubbles.
If it's your will, so mote it be,
by power of earth, air, fire and sea.

MOIRA LEAPT BACK WITH A SQUEAK AS A JET OF blinding cobalt blue flame shot from the tip of her wand and illuminated the water like a lantern. She squeezed her eyes shut against the brief retina-searing flash and blinked to clear the neon squigglies floating like jellyfish across her vision.

The pale blue glow burned onto the backs of her eyelids cast up a memory of Morgana de Moray, fellow water Druid and Moira's own great aunt.

Probably this wasn't the kind of magic Morgana had in mind when she'd given Moira the wand and its matching crown, now stashed in the underwear drawer among a sea of thongs.

But desperate times called for desperate measures, as Uncle Sal always said, and if biblical fish plagues, zombie luaus, ghostly get-togethers, and an ongoing shindig with the Four Horsemen of the Apocalypse and Satan her-sulfurous-self didn't qualify as desperate times, Moira wasn't about to go looking for what would.

Didn't a girl just about need, no, *deserve* a purifying bubble bath for surviving a turd tornado of that magnitude?

"I'll be a pig's pink pecker!" Moira said, finally peeking through her palms to admire the mounds of cloudy foam atop the steaming bath. "It worked!"

Setting her wand on the stand next to the bathtub she'd moments ago cleared of Tierra's green tea bath salts and homemade juniper chamomile soap to make room for a bowl of pork rinds and a glass of whisky, Moira bent to steal a sniff of the spirit's heavenly breath.

She held the smoky amber fumes in her sinuses as she gathered the blood-ruby skein of her hair into a mass atop her head and secured it with a chopstick the way she'd seen Tierra do. The woman was a veritable fount of knowledge when it came to kitchen coiffeur.

Above the sink, the mirror captured her in the oval of it its gilt Victorian frame and held her there. Moira had never been one to linger in front of mirrors. The small toothpaste-flecked shaving mirrors Uncle Sal had kept in the bayou shack where she had been raised had never been much good at showing her more than scattered pieces of herself. Which, she supposed, might have had something to do with the idea of herself she had when arriving in Port Townsend months ago.

The reflection she saw now told a far different story.

Once, a pale strip of flesh on her otherwise tawny shoulder marked where her tank top blocked the low Louisiana sun. Now, the Northwest's endless gray skies had leached all but a golden ghost of her lifelong tan.

Her fingers floated up to trace the oblong scar at the top of her left breast, smooth to the touch, not yet pale. She turned to examine its twin on her back, a purple-red mark hiding in the shadow beneath her shoulder blade.

The place where the bastard known as Conquest to Bible-reading types had put his flaming arrow through her heart. Of course, an arrow hadn't been the only thing Nick Kingswood had driven inside her that day. With knees weakening at the memory, Moira grudging admitted the scars of that joining ran much deeper than she liked to think.

Banishing the invading Horseman from her head, she struck a match across the small box on the counter and lit the four white taper candles set in the east, west, north, and south before snapping off the overhead light.

A man's face swarmed upon the sudden dark.

Moira yelped and grabbed for a towel. "Christ on a corndog! What the hell are you doing in my bathroom?"

"Admirin' the view, mostly." The face clucked its tongue and whistled through the space where his two front teeth should have been. "Damned if you don't look even purtier than I remember."

Moira stared at the face, scrambling for recognition of the features, through which the clawfoot bathtub was still visible. Hair color was impossible to tell given the spectral green glow. Not much of a chin to speak of. Ratty little ghoste-stache like a fungus infecting his upper lip.

It was the eyes that finally gave him away. Well, *eye* really.

Only one of them was focused on Moira's face. The other one had rolled upward to consider the ceiling.

One eye's lookin' at you, the other one's lookin' *for* you, Uncle Sal used to say.

"Skunk Hurley?" Moira asked. "Is that you?"

"I knowed you'd recognize me!" Skunk's face bobbed happily toward Moira, who took a step back.

"Say, Skunk?"

"Yes'm?"

"Seems my Aunt Justine mentioned you'd got yourself dead by trying to breathe bayou water after a night on the 'shine."

"That's about how I reckon it happened. We'd seen us one of them beer bongs on the TV down at Skinny's bait shop and one the boys had a rubber hose—"

Moira held up a hand. Where she came from, the recounting of injuries suffered under the influence of high-octane potables had a way of turning into epics that would shame the Odyssey.

"Point being, you died down in Stumps Bayou, right?"

"Yes'm, that's right."

"So what exactly are you doing *here*?"

"Well now, that there is an interesting story."

"Can it be a short one?" She glanced longingly at the tub, the conjured bubbles already going lacey in spots.

"After they fished me out of the bayou, I watched the boys thumpin' me on the chest for a while and hollerin' at me to breathe and such. But it's like I wasn't *in* my body no more."

"Uh-huh."

"And all of the sudden I see this bright light, just like—"

"On TV," Moira finished for him.

"Right, like on them angel shows. So I start walking toward it like you're s'posed to do, and wham!" Skunk went to smack one hand with the other but missed by a healthy margin, his spectral hands eddying with the current of air as they whooshed passed each other.

Probably down to a depth-perception issue on account of the one eye, Moira figured.

"Wham what?"

"*Wham* a demon with a flashlight pops me upside the head and I woke up here."

"A demon with a flashlight, you say?" This fragrant bit of fuckery had Juicy Lucy Pleatherpants written all over it. It would be just like the infernal walking mattress to funnel all the spirits Death hadn't claimed straight to the de Morays' door just to amuse herself once she'd run out of puppies to kick and orphans' tears to splash into her martinis.

"And may I ask why you felt the need to crawl into bed with my Aunt Justine? You pert near scared the dust off her old cooch."

One of Skunk's eyes looked down at the ground sheepishly. The other had lodged squarely in the region of Moira's towel-clad tits.

"I thought she was you."

Moira felt an involuntary twitch in the hand closest to her wand. "You know, Skunk, it's a damn good thing you're dead already, because if you weren't, I might just have to hitch you to a truck tail-first and drag your sorry ass all the way back to Louisiana."

"Aw come on now. It was dark and—"

"And I'm going to give you to the count of three to get the hell out of here before I use my wand to zap up a ghost gator and feed him your one good eye."

"You wouldn't!"

"One—"

"All right, all right. But don't expect me to come warn you the next time—"

Pop.

Skunk vanished as quickly as he'd arrived with a sound like someone snapping bubblegum. Just like him to show up, be annoying as hell, and take off before relaying any useful information.

Deciding not to pay too much attention to the implications of his unfinished sentence, Moira cracked the window to let some steam escape and stepped into the tub.

Pillowy bubbles climbed the skin of her ankles and calves as she lowered herself into the water, pausing to adjust in increments before sinking up to her neck, eyes sliding closed, head falling heavy against the rolled towel she'd propped at the tub's top rim. With tiny bubbles whispering in her ears, Moira sank a washcloth into the delicious heat and draped it over her face.

Perfumed tendrils of steam tickled her nose with the scents of sage, lemon balm, rosemary, and—butter on top of the ritual-washing biscuit—hyssop.

If it was good enough to tackle a leper, it might could handle the unholy gumbo of demonic zombie-ghost-horsemen cooties Moira figured she'd been hauling around.

She could feel the individual water molecules moving in response to her proximity, sliding over her in an affectionate caress. Her blood rose nearer to the surface of her skin in reply, moving through her limbs in a languid dance.

One lazy hand fumbled blindly at the stand next to the tub, seeking the glass of whisky, but finding nothing.

"Looking for this?"

Moira froze, chills riding down her back as if a bucket of ice water had been sluiced over her.

Without even removing her washcloth, she knew who'd spoken the words.

The one—the only—Nicholas Kingswood.

❧ 2 ❧

Moira tugged the washcloth from her face and found herself rendered momentarily mute by the unexpected sight of Conquest by candlelight.

Darkness made itself his ally, revealing only the parts of him best suited to stunning his prey senseless with an intoxicating mix of fear and wonder. The ponderous outline of his body, feral beneath the thin carapace of tailored shirt and slacks. Long of limb and easy in the way of predators well within their turf.

His eyes, dark thieves that they were, stole flame from the candles around her bath, burning as he stared down at her, whisky in hand. Were the light better, Moira knew they would be the exact shade of the smoky liquid swirling within that glass. Ambient amber lit from realms unfathomable.

She could smell him in the humid room, steam carrying the scent of his skin with its attendant memories. The whole wild weight of him brought to bear upon her.

Nick lifted the glass to his nose and inhaled deeply.

In that moment, Moira marked just how much he favored the wolf both in feature and in aspect—his keen eyes brightening and angular nostrils flaring with appreciation for the scent. She knew the way he moved. With an eerie animal grace and unforgiving sense of purpose.

And then, there was his predilection for taking her by way of canine congress. In the long night they'd spent together, he'd left his share of bite marks on the back of her neck. He'd held her that way as he drove into her from behind.

Moira sank down in the bath, crossing her arms over her hardening nipples, which she was pretty sure he'd already noted beneath the filmy layer of bubbles.

"Macallan," Nick said, sipping the whiskey. "Old. Good."

Nicholas Kingswood's lips were the one feature at odds with a visage perfectly suited to the task of domination. Generous. Sensitive. Soft.

"I wouldn't know." She retrieved her washcloth and pressed it to the area below the nape of her neck where a sympathetic memory plagued the surface of her skin. "I haven't had the chance to taste it yet."

"Where are my manners?" Nick asked.

She had been about to comment that Nicholas Kingswood wouldn't know manners if they stabbed him in the ass cheek with a spoon shank when he descended, hawk-like, upon her. All sudden shadow and sharp hunger.

One of the things Moira found downright vexing about immortals was their ability to move at speeds incomprehensible to the human eye. Even when that human happened to be a witch in possession of all manner of handy Druid powers with which to annoy and astound the common apocalyptic Horseman.

None of those powers would aid her now.

Not when Nick's mouth claimed hers with all the certainty of an invading army, overthrowing all thought and intention with an onslaught of sensation beyond sanity. The taste of whiskey. The scent of smoke. The sound of roaring of blood.

The heat in his lips. The silken slide of his tongue. The unbearable tingle of every follicle as he filled his fist with a handful of her hair.

The feel of him. *Him*. Always him.

Each and every pore in her human body yielded to his immortal matter, offering itself up to his mastery.

Moira could no more refuse him than the tides could refuse the moon.

And in her body's answering, she understood all kinds of things. Why the sun drew the earth into its orbit. Why wolves raised their voices to the moon. Why bolts of velvet nightly unfolded overhead. Why dew separated itself from air to weigh down petals and clover.

She let herself exhale into him the taste ash and rain. The taste of their joining.

Their breath tangled, ragged in the aftermath.

Where the glass had gone, she didn't know. She knew only that she was twice as drunk as she would have been had she finished off the whiskey and had another shot to spare.

"You. Here. Why?" She asked when she'd recovered air, if not the ability to speak in complete sentences.

"Big tub." Nick stirred the surface with one long finger. "Plenty of room for two."

The scrim of foam he'd parted joined again in his wake. "You just want to know if I can do dirty things to you with the water."

A devastating grin carved itself into his cheek and Moira knew part of him was pleased. The same part creating one hell of a tent in his fancy trousers.

Good thing she didn't remember the exact, staggering length and girth of what Nick kept hidden in there.

Good thing she didn't want to touch it.

Not even a little.

And her not wanting to touch it had not a damn thing to do with her wrapping her hand around her wand instead.

Moira swallowed saliva that had pooled beneath her tongue for reasons that surely had nothing to do with Nick.

She attempted to clear her throat, but the sound that came out instead approximated the pained croak of a constipated bullfrog.

Okay. Maybe she did want to touch it.

"Well?" Nick's bemused smile left no question as to whether he'd guessed the direction of her thoughts. "Can you?"

"Please," she scoffed. "I could make you squeal six ways to Sunday with no more than an ice cube and a commercial break. But that don't mean I will."

She thought she saw Nick's lip quiver then. Longing maybe. Or some asshole comment itching to break loose of his tongue. Even money as to which.

"Not even if I lick this whiskey from your nipples?" Nick dipped a finger into the glass and let a single drop hover like a tremulous jewel from his fingertip before collecting it with an unnaturally dexterous flick of his tongue.

Moira prayed the squeak she'd just heard had been Cheeto stumbling upon some hidden treasure in Tierra's compost heap and *not* a burp of unfettered lust squeezing from her throat.

"I'd rather suck a syphilitic skunk," Moira declared with little conviction.

"You mean that?" A cabbage-green glow illuminated the corner of the bathroom as the hopeful visage of one Skunk Hurley materialized above the toilet bowl.

"The *fuck*?" Nick staggered back a step, catching himself on the sink.

Had she been an air witch instead of a water witch,

the sigh Moira heaved might have generated a small hurricane.

A bath.

All she wanted was one measly hour's peace in a solitary fucking restorative bath. Apparently the End of Days was determined to shoot even that straight to hell.

"Skunk, Nick. Nick, Skunk." Moira used her toes to nudge the hot water back on, long past caring who saw what anymore. "Maybe y'all should go grab a beer or something and figure out ways to ruin my life that doesn't involve tag-teaming me while I'm in the tub."

Nick's raised eyebrow seemed to be suggesting that, given different circumstances, he was not opposed to the idea of tag-teaming her in the tub. "How do you know this ectoplasmic turd?"

"Same way I know you," Moira said. "I fucked him once."

She regretted the words as soon as they were out of her mouth. Not because they came out sounding more callous than she'd intended, but because the room darkened in concert with Conquest's eyes.

"This?" The mouth she had admired earlier flattened into a cruel, mirthless line. "You gave your body to *this*?"

"She sure did." Skunk, meanwhile was sporting a shit-eating grin of epic proportions. "Got my foot caught in a crawdad shucker and she humped me all better. She's one of them witches, you know." The verdant ghost whispered this with such simple, guileless wonder that Moira felt an unbidden stab of sympathy for him. As she had the day she'd found him limping home under a barrage of taunts from comelier boys whose mothers would have raced them to the nearest emergency room for an injury half as horrific as the one Skunk had suffered. At the time, she hadn't understood what prompted her to tug him off the old oyster shell path and into an abandoned fishing shack curtained by Spanish moss.

She hadn't known what she was then. What she might someday cause.

But Nick had.

He had known her of old, preparing for her through centuries upon centuries and longer.

Her mind ran out of track when she tried to follow him into the past. She grew dizzy peering beyond her own lifetime, then through the lives of the parents whose passion had made her. Back, back to when the world was new and people hadn't lost their grip on everything that mattered.

"He knows what I am, Skunk." Her voice had acquired a good measure more patience than she had when banishing him earlier. "But you haven't got the first foggy clue what *he* is. You'd best get yourself on out of here before you find out."

"No ma'am." Skunk looked at Nick with undisguised dislike. "I don't believe I'm going anywhere. I don't like the way this suit-wearing shitweasel is lookin' at you."

"You mean with two eyes?" Nick shot the remainder of the whiskey, but promptly sent it back to the air in an atomized cloud when Moira thumped his Adam's apple with her wand.

"You may have an armchair made from the skulls of your enemies, but in my presence, you won't be making fun of the Skunk Hurleys of the world."

Nick rubbed his throat with two fingers as he turned to the hovering specter. "I think it's time you left so Miss de Moray and I can have a discussion."

"And how are you figuring on makin' me?" Skunk managed to look belligerent even without a face of flesh and blood.

"With this." Nick slid the sleek cell phone from his

pocket and performed a rapid series of swipes with his thumb.

"Pfft." Skunk rolled his eye. "I'm dead, remember? What's a piddly little ol' phone gonna do to me?"

Nick said nothing, only waited with the phone pressed to his cheek.

"Nick. You don't have to—"

"Reaper?" A broad grin stretched across Nick's face —an expression which Moira found to be more frightening on him than out-and-out bloodlust. "Yeah, it's Nick. How's Gussy? Good, good. Say, do you still have some of that tincture that reduces ghosts to the spectral equivalent of anal leakage?" Conquest's eyebrows lifted genially. "You do? Excellent. How soon can you be at the de Moray mansion?"

"On second thought, you always could handle yourself," Skunk reasoned.

Poof.

Only when Skunk vanished for the second time did Moira realize she'd forgotten to ask him what he'd meant when he hinted at warning her earlier.

Moira blamed the apocalyptic Horseman towering next to the tub. He had a particularly annoying habit of emptying her head of such useful thoughts.

Alone with Nick again in a room that seemed to have shrunk by half, Moira found herself rambling. "I would have thought the de Moray mansion is the *last* place Reaper would be willing to come. What with our accidentally loosing all those ghosts upon the world."

"It is." Nick loosened his tie with one expert hand and it slid from his collar in a whisper of silk. He carefully laid it across her robe, adjusting it so it hung plumb with the towel rack.

"And Reaper. I hadn't figured him for the type to carry a phone. What with the buckskins, the duster..."

"He doesn't." Off came the shoes. The shirt.

"But you said—"

"I lied." By this time the pants were long gone, and Nick wore only a sardonic expression.

It was a perfect fit.

"Remind me why you're here again?" Moira asked, fully aware he hadn't answered her question the first time.

"I have the whole evening free to fuck you witless," Nick announced. "Julian's off perfecting his melancholy on some moonlit cliff or other. Dru's jerking off to a bag of Red Hots, and Killian made like a mosquito and buzzed off with Tierra to gods know where—"

Moira sat up in the bath, forgetting for an all-important second that she was, in fact, bare-ass naked. "What did you just say?"

"I said Julian is wringing tears from his violin and—"

"No, you arrogant asswaffle. About Killian. Isn't he supposed to be suffering eternal torment at the hands of Lucy in the Sky with Demons?"

"You really shouldn't say her name," Nick admonished. "Somewhere, an orphan just lost his adoption paperwork."

"Is Death out of Hell or what?" Moira hadn't realized was standing until the scar over her breast began glowing like the coals at a goat roast.

And he was staring at it.

The scar.

His eyes coloring with it, pinwheels of fire dancing within them.

Searing pain shot through her, a ghost of the arrow her body had known. Her hand clutched at her chest, finding nothing but the same, strange smoothness of her healing wound. No outward manifestation of the inner agony ripping through her.

Silvery blue light pulsed from the wand in time with her heart, which itself had synchronized with the waves of pain surging along her nerves like an electrical current.

The wand wanted her to do something. To say something.

But now, as they had then, words failed her. Strength failed her.

Moira fell.

❧ 3 ❧

Nicholas Kingswood tasted blood.

Sweeter than any wine. Heady. Drugging his senses with the throb of life and sense of purpose.

Her life. *His* purpose.

The scar on Moira de Moray's breast testified in flesh of their intersection. On the cliff at Siren's Cry, the sumptuous night breathing cool upon their skin, he had nocked his arrow and sent it whistling through her heart.

He remembered the sound the arrow had made when it struck her. The pure pleasure it had brought him. A sensation matched only by the peace he had known when he buried himself within her for the first time.

The memory dragged a savage thrill straight to his cock.

Killing and fucking had always been the two things he was best at. The two things he most enjoyed.

Her scar reminded him of both.

He reached across the distance separating them, fingers seeking the source of the unearthly glow, wanting to feel its heat and smoothness. It retreated from his touch. Downward. Away. Sinking in slow motion as Moira's body crumpled into the bath.

Time took on the odd, stretched quality it sometimes did when Nick's unnaturally long life violently collided with a present shock.

He was hurting her.

And part of him wanted to go on hurting her. To see just how much damage he could cause. Just how much she could take.

He was humanity's bottomless need. Their insatiable desire. The ceaseless search for power, for pleasure.

For pain.

Moira had a bigger appetite than most.

Time with her sisters had tempered her, shoring her up against the darkest of his desires. Drawing her away from the places where their shared shadows had once bled so easily into each other.

Far from regretting the loss, he had relished the chance for an ugly, sweaty brawl with an opponent now more worthy of him than ever.

It was this thought that held him in its thrall, the world around him narrowing until all that existed was Moira, Nick, and the delicious silken thread of fire worming through the air from her scar to his eyes.

An all-together different kind of fire bloomed in his peripheral vision, erasing the room and everything in it for a brief, blinding flash. Nick lifted a protective arm against the intense heat suddenly baking the side of his face.

Whatever hypnotic power had arrested his motion abruptly ceased in that moment, and he was deposited in the present.

In this time. In this place.

In front of the bathtub where Moira's crumpled body slumped limp and pale.

"*Fuck!*" Nick went to his knees, only tangentially registering the water soaking his William Westmancott Ultimate Bespoke slacks.

He registered the sharp pain in his leg with a startled grunt and healthy stream of invectives.

He looked over his shoulder and discovered not a cramp, but a pig. A very small pig with its very small mouth locked onto Nick's not so small calf.

Only then did he understand what he had seen.

The fiery flash had been not some otherworldly warning, but a belch of flame from the infernal regions of the miniature pig's unnatural intestines.

The little fucker was trying to light him up. And not for the first time.

The first time, they were at 30,000 feet, and Nick had been trying to drag the walking bacon from the bag where Moira had him secreted.

His eyebrows and a good measure of Nick's pride had been sacrificed to his unwillingness to listen to Moira's warning not to touch the creature then. Now, he didn't relish the thought of smelling his own nuts cook while attempting to save its mistress.

If save her he could.

Nick was a breaker of shit. A taker of shit.

He could detail several thousands of ways to dismantle a human being. When it came to fixing one, he was drawing a big, fat blank.

His usual method of approaching a crisis (i.e., kill everything and leave) felt somehow incongruous with his desired outcome.

For perhaps the first time in his incomprehensibly long life, Nick asked himself a noisome but prescient question.

WWJD—or, what would Julian do? Julian fucking Roarke would know how to handle this shit. He and his giant encyclopedia brain and tea-soaked diplomatic tongue would have the cloven-footed creature eating out of his hand.

Provided his hand was gloved.

Otherwise there would be some hideous swine

dysentery and the pig's liquefied intestines falling out its mud chute.

He briefly considered dialing Julian's number but then realized he would have to heed whatever counsel he provided, which more often than not contained a laundry list of things Nick was *not* to do.

Pass.

Nick took a deep breath, channeling the calm of his more cultured brother if not his specific advice. An ascot might have helped.

"Look, Frito...Dorito, whatever your name is. We both know you're not so much a pig as a billion-year-old benevolent spirit driving a pig's body. Which is cool. I'm not here to judge your choice of meat suit. But, I'm going to need you to let the fuck go of my leg so I can...do the things that will make Moira better. Understand?"

The little pig's narrowed eyes glittered spitefully in the candlelight. If anything, his grip on Nick's leg tightened.

"For fuck's sake! How are you biting that hard?" Nick said, gripping the edge of the bathtub. "You don't even have teeth!"

The pig growled. Fucking *growled* at him.

"Look, I didn't want to have to do this, but you leave me no choice." Nick made a grab for the stand next to the bathtub, nabbed the bowl of pork rinds and shoved them into the pig's face. "Let go, or so help me gods I will gut you and make you into a magical bar snack." For effect, Nick popped a couple rinds into his mouth and chewed slowly, never breaking eye contact.

It didn't escape Nick that he—Conquest—defeater of nations, slaughterer of entire armies had been reduced to eating *at* a miniature barnyard animal.

Even so, the tactic proved effective.

Pink snout quivering, the pig turned loose Nick's pants and scurried beneath the towel rack.

Thus freed, Nick turned his attention to Moira, whose erratic breaths caused his heart—a mythical entity in its own right—to respond in kind.

Gathering her naked body out of the bath, Nick lifted her whole, wet weight against his chest and sat with her in his lap on the bathroom floor. He pushed wine-dark locks out of her eyes and placed his palm over the scar, still hot against his hand.

Beneath it, her heart fluttered, uncertain and slow.

He had caused this hurt, whatever it was. And if he caused it, might he also be able to take it back?

❧ 4 ☙

Nick was no more of a scholar than he was a healer.

But sacrifice he understood. An eye for an eye. A life for a life. An idea much older than the Bible, and one he was intimately acquainted with. He had tasted her blood, felt her pain.

His own was owed in recompense.

Also, Nick was pretty certain his blood came with an added bonus as he'd been maimed, crushed, stabbed, shot, and beaten thousands upon thousands of times, and he bore not so much as a mark.

So there was that.

Taking up the empty whiskey tumbler, Nick crushed it in his hand. Dark blood welled between the network of shards, a crimson mockery of a cathedral's stained glass. He let the shards fall away.

His bloody palm met Moira's chest with an audible hiss of steam.

Spells and rituals were not within his wheelhouse. The words he spoke were magic to no one but himself.

So he told their story, his hand over her heart.

"Do you remember the day we met?" he asked, watching Moira's face. Beneath the diaphanous skin of her eyelids, the roundness of her eyes moved.

"I climbed aboard that plane, ready to slam a martini or seven and maybe a few stewardesses, and there you were. Sitting in my seat. You know the first thing I thought when I saw you?"

The corner of Moira's mouth twitched.

"Okay, the second thing." Nick bent down until his lips were even with the curves of her ear. "I thought I'd never seen anything as beautiful as you in ten thousand years, and even if I lived another hundred thousand, I never would."

Moira heaved within his arms, her whole body seizing in a spasm that brought to mind a much more pleasant naked memory. He felt her first in-drawn breath rattle through her ribs and drive her upright.

If Nick had mortal reflexes, she would have head-butted him.

And judging by what she said next, that might have indeed been what she'd intended all along.

"If that ain't the soggiest pile of pig shit I've ever heard, I don't know what is."

"It worked, didn't it?"

"Something did," she said, fingers inspecting her chest. "What the—where did my scar go?"

He held up his wounded hand to show her, but the lacerations had already knit tidily closed. "You're welcome."

"For what?" Her eyes narrowed at him in a manner not altogether dissimilar from her porcine protector. "What did you do?"

He should have known better than to hope for tearful thanks and a couple rounds of hearty gratitude fucking. "I undid the damage I had caused. With my blood."

"You gave me your blood?" Moira shoved herself up from his lap and clutched a towel to her chest. "Your blood is *inside* me?"

"It doesn't have to be the only thing." Nick gained

his feet and tugged his damp trousers away from the painful tightness in his crotch.

"How could you do that?"

"It's real easy. You bend over the sink, and I'll—"

Moira's shot to his chest knocked him backward a full three feet. Her eyes widened in surprise and—dare he say it—delight in her newfound strength. *His* strength. "Holy shit. Did you see that?"

Why the everlasting fuck hadn't he called Julian?

"I didn't need to see it," he said, stepping hard on the urge to massage the throbbing spot on his sternum. "I felt it."

"Damned if I don't have the urge to run out and overthrow a small country. Or find an old lady to exploit." Moira wrapped the towel around her and tucked the edge under her arm.

"Do you have the urge to fuck me senseless?" he asked, not completely successful at abandoning all traces of hope from his voice. "Stands to reason if you inherited some of my strength, you might also have inherited some of my libido."

"Not so much fuck you senseless as split your skull with a tire iron. But truth to tell, that ain't new. Cheeto!" The pig wriggled his way out from under the linens and trotted happily around Moira's ankles. She scooped up the creature and nuzzled the disgustingly moist, pink snout. "Did you save momma from that nasty old Horseman? Did you?"

"This *nasty old* Horseman just saved your life," Nick pointed out.

"After trying to suck my soul out of the scar *you* caused in the first place. Forgive me if I don't fall to my knees and gush my gratitude."

"Falling to your knees would be a good start. Of course, I could think of far more productive things for you to do while you're there."

"The more you talk, the less I like you."

"Well, that at least we have in common. How about we just skip the talking and go straight to life-affirming gorilla sex?"

"How about you go tongue-punch a badger's butt?" Moira placed the pig back on the floor and snapped on the lights, considering herself in the mirror. Looking, Nick supposed, for physical changes beyond the disappearance of her scar.

They were both relieved when she couldn't seem to find any.

"Right before I—you, before whatever the hell that was, I asked you a question."

"Yes," Nick confirmed. "Death is out of Hell. It seems your intrepid sister found her way into...that demonic super-slut's domain and hauled Killian's ass back to the land of the living."

"How do you know?"

"Same way I know Lucy's been using Aerin as her own personal puppet. Death sent a raven."

Moira whirled on him, grabbing a thousand dollars' worth of custom-fitted Italian shirt and driving him a foot up the wall.

He could have reversed the hold and had her pinned to the opposite wall in the time it took her to blink.

Could have, but didn't.

Mostly because Nick had never been so turned on in all his life.

"What the hell did you just say?" Her eyes had darkened to the color of the ocean's deepest trenches. Water that had never seen the sun's light or felt its warmth.

"I said Lucy is wearing Aerin like a Givenchy suit. She has been for a while now."

Nick's Bruno Magli loafers found their rightful place on the tile as Moira's grip on him loosened. "How come you didn't say nothing about this when you first got here?"

"You were naked." Nick shrugged. "And when I got done fucking your brains out, Tierra would still be gone, and Aerin would still be possessed."

Moira paced the short path between the bathtub and the door, gnawing the cuticle of her thumb as she walked.

Nick watched her teeth work with perhaps more attention than the action warranted. She halted midstep, the corner of her mouth working upward in a grin that made his insides feel greasy and hot.

"How quick can you get Battle Boy and Doctor Disease here?" Moira asked. "We need to have us a little talk."

$\maltese$ 5 $\maltese$

"**P**ossessed?" Claire repeated the word that had saturated the parlor in Maison de Moray ever since Moira had spoken it. Now it passed along the faces of all who gathered there, leaving shadows in its wake.

And a strange gathering it was.

War, Conquest, Pestilence, and the two de Moray witches who yet remained un-kidnapped by Death or soul-fucked by Satan. Moira had intentionally chosen a time when Aunt Justine was off doing whatever it was she liked to do when she wasn't quietly scowling in corners or looking constipated. The fewer people and/or immortals who knew what they would be discussing, the better.

"Damn skippy," Moira confirmed. "At least, if we can believe Killian baby-daddy Bane. He may be no better than a winged horny toad, but I don't figure it's something he'd lie about."

"And seriously, what the fuck is up with Death taking off with Tierra, anyway?" High color blazed in Claire's cheeks, assisted by the constant fire living just below the surface of her skin. "Where are they? When will they be coming back?"

"Fucked if I know." Nick shrugged, looking about as concerned as he would be if someone had asked him when the post office opened. He'd been in a hell of a snit ever since Moira had evicted him from the bathroom to get her clothes on and insisted he call War and Pestilence over for an impromptu strategy session.

Moira found herself losing patience in the face of his sullen lack of cooperation. "Look, we need Tierra back, and Death needs to get his feathered ass back here and do something about these ghosts. I'm just about sick and tired of spirits popping up in the kitchen, in the bathtub—"

"In my underwear drawer," Claire added. "I wish I was kidding."

"Bane will come back when he's damn good and ready." Drustan Geddes thumbed the edge of a bowie knife that had materialized from the arsenal of weapons Moira suspected he kept strapped to every available inch of his formidable body. "And not a second before. Anyway, you've got nothing to worry about. No harm will come to her as long as she's with him. She carries his spawn."

Flashes of the strange little life bobbing and playing among the ultrasound waves returned to Moira in a soul-rending rush, bringing with it a surge of fierce, protective energy.

"That *spawn* saved Tierra's life," Moira pointed out. "No thanks to the thing that's treating Aerin's body like a timeshare condo. The way she's been acting lately, I should have known."

"Can't say I've noticed much of a difference." Dru drilled at the thick rubber sole of his combat boot with the tip of the bowie knife, looking like he desperately wanted a neck or chest to plant it in instead. But then, War pretty much always looked like that.

Running into Tommy, Claire's meat-slurping, undead ex-boyfriend earlier certainly hadn't eased matters anyhow.

Claire had forgiven Tommy for stabbing her in the

shoulder while he was possessed of a manbun-sporting witch hunter, even if Dru had not.

Moira had lingered near the kitchen door, watching as Dru clotheslined Tommy's feet out from under him when Claire's back was turned.

Planting a boot on the zombie's sternum, Dru had leaned down until his coal-black eyes were only inches from Tommy's. They could breathe the same air...if Tommy breathed.

Not that Moira would have had an easy time breathing if she'd been the one on the floor, blinking up at the hulking vengeance that was Drustan Geddes.

If Nick was the razor-wheeled minds of men who make war, Dru was the weapon they wielded—strength for strength's sake. Spine-shattering, soul-crushing, shocking violence in a black t-shirt and fatigue pants. Being in the same room with him always felt to Moira a little like falling into the tiger's cage at the zoo. Mostly you just hunkered down in a trench and prayed he didn't eat your face.

"If you don't want me to rip your undead spleen out your asshole, I suggest you stay the fuck out of this room," Dru had growled when Tommy had attempted to follow them into the parlor.

Tommy's wide blue eyes had managed to look surprisingly innocent for a reanimated corpse. Moira thought she saw something else flash in them for the briefest of moments. Anger? Fear?

Where in seven swampy hells was Aerin's emotional barometer when you needed it?

"Okay," Tommy had said. "Okay. I'll go. We wouldn't want to upset Claire. Would we?"

Something about the way he'd said this needled Moira. Made her wonder exactly how he meant it.

Dru had looked like he would have preferred to hork a wad of spit at Tommy rather than reply, but he'd left it. Tommy had slapped the side of Dru's boot as he lifted it from his chest and pushed his angular frame back to his feet.

For once, that easy smile Tommy always wore didn't look easy at all. It had looked...smug? He'd winked at Moira as he shuffled into the kitchen, most likely in search of floppy strips of raw bacon.

Moira made a mental note to have a come to Jesus with Cheeto about trotting clear of Tommy, seeing as her familiar was pretty much raw pork on four legs.

"Aerin's linguistic patterns do tend toward the abrasive, which makes variations in her mood and mental state difficult to detect." Julian Roarke's crisp declaration dragged Moira back into the present, ears first. He was the only one in the room with an accent as pronounced as hers, and yet its effect couldn't be more different. "I'll allow Drustan that much. But, what Moira has reported is consistent with my own theories on the matter."

Pestilence was something of an anomaly to her. With his fine, pale skin and features so perfect, he looked stricken under the weight of bearing up such beauty.

Beauty Moira found hard to reckon, having grown up in a place where faces were dealt in measures of over and under abundance. Buck teeth, weak chins, ears like jug handles. A place where men brayed their laughter and slurred their speech. Slumped over barstools, guts and ass cracks aplenty falling out of work-worn jeans, the contrast they formed to the lithe, waist-coat wearing, by-goddess gentleman before her now made Moira's eyes water.

"Theories?" Nick detached himself from the fireplace mantel he'd been leaning against and stalked closer to his brother, who looked perfectly at home on the velvet settee. "*Theories* means you've been brooding about this for a while, haven't you, Jules?"

A gentle incline of Julian's head passed for acknowledgement. "For a time, yes."

"And what is it that has you so convinced?" Dru asked. He had moved on from shanking his boot and was now using his knife to pare the edges of his already-short fingernails.

If Tierra were here, she would be shoving a hand-thrown bowl into his lap to catch the clippings.

If Tierra were here.

The thought pierced Moira with a dart of worry.

"Well," Julian began, looking for all the world like a professor stepping up to a lectern as he rose from the couch. "Through repeated empirical observations on my part, I have documented certain physical reactions to Aerin which are antithetical to attraction."

"How's that?" Claire asked.

"He means he can't get it up for Aerin," Nick offered by way of translation. The speed with which he did so had the ease of a well-worn pattern between them. One that they'd probably been enacting since before King Tut was a horny twitch in his daddy's ballsack.

"Since when?" Dru had abandoned his knife, leaning forward with a sudden interest in the conversation. "You sure as hell didn't have any problems sticking it to her in the alley."

Moira studied the grimace etching Julian's face, appreciating for the first time that being around someone for a few thousand years wasn't necessarily a guarantee that you'd like them any better. Maybe exactly the opposite.

"The reactions I am referring to occurred sometime after that. At first, I thought it might be the product of over-satiation, as Aerin and I...well, we..."

"Hit it harder than Caligula at a Saturnalia festival?" In Nick's case, Moira guessed this probably wasn't a metaphorical comparison. In fact, she wouldn't put it past him to have kept a scorecard on a clay tablet to make sure he'd been keeping up.

"I wouldn't have described it in those terms, necessarily. But, in a manner of speaking, yes. I suppose you could say we made up for lost time. Until..." Julian's smooth brow creased. Moira sensed the depth of feeling behind this expression, the great volume of his knowledge crashing against his inability to make sense of something as simple and as complex as the want of one body for another.

"Until you all the sudden felt like someone up and pissed out the fire in your heart, and you were left scratchin' your ass and wondering where it had gone," Moira said. "The fire. Not your ass. Anyone can see that's still there, of course."

By the look on Julian's face, he had been surprised by the accuracy of her statement. By the look on Nick's, he was altogether displeased that Moira even knew Julian had an ass.

A girl could look. A girl just about *had* to look when she was about to suggest something in which Julian's ass might play more than a backstage role, so to speak.

"All but the gluteal abrasion," Julian agreed. "At first, I couldn't account for the reaction. It wasn't until the next time we had the displeasure of a visit from she of whom I am not fond of speaking that I recognized my body's response. The revulsion, the irritation—"

"The desire to drag your balls through broken glass," Dru supplied helpfully.

Moira felt a blast of heat on the side of her body where Claire was seated. Apparently, this comment had pleased her sister.

She rode the wave of warmth out of her place on the overstuffed sofa, conscious of Nick's eyes on the exposed length of her legs beneath the frayed edge of her denim skirt.

"All right, y'all. I think we all know what it feels like

to be around Lu—the great blond she-whore," she substituted in a rare moment of deference to the Horsemen. "What else do we know about her?"

"If she were a candle, her scent would be Blood of the Innocents and Slut?" Nick offered.

Dru's stony façade cracked ever so slightly at this. "Her shoe size is peasant neck?"

"What she can't have is what she wants most." Claire's eyes darkened to the color of red clay as they sometimes did when her fires were banked and the coals burned deep below the surface. Lucy had befriended her first, after all, and had helped her to bring Tommy back. Moira suspected her sister still suffered a tangled net of emotions as a result.

"Right. And what does she want more than anything?" Moira crossed her arms over her chest, all too aware of the insistent amber gaze making a study of her breasts.

"Aside from a purse made from the skin of a thousand virgins, I'd have to say Jules," Nick said. "But I'll be goat-fucked if I can figure out why."

"Couldn't have anything to do with you following the water witch's tits instead of this conversation," Dru accused.

Heat crawled up the back of Moira's neck and into her cheeks. Funny that the first time she wished she listened to Tierra's gentle bullying about a bra, her sister should be nowhere in the room.

Nick took two long strides into Dru's space, and just like that, the parlor shrank to the size of a saltine cracker, every available molecule of oxygen consumed by the sudden onrush of violent, masculine energy.

Moira planted a hand on Nick's sternum, feeling his heart pound beneath her palm. She tried not to think of the other times she felt it leap like this. Times when she not only felt his pulse, but heard it. Tasted it.

"Y'all knock this off before I turn the hose on you.

And believe me, ain't no one can do it like I can. Isn't that right, Nick?"

A muscle tightened in Nick's jaw. On the smoked honey screen of his eyes, Moira read the memories of tidal waves, cloud bursts, and icy showers—all of which she'd gone to the trouble to arrange for him personally.

He stepped back. In his searing look lived a promise that whatever ground he ceded here, he would reclaim on other fields of battle between them.

And soon.

"Like I was saying," Moira continued. "Lucy wants Julian, but Julian wants Aerin. So Lucy hops into Aerin, and before you know it, she's got a one-way ticket for a ride on the Pestilence Pony." She resisted a glance at Julian, mostly because she already had an idea that his grimaces so far today would pale in comparison to what the term *Pestilence Pony* might conjure. "This is just like the time when we had a nasty old snapping turtle living in the little pond out behind our shack. Every spring, that big, old bastard hunkered down in there and ate the feet off all the little ducklings. Well, one night I got me a chicken carcass and tied it to a rope and waited for him to bite. As soon as he did, I hauled him out of the pond and booted his reptilian butt right back down into the bayou. I mean, I don't know if any of y'all have ever had to fit a duckling for prosthetic flippers, but I'll tell you right here and now. It's a hell of a lot easier to just get rid of the snapping turtle in the first place. You follow me?"

At that moment, Moira could have heard a mouse break wind.

Julian, gallant soul that he was, made the first attempt to wade in. "May I assume that I am the tethered remains of poultry in this colorful metaphor?"

"Yes, sir," Moira confirmed. She'd fallen out of the habit of using formal appellations since coming to Port

Townsend, but something in Julian's attire and bearing seemed to warrant it.

"And you are suggesting that we may be able to lure *the turtle* out of *the pond* by convincing her that the reward she seeks lies elsewhere, i.e., the *bayou*?"

The fact that Julian appeared to be following her train of thought and had not yet made an attempt to cast himself violently off the tracks encouraged Moira perhaps a touch more than it should. "Exactly!"

"Is it just me, or does this sound like a plot from some messed up Disney movie?" Dru asked.

"I was going to go with something Machiavelli might do, but close enough," Nick said.

"Wait a minute." Claire pushed herself up from the couch with a sultry sigh of leather. "So, you're proposing that we lure Lucy out of Aerin by convincing her that he and Aerin are on the outs?"

"That's the idea."

"And exactly how the hell are you going to do that?" Claire asked.

"I believe Moira is suggesting that we make it appear that I've fallen in love with someone else." Julian's silver-blue eyes were alive with thought. Moira could see him tracing the implications and potential outcomes of this plan down many paths at once.

"Yeah." The edge of incredulity in Nick's voice gave this word the weight of a laugh. "But, who?"

Moira took a deep breath and made sure her body was nowhere near the direct path separating Conquest from Pestilence.

"Me," she said.

❧ 6 ❧

"**A**bso-fucking-lutely not." Nick leapt from his station on the couch's arm as if someone had applied a cattle prod to his taint. Which, Moira suspected, was about what her words had been to him. She hadn't expected Conquest to be all together thrilled about the idea of willingly letting his brother Horseman horn in on her, but she intended to make it worth his while at the first available opportunity.

Purely to keep the peace, of course.

"At least hear me out before you object," Moira insisted. "Chances are Lucy's going to be madder than a double-plucked hen when she finds out Tierra sprung Death and they flew the coop. Which means she's going to be looking for vengeance, and I don't know about y'all, but the idea of that demonic old twat using Aerin's powers to carry it out scares the ever-loving sheep dip out of me."

"And me," Claire admitted. "We saw what Lucy did with an army of zombies. I don't even want to think what she might be able to do with the convention of witch hunters that's been camping on our doorstep."

"I'm for slaughtering them all," Dru remarked. This surprised absolutely no one. "Hunting doesn't work so well when you're dead."

"I wouldn't mind acquainting Reverend Bill Blanding with the finer points of Hemorrhagic Peritonitis." Julian's eyes had gone the ephemeral shade of an iceberg's underside. "Assuming we were able to locate them. They seem to be rather at home beneath the city."

"What is it with Christians and catacombs?" Dru's expression was one of nostalgic fondness. The golden age of Rome must have been something like the good old days, or so Moira guessed.

"Eradication. Extermination. Wanton bloodshed and recreational torture. Now *these* are ideas I can get behind." Nick's mood had lightened considerably.

"Satisfying as that may be, it doesn't do fuck-all about Aerin bein' possessed." Moira felt herself become the proverbial storm cloud, darkening the sky of their excitement and making a soggy mess of their plans. She was past caring. Those witch hunters would get what was coming to them, of this she had no doubt. But not before Lucy did. "I was ready to chew open my own wrist after being trapped with that evil whore for a couple hours. Can y'all even begin imagine what it must be like to share your head with her every minute of every day?"

This thought drew a dark curtain over the room in general and Julian in particular. He sank back onto the settee, chin coming to rest on the leather knot of his clasped hands.

"You can joke about Aerin being a foul-mouthed bitch all you want, but she's my sister dammit, and I ain't about to let that malevolent twatsicle treat her like some magical Mercedes. Lucy's had her fun. I think it's high time she got her a mouthful of the misery she so enjoys shoveling down other people's throats."

The ghost of a smile flickered across Julian's lips. "Moira de Moray, I am with you."

"You know *I* am, sister." Seeing the fierce determination in Claire's eyes felt like looking into a mirror, and she was pleased to find the image staring back at her stronger than she'd remembered. Her sister. Her blood.

"Look, I don't want to be the one to shit all over your love-fest here, but how do we know this will even work?" Nick had remained on the outskirts of their circle, pausing now and then to examine details in the woodwork in his restless orbit. "But in case you've forgotten, you're talking about potentially canoodling with Pestilence here."

"Don't be so modest, Nicholas." Julian crossed his ankle over his knee and adjusted the pleat of his trousers. "I think we all know which of the two of us is more likely to give her syphilis."

Nick—resembling a boiled crawdad in both color and expression more every minute—pointed a finger at his brother. "You want to swallow some teeth along with your next swig of centuries-old Bordeaux?"

"Might complement the chalky finish," Dru suggested, drawing a raised eyebrow from Julian.

"If it's the whole infectious disease thing that's got your boxers in a bunch, then relax." Moira stuck two fingers in her mouth and whistled short and sharp. Seconds later, Cheeto came trotting into their midst, her pearlescent wand clasped high in his snout. Moira reached down and took the wand, giving her pig a quick scratch behind one velvet ear in lieu of their usual baby talk.

To Moira's delight and amusement, Cheeto tottered a long, curving arc back to the kitchen, pausing to sneeze a delicate, flaming snot ball on Nick's loafer. It was no bigger than a lit match really, and certainly didn't warrant the florid curses streaming from Nick's mouth.

Claire's hand was clapped to her face, her eyes watering with mirth behind it.

Moira pointed her wand at the offended shoe and put it out with a quick spritz. "See? Good as new."

"Do you have any idea how much these loafers cost?" Nick's black scowl did nothing to dissolve the errant giggle lodged at the back of Moira's throat.

She was tempted to make a jab about Payless, but somehow thought this might hurt her chances of winning Nick to the cause.

"Look, I'm real sorry about your shoe. But my whole point was this," she said, holding her wand aloft. "I'm pretty sure this puppy can tackle anything Julian here can dish out."

"Is that so?" Julian appeared genuinely intrigued. His eyes brightened with the fervor of a scientist as he examined the length of smooth, iridescent wood in her hand.

"Well, it sure as hell did when *someone* shot me through the chest with his flaming arrow."

Nick at least had the grace to look mildly regretful. "Assuming that wand will keep you from getting a wicked case of the clap, what makes you think that you two can convince *the wicked* you're in love?"

"As much as I hate to say it, Nick brings up a decent point." Claire looked from Moira to Julian and back again. "You two aren't exactly what you call a match made in heaven."

Contrary to the assumption made by many when the twang of her bayou patois vibrated the delicate membranes within their ears, Moira was not a fool. She knew what there was to see when others looked at her. Understood that sex was the language she spoke most fluently and any brains she might have were always filtered through it.

And yet, when she'd had even half a chance to read growing up, it was the courtly tales she'd disappeared into. She had long been conscious of a deep ache for a world where doors were opened to her for reasons other than cadging a glance at her ass.

The truth was that pretending interest in a man like Julian Roarke wouldn't require much pretending at all. It was pretending to be the kind of woman *he* might like where her brain started to bog down like a pontoon motor in a weed patch.

"All respect to Plato," Julian said, "but I've found that *like attracts like* isn't always a reliable adage when human courtship is concerned. History lacks no precedent for the coupling of apparently ill-suited companions."

"Yeah, but none of those couples were under the close scrutiny of Satan herself," Claire pointed out.

"That we know of," Dru added.

"What I mean is," Claire clarified, "it won't do us one lick of good if you two aren't actually capable of selling it to Lucy. Maybe we should see what you've got before we commit to the plan."

Moira sought the only other pair of blue eyes in the room. She couldn't help but wonder if this shade didn't indicate an inherent kindness like her own, something not shared with his dark-eyed brothers three.

Claire's eyebrows lifted expectantly. "Well?"

"You're saying you want us to *practice?*" Moira's throat worked over a swallow the approximate size of a duck egg.

"That's what I'm saying." One side of Claire's brick-red lips twisted upward.

"Here?" Julian's voice matched Moira's own for uncertainty.

"Yep," Claire confirmed.

"Now?" Moira gulped.

"No time like the present," Dru chimed in.

Allowing herself one deep breath, Moira turned and faced Julian, still seated on the opposite side of the room. "All right then."

Suddenly, she was back in what passed for a middle school dance in Stumps Bayou. A dark, sweaty basement beneath the reception hall the First Church of the Lamb's Holy Blood loaned out on the weekends to supplement its meager collection plate offerings. Cement cold beneath the industrial carpet. The air heavy with dust and the scent of moldering hymnals. A circle of faces cast in sharp relief by the flashlight pilfered from the custodian's closet. Zydeco music thumping false cheer through the floorboards above.

At the center of it all, an old brown beer bottle, spinning like a centrifuge and Moira, at its outside edge, feeling the pressure flatten her lungs.

She felt just as breathless now.

Julian rose when she was yet halfway across the distance separating them, driven by manners acquired in another time. An older time.

They faced each other, awkward and stiff as two scarecrows, propped together in a field by bizarre circumstance.

Over in the corner, Nick looked like he was being eaten alive by insects from the inside out. Face twitching. Muscles flicking and bunching. A fine sheen of sweat blooming on his brow.

"So, how do you figure we ought to do this?" Moira shifted her weight from one bare foot to the other.

Julian looked thoughtful for a moment. "Perhaps we might begin with an embrace?"

"An embrace." She nodded, grateful for the suggestion. "Okay. That sounds all right. I reckon we could do that."

Neither of them made an attempt to move.

"Shall we?" Julian's arms rose stiff within his tailored dinner jacket. The buttons on his waistcoat winked in the lamplight, catching the strands of the same silvery hue at his temples.

"Sure," Moira said. "That is, if you're ready."

"I am."

"Okay, then."

"Indeed."

"Wow." Dru rolled his eyes. "This is giving me a hell of a boner."

"Hush your face, *Duh*-rew." Moira took a half step toward Julian. "All right. Here I come."

Julian mimicked her movement. "As do I."

"Oh, for fuck's sake." Dru planted a hand squarely between each of their shoulder blades and shoved them together sternum to sternum like two halves of an apocalyptic sandwich.

And then she was hugging Julian Roarke.

❦ 7 ❦

And then she *wasn't* hugging Julian Roarke because his body had accelerated away from hers so quickly that for a brief second, her arms were still in the air where his waist had been. Only when Moira heard the crash did she discover what had happened.

Nicholas Kingswood.

Conquest in his full glory had launched himself across the room and into Julian's body with bone shattering force.

Well, coffee table shattering force anyhow.

The splinters exploded outward more violently than if had someone had taken dynamite to a woodchuck.

On top of the rubble of broken wood, Nick and Julian struggled for purchase. Having initiated the attack, Nick had the benefit of superior position. He managed to get his hands around Julian's throat at roughly ascot level and squeezed with enough force to cause his brother's eyes to bulge as his face reddened.

"You touched my woman, you diseased fuck!" White flecks of saliva gathered at the corners of Nick's mouth. His eyes lit with the same curious glow Moira remembered in the seconds before he released his arrow on Siren's Cry.

"As part of a plan to thwart the Devil, you ignorant

swine pizzle!" Every word was a tortured gasp from Julian's constricted throat.

Nick might have taken Julian's lack of physical objection as a refusal or inability to fight. Most likely because Nick couldn't see what his dexterous brother was doing behind his broad back.

Julian's gloves had *literally* come off.

And what followed would put Moira off oysters for the rest of her natural life.

The long, elegant fingers of Julian's bare hands fastened on Nick's forearms. A look of utter shock was quickly wiped away by the dawning of agony, intense enough to crush Conquest's face into a grimace.

First, the skin surrounding Pestilence's grasp bubbled up into bilious sores. Weeping, the skin beneath them fell away in great, gray slimy sheets. Nick howled in pain and rage but refused to relinquish his hold.

It might have been the sight of exposed muscle, red and raw as a Sunday roast, that finally galvanized War into action. He was on his feet in one second and had Nick in a headlock the next, a bicep roughly the size of a grapefruit flexing around Conquest's neck.

"Let. The fuck. Go." Dru's voice was low and lethal. Enough to have Moira reaching for Claire's hand.

"Three of the four Horsemen of the Apocalypse are having a throw-down in our living room," Claire said. The words were as flat and toneless as if she were announcing she needed to have a pee.

Moira said the only thing she could think of. "And?"

"And nothing," Claire sighed. "I just felt like it needed to be said."

Conquest did not surrender. Not when War threatened to disembowel him with an apocalyptic sword. Not when Pestilence melted his arms into bloody stumps only for Nick to regenerate them and have them melted all over again.

No.

Only when Moira squatted down next to him and spoke one sentence calmly into his ear.

"Nicholas Kingswood, so help me Goddess, if you don't turn loose of Julian right this second, I will never again hump you to kingdom come so long as either one of us lives."

And just like that, it was over.

Nick released Julian's neck. Smooth, tanned skin closed around the mess of muscle and tendon on full display from the elbow down. He stood, brushed a few flecks of gore sticking to the rolled cuffs of his shirt and straightened his tie.

Julian recovered his gloves, neatly tugging each finger into place before rising to his feet and returning a few fugitive hairs to the cue tied at the base of his neck. The red marks where Nick's fingers had been were rapidly fading, along with whatever strange, sudden violence had taken over the room.

Moira had been no stranger to barroom brawls growing up. Hell, it wasn't a Saturday night without one.

But something about watching Julian and Nick go after each other churned the deepening current of dread within her.

This is what it's like.

This is what it's like when the world and all the creatures on it spin ever closer to their collective end. When all is greed, hatred, and hunger. When even brothers tear at each other in blind, selfish rage.

This is what it's like when all that's left is darkness. Vengeance. Destruction.

Opening the Seals may have loosed the plagues, but it was what evil found in human hearts that made it stay.

Was it any wonder Lucy had decided to make this place her home? Her playground?

"You are *so* cleaning this mess up. You know that,

right?" Claire stood over the broken table, her hand on her hip, eyes narrowed at Nick. "If you think I'm picking wads of your skin off the floor, you are out of your immortal skull."

Dru's attention swiveled to Claire, the one spot in the room it never strayed far from in the first place. "He'd be fucking thrilled to clean up, wouldn't you, Nick?"

When Nick began to protest, Moira cleared her throat and folded her arms beneath her breasts.

Right beneath her breasts.

"You have a dustpan or something?" The words sounded like they had been forced through a filter of industrial strength *fuck you*, but for Nick, they represented Herculean strides.

"This way," Moira said. "In the kitchen."

Nick followed her from the parlor through the entryway and into the kitchen, by far Moira's favorite part of the home. Always clean, but never quite tidy, cluttered in a warm and welcoming way. It had been here where she and Tierra had first unburdened their souls of the pain their upbringing had caused. Here she and Aerin had reconciled over fried chicken after their first zombie battle. Here where she and Claire busted each other's chops and shared shots of whiskey.

It felt colder now as Moira walked through it. The various herbs looked blanched and sad by comparison to their cheerful planters—an attic sale jumble of pots and teacups and whatever else Tierra had felt like nestling them in on any given day.

They seemed to miss their mistress as much as Moira did.

Killian Bane, if you're not taking care of her, I will pluck every feather from those flashy wings you're so proud of.

"Broom and dustpan are in there." Moira gestured to the small utility closet next to the pantry. "But I think a wheelbarrow and a shop vac would do a better job for you."

"And where are those?" Nick asked.

"Nowhere," Moira reported. "We don't have either."

"Thanks a heap." Nick bent to retrieve the dustpan as well as an industrial sized black plastic garbage bag. Something about seeing him in this routine domestic situation had Moira's panties migrating to places they oughtn't. "How can an earth witch not own a wheel barrow?"

"Well, we used to have one, but Tierra insisted that Claire burn all the tools those zombies touched after they were done building the shed on account of all the undead cooties they probably had."

"Can't say I blame her." He glanced back at her over his shoulder. "Do you have a better broom? The bristles on this one are all—"

Nick's sharp intake of breath sucked whatever he had intended to say back down his throat. Most likely because Moira's hand had found its way into the front pocket of his pants and around his cock. Her breasts pressed into the warm expanse of his back while her nipples tightened painfully beneath the ribbed fabric of her tank top.

His blood moved as quickly as the rest of him did. In seconds he was full and hot beneath her grip as his knuckles whitened around the broom handle.

"My, my, my." Moira breathed against the space between his shoulder blades. Her hand continued its leisurely exploration. "I ain't never felt fabric like this on the inside of a pocket. What's this made of, anyway?"

"Silk," Nick hissed through his teeth.

"Silk. That explains why it's so...slippery." She slid her hand quickly downward by way of illustration. "I'm slippery, too, Nick. Want to feel?"

Moira peeled Nick's fingers away from the broom

handle and dragged them behind him to find the warmth of her thigh. Upward, under her skirt, across the moisture blooming through her panties.

He tried to turn then, the habit of his dominance rising up as elemental as the very dust from the earth's making and nearly as old. An answering rush quickened in her blood and she pushed him against the closet wall with strength beyond her own. Strength Nick himself had given her along with his blood. The same elixir pulsed within his flesh beneath her grip.

"You didn't like it when Julian touched me, did you, Mr. Kingswood?"

"No."

"I'm afraid he's gonna have to touch me a lot more before all this is said and done." The muscles in his back tensed against her cheek. "But for every time he touches me, I'm going to touch you. Twice as hard. Twice as long. He hugged me, now I'm huggin' you. See how this works?"

He made no answer.

Maybe because she'd tightened her grip on him, working her way upward and over the part of him she knew to be twice as silky as the fabric covering it.

"This plan ain't gonna work if you're bustin' in and shooting everything all to hell every time I get close to Julian. You understand? I'm asking you to cooperate. Not for Aerin. Not even for me. I'm asking you to do it for you. For Nicholas Kingswood. Because every time I pretend with Julian, I'm going to take it out on you."

His big body shuddered with animal pleasure at the proposition, which she'd chosen to phrase like a threat for this very reason.

"Good boy. Now go clean up your mess." She went on tiptoe to bite the muscle at the base of his neck before swatting his ass and releasing him.

Knowing smiles met them when they re-entered the

parlor. The largest pieces of the table had vanished, leaving only odd wood chips and splinters behind.

"Good news is we have some extra firewood," Claire announced. "Bad news is now we're going to have to come up with a story about what happened to the table."

From the way Dru picked splinters off his tight black t-shirt, Moira guessed he might have taken it out and busted it up *by hand*.

"Maybe you oughta go singe it a little bit," Moira suggested. "We can tell Aerin you were practicing a spell that went sideways."

"Not a bad idea." Claire rose from the couch with Dru in tow like a steroid-enhanced shadow. "Be right back."

Nick made quick work of sweeping the unspeakable combination of both immortal and wooden remains into the black trash bag.

Moira followed behind him, dousing the area in Tierra's favorite disinfecting concoction of tea tree and lemon oil when he was finished.

"Would you mind carrying that out to the trash?" she asked Nick, deliberately glancing at Julian, who had retired to the window seat with a stack of books borrowed from the nearby shelves.

A fine white line appeared around Nick's lips as his jaw flexed. "Not at all."

And then there were two.

8

Julian's intense solitude populated the room, filling the space everyone had left behind. He was remote as a statue seated there, the world dissolving beyond the borders of the pages beneath his scrutiny. Moira wasn't sure if it was the direct sunlight filtering through the window or the ugliness that had unfolded only moments before, but his espresso-dark hair seemed shot through with more silver than she'd noticed before.

Slowly and with more care than she used to sneak up on a footless duckling, Moira waded into the silence.

She eased herself down on the cushion next to his, surprised to find herself crossing one leg over the other and tugging her skirt down toward her knee. What was it about Julian Roarke that made everything about her feel as subtle as a drag queen at an Amish barn raising?

"*Medieval Herbs and Poultices*, huh?" She leaned in to peek at an intaglio print of a hydrocephalic monk smashing what looked like a bowling pin into a cup of green weeds. "Don't get attached. I heard there's a surprise twist at the end."

Julian didn't speak.

"So, that went well," she said. "You give a pretty damn good hug, if you don't mind me saying."

It wasn't exactly a scoff, the sound Julian made. More like an exhale, but with feeling.

"Nick and me had ourselves a chat. I think he'll be all right from now on."

"*I*." Julian didn't look up from the text.

"'Scuse me?"

"Nick and *I*," he repeated. "You wouldn't say *me* had a chat. The same rules apply whether it's a compound subject or you individually."

"You don't say." Truth was that Moira knew exactly how that sort of thing worked but she was too lazy to try and school her tongue against following the well-worn pathways in her mind. That, and she had no end of fun annoying Aerin with her hideous grammatical abominations. "Let me try this again." Here, she cleared her throat. "Nicholas Kingswood and *I* conversed at length, and unilaterally decided it would be mutually beneficial if he were to refrain from further displays of aggression in accordance with our plan to prevent one Lucifer the she-demon from facilitating the world's end."

Julian not only looked up from the book, he clapped it closed with his thumb still inside. If he'd had a monocle, Moira was pretty sure he would have dragged it up to his eye at that moment and examined her through it.

"Pardon the cliché, but don't judge a book by its patois, mister."

Scientists measured the widths of atoms in quantities larger than the progress of Julian Roarke's smile. "Well said, Moira de Moray."

"And that's another thing." She slid the book from his grasp and set it back on its stack. "If we're *really* going to get Lucy's cloven-footed goat, you better start practicing some pet names."

"Endearments, you mean?"

"Yes, schnoodle-bum, that's exactly what I mean."

"Schnood—"

"You try to analyze this, and I promise that big old brain of yours is like to explode. Just go with it. Try not to think too much."

Now, Julian Roarke really did scoff.

"Try this. Pick any animal and a dessert you like and slap them together." She counted every crease in his translucent eyelids when he closed them, scanning the vast stores of information living in his head.

"Ocelot tiramisu?"

Moira blinked. "It's okay, darlin'. We'll work on it."

"No," Julian insisted. "I've made a study of every language ever spoken on this planet. I have billions of words at my disposal. I can do this." He took a deep breath, perfect white teeth dimpling one side of his lip in concentration. "Stagtart!"

The biggest, warmest smile she could muster plastered itself on her face. "That was good. The way you put the one word after the other word. And said them together."

Julian's expression was at once sheepish and forlorn. "You sounded just like Aerin then. Struggling to conjure a compliment when truer words are in your mind."

"I know," Moira met his clear-eyed gaze. "I miss her too."

Then she did something that surprised them both. She took his gloved hand in hers.

The warm, buttery leather between her fingers was the last thing she registered before a tidal wave of loneliness threatened to shake her very soul from its moorings.

This was Julian.

In that moment, Moira knew she was perhaps one of the only two women in the Earth's history to reach out a hand of comfort to this man, this being, and that felt like something she might someday be proud of.

But now, it only registered as a profound ache in her

sternum. Her healer's heart called to suffering personified.

"Julian Roarke," she said. "Can I ask you
something?"

"That you may, my little tortoise truffle."

This time, her smile was spontaneous and genuine.
"Hey! That ain't half bad. And the diminutive really
added something I think."

Julian accepted the compliment graciously, waiting
in polite silence for her to continue.

"Anyhow, I was wondering. I don't suppose you've
ever had yourself a good, old fashioned platonic
cuddle?"

One of Julian's dark brows rose in a quizzical expression. "A platonic...cuddle?"

"Yeah, you know. Where you just snuggle up to
someone for no other purpose than to be close to another body?"

"I cannot say I've ever done such a thing."

"Maybe we ought to try it sometime. I have the
feeling it might do you some good, and if whatsher-
hooves happened to walk in on something like that, I'd
bet it would piss her off something royal. Two birds,
one stone and all that."

"I suppose we might endeavor to try it some
evening when we can arrange for the creature in question to interrupt us." The addition of a mischievous
grin to Julian's face peeled at least a decade away from
his careworn eyes.

"All right then. I'd say we have ourselves a plan." She
squeezed Julian's hand, willing whatever solace she
could give to seep through the leather's pores and find a
home among his bones.

And it was precisely in this position, with Julian's
hand in hers, their heads bent in collusion, that Aerin
found them.

$\maltese$ 9 $\maltese$

Lucy's teeth ground together hard enough to send a throbbing pain from her jaw all the way to her temples. Well, technically they weren't *her* teeth, but she felt the pain all the same.

Lousiest fucking day *ever*.

First Killian Bane had slipped from her grasp with the aid of that pregnant cow of an earth witch, and now her soggy water witch sister was simpering all over Julian? *Her* Julian?

Worse still, Julian wasn't just tolerating it. He looked like he might actually be *enjoying* it. And this when he refused to lay so much as a gloved finger on Aerin ever since Lucy had taken residence in her body.

A vehicle Lucy had been enjoying, for the most part. If there was one thing she'd always resented about the way things had down, it's that she'd been denied the opportunity to at least test-drive a human body. Sure, they were prone to all kinds of diseases and dysfunctions and made unpleasant noises after consuming food, but the temporary nature of the vessel itself made everything so deliciously...intense. Midnight voyages with naught but a broomstick between her thighs and velvet darkness sliding across her naked skin. Surrendering to sleep after a difficult day of lies and subversion. The first sip of coffee in a morning still undecided.

Of course, there were other advantages too. Though she had not been able to actively bed Julian while wearing Aerin's skin, she could wander the air witch's mind endlessly, picking memories of their coupling like books from a shelf and lazily flip through them.

Lucy had always suspected Julian Roarke of harboring animal hunger beneath those bespoke suits of his, but even she had been surprised by the ferocity with which he'd taken Aerin against the brick wall of an alleyway their first time. The grainy, unrestrained violence of it still weakened her knees.

Well, Aerin's knees, technically.

Try as she might, she hadn't been able to temp Julian into a repeat performance.

Could the incomprehensible sight before her now be the reason why?

Lucy paused for a moment to savor wave upon wave of jealousy and betrayal surging up from the subconscious pit where Aerin lived now. The denial that followed was like the disappointing aftertaste of an otherwise lovely vintage, the sentiments accompanying it so predictable and boring.

Moira wouldn't do this to me. She's my sister.

Julian loves me. I felt it.

And what do you feel now? Lucy floated this question down to Aerin, waiting for the inevitable reply. This was one of the games Lucy had discovered she enjoyed immensely: tormenting a soul while wearing the body it belonged to.

She really ought to get extra credit for this sort of thing. Queen of Darkness level: Fucking Expert.

Lucy already knew the answer because she felt it too.

Genuine budding affection between Julian and Moira.

But something else too. A trace of rabid jealousy clinging to the air like the whiff of cigar smoke you get after its source has left the room. She would know who it belonged to even if she hadn't had the chance to practice so frequently in the last weeks.

Nicholas Kingswood, a man whose emotional signature was about as deep and complicated as a spit wad. He was somewhere nearby, as were the fire witch and Drustan. Lucy could sense them as well in this pathetic cocktail of family discord.

"Aerin, honey! There you are." The over-brightness of delivery combined with that buzz-saw of a yokel accent made the water witch sound like a braying mule, in Lucy's opinion. "Julian here was nice enough to sit with me on account of I've been worried sick."

"Oh?" Lucy asked. "And what part of Pestilence holding your hand was supposed to make you *less* sick?"

They leapt apart the moment they had seen Aerin, of course, but their proximity on the window seat still felt like ample reason for the indictment.

"I should think you would be glad that I was here to offer comfort to your sister in your absence," Julian said in a voice almost accusatory. "Miss de Moray experienced considerable stress when she received the bit of news that Killian sent to Nicholas by way of raven."

Feeling Aerin's stomach flip was one of Lucy's least favorite manifestations of human fear.

"News?" Lucy struggled to keep her voice neutral. "What news?"

"Tierra's gone." Moira's eyes were large with unshed tears. "Looks like she helped Death bust out of Hell and that bastard took off with her."

"Where?" As soon as she registered the surprise on their faces, Lucy knew she'd asked this with too much excitement and not enough worry. *Oops.* "I mean, what the shit? Why would he do that?" She paced toward the window, wedging herself down between Moira and Julian.

The water witch shifted to accommodate her. As well she fucking should.

"Perhaps to protect her," Julian suggested. "With five of the seven Seals opened and the consequences well upon us, the world isn't exactly the safest place for a woman with child at the present moment."

"If only we could figure out where the raven came from," Lucy said, moving Julian's hand to her knee. If Pestilence was going to pretend *not* to be sneaking around behind Aerin's back, then he could fucking well pretend to be in love with her. "We might be able to find them."

"Fat fucking chance."

Lucy glanced up to see Claire, Dru, and Nick standing in the parlor's oversized entryway. It was the last of these who had spoken.

"The raven left as quickly as it came," Nick added. "We haven't got shit to go on."

"Where on Earth have you been, Aerin?" Claire seated herself on the couch and folded her black leather boots beneath her.

As tempting as it was to launch an offensive, Lucy's first priority was some serious damage control. After all, Killian had finally worked out her identity, and the brood sow could have warned her sisters by now. Judging by the fact that she hadn't been met by burning torches and pitchforks at the door, Lucy guessed word hadn't yet reached them. But if her miserably long life had taught her anything, it was to never assume you had the upper hand.

Especially when all the evidence was there to support it.

"Oh, here and there," Lucy said. *Translation: to Hell and back.* "Business that needed taking care of." *I.e., se-*

lecting a taskforce of her most repugnant minions to search for Bane. "What happened to the coffee table?"

It had taken Lucy this long to notice what had been bothering her about the room. Other than Julian and Moira's pathetically wounded souls tenderly humping each other by the bay window, that was.

Claire slid a nervous glance toward Moira.

"We were all talking about what we were going to do to get Tierra back, practicing a couple spells and such, and Claire up and torched it."

Liar, Lucy and Aerin thought in unison.

"And what did you decide?" Lucy threaded her fingers through Julian's and dragged their clasped hands into her lap.

"Pardon?" Moira asked.

Hard to follow the conversation when you're a filthy fucking liar, isn't it, you hideous hillbilly bitch?

"About Tierra," Lucy clarified. "How are we going to find her and Bane?"

"We figured it might be best if we paired up and searched the area around Port Townsend first. You know, check all the places Bane's been calling home so far. The barracks at Fort Warden. That place out in the woods that, uh, got flooded."

From the looks on their faces, Nick, Julian, and Dru all took exception with Moira's use of the passive voice regarding the unfortunate end of their former dwelling.

"Then we were going to meet up at Manresa Castle at nine o' clock tonight," the water witch continued. "Unless we find Tierra sooner."

"Fine," Lucy said. "Julian and I will take the barracks."

"I'm afraid we already grouped up while we were waiting on you." Moira managed a decent expression of regret. "Nick and Claire, me and Julian, and since you can fly and all, we thought it might be best if you broke off on your own to keep an eye on things from up there while Dru acts as base."

The fresh wave of jealousy oozing from Nick's direction paled in comparison to the blast of hatred, hurt, and despair welling up from Aerin's pit.

Moira is trying to get rid of me. My own sister. What in the actual fuck? How dare she? I will fucking rip every hair from that backwater slut's empty head and force her to eat her own chitlins. And Julian. If that douche lord thought he was lonely before, wait until every human on Earth associates his face with the wellspring of disease.

Well now, Aerin, Lucy thought to her captive. *That's the first intelligent idea you've had all day.*

"Very well," Lucy said, rising on Aerin's best pair of Saint Laurent stiletto heels. "Until nine."

❧ 10 ❧

The world was ending.

Nick didn't need seas of blood or seven trumpets or an angel hurtling through the air crying *Woe! Woe!* and all that happy horseshit to know it. The incomprehensible spectacle before his eyes was all the confirmation he required.

Exiting Port Townsend's only western wear store was none other than Julian Roarke.

In denim.

The brassy snaps of his denim jacket caught the last of the early November sunlight, winking like dying stars as he and Moira stepped out onto Water Street arm in arm.

And of course, the fussy bastard had coordinated his pants to the same hue as the jacket.

If he was willing to give the abominable trousers covering Julian's legs that distinction.

Wranglers.

Julian Roarke was wearing fucking Wranglers. Wranglers so tight, not even the microbes laying in wait within Pestilence's body could fit between his skin and the fabric.

They passed millennia in each other's acquaintance without Nick knowing the precise shapes of Julian's calves and thighs, and now Nick knew not only that, but that Pestilence carried his cock to the left.

Nick was pretty certain he could have gone to the grave twice over without harboring that information somewhere in the unfathomable reaches of his mind.

And it didn't end there.

He got as far as Julian's narrow waist when he was nearly blinded by the flash of a belt buckle bigger than the hubcaps on his Ferrari Italia 458. Above it, Nick could hardly make out the material.

Flannel.

Pestilence, destroyer of entire populations, was tooling around Port Townsend in flannel.

Nick realized he was power walking in their direction only when Moira's eyes rose from the general direction of Julian's denim-clad ass.

From a distant galaxy, Claire's voice called to him.

He had temporarily forgotten they'd spent the better part of the afternoon and early evening pretending to traipse around the wilds beyond Port Townsend in the general area where their home base had been before Moira had power-washed it away.

The memory of Moira wreaking havoc had given him a hard-on not even the fire witch's familiar could banish. The lithe little fox had appeared in the high grasses at the road cut and not let him out of its green-eyed gaze the whole time they walked, killing time.

He hadn't minded Claire. Not really.

In fact, she was pretty decent company for a woman he had no intention of fucking.

Not that the thought hadn't occurred to him once or twice.

Okay, maybe three times, but only because Claire wore leather. But the whole fire witch thing had ruled it out on principle. After his run-ins with the fire-breathing pork chop that was Moira's familiar, he wasn't all that eager to take on another being who might hurl incendiaries at him.

A grudge fuck hadn't been in the cards.

Gods, how he wanted a grudge fuck. It might even release a little of the energy coiled like a viper at the base of his spine.

Yogis had invented a word for that on his account. *Kundalini*. The release of that energy, they had called the *kundalini shakti*.

Nick knew one thing. His *kundalini* was about to *shakti* the fuck out of whoever decided to start shit with him. And there was no shortage of people who wanted to try. He felt animosity stirring up around him like silt from the bottom of a pond in reaction not only to his presence, but also to Moira and Claire's. What the papers hadn't taken care of, Reverend Bill Blanding and his milling, brainless groupies had.

Warning anyone within earshot of the "evil" lurking in Port Townsend.

Even now, pedestrians chose to walk in Water Street's leaf-choked gutters rather than share the sidewalk with the four of them.

The way Nick was feeling just now, he couldn't say this was a bad idea on their part.

"Well, Nick Kingswood," Moira said. "Fancy meeting you here."

"Howdy, you all." Julian reached up to tip his hat, the gesture somewhat compromised by the fact that the article in question was a trucker hat bearing the logo for somewhere called Clem's Crab Cabin.

"You need a contraction in that sentence, sugar." Moira reached up and tugged on Julian's ponytail in a way that made Nick want to break someone in half. "It's *y'all*."

"Right. Yes. Howdy, *y'all*." Julian's rich, studied voice brought an alarming depth to the diction. This, in combination with the way his ridiculous yokel-wear emphasized the spare muscularity of his brother's frame, brought Nick to the realization that he hated Julian Roarke.

Hated his fucking beautiful face and beautiful voice and huge fucking brain and all the things it knew. Hated his ability to make Moira smile. Hated the childlike delight he lit in her eyes and the slack-limbed ease his presence lent to her lovely body.

In fact, if Nick's arms didn't still ache with the memory of the desolation Julian wrought in his flesh, he might have tried to cram a fist through the back of his brother's skull right fucking now.

Moira stood back, admiring her handiwork. "Don't he just look cuter than a gnat's ear?"

"Actually, gnats interpret sound vibration with their antennae," Julian pointed out. "The sound waves are then passed through clusters of cells—and I'm doing it again, aren't I?"

"Maybe just a smidge." Moira held up her thumb and forefinger in a rough approximation of that particular measurement.

"I get that you two are supposed to be nauseatingly in love and all now, but what I want to know is how on earth Moira convinced you to raid Hank Williams's closet." Claire seemed to have remembered that she not only had a mouth, but words to match, her apparent shock only incrementally less than Nick's own.

"Actually, I must admit to finding this attire far more comfortable than I expected." Here, Julian reached up to tug the cuff of his new tawny, tanned-leather gloves. "Did you know that these vests are made from waterproof leather and come equipped with not one, but two concealed-carry pockets?"

"Last time I checked, the only thing you carried concealed was ass-rotting super viruses."

"Oh, he's concealing *much* more than that." An impish smirk darkened one corner of Moira's lips as she cast an appreciative glance right about where a saddle would split Julian's legs.

And Julian, waster of nations, fountainhead of insidious diseases and decay, actually, fucking, *blushed*.

The desire to see that same blood gout from Julian's every orifice rather than flush his pale cheeks was approaching crisis point.

Moira must have sensed the tide of carnage rising in Nick's blood, for she angled her body between his and Julian's and ducked her head to whisper.

"Okay, everyone's got their orders for tonight, right? We all know where we're going to be and when?"

"I'll be waiting in the closet in Julian's quarters with the Grim, ready to cast the exorcism spell we went over," Claire answered dutifully. "Dru will wait with me until you give the signal."

"Perfect." Moira turned to Julian. "And you, mister?"

"I'll be in bed," Julian said. The small hill of his Adam's apple bobbed as he worked over a swallow. "With you."

Nick felt and heard his knuckles creak as he welded his fists to his sides.

"And you?" Moira's eyes softened when they fixed on Nick's, a shift as subtle as a shadow passing beneath the water's surface. A graduation of expression only someone who had watched her face in moments of unguarded pleasure would catch. That he could, that he did, provided Nick with a most welcome stab of savage pride.

"I'll be out in the hall," Nick said. "Not killing anything."

"Good boy." Her voice carried a promise of wet heat that spoke straight to his cock. Whether Julian and Claire had heard this too, Nick didn't particularly care. At the moment, his sole purpose was to finish this business so he could fuck Moira in two with all due haste and expediency.

The end.

Or not the end.

A flash of white in the corner of Nick's vision lured his attention in that direction.

Nick didn't harbor any special pride on the score of his memory. Living as long as he had, he learned long ago to dump all non-essential information every time the sun slid below the horizon. In spite of this, his immortal mind maintained detailed warehouses on two subjects alone.

Everyone he'd ever wanted to fuck. And everyone he'd ever wanted to kill.

The figure etching itself into his peripheral vision landed soundly in the second camp. Slim, small, sliver-haired. Clutching a book to the breast pocket of his linen suit.

The Reverend Bill Blanding. "Oh, that I should live to see such times as sin congregates so boldly upon the streets." His preacher's cadence unfurled itself down the sidewalk like a velvet altar cloth, driving the last of the pedestrian traffic off the street.

In the wake of all that had befallen Port Townsend, the locals had developed a talent for waiting out the weird shit indoors.

Apparently, a showdown with a mob of witch hunters in broad daylight would be no different.

Nick felt Julian's anger kindling like a sudden swarm of bees, the memory of extracting Aerin from the Reverend's clutches all too near for comfort.

"Damned if he don't look like Colonel Sanders," Moira muttered. "Only it's his disposition that's extra crispy instead of his chicken. Anyone ever tell you you're awful uptight?" she asked, turning to Blanding. "It ain't your fingers need licked, if you ask me."

"Stop your tongue, whore." Reverend Blanding held up a bony hand, fingers splayed as if he could pull Moira's words directly from the air. As if in response, figures seeped from the deepening twilight shadows, coagulating in a circle around them.

Nick had seen their kind many times before over the centuries.

Blank eyes turned stony by hate. Empty hearts. Heads aswarm with the greedy anticipation of exacting punishment.

Out of instinct, Nick and Julian herded Moira and Claire between them, reducing the witch hunters' possible angles of attack.

"It's you who might want to stop your tongue, Blanding," Nick said. "That is, if you have any desire to keep it in your head."

"Blanding?" Claire repeated. "As in Reverend Bill Blanding the asswaffle who tried to kill Aerin?"

"The same." Julian's voice had gone low and deadly smooth.

"You see?" Blanding raised his arms in supplication as his eyes scanned the faces of his followers. "By fornication do they enchant others to do their bidding. Now you understand why all who are in league with the enchantress must *also* be destroyed."

Murmured agreement worked its way around the circle.

"Now wait just a toad-suckin' minute there, Colonel Cluck-bucket. The only fornicatin' I ever did with this one here was so he'd agree to kill me, which I'd have thought would thrill you clean out of your linen britches."

"*Moira*," Nick hissed through his teeth. The heat coming off her skin radiated through his dress shirt when their arms brushed.

"No, sir. I ain't about to be bullied by some Bible-beating carpet-bagger with a witch fetish." The same wand Nick had seen earlier in the bathroom at *Maison de Moray* had appeared in Moira's white-knuckled grip.

"We're fixin' to see how Reverend Ratfuck and his boys do with a little synchronized swimming."

Moira's arm swung high with the wand, and there she froze. The sickening sound of rock meeting bone, the awful, unmistakable *crack*, and her body collapsed into Julian's waiting arms.

Later, they would have to have a little discussion about who did the catching when Moira had been knocked the fuck out. But for now, Nick's attention had been hijacked by Claire, who was alternately screaming and gagging as she fumbled for the object that had been hurled with such brutal force at her sister.

Brimstone.

"A man also or woman that hath a familiar spirit, or that is a wizard, shall surely be put to death: they shall stone them with stones: their blood...shall be upon them." Blanding smiled wide enough to reveal the fissure where his dentures met his red, raw gums.

Nick smiled too.

He smiled, because he thought he would have to suffer through the day without killing anyone.

He smiled, because Reverend Blanding thought that if brimstone stopped witches, it would stop a Horseman, too.

He smiled, because they had *both* been very fucking wrong.

Nick had never been much for guns or knives when it came to offing a motherfucker.

To his way of thinking, weapons were kind of like condoms. He understood the need for them in theory but had always resented the distance they created in actual practice.

Using his hands was far more satisfying. Particularly when shattering a man's philtrum—that bony little ridge above the teeth but below the sinus—so the bony splinters could wreak havoc among the recesses below the frontal and temporal lobes of the brain.

So fell the closest of Blanding's minions. Watching one of their brother's faces collapse on itself like a deflated beach ball was sufficient motivation to send a score of them skittering back to the shadows like cockroaches.

"You mind keeping an eye on the ladies here so I can have a chat with the rest of our friends?" Nick asked. By this point, bleeding the pure anticipatory elation of the coming carnage out of his voice required significant effort.

Julian was already slipping out of his gloves and tucking them away in one of his vest's many pockets. "By all means."

Nick stooped and picked up the chunk of brimstone that had felled Moira. "Who threw this?"

"The righteous fear not evil!" Blanding held his tattered leather Bible out like a shield. "Nor will they be dissuaded by the words of the adversary."

"Let me rephrase that." Nick lobbed the mottled gray and poison yellow stone upward and let it fall to his palm with an ominous slap. "Whoever tells me who threw this *won't* get his testicles ripped off and shoved down his throat."

Several arms swung out, fingers at the end of them pointing squarely at a weasel-faced man sporting an old-fashioned friar's robes knotted at the waist with a length of rope. The man's eyes went wide, his gladiator sandals scraping backward with a cartoon character's swiftness.

Reverend Blanding's face had gone bone white as he backed into the protective circle of bodies already shuffling in to surround him. "But behold, the hand of the one betraying me is with mine on the table!"

A surge of pure pleasure bloomed hot in Nick's blood.

The more, the merrier. Every body that put itself between him and Reverend Blanding was one more he'd have the chance to break.

But first...

Friar Tuck's elbows bit into the concrete as Nick came down on his back, knee lodged between the faux-monk's shoulder blades. The air rushed out of the man's ribcage as his lungs deflated in a satisfying *whoosh*. Nick felt a couple ribs splinter like Thanksgiving wishbones when his full weight was brought to bear.

"They *will* be destroyed." Blood dampened the monk's words, choking off the sibilant S into a wet cough. "Kill me if you will, but there will be others."

"If you insist." One quick jerk was sufficient to snap

the man's spinal cord. He shivered out straight like a clubbed fish.

Nick climbed off him before the inevitable void of bodily fluids had the chance to soak through the rough brown cloth of Friar Tuck's get up. Taking the chunk of brimstone from the pocket of his dress shirt, Nick nudged the man over onto his back with the toe of one Italian leather loafer and jammed the rock into his mouth like the traditional apple in the maw of a suckling pig.

With the singular focus he enjoyed only when killing, Nick located the cowering form of Reverend Blanding in what remained of the crowd.

What followed next would remain in Nick's memory as nothing more than a strange collage of color and sound. The world painted with sprays of crimson and serenaded by the lullaby of breaking bones and scattering teeth as he cheerfully worked his way through the pack of witch hunters.

He had a vague sense that he *might* have ripped someone's arm off and beaten him with the wet end at one point, but he could never be really sure. It was entirely possible that he merely picked up the limb after a brush with Julian had relieved it of the connective tissues once anchoring it to its former owner.

There were a few odd body parts decorating Water Street's gutters by that point. Hard to keep track.

Especially after Moira, having recovered her consciousness in addition to a goodly measure of the fighting spirit Nick had grown to...respect, grabbed Julian from behind and commenced to aim him at a second wave of witch hunters bubbling up from a sewer grating like so many rats.

"Moira, what are you—" Startled by the sudden skin-to-skin contact, Julian had spun sharply enough to nearly relieve him of his trucker's hat—a happening

Nick observed with growing interest over the exposed tendons of his current project.

"Just trust me, all right?" At this, Moira yanked Julian's denim jacket down off his shoulders, revealing that Pestilence was not only wearing a flannel shirt, but a *sleeveless* flannel shirt at that.

Which disclosure inadvertently caused Nick to curb check one unfortunate witch hunter's teeth not merely down his throat, as he planned, but clear through the backside of the man's skull.

Collateral damage.

Much like the head Nick inadvertently ripped from its stem when Moira tore open Julian's shirt and vest, sending pearl snaps and buttons scattering in every direction.

Once bared, Julian's torso—a good deal more toned than Nick would have guessed, he was sorry to note—became home to Moira's hands. Her fingers threaded together, making a cage directly over Pestilence's heart as her forehead came to rest against his naked back.

Together, they looked like something you might see on the cover of a romance novel about a lonely rancher—the rancher fed his cattle on the broken bodies of religious zealots.

"Honestly, Miss de Moray," Julian protested. "I don't think now is the time for this kind of—gods! What are you doing to me?"

If Nick had been afraid he would find Moira's hands had migrated to Julian's crotch, he was wrong by several orders of magnitude.

She hadn't shifted one iota.

But Julian had.

Attenuated arms shot straight out from his body in the posture of a sleepwalker. Every muscle of his torso carved in high relief by whatever current passed from Moira through him. From the open palms of his outstretched hands, a dense fog the color of swamp water billowed and swelled, climbing up the legs of those witch hunters nearest them.

Moira had turned Pestilence into an aerosolized weapon.

Dumbfounded, Nick watched in a mix of jealousy and awe as sanguine as the rising screams. *Howls* of pain. Sounds barely even recognizable as human.

Sounds that bred in Nick a fresh wave of jealousy.

"Hey!" Nick called to the leather-clad figure straddling a felled goon and quietly burning him alive from the inside out.

"Kinda busy here, Kingswood," Claire called back.

"Do you see that shit happening over there?" Nick gestured in Moira and Julian's direction with a hand bathed in a cocktail of blood and gore. "Fifteen fucking people. They just took out fifteen fucking people in less than thirty seconds."

"You're counting?"

"*Counting*? Fuck no." Counting implied purposeful effort. Could he help it if he was a businessman whose mind naturally apprehended numbers? Numbers like thirteen. Which just so happened to be how many people whose souls he'd personally freed up for Killian Bane to collect. "I was just thinking maybe you and I could—you know. That is, combining our powers might be an efficient way to address the challenge at hand."

"I'm going to say they have a pretty good handle on this." Claire stood, dusting ashes from her hands as she surveyed the damage. Heaps of broken bodies were piled on the sidewalks, spilling down into the streets. Smoke swiveled up from the eyes and ears of corpses who had gained an appreciation for the fire witch's talents firsthand. "Where's Reverend Blanding?" she asked.

"Son of a bitch!" Nick scanned the wreckage, searching for the telltale flash of white. Nothing. He had gone. Probably sometime while Moira was groping

Pestilence's chest, and it was all Nick could do not to wade through the miasma and end them both.

They were winding down now. Moving together over the field of the dead and dying like a crop duster, giving a little extra blast to those still twitching.

For a man who didn't count, Nick could recall many times when he and Julian had sifted through fields of devastation far larger than what now lay at their feet. In all that time, he had never before seen Julian look as he looked now.

Not because of what he wore on his body, but because of what he wore on his face.

Relief.

Nick understood something in that moment. A truth slipped through the sudden alignment of many windows in the long years of his experience.

For the first time in his entire existence, Julian Roarke had not been required to touch the person he would kill.

The same opportunity Nick longed for and relished with undisguised avarice, Julian had been forced to by Lucy. None of them had been given the choice as to their purpose, but Julian had been robbed of even the manner in which he could carry out his calling.

Until today.

Moira had done this for him. And for a moment, no matter how brief, Pestilence had been freed of his curse.

It was just the sort of kindness that lived within her soul: her essential goodness.

He called his attention to the flickering warmth this thought created in his chest. Cupped his awareness around it as one would cup a candle flame from the wind. If he could hang onto this feeling, protect it from the buffeting of the darker side of his nature, he might just survive what the rest of the night would bring.

"It's about that time," Claire announced, picking her

way toward Moira and Julian. "Do you think *you know who* was watching this?"

"I sure as hell hope so," Moira answered, handing Julian his discarded denim jacket. "If Nick's reaction was anything to go by, watching me and Julian melt those minions together should have just about fried her wires for good."

"*My* reaction?" Nick crossed his arms across a shirt stiff with drying blood. "I was perfectly calm. In control of my faculties the entire time."

"Is that man's leg protruding from his own anus?" Julian inquired, buttoning the jacket against the evening chill rolling in from the Puget Sound.

"He must have fallen on it. Happens all the time on the battlefield," Nick said. It was patent bullshit and they all knew it, but Dru wasn't around to call him on it and none of the others was inclined to argue those kinds of gritty details.

"I guess we better scoot toward the castle," Moira suggested. "We need a little extra time to get cleaned up before show time." She and Claire walked ahead toward the earth witch's borrowed economy go-cart.

Nick couldn't bring himself to bestow the distinction of *car* to anything with fewer than eight cylinders.

"Nicholas," Julian said, slowing his gait to buy them some privacy. "May I ask you something?"

"Sorry," Nick replied. "I'm fresh out of sheep and I know for a fact you don't have a sister."

Julian, master of diplomacy, bestowed a perfectly-seasoned courtesy chuckle. "Actually, I wanted to ask you something about Moira."

Nick stoked the little flame in his chest, banking its power. "I'm counting on you not to ask me anything that will make me want to kill you. Again."

"When she touched me—"

"Too late."

"Allow me to rephrase." Julian's hands folded together behind his back, the gesture completely at odds with his current attire. "You have touched her more—intimately—than anyone. Have you found her capability to heal communicable in that fashion?"

"You mean, can she heal people just by touching them?"

"Precisely."

Deep breaths, Nick. Deep breaths. "The way I understand it, she heals people by fucking them."

"Oh." Julian, crestfallen, considered the pointy toes of his ostrich skin boots.

"Why?" Nick asked.

"Nothing. It's nothing."

But Nick already knew what his brother had been getting at. He paid at least that much attention in his conversations with Julian, ever the scientist and student of his own condition.

Pestilence was contagious.

Both infected and infecting in nature. If Aerin could provide him with a portion of her sensitivity to emotional signatures, could Moira not impart to him the ability to heal? To undo a measure of the desolation he wrought?

Nick, whose own nature inclined him toward an understanding of unconquerable desire, felt the all-consuming need rolling off Julian in thunderous waves.

It was a shame Nick would have to burn the entire world to the ground before he could allow Moira to heal Pestilence in that way.

That was the trouble with natures.

One could occasionally outrun them, but never escape them.

"Let's get back to the castle." Nick beeped open the Ferrari's doors with a remote key fob. "I need time to practice not killing you. And my suit is a fucking mess."

MORA

❧ I 2 ❧

"I say, I feel myself a sudden urge to wrassle a gator and also shuck some crawfish."

Moira fought the urge to giggle, not only because giggling when you were wearing nothing but a boob tube and panties made all kinds of jiggling not only possible, but inevitable, but also on account of the icy earnestness in Julian Roarke's eyes.

Goddess bless him, he was trying.

"Oh, yeah," Moira agreed a touch too enthusiastically. "That was real good. Only..."

"Only what?" Julian rolled onto his side, facing her beneath the downy warmth of the duvet. And Moira had no doubt that a duvet it was, because in Julian's suite of rooms in Manresa Castle, only a duvet would do.

Dark wood, plush carpets, endless bookshelves, and more reading lamps than most people had underbritches back home.

He was bare chested, though Moira was pert near certain he was wearing *something* on his lower half. They sort of kept their backs to each other as they had stripped down just enough to be convincingly bollocky bare-assed when Lucy/Aerin busted her way in about ten minutes from now while still minimizing physical contact.

"Only, no one really wrassles gators any more down in Stumps. Not since the local game warden caught Cleevis McQuee doing much more than wrasslin' one out behind the Hoodoo Shack one night and they outlawed recreational wrasslin' for the whole parish."

They both looked up when a dull thump on the other side of the closet door rattled a painting on the wall. Claire and Dru were already in position.

Which position that might be at the moment, Moira couldn't hazard a guess.

Lord knew she wouldn't blame her sister one lick for doing a little recreational wrasslin' of her own after being trapped in such small space with the likes of Drustan Geddes.

Truth to tell, that had been part of the reason she insisted that they lie in wait in the closet together anyway. Tommy wasn't getting any fresher, and Moira didn't like the way she caught him eyeing the parts of her that would make for the best eating.

"I suppose that makes sense," Julian allowed, leaning on his elbow. The bed shook gently with his laughter, which somehow managed to be both dignified and charming. "You are refreshing, Moira de Moray."

"So is this," Moira said, lifting her wine glass from the adjacent nightstand and taking a sip. "What did you say it was?"

"Chateau d'Yquem. From the Girondes region in Bordeaux. One of my favorites."

"Well, it's a far cry from the 'shine. Doesn't make my nose run or my eyes bleed or anything." She took a larger swig than was perhaps customary for one savoring a vintage that probably cost more than Moira's first car. "Time's running low. Should we practice?"

It was a good thing Julian hadn't been sipping at his

own wine, for Moira was pretty damn certain he would have done a solid spit take. "Practice?"

"Yeah. You don't think Loosey Goosey will be mad enough to hop on out of Aerin if she doesn't really think you were giving me the bone, do you?"

Moira wouldn't have thought it possible, but Julian actually blanched paler still.

"It's all right, sugar. Come on over here."

"Over *where*?" Julian eyed the remaining room between them. "We're already in the same bed."

"I'm not sure what Nick's been telling you, but that ain't all there is to it."

"But—"

"Oh, for the love of lard." Using what remained of the extra strength Nick had gifted her with earlier that day, Moira grabbed Julian by the hips and rolled him on top of her. He was quick to transfer his weight to his hands, making sure his pelvis didn't connect with hers at any angle.

"We could put a Bible between us if you'd prefer," Moira suggested. "Or you could just lighten the hell up and realize that this is no different than when I put my hands on you earlier to get rid of them witch hunters."

Julian vanished from behind his eyes for the space of a few seconds. Their darkening marked his return. "I wanted to thank you for that."

"For what?"

"For what you did today. I can't adequately put into words what it meant to me. Not to have to—"

"Don't mention it." Moira remembered then what it had been like to hold his body to hers. To feel the loneliness seeping from his bones. He had been all angles at first, rusty from disuse and accustomed only to shaping himself around the empty space where his love for Aerin lived and breathed.

With the mutability of her element, Moira had let

herself slide into the void her sister left behind, filling it in, if only for season. Only for the sharing of pain.

"No," he said. "I need to. You see, because of who I am, *what* I am, I felt what it would be like. If I were able to do more than just destroy. Just for a second, through you, I knew how it would feel."

His arms had relaxed as he talked, the weight of his body becoming tangible on her skin in the places where gravity chose to join them. The belly. The thigh. Ankle and foot.

"And how did it feel?" It wasn't sex lowering Moira's voice to its smokier registers, but another kind of longing. The healer in her stirring, turning, rising.

"Exquisite." It was little more than a whisper. The desire in it not for her, Moira knew, but for what she had made him feel.

Julian's dark hair brushed her cheek as his face lowered toward hers.

All at once, Moira could smell his skin, and his lips, the blood in them, and she knew exactly how Julian Roarke would taste with the singular, prickling awareness that came only before a first kiss. The first taste of someone new.

In the last seconds before their lips met, Julian's body went rigid beneath her fingers as his gasp stole what little breath Moira had been able to conjure.

"She's here," he said.

LUCY MOVED DOWN MANRESA'S DARK HALLS AS quietly as the many ghosts who had made it their home. Restless spirits she had pressed into her service with the promise of an afterlife she had no intention of providing.

Still, it had been enough to convince them to spy on the de Moray sisters and Horsemen alike. Even the lovesick Skunk had crumbled at the prospect of a one-way ticket out of Earth's limbo, informing her of what had passed between Nick and Moira in the bathroom. No wonder the little slut couldn't keep her hands off Julian.

She'd received a healthy helping of Conquest's legendary libido.

From her station on the roof of the Palace Hotel, Lucy had watched the spectacle unfold, numb with shock and horror. In all her millennia, she had never witnessed anything so reprehensible. So wantonly and violently unnatural.

Julian Roarke...in *Wranglers*?

Even the memory set Aerin keening from her personal purgatory at a decibel to shame even the most odious banshee.

And the way Moira had plastered herself all over him to exterminate the witch hunters. It shouldn't have been possible. *Wouldn't* have been possible had the soggy skank not inherited Morgana de Moray's wand.

Lucy's hand flashed out, her razor-sharp nails opening long gashes in a dowdy eighteenth-century oil painting as she passed.

Would that it were the water witch's face.

The melancholy chimes from a grandfather clock downstairs tolled a quarter past eight.

Where the fuck *was* everyone?

She'd found the library deserted despite the clear emotional signatures informing her that Nick, Julian, Moira, Claire, and Dru had been there, and recently.

"Hello?" Lucy waited, wishing for the first time in the several weeks that she had access to the hearing capability of her own, immortal body.

At first, she thought she heard an echo but quickly realized she was standing in the middle of a small, carpeted hallway. Also, last time she checked, echoes generally sounded like at least some part of what had been originally said.

This sound hadn't been anything like "hello."

More like the sound someone might make if they were in severe pain.

Splendid!

Lucy sprinted down the hall, visions of medieval torture devices dancing in her head. She froze mid-step, one of Aerin's stilettos hovering above the refurbished carpet.

Julian's suite.

The sounds were coming from Julian's suite.

She pressed her cheek to cool wood faintly scented of some citrusy furniture polish and listened.

Rustling. A thump. Another thump. A gasp.

"Yes, Julian! Yes! Give me that vitamin D, you virulent stud!" Moira's swamp-sludge twang was as unmistakable as it was inimitable.

Lucy jerked back as if slapped, unable to manage the sudden onslaught of Aerin's rage. The force of it sent her staggering backward, stomach lurching, knees weakening as Aerin's body revolted against the heartbreaking, gut-wrenching insult of what her own sister was doing.

Unwelcome tears blurred Lucy's vision and spilled hot down her cheeks. She swallowed the bitter taste of bile.

No. This couldn't happen. This could not be.

Every feeling Lucy had suppressed over the past weeks came surging up from Aerin's pit and she was drowning.

Fear. Misery. Desperation. Self-hatred. Despair.

"Prepare to be infected by my love, Moira de Moray!"

Clutching a nearby tapestry, Lucy clawed her way to her feet. Oh, they would pay for this betrayal. With blood, and bone, and suffering greater than any mortal or immortal had yet experienced in the history of this wretched planet.

Now.

The door broke open under the pressure of Lucy's well-aimed kick. Unfortunately, so did the stiletto heel of Aerin's shoe. Lucy no longer cared.

She limped into the room, hair stuck to her face with sweat and tears, shaking and crazed with the desire for retribution.

Hell had assembled itself around her. Not because she had conjured it, but because the vision unfolding before her eyes was as close to eternal torment as Lucy had ever strayed.

Julian's knuckles paled from the effort of grasping the headboard. The long muscles of his back tensed and slackened in time with lean hips bucking beneath the blanket.

And *her*.

Moira de Moray writhed beneath him, dark hair flooding over the pillowcase in the disheveled eddies and whirls of passion.

A red polished claw raked down Julian's back and disappeared beneath the bedclothes. In the next instant, his head whipped backward, his throat becoming a long, pale arc that Lucy would have liked to rip out with her teeth. His unhinged cry of pleasure was soon joined by Moira's—a shriek that split the very air molecules, freeing the water they held to fall on Lucy's skin in a chilling mist.

So absorbed were they in their shared climax that neither had even noticed her enter the room.

She would *not* be ignored.

Lucy grew beyond the limited container of Aerin's body, marshaling the darkness she had been forced to relinquish while inhabiting a human form. It bled into Aerin's body, sliding between her cells, seducing her innate abilities into a twisted tango with her own.

Wind whipped the bed curtains and made a blizzard of the papers on Julian's desk. Books blew open, their pages piling from one side to the other on the sudden gusts. The locks Lucy had bound into a chignon at the back of her head escaped under the pressure, climbing before her eyes like black cherry flame.

"*Now, Claire!*"

Lucy barely had time to register the closet door flying open before strong hands closed over her biceps, dragging her backward, pinning her to the wall.

Nicholas. And Dru.

Her own curses and promises of retribution were lost, eaten up by the cyclone unleashed within the room.

Moira and Claire chanted over the maelstrom, a wand in the first witch's hand and a book in the second's. Julian stood apart, an expression bearing equal parts hatred and hope on his face.

Tricked.

Lucifer, the mother of lies had been tricked. Betrayed. And by her very own henchmen.

The chamber filled with a silvery light—vile, slippery, loosening Lucy's grasp on Aerin's body, prying her out of every space where she yet held dominion.

She was already sliding from the grip of War and Conquest when a blinding flash of green bloomed large, rendering all present in the hue of a night vision camera.

"Tierra! *No!*" The water witch's scream pierced the swirling maelstrom of color and sound.

And as it is for so many, Killian Bane's face was the last thing Lucy saw before she descended into the swarming dark.

❧ 13 ❧

Moira, Tierra, and Claire knelt over Aerin's prone form, the four of them held by a strange, sacred silence.

Aerin was alive, but there was no telling how long Moira or Claire would be if Julian continued to pace and sigh in such close proximity.

Nick and Dru had been kind enough to escort him to the library in search of a drink after he'd been the accidental progenitor of a bacterium that ate through all the bed curtains and half the area rug.

Tierra twisted the strand of amber beads at her throat. "Will she be okay?"

"Don't know yet." Moira looked up from Aerin's face to find Tierra's green eyes darkened by worry. "The exorcism spell Claire and I were casting was in the *two witches, one wand* section of Grim. The extra power might have cooked her kooky."

"Didn't you ever watch Ghostbusters growing up?" Claire chided. "*Never* cross the streams."

"I'm sorry, okay?" Unshed tears pooled in Tierra's lower lids. "When I saw you two casting a spell at Lucy—"

"At Lucy?" Moira asked. "Since when was going blind as Dr. Lector a side effect of being knocked up?"

"But I did," Tierra insisted. "I saw Dru and Nick holding *Lucy* down and you two chanting a spell and Lucy writhing and spitting."

"Maybe the *bun*," Claire said, glancing at the gentle swell beneath Tierra's flowing peasant dress, "has some kind of x-ray vision that can spot demonic spirits."

"I s'pose that's possible." Moira mopped Aerin's pale brow with a damp cloth. "But then, we wouldn't know what the tadpole's been up to lately on account of you deciding to have yourself a little babymoon with Death."

"That is *not* what happened." The bracelets ringing Tierra's arms gave a fierce little jingle as she folded her arms across her growing bosom. "Killian abducted me. I didn't have a choice."

"Yeah. You look like you've been pure miserable." Truth was that Moira had been delighted to see her sister again. Relieved she had made it back to them safely. But the gladness she felt had quickly been boiled away when she'd observed the healthy, rosy glow of Tierra's cheeks and the beginnings of a bronzy tan on her chest and arms.

It was the kind of look folks always brought back from places where drinks were named after natural disasters and fluffy, white towels appeared in the hands of broad-chested cabana boys.

"You shouldn't have just run off like that without telling us where you were going." Claire said this with the relish of someone who had been on the receiving end of the same admonition from Tierra's lips a time too many. "At the very least, you could have left a note."

"I did!" Tierra sat back on the heels of her sandals, indignant. "I specifically told Jinx to make sure you read it if anything happened to me."

"Have you forgotten you're the only one who can talk to land critters?" Moira asked. "Meeeeaaww sounds just as much like *watch out, I'm fixin' to bend a cat biscuit* as it does *by the way, Momma's gone off to Hell*. What if something had happened to you?"

"Look, I didn't fly all the way back from paradise just to be given the third degree." Tierra pushed herself to her bare feet and propped a hand on her hip. "I don't owe you or anyone else—"

Aerin's torso jerked upward at a ninety-degree angle to her legs, and for one horrifying moment, Moira prepared herself for a projectile stream of something like pea soup. Her sister's gasp sounded exactly like the first breath a drowning man draws after horking up a chestful of water.

"Aerin!" Moira had to stop her hand from bestowing a mighty clap on the back, settling instead for rubbing a circle between her shoulder blades. Another couple ragged breaths, and she seemed to recover the art of working her own lungs.

"Lucy," she croaked. "She—I didn't—I couldn't—"

"We know, darlin'. We know all about it. She's gone now. She can't hurt you no more."

"How do we know?" It was Claire who posed the question, though it had already been scooting around the channels and locks of Moira's mind. "That's just the sort of thing Lucy would say to make us believe that she'd been evicted."

Fortunately, Moira already had a surefire test in mind.

"Come on in, Julian." Maybe it had been their tag-teaming the witch hunters via bio warfare. Maybe it had been the split-second she'd thought she felt a plague of stiffy invading Pestilence's trousers while they were dry-humping—a nice gesture on his part. And a hell of a part it was, she couldn't help but notice.

Whatever the reason, Moira sensed a tenuous connection where there hadn't been before. One defined not by lust or romantic attachment, but a deep, mutual admiration and understanding.

A friend.

Moira had a friend.

A highly infectious friend who she could feel hovering outside the door.

Julian had recovered his shirt, if not all of the polish and poise he usually operated with. He stood in the doorway, Nick and Dru looming behind him like sentinels from another time.

Which, Moira supposed, they were.

Aerin rose to her feet, denuded of their expensive heels by virtue of Lucy's struggle toward the end of her residency.

They approached each other slowly, carefully, the remaining distance between them finally broached by Julian's outstretched hand.

Aerin regarded it for a moment with the suspicion of a wild animal approaching an offered treat.

"You have nothing to fear, Aerin de Moray," Julian promised. "Not anymore."

With the measured progress of growing grass or shifting tides, Aerin slid her palm into Julian's, letting out a little cry when he crushed her into his embrace.

"It's you," he breathed into the top of her head. "It's really you."

Moira's exhale felt like it might never end.

"Don't get too excited," Aerin mumbled into Julian's shirt. "It may be months before I can recover my lady boner after seeing you in shit-kickers and hillbilly haute couture."

"Perfectly understandable, of course." Julian pressed his lips to her hand, then turned it palm-up to kiss her wrist.

"At least a week," Aerin amended, settling for days, then hours by the time he kissed her ear, and everyone quietly excused themselves from the room.

"I need a drink." Dru shuffled toward the stairs.

"Or seven," Claire added, trailing him at a healthy distance.

Moira and Nick waited to hear their footsteps upon the wooden stairs, their silence a contract whose terms they had both understood and accepted long ago.

Then they fell on each other, ravenous.

They worked down the corridor with the stumbling graceless lurching of a creature newly born. Shoving up against walls to maintain their balance rather than turn loose of each other's bodies. Hands diving beneath each other's clothing, mouths fused, tongues spelling unspeakable intentions.

At last, Nick took responsibility for their progress by lifting Moira off her feet, scissoring her legs around his waist so he could carry her the last few yards to his room.

And then they were falling backward onto the bed, the remaining layers between them peeled away in the work of seconds.

Nick stilled inside her.

For an absurd moment, Moira thought the force of their passion had pricked Nick's eyes with pinpoints of blood-red and cast a crimson pall of lust across his languid features.

But his gaze remained fixed on the window. Frozen. Hypnotized for reasons that had nothing to do with their joining.

She looked, too.

The Puget Sound was a landscape painted in blood.

All of it hemorrhaged from the great scarlet wound of the swollen moon dipping low above the waves.

"And the moon became as blood." Nick's lips moved in a kind of dreamy recitation. He stared down at her then, his eyes clinging to rubies within their depths. "The sixth Seal has been opened."

CLAIRE

CINDY STARK

❊ 1 ❊

That was the most reckless thing she had ever done, and she would pay for it.

Claire de Moray peeled her leather jacket from her shoulders as she fled down the hallway in Manresa Castle, away from the scene of Lucifer's defeat and away from Aerin's and Julian's tender reunion.

But mostly away from Drustan Geddes.

War.

Second Horseman of the Apocalypse, and the man who stirred the smoldering embers inside her with just a look, making her burn with need.

Moira had insisted it was a good plan, and it wasn't like Claire had been completely alone with Dru. But thirty minutes sharing a small closet with the virile Horseman, listening to Moira and Julian pretend to make love in order to lure Lucifer into a trap, had used up every bit of reserve she had to resist him.

Sacrifice, she reminded herself. It was all about the sacrifice to exorcise Lucy from Aerin's body and save the entire world from total destruction. No biggie. Certainly nothing a stiff drink and ice bath couldn't cure, right?

Goddess knew, after the past few weeks, working in close proximity with the Horsemen in an effort to rescue her sister, Claire's reserves had already been lagging like a tired horse. With her sense of sight diminished in the darkened closet, other senses had dominated.

Dru's seductive scent of gunpowder and leather had teased her. She could practically taste the licorice on his lips, reminding her of the first time he'd seduced her. The illusion of them together had been incredible. *Just one touch*, her body had begged. As it was, she had trouble sleeping, remembering his fingers caressing her skin and the whisper of his voice in her ear...although that could actually be him sneaking into her thoughts, the bastard.

How would she ever forget him if she couldn't get him out of her head or her heart?

Should she bother to try?

She had succeeded in hog-tying her urges and keeping her hands to herself, but by the time she and Dru had exploded from the tiny enclosure to battle the Devil and evict her from Aerin, Claire's resolve had weakened and left her thirsting dearly for something she shouldn't want.

Hence her hasty escape.

"Claire."

Dru growled her name from behind, ensnaring her in his powerful trap. She stopped and glanced over her shoulder. His massive form filled the narrow hallway as he stalked toward her like a predator narrowing in on his prey. An olive-green cotton tee clung to his broad chest, emphasizing chiseled muscles honed from years of wielding a mighty sword, the same weapon that had permanently left open a portal for him to communicate with her heart.

If she had only known the hidden options that came along with his stolen sword.

As Dru approached, unwelcome excitement and fearful nerves burst over her like summertime fireworks. If she'd thought she could escape him, she would have run. As it was, she feared this slayer would hunt her until the end of days.

Which, in reality, might not be that long if they kept opening the Seven Seals of the Apocalypse like they were endless birthday presents.

Before Dru could reach her, fear won out, and she turned and hurried for the stairwell. Not one to be cowardly, she hated that she caved to her baser fears. She feared nothing. Not death for it would end the planet's curse and save her family. Not pain. She'd experienced enough of that in her lifetime to know it couldn't last forever.

But she feared War.

Not because he would hurt her. But because he might try to love her.

She never reached the first step. Strong fingers encircled her arm, stopping her as effectively as if he'd knocked her flat.

She whirled around, prepared to deliver another venomous criticism that might continue to keep Dru at bay. Words seemed to be her only protection against the powerful warrior. He had sporadic access to her thoughts, but her words seemed to make him doubt.

Something in his eyes stopped her. "We need to talk."

No. Allowing him near her would cost her the battle. He expected a civilized conversation, and that would undo her. The connection wrought by forces far older and more powerful than her already allowed him too much insight into her thoughts.

"I need a drink," she said instead of addressing his statement. The fierce encounter with Lucy had drawn far more from her than expected for such a simple spell.

"I'm buying," Dru responded, not realizing her excursion into the lounge was an excuse to leave him. He slid his hand down her arm and entwined their fingers as they descended the stairs.

At the bottom, she stopped, fueled by frustration, and faced him. With a quick jerk, she broke his grip on her. "I don't need you to hold my hand or buy me a drink. In fact, I don't need or want anything from a man like you. Just because my sisters have lost their ever-loving minds and hooked up with your brothers, doesn't mean I will. Got it?"

The momentary silence sucked the air from the room like an atomic bomb.

Dru personified the image of an epic warrior. Proud and arrogant. Massive chest and thighs. Arms that could crush boulders. No doubt many had paid homage to the gloriously built machine of a man born only to fight legions of battles upon which many had sacrificed their lives in the name of God and honor. She would not follow in their foolish footsteps.

He narrowed his gaze. "Don't lie. The closet damn near incinerated trying to contain what's between us." The timbre of his words vibrated her very existence.

Exploring what had blossomed like a fireball between them would never happen. First, she owed her loyalty to Tommy. He might only be a shell of his previous self, but she was the one who had taken his life, and she couldn't destroy him again.

"Fuck Tommy," War growled in a low voice.

She jerked in response to him invading her thoughts. "Stop that," she hissed, mentally burning any emotional ties she could locate. The more time she spent near him, the more intertwined they seemed to become.

"I've noticed it, too." His eyes glittered with triumph.

"No." She shook her head. "You can't read every thought I have." Their connections had been scattered at best until recently, sometimes feeling as though he was in the same house, other times only a distant echo.

"I can read you right now." He moved a step closer, forcing her to retreat, which only served to press her back against the gold-papered walls. "It seems the close proximity in Julian's room has allowed me full access to your every thought and emotion."

"Let me go." She shoved her palms against his chest, but he didn't budge.

"Don't be afraid, Claire."

Panic and vulnerability clashed inside her, and she desperately tried to shut down her thoughts.

Tenderness on the warrior's face nearly undid her. "You can trust me."

"No, I can't. I don't want to. I want you out of my head and out of my heart—"

His eyes smoldered in victory, drawing her fears to the very topic she wished to hide from him. If she let Dru in, she'd damage him with her love like she'd done with Tommy. Destroying Dru would kill her.

"You can't hurt me." He lifted a hand to her cheek. "There's nothing physical you can do that I can't recover from. I've been alive for thousands of years, Claire, waiting for you, waiting for this moment in my life. I've kissed you once, and it wasn't nearly enough."

"A kiss is one thing." Her thoughts spun as she tried to comprehend. "I share a power that's strong enough to end this world. How do you know I can't hurt you?"

"Doesn't matter either way. If I'm going to go, then I'll die knowing what it's like to be inside you first."

His words forged a shiver inside her that wouldn't stop.

He wrapped a powerful arm around her and tugged her hard against him, the impact stealing her breath. The moment their bodies touched, hers molded to his as though two parts of a long-lost artifact had been brought together. His midnight gaze bored into her, daring her to argue further. "We've been apart for too long."

He gave her a fraction of a second to protest, but her words had deserted her like the most cowardly traitors.

With his free hand, he anchored her face between his fingers and lowered his lips to hers.

Wild sparks flew left and right like a fierce clash of swords. Formidable energy surged through her veins and branched out in every direction like lightning searching for earth until each cell inside her burned with a power that could consume the masses. Dru's touch resurrected the traces of his influence that had lingered in her blood since she'd possessed his sword, sleeping soldiers awakening to battle for their master's great cause.

Her focus narrowed to the feel of his delicious, commanding mouth on hers, to the softness of his lips and the power that pulsed beneath. Each kiss, each slide of his tongue against hers seared into her memory with stunning clarity. She gripped his shirt as her heartbeat fell into line with his, the synchronicity sweeter than anything she knew.

Goddess help her.

When Claire melted against him, defeated in her battle against desire, Dru broke the kiss. Fierce intensity flooded her with a lucidity she'd never experienced. Much like a high on an as-yet undiscovered super drug.

She expected him to revel in his victory, but he seemed as surprised as she did by the force of their bond. A low growl rumbled in his throat, and hot testosterone pulsed in the air around him. "Don't deny this, Claire. Don't deny me. I can see the desire burning in your eyes."

She blinked rapidly in an attempt to erase what he might have seen.

"Come back to my room with me, or we'll continue

this right here." He delivered his ultimatum with a confidence born from years of triumphs.

If she faltered, she would not only break her vow to Tommy, she'd likely lose herself as well. She gulped in breaths of air as she twisted from his grip. "You might weaken me with a kiss, but you'll never completely conquer me." Instead of heading toward the stairs like he would have expected after his command, she strode toward the lounge.

Inside, she was surprised to find the young butler, who had welcomed her into the house the first time she'd visited, tending bar. A handful of the groundskeepers and hotel staff ate their dinner at the cozy tables. Manresa was certainly large enough to house the Horsemen and many others if they so chose, but she was surprised any had decided to stick around with the big, bad men of the Apocalypse storming about the castle.

Then again, where did one go when his hometown collapsed around him? And she knew the Horsemen would pay well to keep the place in working order and indulge in their creature comforts. After all the years walking the earth, luxury was theirs for the asking if they wanted it.

Claire claimed a barstool covered in the softest red velvet, anchored her elbows on the well-worn bar, and willed her ragged breaths to return to normal. "Fireball whiskey," she called to the butler when he glanced her way.

A tingling awareness crept across the back of her neck like a lover's seductive kiss. *Dru....* Always the same signature sensation when he was near.

She steeled her spine and focused on the numerous bottles sheltered behind the bar, not willing to give him the gratification of knowing how he affected her.

A satisfied chuckle echoed from somewhere behind her. The seductive consciousness moved from her neck to caress her shoulders. *Goddess-dammit*. Finding a spell to block him from her thoughts would be the first thing she did in the morning.

No, you won't.... His thoughts invaded her mind.

Her eyelids fluttered closed as delicious unseen fingers massaged tension from her body. *It's not real*, she reminded herself. Dru's capacity to make it seem as though he touched her had fooled her in the past, but now that she carried a piece of him inside her, she could distinguish the difference between a lovely illusion and the incredibly powerful seduction of the man in the flesh.

It's real. Let me show you how real.

She stiffened when his imaginary touch moved to her breasts, cupping her. Strong thumbs crested her hardened nipples. She gripped the bar and gasped at the delicious sensations.

"Ma'am?"

Claire flicked her eyes open and found herself staring into the young red-headed butler's blue eyes. "I'm sorry. What?"

He dropped his gaze to her breasts as he placed her drink on the bar. Lust lurked in the shadows of his expression. "You were...." He cleared his throat. "If you need some company, I could help you with..."

"The lady doesn't need help from anyone but me." Dru's threatening reply came from somewhere beyond her shoulder, sending the butler stumbling backward.

"Sorry, sir. I didn't mean...please forgive me."

Dru didn't respond, but Claire could well imagine the look he fired at the innocent man.

"I'll just..." He quickly retreated to the other end of the bar where he wiped down the gleaming wood in front of him, constantly flicking nervous looks in her direction. A Middle-Eastern man dressed in a traditional brown and gray Moroccan *djellaba* came up next to him. The older man with a bushy salt-and-pepper moustache whispered something in his ear as though counseling him.

The butler nodded to the man in understanding and didn't look her way once after that.

Claire gripped her glass and swiveled on her seat, her knees bumping Dru's thighs as she came face-to-face with War. "*Leave me alone.*"

He shook his head in slow succession. "You know I can't do that."

By slow degrees, she became aware that, though few in number, each man in the room watched her. She narrowed her eyes in suspicion. "What did you do?" She couldn't know for certain if they all really stared or if he'd conjured another illusion. Her clarity only came where Dru's thoughts and body were concerned.

"It's not me. It's you. You've given every guy in here a hard on. They sense the unfulfilled need pulsing inside you for me." He grinned wickedly. "It's only going to get worse if you don't address it."

Anger flared. He'd done this to her, made her a spectacle to everyone in the room. "Fine. I'll go home and fuck Tommy."

"*The hell you will.*" His voice boomed and rattled the glasses hanging above the bar.

She gritted her teeth as a slender man with short blond hair stood and gawked at her with a lusty gaze. A portly man clad in dirty overalls did the same. She had to wonder for a moment if they would turn into fucking zombies.

"Don't you think about going for her," the hefty man warned and blocked the slender man's path. "She's going to be all mine."

"Damn you," she whispered to Dru.

"If you weren't so damn hot." He grinned.

"I hate you." One of these days, she'd show him her prized Indian bowie knife. He'd soon learn he couldn't always manipulate her.

His snort fanned her irritation. "Grab your drink, and let's take a stroll around the grounds before you drive these men insane."

He left her no choice, but she still wouldn't comply like a lowly soldier. Instead of following his direction, she lifted her shot, downed it, and slammed the glass on the bar. With annoyance threatening to explode like a match hovering over gasoline, she pushed past him and headed out of the room, just as the portly man threw the first punch at her would-be slender suitor.

The moment she exited the building, her lungs deflated in shock. She stumbled and grabbed for a nearby column to steady herself as a fearsome and wild sight exploded on the horizon before her.

"Dear Goddess," she whispered as she drew shaking fingertips to her mouth.

❧ 2 ❦

Dru, obviously not expecting Claire to stop so suddenly, slammed into her with the force of a warhorse. She grappled for purchase even as he snatched her with a strong arm to keep her from tumbling down the stairs.

"Oh...*fuck*." His words rolled like a carpet of devastation. "I've seen some bad shit in my life, but this is...eschatological."

The scarlet moon hovered over the Puget Sound and bled into the water, mortally wounded and leaving the once-picturesque Port Townsend cast in an eerie red glow. If Claire had wondered if the end of times was upon them, she could no longer doubt its untimely arrival. An unwelcome tingle scampered beneath the surface of her skin, as though something buried deep had been awakened by the ominous manifestation. As though subconsciously she'd been waiting for this.

Cold fear drained through her like embalming fluid. The innumerable hurricanes, earthquakes, and tornados were bad. Random murders, over-zealous ghosts and freakish zombies were bad. But this was downright scary as shit.

She gripped Dru's hand. "What's happening?"

"The spell you and your sisters cast in Julian's room must have opened another fucking Seal."

She recoiled from the accusation hurled at her.

"No." Her voice shook as she answered. "We couldn't have. Only three of us performed the spell, not four. It was supposed to only be Moira and me in order to keep things under control, but Tierra showed. Still, Aerin was out of commission."

He stared across the grounds toward the Sound, clenching the muscles in his chiseled jaw. "If the spell carried enough energy to boot Lucy from Aerin's body, then who knows what kind of bad mojo came from what you did. Did you and Moira consider that before you charged ahead? Many good armies have been defeated by lack of forethought by their leaders."

She gripped the fear that coiled wildly through her, trying to control it before it brought her to her knees. Hell. Maybe that's what she needed to do. Fall to her knees and beg the Goddess for mercy.

Dru turned her to face him, and the sight of his eyes drilled into her like a thousand needles. "Are you sure Aerin didn't help, Claire? She was inside, fighting to get out. She could have."

"I don't know." She could scarcely believe the world hovered on the brink of complete annihilation, and it was all their fault. Again. "We never wanted this to happen. You have to believe that."

"What you *wanted* doesn't mean a damn thing when you can't control what you're doing. Every action has an equal, opposite reaction. It's fucking physics, Claire. Now can you understand why I originally took your power? I couldn't kill you, but I could find no other way to prevent the end of mankind."

His words devastated her, smothering the fire inside her until she could barely breathe. He was angry and rightfully so. Up until this point, she wasn't sure if she'd taken the Apocalypse seriously. Yes, bad shit had happened, and it had frightened her and her sisters, but there had still been Seals between them and the end of times.

Now they had only one. One Seal. Who knew how fragile it was? The whole fucking thing was a time bomb waiting to detonate. "We're not trying to end the world, Dru. How can loving and protecting each other bring about such desolation?"

"The four of you aren't powerful enough to stop a prophecy."

He was right. Utterly and devastatingly right. She couldn't continue to play with literal fire when she had no idea what the hell she was doing. There was a solution though. "Kill me, Dru. Carry out the command you were given. I was never meant to be with my sisters. Never meant to be with you."

Dru cursed beneath his breath. "Don't get all dramatic on me." He pulled her against his chest, and she accepted the solace he offered. "Stop counting bodies before the war is over. We still have a chance."

"I only ever wanted a family, a place to belong. Goddess finally granted it, but she's cast our happiness with a plague." She lifted her gaze until his dark eyes met hers. Intense shivers cascaded over her like acid rain leaving her cold inside. "What can we do? I don't want to hurt my sisters, don't want to bring about their or anyone else's destruction. We have to take this seriously."

"Okay, then. There is another solution beyond snuffing out one of you."

She lifted her brows in hope. She would do anything.

"Never cast another spell with any of your sisters. Intentional or accidental. Scatter across the globe and never see each other again."

He may as well have handed her a death sentence.

"Goddess help us." Tierra's grave tone reached out from the lawn below them.

Claire jerked her head toward her sister's voice, surprised to find that Tierra and Bane had joined them. Death wrapped his arms about Tierra in a protective gesture. Tierra had folded hers across her expanded stomach, guarding the tiny treasure who grew inside.

"Tierra," she whispered and pushed from Dru as Tierra broke free from Bane. Claire opened her arms to her sister, and Tierra accepted her embrace, squeezing her as though it might be for the last time.

"This is my fault," Tierra said as her horrified gaze shifted to the havoc they'd wrought. "I should have stayed away. But I'd been gone so long, and I sensed you needed my help. I should have trusted you and Moira to handle this. I forget you're not the same women who showed up on my doorsteps all those months ago. I'm so sorry."

Had it only been months? It seemed as though years had passed since she had climbed from the plane after traveling from Bali. "Don't blame yourself, Tierra. It's done. None of us could have known. For all we know, Moira and I might have caused the same without your help. We've been dabbling with things we shouldn't."

"I knew what would happen." A woman's scratchy voice tumbled down from above like marbles of hail on bare skin.

Claire nearly fell back as she tilted her head skyward, looking for the mother of all evil.

"You've done this. All of you." Lucy leaned over the rooftop balcony above them, her features as solemn as a pallbearer. Her once-styled blond hair hung limp about her shoulders, her perfect skin now cast with the grayish-tinge of the dead. Apparently, occupying another body took its toll. "You've brought damnation upon mankind. I've tried to help you. Tried to stop all of you, and *look what you've done.*"

"You!" Tierra thrust a bejeweled finger at the Devil but failed to finish her sentence. Death held her tightly to him, as though afraid of what might happen if he let go.

War had no such reservations. He released Claire's hand and faced upward. "You can blame no one but yourself, Lucifer. You want eternal power, and you're willing to sacrifice everything to get it. If we're going to save this fucking world, you're the one who needs to be stopped."

Her shrill laugh split the fearsome night. "You can't kill me, Dru. *I own you.*"

"Do you now?" He surveyed the stone ledge above him. "Or are you weakened because of what you've done to Aerin? I'm going to guess the latter."

The confidence on her weary face flickered. For a long moment, no one moved. Then Lucy bolted away from the edge. Dru jumped and grabbed hold of the stone ledge and propelled himself up onto the balcony. His muscles bulged as he ripped his weapon from an unseen sheath and pulled out his immortal sword that had sent many souls to Death.

The swift, powerful act blasted sexual heat through Claire. As much as she wanted to hate Dru, the ties that bound her to him were unbreakable. Might be the traces of his sword left in her system or the fact that he'd once housed her Fire.

"How did he do that?" Claire mumbled beneath her breath. If she could manage to pull her knives from thin air...

He flashed a darkened gaze toward her, striking quick as lightning. *I'll show you later,* his promise echoed in her mind. *When I have you in my bed.*

Dru bellowed a war cry that defied the ages and charged after the Devil.

Claire eyed Tierra but didn't move. Tierra did the

same, her green-eyed gaze swishing between Claire and Bane.

"Shouldn't you go after him?" Tierra asked her Horseman.

Death puffed out his chest. "And leave you and the baby vulnerable? No."

"How many times do I have to tell you? Stop making decisions for me and my baby."

"*Our* baby."

Anger flared in Tierra's expression, and she growled her frustration. "I don't need you to babysit me. Don't need you to steal me away from my family. In fact, I don't need you at all. You're the one who put me in this damn situation in the first place." She fisted her hands and propped them on her hips.

Claire slid her gaze toward Bane to watch his reaction. She thought for sure he'd come back with a verbally defeating blow. Instead, he wrapped his arm about Tierra's shoulders.

"You don't mean that."

"Yes, I do," she ground between clenched teeth. "If I had Dru's sword, I'd slice off those wings and punish you for good."

Death actually looked affronted.

"You want to do some good?" Tierra continued. "Then stop this madness. Use your power to save the world so our child isn't born into this Goddess-forsaken mess."

Tension tight enough to pluck stretched between them for several long moments. Then Bane nodded. "I'll do this for you, Tierra. For you and our child."

His nostrils flared as he glanced at Claire, and she pondered the phrase "peaceful death". There would be no peace when this massive man came to claim you.

"Take her home, Claire," he said. "Double...*fuck*, quadruple your wards. I'll be back soon."

Pride flickered across Tierra's face, but she remained silent.

"I'll take care of her and the wee one," Claire promised.

Death cast one more longing look toward Tierra and then spread his massive wings. Claire's hair fluttered against her cheek as he disappeared into the hellish sky.

"Think they'll be okay?" Tierra twisted the bangles on her wrist as she stared at the space he'd just occupied.

"I thought you were pissed at him." Though Claire knew better than to dismiss the love her sister and Death had for each other. Tierra could deny it all she wanted, but Claire was an expert on fire in the veins. Those two definitely had it.

"Just because I'm mad, doesn't mean I want him to get hurt. It's true nothing can kill him." She paused to swallow. "But he can feel pain. They all can. When I found him locked in Hell... it was horrible, Claire. Truly horrible." Tears welled in her eyes.

Claire took Tierra's hand as desolate fear rang hollow in her heart. "I know. I worry, too." She silently prayed to the Goddess for their safe return.

❄ 3 ❄

A heavy rain pounded against the windows in the kitchen of the cozy Victorian house Claire shared with her sisters. The skies might be the color of her stiletto sword, but at least they weren't bloodshot at the moment. Unfortunately, the scarlet forewarning of the end of times would rise again that evening, just like it had each night for the past week, a looming threat that chased away any remnants of sun and Claire's hope for a happier tomorrow.

The last fragile Seal remained intact, but who knew what slight spell might shatter it and send them all into oblivion. As it was, the world crumbled around them, showing the wear and tear of the last days. At first, she and her sisters had been glued to the TV watching reports on horrific floods and earthquakes, failing countries and pervasive wars, but the devastating news was too much, especially knowing they brought about the unimaginable catastrophes.

Watching a shocked child covered in blood, the sole survivor in her family after a bomb decimated the rest of her kin nearly undid Claire.

But here in the kitchen, closed off from the rest of the messed up world, the simple, mundane task of making breakfast provided a respite Claire desperately needed.

Tierra stirred honey and buckwheat into waffle batter, her usual humming absent. Claire allowed herself a small bittersweet smile as she brewed chai tea. She and her sister had finally agreed upon a morning drink that they both enjoyed.

"Good thing I stored away all that flour in the cellar," Tierra said.

"Not to mention all the vegetables in the garden. No one grows them like you." Food had become a scarcity in their small seaport town.

Tierra beamed at the compliment. She had used her magic to create a community garden where anyone could harvest what they needed since desperate residents had long-since looted the local grocery stores. With Tierra's verdant thumb, no one in their community went hungry, except those few who refused to accept help from a witch. As soon as someone picked a tomato, another would grow in its place.

Witchcraft could create good things, too, and if Claire wasn't mistaken, her powers had increased since the opening of the last Seal.

When the teakettle shrilled, Claire lifted it but quickly returned it to the stove as the floor beneath her rumbled, rattling all the dishes in the cupboard. She slid a worried gaze to Tierra who mirrored her emotions. When it stopped, Tierra poured batter on the griddle and closed the lid as though minor earthquakes were an everyday occurrence in Port Townsend. Which they sort of were now that the sixth Seal had been shattered.

"Breakfast will be ready in a minute," Tierra said a little too brightly, trying to cover her concern. Neither of them had seen or heard from Dru or Killian since they'd taken off in the night after Lucy.

"Great." Claire smiled and tried to focus on the moment and not what hovered on the horizon. She gathered the plates, cups, and silverware they would need.

Happy whistling brought Claire's head around sharply.

Tommy appeared in the doorway of the kitchen clad only in a towel. Her jaw slackened as her eyes bugged in disbelief. The man...er, zombie wouldn't quit.

He lifted suggestive brows and grinned as he walked with a sexy swagger to the stove, lifted the tea kettle, and poured a cup.

Oh...Goddess. She forced her mouth closed and glanced at Tierra, hoping she wouldn't notice anything out of the ordinary. Tierra lifted a hand to her nose and rolled her eyes. Aerin or Moira wouldn't have been so nice.

Claire refocused on the undead love of her life. Make that her previous life.

No...she still loved him. Death didn't kill a love that strong.

"What are you doing?" she asked cautiously, working to keep her gaze from drifting to the towel slung low on his hips. If he had been alive, she would have melted on the spot, but there was something about the sickly color of his skin that didn't quite do it for her.

He stared at her for a long, languishing moment as though to mentally communicate his thoughts. "Getting tea."

She snorted softly. "You know you can't drink that." It would go right through him, and her sisters had long since lost patience with Tommy and the messes he created trying to live a normal life.

"It's for you, love."

Love? Tommy hadn't used that endearment once since she'd accidently brought him back from the dead.

"Come, sit down." He set the cup on the table and pulled out her seat.

She kept her footsteps slow and measured, trying to

piece together his intentions. Instinct warned her something was off, but she couldn't pinpoint what.

He'd caught her off guard once when he'd been possessed by a vengeful ghost. The butcher knife he'd stabbed her with had hurt like a bitch, but he seemed to have all his faculties today. At least as best as he could. With his lack of clothing, the only place he might have a weapon would be under that towel, and what he had there would only shoot blanks.

"Tierra?" Claire pleaded with her eyes for her sister to join her. "You're eating with us, right?"

Tierra shook her head as a repulsed look twisted her features. She placed a hand over her mouth. "Not much of an appetite this morning. I'll take some tea with me. You eat this waffle. I'll grab something later when my stomach settles."

She wanted to label Tierra a coward for deserting her, but the fact was, Tommy's undead odor *had* grown stronger after the breaking of the sixth Seal. Claire had no idea what that meant, but it couldn't be good.

"I'm glad she's gone," Tommy said in low tones as he settled into the seat beside her.

She glanced sideways, wishing she could un-see the vast amount of pale gray skin he exposed. "Where are your clothes?" She used the excuse of buttering her waffle to break the constant visual contact with him.

His once-brilliant eyes had dulled to a matte blue. "Didn't think I'd need them this morning."

The sight of him sometimes offended her, too. She couldn't lie. Definitely did so now, but how could she complain? Seriously, how many people wished they could have one more moment with their loved ones? She was the one who'd killed Tommy, who'd separated his soul from his body in the first place. A bad side effect from a spell she'd cast had used unseen forces to piece him back together again. If he stunk, she was to blame.

"It's kind of chilly in here." Not that he still experienced temperatures. She ate a forkful of waffles and tried to breathe through her mouth to lessen the smell of decay that had slaughtered her appetite, too.

His chuckle spread throughout the room like a newbie trumpet player, grating against her nerves. "Remember when we lived together before? You'd make breakfast while I showered."

"Yes," she said in an effort to encourage him to continue. *He had just showered and still smelled like an old dog's breath.*

He put a cold hand over hers where it rested on the table, and she tensed. She'd wished, *had tried*, to force herself to allow him to touch her, but each time he held her hand or caressed her cheek, she cringed. "You were always ravenous before breakfast, but not for food," he continued.

She closed her eyes understanding the direction of his thoughts. She'd wanted him desperately back then because, instead of food, making love had been her sustenance.

The tables had turned, and he wanted her now.

The few bites of waffle she'd eaten lurched in her stomach at the thought of them having sex. She expelled a large breath and prayed she could maintain her sympathy for him.

"Tommy, that was back then, back before you were a..." She couldn't bring herself to say *corpse*. "Before I killed you."

His smile grew bigger. "I know, Claire, and I think I understand your reluctance now."

But how could he possibly and still retain an expression that bordered on flirtatious and menacing?

"You've been carrying around a shit-load of guilt. That would kill anyone's sex drive." He tightened his hand around hers, and she was again reminded that undead didn't mean loss of physical strength.

He stood. "I forgive you, Claire. You didn't know what you were doing. I know that now, and I forgive you. With that said, there's nothing to stop us from reconnecting." With a glint in his dull eyes, he whipped the towel from his hips.

She choked on a breath.

He stood in all his sinewy, grim splendor with a shitty grin on his face. She fought to keep her gaze averted, but sick curiosity won out. Aw...damn. His once-glorious manhood remained nothing but a shadow of its former self.

"It's now a grower instead of a shower," he reassured her.

She lifted a hand as she pushed back from the table. "I'm sure it is. But I'm not..." Her guts rumbled like a blender without a lid, and she clamped a palm over her midsection as she ran from the room.

"Should I meet you in the bedroom?" he called after her.

❧ 4 ❧

Claire nearly flattened Tierra in her haste to reach the upstairs bathroom. She lifted the toilet lid and heaved nothing but air. "Open the window," she said with a gasp when Tierra appeared beside her.

Her sister complied. "Are you okay?"

"Fine." Claire stayed hunched over the bowl with her hands on her thighs, blessing the cool tendrils of rain-soaked air that rushed in to erase Tommy's scent.

"It's not morning sickness, is it?"

Claire turned her head and burned Tierra with a glare. "Who the hell do you think I've been having sex with?"

She widened her innocent gaze. "Not Tommy, I guess."

Claire's abdominals contracted, threatening to heave once again.

Tierra quickly rattled off a spell that quieted Claire's uneasiness. She shrugged when Claire eyed her with a questioning look. "Something I learned out of necessity." She slid a protective hand across her swollen belly.

"Thank you." Claire inhaled a deep breath and stood.

"Dru, then?" Tierra probed, reigniting her ire.

"No, Tierra. I, unlike the rest of you, have not slept

with a man, alive or otherwise, since I've come to Port Townsend." Unless she wanted to count the fantasy sex Dru had conjured when he'd held her captive. Which was better than any real-life sex she'd had, but... "I've had more important things on my mind instead of creating the Antichrist."

Seconds ticked past as tension overpowered the air. When Tierra spoke, her voice shook with emotion as the earth trembled and rattled the potted fern sitting on the counter. "Don't get all sanctimonious on me. You and the other two are the ones who told me I needed to get laid. *Remember?*"

Tierra volleyed another angry look before she strode out of the room.

Ah, shit. Tierra was helpful one minute and overly-sensitive the next. Damned hormones. Not to mention Claire's words were anything but sisterly. No one wanted her baby to be called Satan's spawn.

As Claire hurried down the stairs after her, Kai joined in, his bushy fox-tail almost tripping her in an effort to be first to the bottom.

"I'm sorry," Claire said as she caught up with Tierra on the porch. The rain had eased to a drizzle, and Claire gulped in the fresh, crisp air. Tierra dropped to a cushioned Adirondack chair as gracefully as a pregnant lady could, her bangles tinkling as she did. Claire folded into the seat next to Tierra, petting Kai's fur as she tried to get her sister to look at her. "I didn't mean what I said about buying into all that Antichrist nonsense. I didn't think and just spoke out of fear."

When Tierra looked up, her eyes were dewy like the lush grass. "How am I not supposed to think about it, Claire? The idea haunts me constantly. When I close my eyes and try to tune into the little being inside me, everything seems fine. But then things happen...odd things, and I worry."

Even as she spoke, the bulge beneath her flowy bohemian blouse rolled hard enough to make Tierra catch her breath.

Claire buried the uneasiness inside her and took Tierra's hand. "Whenever I'm around you and the baby, all I sense is love and goodness. Just because Death is the daddy doesn't mean a thing." That much was true. The baby's actions might be odd, but they didn't seem evil.

Tierra shook her head in distress. "How could I have fallen for him? Of all people? Death is everything I'm not. Yeah, the sex is great, but he's constantly trying to control me, and I'm not having any of that. Plus, he collects *dead* things."

The fact that any of this could be happening blew Claire's mind. Even so, getting all panicky wouldn't help. "It's all in the way you think about it, Tierra. Life is a cycle. There can't be life without death, and really, death is the first stage in the rebirth of living matter. Killian takes what once was and allows it to be again."

Tierra thought on that for a moment, compressing her lips into a thin line. She blinked a few times as she nodded. Her anger at the unknown still burned, but Claire sensed the fiery emotions lessening inside her sister.

"Doesn't mean I forgive him for everything he's done, including impregnating me, binding me to him, *and* whisking me away from all of you. I needed to be here to help with Aerin, to support you."

Claire snorted. "Let's be honest. Death doesn't have the greatest timing in a lot of things." Rarely did he take someone when they were ready to die. Most of the time his work was messy and painful.

"Right?" Bashing her lover did seem to bring Tierra some relief, and Claire was all for that. She couldn't imagine being pregnant...ever...but especially not when times were hard and uncertain. Bringing a child into this disastrous world was insane.

"Men," Claire said with a frustrated sigh. "It's lucky we're the physically weaker sex, or they'd probably all be dead."

Tierra's lips twitched, hinting of a smile, bringing about the lighthearted feeling Claire had experienced earlier before Tommy had walked in all naked and disgusting.

"Speaking of death and men..." Tierra's brief happiness dimmed as she pinned Claire with a pointed look. "I don't want to be rude, but you have to do something about Tommy."

Tierra rubbed knuckles across her nose. "He stinks worse than ever. I think he's rotting...more than he already was...not that I know exactly how these things work. I've tried cleaning spells and cans of air freshener, but nothing takes away the stench." She inhaled a quick breath and continued. "I know you love him, but Moira and Aerin have practically moved into Manresa Castle just to be away from him. This is their home, our home, and, I'm sorry, but Tommy can't stay any longer."

Claire dropped her hands into her face, well aware her boyfriend, such that he was, had become an issue she could no longer ignore. She'd kind of hoped the smell of rotting fish had all been in her head. "I know. I know," she mumbled through her fingers before lifting her head. "I just don't know what to do about it. I made him this way, Tierra. I stole his life from him, and now I'm supposed to kick him to the curb because he's a little stinky?"

Tierra snorted. "He's more than a little smelly. He's killed what appetite I had left. And Goddess knows if you don't do something quick, Killian will use it as an excuse to try to kidnap me again."

"Okay." It had to be done. "Just give me a couple of days to figure it out, okay?"

"Two, Claire. I can't tolerate more than two."

She released a sigh laced with toxic worry and rested

her head against the back of the chair. Sea birds torpedoed each other in the distance, sending feathers flying and bodies dropping as the salt-tinged air swirled around her. Ominous clouds hovered like a battalion catching its second breath, promising a blister of rain before the day ended.

"Do you ever wonder what might have happened if you hadn't sent out that call to us or if one of us had chosen not to come?" She shifted her gaze to Tierra who sat with her eyes shut and her hands resting on her swollen stomach.

A silent moment stretched between them. "I've thought of that so many times and wondered if there's anything we could have done differently that might have kept us from where we are now."

"And? I only ask because I'm feeling awfully selfish for wanting to be with my sisters. Dru said we should separate and never see each other again." The idea was a dagger to her heart. She'd never known love like she had with her sisters, never realized how deep the hole was until they filled it. Asking her to leave was beyond cruel.

"Aunt Justine and the coven did exactly that when we were little. Then I brought you back." She lifted her green eyes to Claire, resurrecting that odd feeling Claire had when she'd first looked into faces so similar to hers. "I couldn't deny what burned inside me any longer, Claire. We couldn't fight something this strong, even if we would have known in advance what might be in store."

That's what she was afraid of. "If what you're saying is true, then at some point, it's fated we'll open that last Seal."

"I pray to the Goddesses that won't happen, but I worry that it's already too late. Do you sense it, Claire? A strengthening of the elements? More fires, storms, and earthquakes? Mankind grows weaker as they increase, and I'm not sure how long until we succumb."

"I don't feel weaker, Tierra. Even now, an inferno roars inside me as though my human shell can barely contain it."

"I thought it was the baby doing that to me."

Claire reached over to clasp her sister's hand, needing the strength and solidarity Tierra offered. "Maybe the change is helping us, too. Maybe it's not about lessening our powers to avoid the last Seal. Maybe it's about strengthening them to help control what happens afterward."

Tierra pondered that for a long moment. "And if you're wrong?"

"Then we're all dead."

❧ 5 ❧

"We can't just sit here, Tierra." Frustration thundered through Claire. "We need to *do* something."

Tierra spread her hands and gripped her head like a basketball. "*But what?* My head already feels like it's going to explode. I agree we've grown stronger, but what the hell do we do with it? I keep thinking the answer is on the tip of my tongue, but I can't spit it out."

Claire was about to respond that she felt the same when a fiery rock the size of a grape whistled through the air like a bullet, hit the house with a thump and landed near their feet, hissing as it made contact with the lush grass.

They both jumped out of their seats, looked at the offending stone, and then at each other. Together, they cautiously made their way from beneath the protection of the porch.

"*What the hell is that?*" Claire peered at the smoldering gray rock that spit and hissed as stray raindrops pelted its uneven surface and evaporated.

Tierra glanced skyward. "I'm not sure. A piece of a comet, maybe? I've heard others in town talking about the sky falling, but I assumed they were kidding."

Claire wished. "I thought we'd warded the yard to

keep out zombies and flying fish. You'd think it would work on missiles comprised of ice, rock and stardust."

"Agreed." Tierra reached for a stick lying on the ground near them. Before she could grasp it, the slender wood rushed toward her hand, and Tierra wrapped her fingers around it.

"That's a neat trick." Claire eyed her warily. "But I thought we agreed not to do magic for now."

Tierra looked at her with rounded eyes. "I didn't do it on purpose. I swear. Maybe it was the baby."

"Oh, sure. Blame everything on the kid." As Claire spoke, a large evergreen a few feet behind Tierra moved, seeming to take a step toward them.

Claire blinked, realizing the shrub hadn't moved, but a camouflaged man had emerged from the greenery with a lethal-looking dagger in his hand. "Tierra, drop!"

Her sister didn't hesitate to curl onto the grass protecting her child.

"The spawn of Satan must die!" The ominous figure lunged for Tierra with his knife outstretched.

Claire thrust her leg into the air. A loud grunt escaped the assassin's throat as Claire's boot connected with his sternum. She shoved again and knocked him on his ass.

"Get inside!" She yelled at Tierra and stalked toward the man as he clutched his chest with one hand and grasped for the knife he'd dropped a few inches from his fingers.

"I can help!" Tierra cried.

"No," she ground out. "Protect the child. I've got this."

Tierra ran for the porch as two more camouflaged men emerged from the bushes. "There are more, Claire!"

"Shit," Claire hissed as she pressed the heel of her boot on the man's wrist, keeping him from reaching the dagger. She needed to take care of this one first.

"Threatening me with a knife is a fatal mistake, asshole. That's like trying to use my best friend against me."

She wrapped her fingers around the hilt of the assassin's knife and found herself on the ground a millisecond later. Dark eyes glittered behind his black ski mask as he gripped her wrist with powerful fingers and straddled her. She struggled to keep her hold on the knife.

"Bastard," she groaned as she wrapped her legs around him and tried to throw him off.

Kai shot out a tremor that knocked the other two to the ground before they reached the porch, but that would only deter them for a bit.

A small rock sailed out of left field and slammed into her attacker's cheek, surprising them both.

"*What the fuck?*" he growled.

Claire twisted her head in time to see Tierra conjure another from the safety of the house and send it sailing toward him. "*More!*" Tierra's tactics just might tip the scales and save her ass.

Her plea increased the frantic struggling between her and the assassin. With amazing strength, he pried the knife from her hand. She gripped his beefy fist with hers as he used the weight of his body to angle the knife downward.

The ground rumbled, but the rolling movement didn't dissuade the bastard on top of her.

In her peripheral vision, Claire caught sight of the next rock flying toward her and focused her energy on it. The brief lapse in attention allowed her assailant to bury his knife into her bicep, but by the time the rock slammed into his head, she'd turned it into a flaming fireball, just like the comet that had landed a few minutes ago.

He screamed in pain as he scrambled off her and struggled to get to his feet. Another hit him in the back, and he tripped.

After that, Tierra's rocks came one after the other. Claire set them all aflame while she struggled to pull the knife from her arm. The second and third assassins clamored to stay upright as they dashed and stumbled toward the gate, screaming as Tierra's fireballs nailed them with precision, but the first attacker seemed determined to complete his mission.

He loomed toward her, now blocking fireballs with his gloved hands.

"You'd better run while you can," Claire said to the man as fear mounted inside her.

Instead of heeding her warning, he pulled another knife from behind him and threw it at her without breaking his stride. The blade sunk deep in her thigh.

"*Mother fucker*," she growled at the pain.

She jerked the knife from her leg, paused for a brief moment to aim with precision and then sent the knife whooshing through the air. It hit him dead in the chest, and he dropped. Hot anger and fear propelled her forward. When she reached him, she jerked the knife free. "*I warned you not to fuck with me.*"

Disbelief radiated from the eyes behind the mask. With a quick tug on the knitted hat, she revealed his face. She couldn't say she recognized him.

Blood covered his mouth and smeared across his cheek. He tried to speak but only sprayed more blood with each breath. A lung was her target, and she'd hit it.

"Your first mistake was trying to hurt my family." She kicked at him as hot tears burned her eyes. "Your second was thinking you could use a knife against me."

Tierra wrapped a hand around Claire's forearm, startling her. "He's one of the witch hunters."

Claire swiped at her tears. "Are you sure?"

The sound of squealing tires infused Claire's blood with more adrenaline, and she turned, ready to attack. Dru barreled from his Hummer and sprinted toward her, jumping the gate instead of slowing to open it.

"What the fuck happened here?" He took in the man lying at Claire's feet and then stared at them, his expression demanding an answer. Before they could respond, Killian swooped in and landed next to Tierra.

"He tried to kill us, to kill the baby." Tierra's voice wobbled. "Claire stopped him."

Dru pierced her with fearsome eyes, and then a smile turned his lips. "That's my girl."

"Fuck," Killian cursed beneath his breath. "I knew I shouldn't have left you."

"I'm not finished yet." Claire separated from the others and strode through the house. She grabbed her motorcycle key from her pocket and kept right on going until she was out the front door. Pulsing fury overrode the throbbing in her arm and leg. She had enough of those bastards and the constant threat they posed to her family. It was time someone did something about them.

She winced as she threw a leg over her motorcycle. With the key in the ignition, she started and gunned the motor. Dru sprinted toward her from the direction of the house and held up his hands as she revved her engine.

"Where do you think you're going?" He scoured her with his gaze and didn't seem too happy with what he saw. "You need to fix your wounds before they get infected."

"To erase the witch hunters once and for all. If you don't move out of my way, I'll run you down, too." She angled the handlebars slightly away from him and threw it into gear. The bike sprayed gravel until she reached solid asphalt. Her wild engine drowned out the sound of Dru calling after her.

Wind whipped fiercely through her hair as she sped down the road. She wasn't sure if she was headed in the right direction, but something compelled her up the sloped streets of Port Townsend. She wound through tree-lined roads and vintage Victorian homes, the compelling feeling inside of her growing stronger. She needed to end this, but first she needed to find the witch hunters. Taking out one or two did no good.

As she reached the gated entrance to Fort Worden State Park, a massive truck veered toward her. She had a split second to decide and chose to lay down her bike in an effort to keep from being flattened.

Dirt and gravel viciously dug into her leathers, as she slid to a stop. Every bone and muscle inside of her screamed bloody hell. With her heart pounding wildly and her breath coming in deep rasps, she scooted from beneath her mangled bike.

"*Son of a bitch.*" She couldn't stand yet and take in the full damage, but from where she sat, the crash had mangled her bike something fierce.

The sound of a loud engine roared, growing ever closer. Claire stuffed a hand in her jacket to ensure she still had the dagger. Dru's signature essence reached out to her just as his menacing Hummer came into view.

His tires screeched as they skidded to a stop. Dru was out the door and by her side before she could blink.

"God dammit, woman. Are trying to get yourself killed?"

"Goddess," she managed.

"What?" His emotions were a mixture of fury and frustration.

She tried to use her hands to sit up straight, but the fall had left her palms torn and bloody. "Goddess, not God."

"Hell Almighty. Who gives a shit right now?" He squatted beside her, assessing her with angry eyes. "Don't ever run out on me like that again. Especially not to do something stupid."

Her heart still thudded like a racehorse in full throttle. "Those bastards have run out of time, and I intend to stop them."

"*Fuck*. You're bleeding everywhere. If this doesn't show you that you shouldn't be reckless, then I'm going to." Before she could argue her case, he scooped her up and strode toward his truck.

For just the briefest moment, she closed her eyes and leaned her head against his chest, connecting with and soaking up her fire that burned inside him.

"That's right. Take all you need."

She wanted to say something snarky, but she needed to gather her energy first.

Dru placed her gently inside his SUV and closed the door. She watched as he strode around the front of his Hummer. She hadn't been inside this vehicle since the first time he had kidnapped her. She'd been so frightened of him back then, so confused by the fire that burned inside her that she didn't understand. Things had certainly changed since then. He still scared her, but not for the same reasons.

Dru jumped into the driver seat with an easy, lithe grace and started the engine.

"I didn't need you to come rescue me. I can take care of myself quite fine.

He slid a sarcastic look in her direction. "Looks like it."

"What about my bike?"

"Pretty sure no one's going to steal it in that condition, and your well-being comes first." He steered his vehicle around a corner, and Claire found herself distracted by the lovely way his triceps flexed. "If that's what it takes to keep you distracted, feast away."

She whisked her gaze to his eyes where she found sexual attraction forever smoldering. "I hate you." She focused her gaze out the front window and purposely focused on flowers growing in people's yards. *Wow, look at all that lavender. I bet it smells heavenly. Such beautiful clumps of purple. I've never seen anything so lovely.*

He chuckled. "Hide it all you want, Claire. I know

you want me." Without missing a beat, he continued. "Is Moira still with Nick?"

"I think so. Why?" She'd fold her arms across her chest if it didn't hurt so damn much to move.

"Good. She should be able to patch you up."

Claire knew she'd get an earful along with Moira's tender care.

"That moment, Claire. That instant when you must have realized you were in danger..." Dru whispered a swift, harsh curse beneath his breath and shook his head. "You scared the shit out of me."

"You sensed it?" she asked cautiously.

"I fucking lived it, and I never want to do that again."

His words touched her heart in a way no one ever had. "*Really?*" He'd been worried?

He shot a look toward her that said her question offended him. "Yes, really. I know you don't believe it, but I care about you, Claire. I didn't ask for this bond between us any more than you did. But there it is. Why do you think I couldn't kill you when that's what I'd been born to do?"

❦ 6 ❦

"What the Sam Hill did you do? Try to eat gravel pie?" Moira shook her head in disapproval as she helped Claire peel the tattered leather jacket from her shoulders. Once Claire and Dru had reached the castle, Claire had insisted she walk inside without assistance, but she had to admit climbing the stairs to Dru's room had been a bitch. He'd forced her to lay on his bed while he'd retrieved Moira.

Claire sucked in a quick breath as air hit her raw and ripped flesh. "Careful," she hissed.

"Careful? Why should I be careful when you weren't? More than once, you've tore off down the street on that two-wheeled corpse-maker of yours and didn't give two figs about those of us worried at home." She narrowed her gaze and leaned closer, two burgundy braids swinging forward over her shoulders as she did. "That don't look like road rash to me."

"It's not." Claire didn't want to talk right now, didn't want to explain. She wanted her wounds covered and a soft pillow to crash on.

Moira paused and placed her hands on her hips. "Make with the explanation, woman."

A disturbance in the air briefly stole Moira's and Dru's gaze as Aerin and Julian pushed into the room.

"What the fuck?" Aerin took in the scene with one quick look. "Who hurt you?"

"Witch hunters," Dru supplied.

Moira lowered her brows in a frown. "You just said she dumped her bike."

"Oh, my God," Aerin said. "You're bleeding."

"Goddess," Claire and Moira corrected in unison.

Aerin rolled her eyes so hard, Claire thought they'd get stuck in the back of her head. "I don't give a flying fuck. Tell me what happened."

Claire dropped her head backward with a sigh. "Listen closely, because I'm only going to say this once. Then I'm going to take some pain meds and escape this nightmare."

Hang in there, baby. Dru's words wrapped around her like a warm hug.

She inhaled a breath and let it ease out of her, reaching for the fire inside that seemed to help with the pain. "Witch hunters showed up this morning and tried to split Tierra's gut like a ripe watermelon."

Moira gasped as Aerin added another, "What the fuck?"

"I tried to fight with knives, but I would have been lost without Tierra tossing rocks that I turned into fireballs."

"I thought we decided we weren't using magic together." Aerin gripped Julian's hand. "That's why I've been staying here and not at home with everyone."

If it wouldn't hurt terribly bad, Claire would have snorted and pointed out she knew exactly why Aerin hadn't left Julian's side.

"Our magic just happened, okay? The world didn't fucking end, and they would have gutted our sister otherwise." Goddess, she hurt.

Dru moved in closer and put a reassuring hand on her calf. She wished he would quit being so tender. It was harder to push him away.

A hint of a smile quirked on his lips, but he didn't look at her.

"After that, Claire jumped on her bike like a reckless warrior and raced after them. But her tactics resulted in her eating *gravel pie*, as Moira said." Dru nailed her with a pointed look.

Claire growled her frustration. "All of you, get out. I'm hurting here, and I don't need a lecture."

"All of you out." Moira shooed at them.

"I'm staying." Aerin folded her arms and moved in closer.

"Fine." Moira directed her commands to Dru and Julian. "You boys get along. I can't work with y'all hanging around here like a bunch of hard-up vultures on a discount meat wagon."

Dru reluctantly followed Julian out into the hall. "I'll be next door," he said with a jerk of his head before he disappeared from sight.

"Help me, Moira," Claire said with a tired sigh as she glanced down at the jagged tear in her jacket that shimmered with blood. "I know I messed up, but could you help me before I bleed out?"

"All right. But don't think I'm goin' to forget." Moira glanced over her shoulder toward the dresser. "Aerin, see if there's any scissors in that first aid kit Dru brought."

Aerin dug through the white plastic box before she pulled out the tiniest pair of scissors Claire had ever seen. "These scissors couldn't cut off a bandage."

"If they can cut at all, they'll do." Moira scooted out of the way. "I want you to slice up the sides of her pants so they're easier to take off."

"No," Claire cried instinctively. "You'll ruin them."

Moira scoffed. "Honey, they have more holes in them right now than a beer can on a fence post. There's no saving them."

Claire pouted. "They were my favorite, and I'll never find a new pair in town."

"Tough shit, lady." Moira smirked.

Aerin seemed to take her own amount of perverted pleasure in sheering up the leg of her pants. Claire squeezed her eyes shut and held her breath as they stripped leather from her battered body. She probably deserved their anger.

"Well, I'll be fucked." Aerin spit out her words. "Those motherfuckers got you twice. I wish they were here right now. We'd slam them with enough magic to knock them on their asses for good."

"We can't keep using magic," Moira reminded her.

"Then how the hell are you going to heal Claire?"

Aerin's question seemed to stump Moira for a moment and then her aquamarine eyes brightened. "If Claire and Tierra used enough powers to send those witch hunters packin', then a tiny bit of mine won't hurt. But you should get gone, and Claire, you have to promise not to help none, okay?"

"Okay," Claire whispered. As it was, she just wanted to fall into the deepest oblivion and never wake up to see the mess they'd made of the world.

Hours later, she woke to roaring flames dancing in the fireplace in her bedroom. Her first question was how long had she been out? Red shadows crept up the wall, letting her know that night and the bloody moon had risen. The second was how the hell did she get home?

She gingerly tested her body and glanced at the wounds she'd sustained earlier in the day. White bandages covered stab wounds, and she slowly peeled them away to find scars that looked weeks old instead of hours. She had succumbed to the heavenly retreat of exceptional painkillers Nick stocked in his room before Moira had finished her work. She'd have to thank them both later.

Slipping into her crimson silk wrapper, she stuffed her toes into red fuzzy slippers and made her way downstairs. Murmured voices and the scent of something warm and spicy drifted from the kitchen.

"Hey," Claire said as she stumbled in.

"Well, if it isn't Asphalt Annie," Moira said.

"Hush," Tierra said. "Don't forget she saved me and the baby today."

Claire eased herself into a chair. "Go ahead and take your shots. I deserve them."

"Dru brought your bike back." Tierra poured something that smelled heavenly into a cup and passed it across the table to her. "I'm glad I saw you before your bike, or I would have freaked out."

"We've been discussing options." Aerin passed the sugar bowl. Tierra had managed to sway all of them into drinking various teas, but Claire hadn't found one yet that she didn't like sweetened. "While you've been sleeping it off, we've come to several conclusions."

"It's like we talked about earlier," Tierra said. "Ever since we opened the sixth Seal, powers have shifted. We seem to be stronger, but so does everything else."

"Some of us have agreed that we might not want to continue to use our powers." Moira shifted a sly glance toward Aerin.

"Yes, I'll admit it. I'm the first one to say fuck that shit. We have every right to use our powers." Aerin poured a shot of whiskey into her coffee. "First of all, you know we won't be able to stop. It's only a matter of time before one of us fucks up and uses a spell on accident. Magic is our power. We needed to protect ourselves. Who's to say we should try to stop the Apocalypse? Maybe we should embrace what's to come. Maybe we're going to be the goddesses of the new world."

Tierra inhaled a sharp breath and covered her mouth. "That's blasphemous," she whispered from behind her hand. "Don't let Aunt Justine hear you say such things."

Aerin rolled her eyes. "You're all a bunch of pansy-asses. You'd be dead in a day in the corporate world." She rested her forearms on the table and leaned forward. "Can you imagine the massacre that would've happened today if Claire and Tierra hadn't used their magic?"

"She's right." Tierra covered her belly as she shifted careful eyes toward Claire. "Something else I should point out. I don't know how I could have forgotten this, but remember when I was in the Standing Stones and I spoke to our mother? She told me then we must always stick together, be as one. Dru's idea of scattering us across the globe is out of the question."

Moira cleared her throat. "Also, I discovered a section in Grim that tells us to use what's rightfully ours and not be afraid of the future. If that wasn't directed toward this moment in time, then I'll be a frog's plum sack."

Their words shifted inside Claire's mind like blowing sands in the Syrian Desert and finally settled into place. "You don't need to convince me. I don't like the idea of a battle because people get hurt. In fact, scares the hell out of me, but that doesn't mean I'll back away. I have faith that we'll find a way to make this okay."

Her sisters nodded in unison. "Except maybe we shouldn't go all hog-ass wild with it," Moira said.

"Agreed," Tierra said quickly.

Aerin scoffed. "We can't be afraid of this, and we can't ignore our magic. I have a theory on how the witch hunters accessed the property today. If our magic is stronger, and the spells that are protecting our house are weak-ass shit that we conjured in the first days, it's no wonder we're being barraged by comets and attacked by assassins. Instead of running and hiding, we need to fix it."

"What exactly do you propose then?" Claire asked as the hairs on her arms rose in warning. What Aerin said made sense. They needed to secure their home, or their world would end first. If they didn't have the baby to worry about, it might have been a different story, but that innocent child needed the best from all of them.

"As it so happens, I've also been studying Grim." Aerin pointed to the ancient tome resting in the center of the table. "End of Days," she said clearly to Grim.

The book covered with dried human skin wiggled and then flipped open, an unseen hand whisking through the pages until it came to a dead stop.

Aerin grinned at them all. "Like most people I deal with, I've created a mutually beneficial relationship, so he gives me what I want."

Moira lifted a perfectly arched brow. "Grim, show me the spell on how to make cheese from a plain ol' glass of milk."

The book fluttered again, and sure enough, there was actually a spell for cheese.

"What?" Moira said looking at all of them. "When the moon turns as red as a bull's pecker, a girl needs her comfort foods." She shifted in her seat. "My point is, Grim don't have an ass to kiss anyhow. You just have to ask nice."

Claire eyed the wise tome, wanting to ask about spells that would seal off her thoughts from Dru, but she'd have to wait until she was alone with the book. "Okay, then. Grim, show us the spell we'll need to protect our house against our enemies in the darkest of times."

Pages flipped one way and then the other, as an electric shock passed through Claire's body. Finally, the book stopped and rotated until Claire could read the text. "I'll be damned."

Aerin leaned closer as Tierra and Moira jumped from their chairs so they could hover over Claire's shoulder and read the spell.

"Frog's breath?" Tierra muttered. "How the hell will we get that?"

"Well, for starters, you'll need some ice cubes, a tennis racket, and Elvis's first—" Moira stopped mid-sentence when she saw all three of her sisters staring at her open-mouthed. "Y'all never mind about the frog's breath. I'll take care of it. What else?"

"The rest of the ingredients seem pretty easy, except..." Claire paused.

"Except it will require all of us to participate." Aerin turned her blue-eyed gaze toward each of them. "I refuse to be afraid."

Claire inhaled a deep breath and focused on her intuition, looking for any kind of sign that might steer her in a less dangerous direction. Nothing surfaced. "I'm in."

Tierra chewed on her bottom lip. "I'm not so sure."

"Do you want to leave *it* unprotected?" Aerin stared at Tierra's belly with a purposeful look before she met Tierra's gaze again.

"Okay. I'm in," Tierra said in a rush.

"Well, fish spunk. I ain't never backed out on a dare. Why start now?"

Where Moira managed to come up with frog's breath, Claire would never know. To be honest, staring at the small, clear bottle, Claire wasn't sure there was actually anything inside.

"You sure about that?" Claire asked as Moira pulled the stopper and dumped what invisible thing she had into the boiling cauldron.

Moira snorted. "Don't ever doubt a water witch. Just ask Nick *I'll screw anything that moves* Kingswood."

The four sisters snickered as Tierra stirred the contents.

"That's everything then." Tierra scraped the edges of the pot before she tapped the wooden spoon on the side and then set it down. She lifted hesitant eyes and focused in turn on each of them. "Are you sure about this?"

"We're sure." Aerin opened the Grimoire she'd been cradling in her arms, skipping right past the moment for any of them to voice second thoughts. "Can everyone see the words?"

They all nodded.

"On the count of three, then." Aerin exhaled a deep breath. Claire grabbed Tierra's and Moira's hands as she took one last look around the room crammed with herbs and flowers thriving in gorgeous pottery. If they were about to blow the Earth to smithereens, she needed a hand to hold and a memory to cherish in her final seconds. Both sisters squeezed back.

Aerin counted down, and they all began.

*"By the power of four, we call upon the elements
to provide us the protection of thee.
Open the land, raise the seas, or burn the winds, whatever
needs be,
By earth, air, fire, and sea..."*

❀ 7 ❀

Claire stared into each of her sisters' eyes...silver, emerald green, and aquamarine as the ground rumbled angrily beneath them. Aerin, eyes wide, dropped Grim on the table and grasped Tierra's and Moira's hands, completing the circle. Synchronized buzzing hummed through Claire's veins, churning her fears.

A strange violet mist rose from the cauldron, swirling around them before disappearing through the screen door. Then, nothing.

None of them moved as they waited for the final blow of fate's hand that would snuff out all life. Seconds passed, slowly easing upon a minute. Then another.

"Welp, guess we didn't end the world." Moira gazed around the room, confident in her assessment.

"Did the spell work?" Tierra asked.

Aerin shrugged. "I guess we won't know until someone tries to get in. Claire, maybe you should ask Tommy to leave and then have him try to return."

"Funny," Claire replied and narrowed her eyes.

"She was serious, Claire." Moira nodded, her gaze kind but firm. "The Tomster needs to go. He smells worse than week-old fish guts. In the sun."

"I already told her the same." Tierra fired a warning gaze at Claire. "She has two days."

The pressure snapped the thin line holding Claire together. "Stop harping on me. I'll take care of it, okay?" Though how, she didn't know. She couldn't send Tommy out in the streets alone. That would be cruel. Maybe she and Tommy could get an apartment or a little house somewhere close by so she could visit her sisters whenever she wanted or whenever she needed to escape Tommy's smell. Which would be daily...if not hourly. Goddess help her.

"Ladies." The baritone caused them all to jump. Claire whipped around, knocking one of Tierra's gorgeous mugs with her elbow. She winced when it shattered on the floor.

Tommy stood in the doorway between the kitchen and the porch where they brewed. Thankfully, he wore clothes this time. "What is it, Tommy?" Claire refused to meet Tierra's gaze.

"I need to talk to you, Claire."

Her sisters broke apart, chattering and relieved.

"Seems like a good time," Tierra said as she passed.

"Do it," Moira whispered.

Aerin choked on the vile air but managed a word. "Now."

Claire waited until her sisters disappeared to face Tommy...except they hadn't exactly left them alone. She sensed their presence nearby. Probably hiding in the kitchen so they could listen. She opened the screen, watched them scatter away, and then closed the thick wooden door between them.

"Do you want to sit out here or maybe go for a stroll in the garden?" Claire eyed the bushes and trees cast in menacing shadows. She hoped their spell had worked because she'd left her room without bringing her favorite dagger with her.

"Doesn't matter much." He glanced about the enclosed porch with his brows furrowed. "This is okay."

She waited for him to sit on a wicker chair covered with a floral cushion before she chose the one farthest away from him. Thankfully, a lovely breeze blew in off the Sound.

"Nice robe." He eyed her chest, and she realized her sash had come loose, revealing the crimson lace bra she wore beneath. "Matches the moon."

"Thanks." She yanked on the ties, securing them in place. "What did you want to talk about?"

Dark lashes framed dull blue eyes that she'd once drowned in. "Your sisters."

His answer surprised her. "My...sisters?" She wasn't sure what she expected him to say...maybe another sexual proposition...but not anything about her sisters.

"They're getting on my nerves. Aerin walking around like she owns the world. Moira won't even look at me, and I'm damn sick and tired of that disgusting air freshener Tierra constantly sprays. I get that you're all probably embarrassed because you smell, but that lilac stinky shit doesn't come close to covering it."

She opened her mouth but no words formed.

"You guys are casting spells, shaking the shit out of the earth," he continued. "It's making things tough for everyone, and I can't sit around and watch it anymore."

"You can't sit around...?" She blinked a couple of times, trying to formulate a response.

"Oh, God." He dragged gray-tinged fingers through his long, dull hair. "It's not even that, Claire. I could tolerate those things if I knew you really loved me."

"Tommy—"

He silenced her with a raised hand. "I know a part of you loves me, Claire. I sense it in that loud beating heart of yours. But I need physical love, too." He pinned her with a serious gaze. "I've found someone new."

It took her a moment to process what he'd said. "You..."

Irrational emotions flooded her brain, and she swam like crazy to steer clear of the pain. "*You're cheating on me?*" It shouldn't have hurt because they hadn't had a real relationship for years, but it did.

He stood and glared down at her. "Are you going to deny sleeping with Dru? I've watched the way you two are together. Don't lie to me."

"I haven't cheated." Not exactly, anyway. Though she'd thought about it many times.

And there had been that one time in his basement and the other on her roof, but she and Dru had never *really* touched each other.

"I might be dead, but I'm not an idiot. I see the shit that's going down. It's only a matter of time before you cave, and I'm tired of him wielding his sword like he's the *mightiest fucking soldier* who ever lived."

Uh...Dru *was* the fiercest warrior on the planet, but now might not be the best time to mention that.

"One of these times, he's going to get really pissed and chop off my fucking head. Then where will I be, huh? Deader than dead? I don't need that constant worry."

"So, you've found someone new?" She should stop being so selfish and be grateful. Tommy deserved someone who could really love him.

He nodded, a bittersweet expression on his face. "Gertie. She's a spirit of sorts who was recently chased out of a certain castle by some older Middle-Eastern dude. We're going to find a place on the edge of town where no one will bother us."

"A spirit? How will you..." She wanted to say fuck, but that seemed rather indelicate at the moment. "How will you be together?"

He glared at her for a long moment. "She's a succubus, okay? Doesn't matter. Our sex life is none of your business. I came to say goodbye, not listen to you judge and preach to me."

She tucked in her bottom lip and stood. With only shallow breaths, she moved forward until they were face-to-face. "I'm sorry this didn't work out for us, Tommy. It hurts me more than you know. I don't know how many days we have left on earth, but if Gertie makes you happy, then I can be glad for that."

He nodded, his expression solemn. "Thank you."

"Can I have a hug?" She opened her arms, and he stepped into them, crushing her against him. For that moment, it didn't matter that he had the warmth of the arctic tundra or smelled like rotting vegetation under the hot sun. She loved this man, deeply, and he would always own a sacred space in her heart.

He pulled back, and she swiped at the tears hovering beneath her eyes, embarrassed at her show of emotion. "I'm sorry, Claire. I didn't want to hurt you."

She shook her head, the large knot in her throat choking her words. "It's okay. Just go, and be happy, Tommy."

He paused for a long moment, and she wondered if he changed his mind. Then he turned from her, strode down the back porch steps and faded into the red-tinged darkness of night.

A sob erupted from the deepest part of her soul, and she clamped a hand over her mouth. Scalding tears burned her cheeks as she once-again mourned the loss of her first love.

This was for the best. For both of them. But, she had to wonder if she'd ever see Tommy again. He deserved someone who loved him, someone who lit up when he walked through the door. Someone who didn't look at him as a burden she would carry for the rest of her days.

She should be happy. *They were both free.*

Another sob wracked her body, and she doubled over and hugged her knees.

The moist air around her sparked with electricity, and she looked up, afraid she'd find another assassin.

Dark and dangerous, Dru stood above her, his gaze stark with concern. "Come here," he commanded. "He's not worth your worry."

She stood, her legs shaky, and then she rushed into his embrace as another sob escaped.

"It's okay." He stroked her hair as she bled painful emotion. The physical wounds she received earlier were nothing compared to this. It was a ripping, a rending of the heart, and she collapsed against him, unable to bear the weight of it.

He leaned away and tilted her chin upward. She sniffed, trying to regain control over her tears. This man wouldn't understand any of her feelings. He'd never known abandonment and heartbreak like she had.

"You're wrong, Claire. I do feel it. Your heart has become my heart."

She squeezed her eyes shut, wishing he could understand, wishing that he couldn't read her so easily. "I feel so guilty because there's part of me that's glad he's gone. But I will miss him desperately."

"I wish I meant that much to you." A strange, overpowering essence that she recognized as Dru tugged at her heart.

"Oh, Dru." With shaking hands, she cupped his face, reveling in the rasp of whiskers against her fingertips, admiring the strength of his jaw and the softness of his lips. "I don't know if I'm capable of giving away my heart again, but I'd really like to give you this."

She tugged his head down, her fingers gliding across the stiff ends of his short hair, and she kissed him. Tentative at first, and then lingering a little longer.

He returned her kisses, but otherwise remained motionless while she explored his mouth and the sensuous way his tongue tangled with hers. She slid her fingers along the corded muscles covering his broad shoulders, soaking in the feel of him.

The man was larger than life in so many ways. He should have been too much for her, but he wasn't. His warrior soul clicked with hers in a way she hadn't known could exist, and he terrified the hell out of her.

"I should go inside," she said as she stepped away.

He planted firm hands on her hips, reclaiming her. "Why?"

She fought to keep her mind blank, recognizing how vulnerable she was to him at that moment. "It's been a really long day. Fighting those assholes and wrecking my bike." She sniffed and blinked furiously. "And then Tommy. I think what I need most is sleep."

"You could come back to my room and sleep with me," he suggested. Her body responded to his words, and she had to battle the urge to give in. This man would love her like she'd never been loved before.

"Don't be afraid, Claire. A valiant warrior faces her fears and forges ahead. You never know what may be waiting for you on the other side."

Her breaths came faster, bordering on hyperventilation as her insides melted to liquid fire. She wanted to lose herself in him so badly. But she was afraid she'd be lost forever then.

She took another step backward. "Goodnight, Dru. Thank you for coming to check on me."

His expression flattened to the hardness he'd worn when she'd first seen him at the airport. "I'll always be here for you, Claire." He fisted his hand and placed it over his heart.

Oh, Goddess.

She turned and fled from the man who'd turned her world upside down.

❧ 8 ❧

When Claire walked in, Moira sat at the kitchen table reading a tabloid, her long legs stretched out and resting on a nearby chair.

Moira looked up, her lovely eyes filled with concern. "Everything go okay with the Tomster?"

She nodded, but didn't trust her voice to speak. She collected a bottle of their strongest whisky and a shot glass etched with a skull and crossbones before she dropped into the chair next to Moira. Claire poured amber liquid almost to the brim and then slammed that puppy home.

Molten alcohol burned a fiery path all the way to her stomach. She inhaled as the strength of it soothed her and shifted a sideways glance at Moira who still studied her with knowing eyes.

"Did you tell him he has to move out?" she prodded.

Claire half-laughed, half-cried. "*He* actually broke up with *me*."

"What?" Moira dropped her feet to the floor and leaned forward. "You gotta be kidding."

"Nope." Claire poured herself another glass. "Said he had enough of you guys not treating him right and that we all smelled."

Moira busted out in a laugh. "If that ain't funnier

than a three-legged mule tryin' to tango. We don't stink."

Claire snorted. "I guess things have changed for him."

"Well…there's truth to that. And not necessarily in a good way."

"Depends on who's talking. What one finds disgusting, another finds attractive." She tipped back the whisky she'd poured and then met Moira's gaze. "He left me for another woman. A succubus, no less."

"Yeah, that'd chap my ass right and proper. If that succubus is half as good at possessing people as she-Satan, he'll be having all kinds of kinky sex with every woman in town."

The thought of Tommy with all those women, even if they were taken over by the same spirit, turned her stomach. "I don't want to talk about it."

Moira's expression softened. "Don't you worry. Let him pass that dead, diseased dong of his to a few desperate hussies. The time has come to pay the pig farmer."

"Piper?"

"What?" Moira lifted questioning brows.

"Never mind." Claire eyed Grim who rested near Moira's elbow. "Okay if I take Grim for a while? I wanted to study a little more."

"Knock yourself out." Moira pushed the tome toward her, and Claire cradled it against her chest. Something akin to family ties wrapped unseen tendrils around her.

Claire scooted her chair back but didn't stand. "Do you ever think about our mother?"

Moira considered her for a moment. "Sometimes. I do wonder what life would have been like if she'd lived, and we'd all grown up together."

"She obviously loved Tierra more. And you, too."

"What gave you that idiot notion?"

"Tierra stayed with the family while the rest of us were scattered. She has her crown and wand, and so do you."

"Those don't have anything to do with our mother. Tierra received hers from Malcolm de Moray, and Morgana de Moray brought mine after I made like a shish kabob and fell into the Sound. Why do you blame her?"

Claire shrugged. "I don't know. I just keep thinking there must have been something she could have done to save us from all of this."

Moira pinned her with a solemn gaze. "Maybe she did. Maybe that's why we're alive instead of drinking mud soup with the fishes. 'Sides, Aerin doesn't have hers yet, either. You're just gonna have to be patient."

She tried to find comfort from Moira's words. Maybe their mother had loved them beyond words, beyond a lifetime. "I just miss her and wish I could have known her."

"Me, too." Moira turned the page of her tabloid and widened her eyes. "I'll be damned." She looked up with alarm blazing in her cool eyes. "I thought it was bad when I'd read that the Queen beheaded the prime minister, but look at this."

She turned the magazine and shoved it toward Claire, pointing a finger to the photo of nothing but sand. "Pyramids have all sunk into the ever-loving ground. Gone. Just like that."

"No." Claire couldn't believe that. "Someone must have taken a picture of an empty desert, and they're now claiming it's where the pyramids were."

"If you don't believe me, then look at this." Moira flipped back a couple of pages and touched her finger to a photo of what looked like a pile of broken limestone and marble. "The Leaning Tower of Pisa toppled like a preacher's wife at a whisky social. At the rate we're going, it's only a matter of days before Rome falls again, I reckon."

Claire wished she could say it was all a bunch of bullshit, but for once in her life, the tabloids had probably gotten something right. "I can't think about this right now, or it's going to blow my mind."

"It's okay. I understand. It's a lot to take in. Right now, you need rest. You've had a bitch of a day. We'll tackle the Apocalypse tomorrow."

In the safety of her room, Claire crawled into bed with Grim and patted her quilt to invite Kai to join her. The gorgeous red fox with intelligence glowing from his obsidian eyes curled into a ball at her feet. His fiery energy blended with hers, soothing her tormented soul.

"Hello, Grim." She traced soft fingers down the rough skin of the book, working to keep her mind blank until the very last second. "Show me a spell that shields my thoughts," she blurted out quickly.

Something sharp twisted in her gut, infusing her with sadness and pain as the pages flipped furiously in front of her. She swallowed and ignored the torture going on inside her as she scanned the spell.

Nothing but an incantation. No sacrifice. No concoctions. Just lethal words.

Before she could change her mind, she recited the spell, the discomfort inside her increasing until it finally popped. Like literally made a loud popping sound that came from somewhere in the vicinity of her heart.

She inhaled her relief. Waited for a moment to see if it would sustain itself, and it did. Then cautiously, she searched for a trace of Dru's essence and found nothing but a cold, barren cavern where he'd once been. An incredible ache rolled through her. In an effort to fight it off, she wrapped her arms about her middle and curled onto her side.

Goddess, she thought watching Tommy go had been torture. That was nothing compared to this.

Kai whimpered and moved closer, touching his nose to hers.

She tried to breathe through the pain as she placed a hand on Kai's fur. She'd survived losses before, and she would this one as well. If she could live without her fire—well, maybe that wasn't the best comparison.

She closed her eyes and inhaled the fiery energy burning in her room until the fireplace went dark. It wasn't as if she was cutting off Dru completely, but she couldn't afford to have him haunting every thought. She had to think about thwarting the Apocalypse and saving the world first, and didn't have time to be distracted by a hot guy who could kick Hercules's ass with his pinkie toe. Even more so, if she and her sisters ever decided to do something drastic, then Dru couldn't know.

A woman needed her secrets.

ϗ 9 ϗ

"What's got your dick in a twist?" Nick asked as Dru dropped into the seat across from him.

Thankfully, none of the castle workers remained in the lounge this late except the red-headed butler. "Who says I'm pissy?" When the butler finally gained the courage to look in Dru's direction, Dru nodded for him to bring his usual drink.

"I do." Nick held his gaze as he removed his cuff links and dropped them to the small table between them. "If I was a betting man, and I am, I'd say you need to get laid."

Dru cursed under his breath, not happy that his fellow Horseman could read him so easily. "You don't know dick."

Nick rumbled out a hearty laugh as he rolled up his sleeves. "You still haven't spoken to Claire."

He downed his shot of whisky the moment the butler set it on the table. "I've been too busy hunting down *our favorite lady* to worry about Claire. Claire will come around when she realizes she was wrong." She had no other option.

Nick was smart enough to only respond with a nod.

"What about Moira? Why aren't you with her tonight?"

Nick snorted. "I wore her out. Said she needed alone time with that pig of hers. They were going to paint their toenails."

Dru chuckled despite the ache in his heart. "That's the best thing I've heard all day. Trumped by a pork chop."

"Fucking pig," he muttered and then lifted his gaze to Dru. "Anything new on Her Royal Darkness?"

"No. I know she's still here, but she's gone completely underground." Which pissed him off almost as much as Claire and her irrationality. Claire might think she'd cut him off, but he wasn't that easy to outmaneuver.

"Give Lucy time. I've never known a narcissist who could stay out of the limelight for long. She'll be back."

"No doubt," Dru commented. "But I'd like to get to her before she regains her full powers. Take her out once and for all."

"Might already be too late."

The butler returned to their table and placed a sizzling steak and baked cheesy potatoes in front of Dru, easing his ire. "Thanks."

"You're welcome," the timid butler managed to say.

"Looks so good, I believe I'll let you live another day." Dru sent him a fierce stare.

"Thank you, sir." The young man ran from their table.

"You're scaring the shit out of him." Nick laughed.

Dru focused on his steak as he slid a knife through the meat, releasing juices onto his plate. "Punk kid flirted with my woman. Can't let him think he can get away with that." He met Conquest's gaze and shoved the chunk of beef into his mouth.

Nick's phone vibrated, and he snatched it from the table as though he'd been waiting for the message. He read whatever had popped up on his screen and then grinned. "Looks like I'll be sleeping at Moira's house tonight." He swiped his cuff links from the table and stood.

"She summoned you, did she?"

"No one summons me. But yes, I'll indulge her for tonight. I don't know if Claire is anything like her sister, but if she is, you'd understand why I have no more time to sit around and talk shit with you."

Dru snorted. "You're pussy-whipped."

"That reminds me. Moira asked that I bring the cat o' nine tails for the evening's festivities." Nick smirked. "Good luck with your celibacy."

Dru growled the moment Nick walked out the door. The butler, who'd been midstride to his table, turned and scurried away.

Dru dropped his head into his hands and then scrubbed the scruff on his jaw. He had to figure out a way to reach Claire before he went insane. Half of him wanted to wring her neck for what she'd done. The other half ached to hold her and love her until she felt safe enough to let him in again.

⚜

CLAIRE DIPPED AND SWOOPED IN THE NIGHT SKY, loving the exhilarating feel of wind in her hair as she broom-flew over the Victorian seaport she now called home. Flying sure as hell beat lying in bed, fighting to erase Dru from her mind as easily as she had banished him from her soul. Keeping her broom in the sky required all of her concentration which was why she'd chosen it. She'd never command the heavens like Aerin did, but with her bike mangled, this was her only form of escape.

To be honest, soaring through the open air was pretty damn awesome. The fresh oxygen rushing past her was raw fuel to her fire and sent her heart racing. She'd left her sisters at home, oblivious to her escapades, all three of them otherwise occupied. They wouldn't miss her. And for a few moments, she missed no one.

In fact, her sisters hadn't missed her the previous two nights when she'd done the same. Claire smiled, reveling in her freedom. The world could end tomorrow, so she needed to enjoy the moment she had right now.

She doubted anyone in town who happened to look toward the heavens would notice her. The quarter moon currently cast in the sky didn't glow as brightly, and she'd dressed in black leather as camouflage.

Still, this wasn't only a joyride. She had a serious mission to accomplish. She'd located the witch hunters her first time out, and she intended to gather more information before she formulated a plan and presented it to her sisters. She'd surveyed the area for several days now, getting a good visual of the outlay of an old World War I army battery that seemed to be the witch hunters' home base. Most of the vicious bastards ventured forth during the day and then returned to their cement hive at night like nasty wasps.

If she accomplished nothing else before all was said and done, she would destroy their camp with all of them in it. For now, though, she zoomed along the coastline one more time, not quite confident enough in her skills to skip across the Sound.

When she'd done her best to fill the empty vastness in her heart with the thrill of racing through the night sky, she aimed for the lighthouse and Kinzie Battery beyond. She stayed high in the sky as she soared over Fort Worden and only dropped when she had the full cover of trees below. A stray branch knocked her off-balance as she descended, and she tumbled the last six feet to the ground with her broom whopping her on the ass when it landed a second later.

She groaned as she picked herself up and brushed

dirt from her leathers. "Those things need to have a self-landing mode or something," she grumbled as she reached for the broom handle. She stored her ride safely beneath the same large pine as she had the two nights before and then crept closer to the cement shell of one of many World War I batteries.

Walking as silently as Kai might through the cool, pine-scented air, she crept closer to the secluded spot she'd discovered on her first escapade. She'd only meant to confirm the witch hunters' basecamp was at Fort Worden like she suspected, but she'd been surprised by the sheer number of them hiding out there. Originally, she estimated maybe fifteen or so, but last night, she counted more than fifty circled around the outside cement pit filled with a blistering fire that seemed to be their gathering spot. Tonight, if they all congregated in their spot again, she intended to take a peek inside the cement battery.

She slowed as she reached her vantage point and dropped to her belly before peering down the hillside. The fire that normally roared in their pit lay dormant, disappointing her. She used it to count the number of people and memorize their faces. The fact that the witch hunters weren't all there this evening also messed up the attack plan she'd begun to formulate.

A disturbance in the atmosphere chilled her. Just as she stood, intending to retreat, something snapped behind her. Claire whirled around, but no one was there. Her heart squeezed in panic as she scanned the area, and she did her best to remain calm. With no one in sight, she walked quickly and quietly toward her broom.

She had a hundred feet left to go when a black-clad figure shifted from the shadows. Then another and another. She reached for the knife sheathed at her side. Just as she touched the hilt of the blade, two strong arms banded around her, knocking her to the ground. She reached for the fire inside her until a bruising blow to the back of her head stole her consciousness.

COLD WATER SPLASHED CLAIRE'S FACE. SHE CHOKED and sputtered against the shock of it, trying to gain her bearings. Each movement caused her head to pound with the force of a thousand hooves. The dank smell of moisture clogged her throat, and cold from the cement floor where she lay had long since seeped into her bones, chilling her to the core. The glass of wine she had earlier threatened to reappear.

She dropped her gaze to the spot on her chest that burned her with pain and made it hard to breathe. A leather cord held an icy stone against her skin, the shock of it ripping a cry from her throat.

Blinking rapidly, she cleared her eyes and focused on fat, leather-clad legs standing in front of her. She shifted her gaze upward.

A man with a dark beard and black felt hat stood over her, holding a battery-powered lantern. Evil intention burned in his eyes. He kicked at her with his booted foot. Instinctively, she tried to block him, only to find her hands had been shackled to a thick chain anchored in the middle of the room. The tip of his boot landed hard against her thigh, and she cried out.

"Did you think we wouldn't notice you'd been spying on us, witch?"

She searched for her fire but couldn't access it. "What have you done to me? Let me go."

Sadistic laughter echoed through the cavernous room. "No, witch. You won't be getting free this time. There's no one to save you. Your sisters are all home, and the Horsemen are otherwise occupied with women. While you were checking up on us, we were watching you."

Dru? With someone else? Deep, piercing pain stabbed straight into her heart. The witch hunter's words cut more than the iron shackles about her wrists.

He nudged her again with his foot. "I've come to give you one last chance at salvation. Tell me how to remove the spell protecting your house, and we will kill you and your sisters quickly. Refuse, and I'll personally make sure your pain is unimaginable."

"*Fuck you.* Let me go, and I'll offer you the same deal."

"Still cocky after all these years, Tierra de Moray. My mama told me what you were, years ago. She said all witches deserved to die. Should have listened to her then. Would have saved all of mankind a heap of trouble."

He thought she was Tierra? "Fuck you." Did he not realize Tierra was now pregnant?

"Such a dirty mouth. Don't remember you being so vulgar back in school. I guess your true colors are showing." He chuckled. "I have to say I'm glad you didn't accept my offer. The sounds of your screams will be music to my ears."

He took several steps toward the exit before turning back. "Might want to take a few minutes to make peace with your God. You'll be meeting him shortly."

"Goddess!" she tossed at his retreating back and heard him laugh in response. Anger burned inside her as he strode away, and she released an irate growl. "I swear to Goddess I will kill you!"

She gritted her teeth and squeezed her eyes shut, wishing desperately she could reach out to Dru. She'd jumped the gun far too many times in her life. The price of this one might *be* her life.

❧ 10 ❧

Claire struggled against her restraints again, furious that they held her in place. Her head throbbed like she'd been hit with a ten-pound boulder, making it hard to keep her thoughts clear. Nausea turned her stomach into a tempest-tossed sea. "*Son of a bitch.*" She flicked her gaze to the sheath at her side, angry all over again that it was empty. But, of course, they wouldn't leave a dagger with her.

After everything that had happened, she should have been better prepared.

She filled her lungs with precious oxygen and tried to will away her panic and block the vicious amulet hanging about her neck. This wasn't over yet. She'd escaped equally dangerous situations, and if she kept her wits about her, she might do the same this time. Goddess help her.

She closed her eyes and sent out frantic tendrils of thought in each direction, searching for any source of heat or fire. The cold cement surroundings didn't aid her exploration, and she cursed the fact that the witch hunters hadn't worshipped a bonfire that night like they had the others.

Quickly, she took stock of her resources. Fire wasn't an option, at least for the moment. She wished to hell she'd had Dru teach her how to create an illusion, if that was at all possible. She'd make those freakish witch hunters believe they were all burning in hell.

She had her words...which hadn't helped so far since the asshole who held her was more likely to kick her than talk. Though he did think she was Tierra, in which case she might try to fake a childhood relationship with him and beg for mercy.

"They're about to crucify you, and you're meditating?"

Claire ripped open her eyelids to find Lucy crouching nearby, staring intently at her.

Claire snorted a delirious laugh, unable to maintain her dignity any longer. "As if things couldn't get worse. What the hell do you want, She-devil?" If Lucy thought she could possess her like she'd done with Aerin, she'd better reconsider.

Instead of taking offense, Lucy smiled. "I like that... She-devil. It has a nice ring to it, don't you think?" Satan looked better than she had the night Dru chased her off, but she hadn't quite cast off the haggardness that dulled her perfection.

Claire released a slow breath, trying to keep her stomach under control. If she tossed her cookies in front of the Devil, she'd never live it down.

She'd once feared this woman, had also once thought of her as a friend until she'd learned better. It wasn't that she didn't have a healthy respect for Satan, but Claire had found her own set of powers. Maybe she hadn't yet honed them like Lucy had hers, but they weren't laughable, and she and her sisters had grown stronger every day. "If you've come to kill me, get in line. There's a bunch of crazed motherfuckers congregating outside that get a go at me first."

"I admire you, Claire." Her smile grew wider. "Your courage and grace. You and I have a lot in common."

"Like what? Our beauty?" Claire said with a gasp as her control slipped.

Lucy snorted. "I wouldn't go quite that far."

And that was the end of Claire's patience. "Look, say or do what you need to, and get the hell out. I need to formulate some sort of retaliation before I let these idiots take my life." If it wouldn't leave her sisters at a greater risk, she might go along with the show just to end the torture for everyone. But they needed her, and she needed them.

Lucy waved away Claire's worries with a flick of her wrist. "Don't worry about them. They believe you're the earth witch, and they intend to burn you at the stake."

A sarcastic laugh escaped Claire's lips. Wouldn't they be surprised when they tried to burn her? If she could escape the influence of whatever damned thing they'd placed about her neck, this might actually work in her favor. It gave her a fighting chance to say the least. If they put her anywhere near flames and she found a way to access her powers, they'd all be toast.

Like literally toast. Black, burned, disgusting toast.

Lucy inched closer, studying Claire and then her bonds. "Oh, how they love those amulets. I know that neither of us cares much for the blithering idiots, but you have to give them credit for figuring out that much. When they first came to Port Townsend, I labeled them all Neanderthals. They've come up a bit in my estimation."

"If they're such Neanderthals, then you shouldn't have a problem removing whatever they've tied around my neck." Maybe if she played on Lucy's ego, she'd help her.

Lucy scrunched up her features. "Eww...no one wants to touch that."

"*Are you serious?*" Claire ground out the words.

"Fine." She rolled her eyes. "I may be inclined to help, but you must hear me out first."

Well, she'd be damned. Lucy asking instead of demanding. "Speak it."

Lucy released a dramatic sigh. "I know we've had our differences, Claire."

She snorted. "You've tried *and failed* to kill my family."

Satan tucked a bedraggled curl behind her ear. "If you could listen for a moment and try to see things from my point of view. Honestly, I have nothing against you and your sisters personally. Well, except that bitch Aerin. But the rest of you are just in the wrong place at the wrong time. It's what you represent that behooves me to take the action I must in order to save the world."

"I thought you wanted to end the world." Wasn't that why she'd tried to take over Aerin's body? Well, that and to sleep with Julian?

Lucy scoffed. "Why would I want that? I like things the way they are. People *worship* me. If you ladies succeed and bring about the Apocalypse, what will become of *me*?"

The pounding in Claire's head grew stronger as she tried to make sense of Lucy's motivations. "Stop. Just stop. You're talking in circles, and I can't make sense of it. There's a reason you're here. Say it."

Lucy blinked several times as though taken aback, her fake lashes fluttering against her cheekbones. Then the dumb blonde routine fizzled, and Claire was left with the ruthless demon spirit she recognized beneath Lucy's once-beautiful exterior.

"You prefer that I speak to you woman-to-woman? Fine. Here are the facts. Infantile idiots that you are, you've managed to break six of the seven Seals. That leaves one, *only one*, between what we have now and complete, utter devastation. Are you all prepared to undertake that ominous, colossal event?" If her words didn't cut to the heart, her furious gaze did.

"No." Claire swallowed and wished she could stand to face her foe. "That's not our intention at all."

"Then what the hell having you been doing? You four are imbeciles who need to be stopped before this goes any further. You say you love your family, love the Antichrist that Tierra carries, which, I'll have you know, is *not* my spawn. The next person who speaks those words will know my fury." She cleared her throat as though to reset the conversation. "Claire, I would like you to consider ending your life before you all end the rest of us. I know it's a great sacrifice on your part, but you mustn't be selfish. Not in these dark times."

Claire opened her mouth but couldn't speak. She'd had similar thoughts in the past, but...selfish?

"Don't answer me now. Take some time to think about it." Lucy glanced over her shoulder as male voices grew nearer, and she thrust a folded piece of paper into Claire's bound hands. "Take this. I call it my cyanide spell. It's come in handy a time or two."

"Obviously you didn't use it on yourself," Claire pointed out.

"As if." She snorted. "I'm not the one causing problems." She looked again in the direction of the voices. "Think about my suggestion for a day or two, and then we'll talk."

Lucy took two steps away and then hurried back to Claire. She pulled a bejeweled dagger from between her breasts and slit the leather cord, allowing the stone to fall into a cloth pouch she carried. She replaced the cursed talisman with a similar looking stone. "There."

"Can I have the knife?" Claire asked, now able to inhale a complete breath again.

Lucy hesitated for a moment. "No," she said with a decidedly flippant tone. Before Claire could beg, Lucy slipped quietly into the darkness a few seconds before the group of witch hunters appeared.

Eight men dressed in Puritan-period clothing circled the edges of the room, leaving her in the middle. The white collars of the ominous apparitions glowed against their black coats, reminding Claire of the distinction between heaven and hell, good and evil. The men all carried similar battery-powered lanterns and glared at her as though she were Satan.

The world had gone completely mad. Was that also part of the end of days? Maybe mankind had gone too far in destroying the world and each other, and it was time to be done with it.

The asshole who addressed her earlier stepped closer. "Tierra de Moray, you are hereby charged with practicing witchcraft and sorcery. The fathers would ask what you have to say in your defense."

Claire paused to glance at each one of them, memorizing their features, promising with a look that they'd all die that night. She returned her glare to the first asshole. "Excuse you, sir, but fuck you."

Gasps from several of the men echoed through the room, but asshole's smile grew bigger. "If convicted, you will be punished by death."

"Well, in that case...fuck you."

Another man with a long gray beard moved forward. "Is that your final answer?"

She paused for a long, breathless moment. *"Fuck...you."*

Claire stumbled through the maze of cement tunnels and rooms as the leader of the witch hunters jerked hard on the long chain attached to her shackled wrists. The rest of the men followed behind her, their excitement echoing off the walls.

They had captured a witch, and they intended to watch her burn.

Claire played along, acting feeble and tossing hateful barbs like they were grenades. They only laughed harder.

The moment she stepped from the cement battery into the crisp Port Townsend night, her power growled restlessly as fear slithered over her. More than a hundred had gathered to watch her execution, many more than she originally expected. The second one of them lit a match, she would gain control, but her hands still remained shackled, and anyone could throw a knife in her direction and take her out before she could retaliate.

She narrowed her gaze and stared at them as they hurled insults at her.

"*Evil witch.*"

"*Satan*"

"*Burn for what you've done.*"

Such idiots. She'd done nothing but love and protect her family. Exactly the same as they would have done for theirs. Just because she was different didn't make her bad.

Something hard hit her in the neck, and she swung around as a small rock tumbled to the ground. She turned an angry gaze toward the crowd, and they stepped back as though fearful she would reach them.

Asshole jerked her to the center of their gathering area and into the circular cement pit they used for fires the previous nights. Ashes scattered about her feet, cold and void of life, leaving her with an ominous chill. He attached the chain to another stake that had been bolted into the ground and moved away.

Voices from the crowd grew to a whispered frenzy as the witch hunters approached her, each with an armful of lumber. They dumped their loads unceremoniously at her feet, some of the pieces striking her legs.

A shiver of fear over what was to come rippled through her. She worshipped fire. Trusted it immensely. She used it as a tool or weapon more times than she could count. But she'd never actually stepped into a raging bonfire, and that's exactly what they intended to make.

When the logs were piled as high as her knees, a hush fell over the crowd as a few of the men tucked dried leaves and twigs between the pieces of wood.

"Thou shalt not suffer a witch to live." Asshole's voice rang through the quiet night.

A moment later, the hoard of people began to chant the same words over and over. *"Thou shalt not suffer a witch to live. Thou shalt not suffer a witch to live. Thou shalt not suffer a witch to live."*

Waves of hatred from the crowd washed over her, and she wondered how they could despise her so much when they didn't know her.

A short, stocky witch hunter with raven black hair

approached the leader and opened a box. Asshole re-moved a long match and held it up for everyone to see. Cheers and encouragement echoed through the crowd.

"Stop!" Claire shrieked before he could strike the match.

A malevolent smile twisted his lips. "Do you wish to beg for mercy?"

Goddess, she hated him. "I wish to give you one last chance," she said loud enough for everyone to hear. "If you value your life and what's good and right with this world, you'll stop this madness. Leave. Go home to your families."

"*Thou shalt not suffer a witch to live. Thou shalt...*" Their chanting began again, growing louder and louder with each round.

Dammit.

Though the sounds of the mass had reached a zealous pitch, she swore she could hear the scraping of the match against cement. A second later, the sweet scent of sulfur filled her nostrils. Jolts of electricity sparked inside her as the leader touched the long match to the kindling. Voices dropped to whispers as leaves and then twigs caught the flame and crackled.

"Your sisters won't be long behind you." Asshole stepped back as flames licked greedily at the dried wood.

She froze for a long, fearful moment, and then loving acceptance and exhilarating power leapt from the flames to encircle her. Her legs threatened to buckle, but she gratefully accepted the gift. Tendrils of smoke curled into the air, and she filled her lungs.

She had nothing to fear. Fire would not harm her. She and the flames were one elemental force bonded forever.

Claire smiled at the group of witch hunters who ob-served her with smug expressions. At first, they con-tinued to watch, unaffected by her grin, but then one by one, they slowly lost their confidence. She held her shackled hands to the flames until the heat softened the metal about her wrists and she was able to slip free of the restraints.

With a burst of energy, she stood. Flames flew outward from the tips of her fingers, encompassing her with a mighty roar. Her whole body burned with staggering, powerful fire, and she fought to control the angry beast.

This was much more magic than she'd ever experienced. Far too much. *She wasn't ready.*

"Fear not, fire witch. The flames you see are you." The face of a beautiful woman flickered in the flames.

Claire blinked furiously, wondering if she had actually died in the fire. "Who are you?"

A calm smile crossed her lips. "My kin on this earth called me Kenna. I was sister to Malcolm de Moray. You and I are of one, and my blood flows through you now. Do you sense it?"

Fiery energy pushed Claire's boundaries, making her feel as though she might split in two. "I sense it, but it's too much, too hard to handle." She forced her breaths to slow, hoping the lessening of oxygen might lower the energy.

"It's not too much. You are strong. You and your sisters. Use your powers wisely and never fear to do what's right. Always trust yourselves, and you will forever have what you need." With those words, the wavering vision dissipated like wind chasing away smoke.

Claire wanted to cry out for her to return, but somehow, she knew her attempts would be pointless.

This fire was hers. She owned it, and she must embrace that.

With a prayer on her lips, she filled her lungs until she feared they might burst and let her energy explode outward from her like a detonating bomb.

THE TIRES ON DRU'S HUMMER SQUEALED THROUGH the night as he raced toward Fort Worden, uncertain what Claire's incredibly powerful energy signature meant. Their bond might not be what it once was, but one spell could not break what had been forged between them.

Formidable flames shot from the tops of the trees near the shoreline. At that point, Dru abandoned the trivial roads and drove his SUV in a direct route over the large expanse of grass that encompassed much of Fort Worden until he came upon a crazed mass of people running in his direction. Hatred for Claire vibrated around them like a black aura.

Witch hunters.

If they hurt her...

He jumped from his vehicle, pulled his sword from its magical sheath, and raced toward them with a war cry bellowing from his lungs. The witch hunters wanted Claire dead, so he couldn't allow the sadistic bastards to continue living.

People halted in their tracks, expanding fear rampant on their faces as others behind them crashed into those ahead of the pack, toppling over them like a mass of ants trying to flee an enemy.

Many scrambled to their feet and retreated toward the flames. Others cowered and screamed for mercy. He saw them as nothing but a threat to the one he loved as he carved a bloody path toward the massive flames.

When Claire came into view, he nearly fell over himself.

She stood serene as otherworldly flames swirled around her body. Her hair danced about her shoulders, tendrils of fire playing in the night. Atop her head sat a ruby-encrusted crown that glinted in the firelight, and she held a wand in her hand.

"*Son of a bitch.*" Fire had finally bestowed upon her the gifts of her ancestors, and he had a feeling she'd be fearsome to behold when she reached her potential.

Though she faced in his direction, he was certain she didn't see him, didn't see any of the commotion that exploded around them.

He raced toward her until he reached the perimeter of the fireball that surrounded her. She was close, but not close enough, and he yearned to pull her into his arms and know that she was safe.

Flames licked at him, teasing him with their touch, but not burning. He watched with fascination as curls of fire coiled about his boots and then crept up his calves. His sense of self-preservation screamed for him to take a step back, but he couldn't get over the fact that his boots didn't burn.

When he glanced back to Claire's face, he was shocked to find her staring at him intensely. Slowly, she lifted a hand and held it out to him.

He paused for a long moment, unsure if he could embrace complete trust. Besides his brothers, he'd never trusted another soul who'd inhabited this earth during the endless years he'd roamed the valleys and mountains. The burning ache to take her hand urged him forward.

Ah, fuck. He'd never been a coward before, and he refused to be one now.

He gripped her hand and stepped into the most exquisite fire he'd ever encountered.

The second Dru wrapped his fingers around Claire, she tugged him toward her. "You're here," Claire said, grateful that he could share this moment with her. A massive wall of flames swirled up around them, encompassing them in a fiery cocoon, just the two of them. Horseman and witch.

Her Horseman responded by wrapping his strong arms around her and crushing her to his chest. "Dammit, Claire. I needed to know you're safe. It wounds me deeply every time something like this happens."

She pulled back to view his face. Tenderness in the warrior's eyes nearly undid her. "How did you know what happened? Where I was? I blocked our connection."

"I should throttle you for that. And I plan to later. When are you going to get it through your thick head that we're bound to each other?"

"I cast a spell, and I know it worked." She glanced at the wild fire dancing around them and then touched her fingertips to his cheek. "Are you really even here?"

He placed his hand over hers. "One spell can't break what we have, Claire. You only closed your side of the door. You made it more difficult to find you whenever I wanted, but you didn't completely severe the connection."

"I don't know if I should be angry that it didn't work or grateful." She would have a word with Grim.

He cupped her chin. "Grateful. Even if you won't admit it, you need me. You want me."

She inhaled sharply, her attraction to him cutting her to the bone. He spoke the truth, and she could no longer deny it.

He grinned.

"What?" She narrowed her gaze in uncertainty.

"Heard that. Felt that here." He placed a hand over his heart. "You're mine now."

She nodded as she studied his fierce gaze and strong jaw. Could he really be hers? Could he fill those empty spaces in her heart?

"Yes," he whispered as he lowered his mouth to hers and held her tightly against his strong body.

The fire around them intensified, mirroring what she experienced inside.

Do or die, this would happen.

"That's what I've been saying all along," he murmured against her lips.

She drew her fingertips over his muscled back, reveling in the hard curves, before drawing them down to his trim waist.

He pulled back, watching her with lust-filled eyes. "Damn, woman. These are some badass flames. I could have used you throughout the ages, fighting by my side."

"I wish I hadn't gone this long without you, either." She drew a finger along his moistened bottom lip and then touched hers.

"Let's get out of here," he said. "I love your flames, but I wouldn't want you to forget yourself in the throes of passion and set my balls on fire."

She laughed and mentally lowered the fire around

them until nothing but ash remained. Together, they glanced over the devastating carnage.

"I didn't want to hurt them. I gave them a chance to leave, but they refused."

He placed a finger against her lips. "Shh... This tragedy lies at their feet. They made their choices. I know it's hard to see such devastation. Believe me, gruesome doesn't come close to describing my first battle and many after that. It is what it is. Death and his reapers might be pissed because they'll be working overtime to catch up."

His attempt to soothe her didn't help.

"You did what you had to do." He held her close to him, shielding her from much of the horrific sight as he led her up Artillery Hill.

"I need to get my broom if the witch hunters didn't already take it. Also, I have this." She held up the ash wood wand that had arrived in her hand after Kenna departed. "I'm not quite sure what to do with it."

He laughed. "I guess that's something you'll have to figure out with your sisters. You've been crowned as well."

She lifted surprised brows as she placed both hands atop her head. Her fingers met with metal. "With everything that happened, I didn't realize it was there." She slid it from her hair as she slowed her steps and then stopped.

The sight of her crown stole her breath. Large rubies glowed in the dark night, set deeply into intricate swirls of gold that simulated flames. So pretty. Too pretty to be hers. "How can I accept this? It's so beautiful, and the power radiating from it is incredibly old. It's too much."

Dru took the crown from her and placed it back on her head. "Looks good on you. If I had any doubts you were the one who'd end my life as I've known it, I no longer do. This is meant for you and you alone. You can no longer deny who and what you are."

Her insides trembled. "The fire witch prophesied to help end the world."

He smiled. "My fire witch, and we'll see about ending the world. One solid Seal remains in place, and we're going to keep it that way."

They walked through the silent night, the atmosphere a complete contrast to what she'd experienced. "Did I kill them all?" she asked quietly.

"I took out my fair share, but plenty of them got away. No doubt they'll regroup and try again."

"We've got to stop them, Dru, before they succeed in killing one of us."

"Agreed. I'll talk with my brothers. It's better if we take them out. It will prevent you from accidently opening a Seal, and I know Julian wouldn't mind sharing his secret handshake with them."

She rolled her eyes, but he did manage to coax a smile from her.

He drew her along until she reached her broom which remained safely stowed where she'd left it.

"Do you want to ride it or bring it in my SUV? We could meet at the house or the castle. Your call."

She hesitated. "Do we have to leave? I don't want to go home just yet." She was excited to show her sisters the intricate crown and wand, but explaining how she'd come by them would require some precise verbal maneuvering.

He pulled her close, his warm breath tickling her ear. "We can go wherever you want. I'm not concerned about the witch hunters attacking again. What remains of them have scurried into hiding. How about we walk instead?"

She nodded, loving the idea. She held his hand, strolling as though they were a normal couple out for a romantic midnight date. They kept going until they reached a second battery, remnants of a cement barracks surrounded by soft grass.

A hush fell over them, as though they'd entered another realm, one devoid from hate and anger and filled with only loving nature. They crossed a broken fence with a dangling sign that read, "Falling can be Deadly", and continued until they reached the edge of a grassy cliff. The beach stretched out below them, a barrier between them and waves that softly lapped at the shore. With the exception of the red moon, this might be any average night in Port Townsend.

Except he was War and she was a witch.

She stowed her items in the tall grass along the edge of their outcropping and stepped into his open arms. "Look at that," she whispered as he cradled her against him. "So beautiful."

"A lot of falling stars," he responded.

"If we pretend they aren't a sign of the times, they're stunning."

"Mmm..." He kissed the top of her head, and she closed her eyes for a long moment. The heat from his body called to her, and she ran her hands up and down his back, memorizing the feel of him and how her body responded to his presence.

She opened her eyes and lifted her gaze to meet his. "Make love to me, Dru."

He growled his approval and captured her mouth in a heated kiss. She wrapped her arms about his neck as he lowered them both to the ground.

"I knew you'd see things my way." He kissed along the curve of her neck.

She punched him, but he grabbed both hands and held them above her head. His power and virility shocked her. "I should light your ass on fire right now."

"But you won't," he taunted.

"How do you know?" She squirmed beneath him.

"Because you want this as much as I do." He released her hands and buried his in her hair, providing a cushion for her head. He lowered his mouth to hers, kissing her softly at first until their kisses grew much stronger.

She tugged at his shirt. He'd conjured a fantasy once where he'd allowed her free access to his body. She wanted that again. "I've ached to touch you for so long. Your fantasy wasn't nearly enough."

He sat back on his haunches, straddling her with powerful thighs, and jerked the t-shirt over his head in one swift move. She hissed in a breath as he towered over her, all ripped muscles, drawing every bit of heat to her core. "Come to me."

He grinned and shook his head. "Not until I have that leather off you." With careful movements, he slid down the zipper on her jacket exposing her wispy black lace bra. "Is that all you have on underneath?"

"What else do I need?" she teased.

"Nothing." His smile grew wider as he scooted back enough that he could reach the button on her black jeans. "No leather pants?"

"Ruined them in my crash." She was still pissed about that.

"Serves you right then." He unzipped her pants and slid his hand down the opening.

She tensed as his fingers reached her panties.

"Damn if you're not the hottest thing I've ever seen."

"I'm a fire witch, honey. What did you expect?"

He moved to the side and pulled off her jeans, dragging her panties halfway down her legs as he did. "Fuck," he whispered as he cupped her mound, drawing another gasp from her as shivers erupted from her head to her toes. "I had high expectations, but you've exceeded them all."

He finished removing her panties and then ran his palms up her thighs, retracing the path to the aching, hot moisture pooling at her core. When he dipped his fingers inside her, her hips came off the ground, far too eager for his touch.

"Take off your pants," she said, her words barely more than breaths.

He did as she ordered, revealing a body that could only be described as utter chiseled perfection. He'd taken down countries with that massive chest and incredible arms. Now, he would love her with the same.

He slid her jacket from her shoulders before popping the clasp at the front of her bra. "Goddess, I want you."

She laughed. "You said Goddess."

"I'll fucking thank everyone I can just to have the privilege of being with you."

She opened her arms to him. "I never knew you were such a charmer, Dru. I thought you were all manly beast."

He growled. "I'll show you manly beast." He sucked a hardened nipple into his mouth, and her eyes rolled back as exquisite pleasure washed through her.

She slid her fingers through his hair as he loved one breast and then the other.

"Dru," she whispered when she found her voice. "I think we can do away with all the foreplay. If I don't have you inside me right now..." She caught his lower lip between her teeth and nipped.

"Fuck foreplay." He caught her gaze as he situated himself between her parted thighs, his gaze feverish with desire. "Claire," he whispered as he slid into her.

She cried out in pleasure as he filled her. Not only did his body bond with hers, but some part of him coiled tightly around her heart and soul.

Dru thrust over and over, filling her until she feared she'd explode. Desire flowed like molten lava through her veins, singeing her in a most delicious way. She worked to control the heat building inside her, wanting it to last as long as possible, but Dru surged forward in relentless passion until she experienced only the feel of him, the incredible taste of his mouth on hers, the way his body had become one with hers.

"I promised you once that I would fuck you until you couldn't remember your name." His rough voice drew her like a flame in the night. "Do you remember that, Claire?"

"Yes," she whispered, ready to come apart at the seams.

"I promised I'd take you until you wanted nothing more than to make love and make peace for the rest of your life."

"Yes," she gasped as he hit a particularly sensitive spot.

"Say you take me, Claire," he whispered against her ear as he repeatedly filled her and then retreated.

"Take you?" she asked breathlessly, remembering the words Tierra had spoken that had bonded her forever to Killian.

"Take me, Claire. Take me forever. I cannot live without you."

Her heart crashed in on itself. This man would forever own her, and she couldn't survive without him, either. Not now that she'd known him inside and out.

Her breaths came fast as she tried to hold onto sanity long enough to answer him. "I take you, Drustan Geddes. All of you. Forever."

"And I take you, Claire de Moray to be mine for eternity."

Something hot and electric exploded inside her, and she clung to him as wave after wave of passion broke over her.

"Yes," he hissed as he whisked her from one climax directly into another.

"Dru," she gasped.

His chest heaved with exertion as he caught her gaze and smiled at her.

He believed he'd been cursed with the power to destroy through war, but she could no longer buy into that. He might be a master in the arts of battle, but he had the capacity to love far more than that.

She'd believed no man alive could love her like this without her stealing the life from him. She'd been wrong.

The power generated by their lovemaking was bigger than the both of them.

"Claire," he groaned as he thrust into her at a frenzied pace. She held him tightly to her as he sought for what he'd given her so many times.

He released a passionate curse in a language she didn't understand and then stiffened as he buried himself deep inside her. The great immortal brought to his knees by love.

By slow degrees, reality snuck inside their precious bubble as crisp night air filtered around them, cooling their bodies. Dru stayed where he was, planted inside her, breathing heavily. Claire wrapped her arms and legs around him and held him close.

"You pledged yourself to me, Claire. It can't be broken."

"I know," she whispered in return. "I don't regret it." She paused for a long moment. "Do you?"

"Nay. I'll never regret loving you." He moved his hips, his cock hard once again.

"Already?" she asked with a laugh.

"I'll stop if you want," he mumbled against the side of her neck where he nuzzled.

"No." Her words had grown breathless. "Love me for as long as we have, Dru."

When he'd taken her again and she'd shattered more times than she could count, he took his pleasure once more. The feel of him shuddering against her brought almost as much gratification as when she'd done the same. He exhaled a deep sigh of satisfaction and rolled from her, pulling her on top of him where he cradled her against his thundering chest.

"I never knew Horsemen could be so...virile." She laughed at her choice of words.

His laughter rumbled from deep in his chest. "Trust me. There are a lot of things you've yet to learn about immortals."

"No wonder my sisters have kept your brothers close." She closed her eyes on a groan. "Damn. How am I going to explain us, let alone my crown and wand?"

He squeezed. "You'll figure it out. I'm just glad it's you and not me. Those sisters of yours could bring legions to their knees."

"They might do much worse to me. Maybe I shouldn't tell them."

He turned her face toward him and placed a soft kiss on her nose. "No more secrets, Claire, between any of us. If we're going to stop the Apocalypse, we need to work together."

She stewed on that for a moment and then released a long sigh. "Better now than never then. I have something I need to tell you, too. Julian and Nick were already at the house when I left. Call Killian and see if he can join us there. I know it's late, but I don't think we should wait."

Claire's sisters sat around the kitchen table watching her with bleary eyes. Julian and Nick hovered in the background along with Dru. "Killian should be here any minute," Claire promised.

"Is his presence really necessary?" Tierra shot Claire a secretive look.

"We're all necessary," Dru answered.

Tierra grumbled and then stood. "Fine. I'll brew some tea."

"Too early in the morning for that weak-ass weed water. Y'all need coffee."

"I'll make it." Aerin jumped to her feet.

Claire shot a nervous glance at Dru. The thought of coming clean to her sisters twisted every fiber inside her into a never-ending Celtic knot.

It'll be fine. Trust them. Dru's thoughts crossed the distance and strengthened her resolve. She was his and he was hers, and nothing could change that. Their pledges had shattered her spell and brought them even closer than they'd been before. Together, they would battle whatever hovered on the horizon.

The sound of something landing hard on the porch drew their attention, and a second later, Killian walked through the door. Claire watched as Tierra's face lit up, but then Tierra quickly busied herself at the teapot.

"I got here as quick as I could," Death said. "I'm almost certain I've tracked down our target. I haven't been able to catch up with her, but I believe she's taken up residence in the catacombs below town. I lost track of her right before you called, Drustan."

"Speaking of Lucy," Claire said.

"Shh..." Dru cut her off. "Do not speak her name. She may hear you."

Claire threw up her hands in defeat. "Fine. Speaking of La Reina de demons...can I call her that?"

Julian nodded his approval.

"She's one of a few things I need to tell you about." Claire glanced at each of the occupants in the room, hoping she wasn't making a huge mistake. "First, I should probably start with this."

She lifted the red silk tote bag she'd rummaged from her room, inhaling deeply as a frisson of energy filtered through her. "I encountered a small skirmish tonight while I was in town."

Moira lowered her brows. "I thought you'd gone to bed."

"I did." She drew out the last word. "But I couldn't sleep. I get restless sometimes, and the only thing that settles my soul is a ride on my bike. Since I couldn't very well do that, I took to the skies on my broom."

"How was it?" Aerin asked, her eyes lighting up at the topic of flying. She was still rough around the edges after her possession but getting better every day.

"I loved it. So beautiful at night, even with the red moon."

"Skirmish," Tierra reminded her.

"Yes." She exhaled. "I came across the witch hunters. Found their base camp, really."

"*What?*" Aerin and Moira exclaimed in unison.

"And they found me," Claire added before they could get too excited.

Julian glanced at Nick and then back to Claire. "And yet here you are."

She swallowed. "I'm lucky to be here."

"Bastards held her with the same type of amulet that they'd used on Aerin," Dru said.

"They thought I was Tierra. They wanted to burn you at the stake." The thought of that bruised her heart.

"No." Tierra wrapped protective hands across her body. "What happened?"

Claire dropped her face into her hands for a brief moment. She was terrible at giving detailed explanations. "I'm just going to spit this out."

"Please do," Aerin said.

"They tried to burn me. I gave them a chance to retreat. They refused and lit the pyre. Big mistake."

"Fucking huge, I'd wager." Nick inched closer to Moira's chair.

"Damn straight," Dru said. "You should have seen her. She blasted the shit out of everyone in the vicinity. She wasn't on fire. *She was fire.*"

His passionate words heated her cheeks. "While I was in the fire, Kenna de Moray, our aunt who lived long ago, gave me this." She pulled out her wand. "And this." The rubies in the crown glittered red while the gold reflected the kitchen lights.

"*Son of a bitch.*" Aerin slammed a fist on the table. "Where's my fucking crown?"

I'm sorry, she mouthed to her sister.

"I need a cigarette." Aerin glanced angrily around the room.

"I could light it for you," Claire offered and flicked a flame from the tip of her finger.

"No," Tierra said with enough force to draw everyone's attention. "Don't encourage her. Not when she's still this weak."

Shit. What to tell them next?

Us. Dru joined her and wrapped a possessive arm around her shoulders.

Yes. That. "Also, Dru and I pledged ourselves to each other forever." She squeezed her eyes shut when voices erupted in the room.

"Son of a sasquatch taint," Moira said, looking from Tierra to Claire. "What is it with y'all? You let someone slip the salami, and it's all eternal vows and demon spawn. Couldn't you wait for a hot minute and let someone throw you a damned bridal shower or something?"

"Spare me the fucking bridal showers," Aerin muttered before pouring herself a steaming cup of coffee. "Or shoot me."

Claire stared at everyone who'd now become her family. She'd stirred them up, and their words came at her like angry, buzzing bees. "That's not all," she said loud enough to be heard.

Dru turned to her with a quizzical look. *There's more?*

"You said we shouldn't keep secrets," she said to Dru. "The she-bitch visited me while they held me captive. She offered me something she called a cyanide spell. She asked me to consider killing myself to save the world."

"I'll fucking kill her." Dru strode toward the door.

Killian opened it. "I'll help you."

"Stop!" Nick commanded. "You're going about this all wrong. Am I the only one who sees an opportunity here?"

"He's right," Julian said as he slid a hand down Aerin's arm and she placed her hand over his. "Did she give you the spell?"

Claire frantically dove for her pocket. She'd stuffed it in there, but so much had happened since then. Still, the crumpled piece of paper waited for her at the bottom and she pulled it out.

"May I have a look?" Julian held out a hand.

"He's quite studious," Aerin said by way of encouragement.

Claire placed it in his hand, and they all waited silently for him to peruse it.

"Seems a straightforward suicide spell," he concluded.

"For once La Reina of the damned tells the truth," Killian said. "I don't believe it."

"If it's a suicide spell, is there a way we can use it against her?" Claire slid her gaze to Dru. "Kind of like we did when I stole back my fire."

"I haven't forgotten that." Dru's grin promised no mercy.

"You started it," she countered.

"Stop the flirting. This is serious shit." Aerin glanced between them with an annoyed look. "Fucking newlyweds. Ugh." She turned and smiled at Julian. "Tell us what else you know."

"Normally, I'd say no, but she is in a weakened state. It might be possible." He studied the paper for a few more moments. "The ingredients are all soluble, so if you could get her to drink it..."

"Can't kill a duck by sittin' on your ass." Moira shot a look at Claire. "I say we do it."

"No way." Dru glared at all of them. "No fucking way. I just claimed Claire. I won't lose her now."

Claire gripped his hand. "I'm not afraid of her, Dru. After tonight, I know I'm a lot stronger than I was. If it doesn't work on either of us, she'll think I did the spell wrong. She'll have no idea that we tried to use it against her."

"How will you get La demon to come forward?" Tierra asked. "The guys have all said she's in hiding."

Nick smiled at Claire. "All you have to do is call her name. She wants this. She'll come for you, Claire."

CLAIRE SAT ALONE ON THE STEPS OF MANRESA CASTLE except for two crystal goblets and a bottle of the most expensive wine she'd pilfered from the castle's extensive stock. A sliver of the blood-red moon hovered overhead, and she shivered under its watch.

She and her sisters had worked for a week to figure out a way to coat both glasses with the rubbery cyanide concoction in order to remove any suspicions Lucy might have about having one last drink with her. They'd needed several more days to work up a spell to protect Claire from the toxins, and another day to create something that looked similar to the product of the original cyanide spell.

Claire could hold the poison in her mouth as long as she wanted, but she couldn't swallow. Dru had argued furiously, but in the end she, with the support of everyone else, had won.

The worst that could happen would be that Lucy would catch on, and Claire wouldn't drink either. Or she could always spit it out. As an extra protective measure, she'd brought her wand and proudly wore her crown of fire. Also, her sisters and the Horsemen hid out upstairs, far enough away that Lucy wouldn't fear them, but close enough to come running should she need help.

The fact that Dru could read her every thought was the only thing that finally convinced him.

"Lucy," she whispered into the darkness. "I'm ready to do your bidding."

She listened for any movement, but nothing but the breeze in the trees made noise.

"Lucifer," she said in a louder voice. "I'm ready, but I

can't do this alone." She dropped her head into her hands, pretending to be torn by her decision.

"Hello, lovely." Lucy's smooth voice came from the shadows along the edge of the castle. "I'm here to help."

Claire did her best to look pensive. "I want to do this, but I can't do it alone. I can't ask my sisters. They wouldn't understand. They'd try to talk me out of it." She let her words ramble in a distraught fashion.

"Shh... Calm yourself." Lucifer approached cautiously, scanning the perimeter. "That's a beautiful crown you're wearing."

"A gift from my ancestors. One I shouldn't have accepted. It's made me even more powerful, and I can't contain it. If I don't do something now, I'm going to kill everyone I love."

"Don't worry." Lucy sat next to her and patted her hand. "I understand. It's what I've been trying to tell you all along. I'm not a mean person. My job is to punish those deserving it, and I certainly wouldn't have chosen for you to die. But that's just it. Someone chose you or one of your sisters. One life for many, you see."

When Claire didn't readily agree, Lucy continued. "I sense a warrior's spirit in your heart, and I think you can understand that concept. Perhaps this is something you've learned from the massive amount of time you've spent with Dru."

Panic spiked inside. *Could she sense Dru's essence inside her?*

Claire swallowed and lifted the bottle of wine. "I want to go out in style. I brought my crown and the best of wines."

"You do look very pretty." Lucy gazed longingly at her ruby-encrusted crown.

"You can have it when I'm gone if you'd like."

Lucy's eyes sparkled. "Really? That is quite generous of you."

"I don't want it. Won't need it." Claire blinked several times as though holding back her tears. "Will you drink with me? One last exquisite taste of life on earth?"

The devil arched an almost perfect brow. "Do you have the cyanide pill?"

Claire opened her fist and held it out.

Lucy took it between two fingers and held it up to inspect it in the waning light. "You've done beautiful work, my dear. You should be proud."

"My last spell," she said wistfully.

"Your most important spell," Lucy countered.

Claire lifted the bottle of wine she'd already opened and filled both glasses. She held one out for Lucy, and Lucy exchanged the cyanide pill for a glass.

"To mankind and the sanctity of Earth." Lucy lifted her glass for a toast.

Claire held her gaze as she tapped Lucy's glass with hers. "To mankind and earth."

Lucy watched with suspicious eyes as Claire set the pill on her tongue. Before Claire could drink, Lucy took hold of Claire's glass and pressed her own into Claire's hand. "I hope you don't mind. It's nothing personal."

Claire shrugged her shoulders as though it made no difference and lifted the cup to her lips. She took a small amount into her mouth and pretended to swallow. Lucy smiled and did the same.

"This is delight—" Lucy arched her neck and gasped before she turned her coal-black gaze to Claire, fear swirling in her eyes. Claire couldn't move fast enough to avoid Lucy's tackle. She hit the ground hard, spitting wine as she did, but the fizzle down her throat screamed that she'd hadn't expelled it all in time.

Lucy hacked and pointed a threatening finger as she scrambled to her feet and ran, stumbling, into the night.

Claire grabbed her own throat as something akin to a fireball swelled within. She dashed up the steps and into the house, wanting to scream for help as everything inside her scorched with the force of a wildfire in a parched forest.

It burned.

Like she burned.

Clarity slapped her, killing her panic. She halted, closed her eyes and focused all her attention on the acid poisoning her system. She could burn hotter than it could. She didn't know how, but she could.

When she felt she'd compiled enough pressure to expel it, she opened her mouth and blew the toxins from her body. Searing flames roared from her like an infuriated dragon. The force of it blew her backward toward the door as it morphed into a massive fireball that shook the castle walls when it exploded. A second later, another one detonated. Dust and chunks of debris fell from the ceiling.

Her excruciating screams rippled through the fire as the second floor collapsed onto the first.

"*No!*" She choked as smoke and flames swallowed the building. *Her sisters were in there.*

Dru. Everything she loved and lived for.

The Goddess could not be that cruel.

She gathered her strength, harnessing everything she had to extinguish the fire. With a prayer on her lips, she whispered words to kill the flames. A colossal fireball blasted into the night, battering her with a chunk of wood.

"Noooo!" Claire screamed through a parched throat, but the beloved old castle, with all inside, shuddered and crumbled to the ground.

Watch for the exciting conclusion to the Witches of Port Townsend series to be released October 2017.

ABOUT CYNTHIA

Cynthia St. Aubin wrote her first play at age eight and made her brothers perform it for the admission price of gum wrappers. A steal, considering she provided the wrappers in advance. Though her early work debuted to mixed reviews, she never quite gave up on the writing thing, even while earning a mostly useless master's degree in art history and taking her turn as a cube monkey in the corporate warren.

Because the voices in her head kept talking to her, and they discourage drinking at work, she started writing instead. When she's not standing in front of the fridge eating cheese, she's hard at work figuring out which mythological, art historical, or paranormal friends to play with next. She lives in Colorado with the love of her life and three surly cats.

Cynthia loves to hear from readers.

Visit her: http://www.cynthiastaubin.com/
Email her: cynthiastaubin@gmail.com

ABOUT CINDY

Amazon bestselling author Cindy Stark lives in a small town shadowed by the Rocky Mountains with a kindle of kitties, working her way toward official Cat Lady status. She writes fun, witch cozy mysteries, emotional romantic suspense, and sexy contemporary romance. She loves to hear from readers!

Cindy loves to hear from readers.
Visit her: www.CindyStark.com
Email her: CindyStark19@gmail.com

ABOUT KERRIGAN

Kerrigan Byrne is the USA Today Bestselling and award winning author of several novels in both the romance and mystery genre.

She lives on the Olympic Peninsula in Washington with her wonderful husband and Willow the Writer Dog. When she's not writing and researching, you'll find her on the beach, kayaking, or on land eating, drinking, shopping, and attending live comedy, ballet, or too many movies.

Kerrigan loves to hear from her readers! To contact her or learn more about her books, please visit her sites:

Kerrigan loves to hear from readers.
Visit her: www.kerriganbyrne.com

ABOUT TIFFINIE

USA Today Bestselling Author Tiffinie Helmer is always up for a gripping adventure. Raised in Alaska, she was dragged "Outside" by her husband, but escapes the lower forty-eight and returns to her beloved Alaska every chance she gets.

A mother of four, Tiffinie divides her time between enjoying her family, throwing her acclaimed pottery, and writing of flawed characters in unique and severe situations.

Tiffinie loves to hear from readers.
Visit her: http://tiffiniehelmer.com/
Email her: Tiffinie@TiffinieHelmer.com